ALSO BY AYELET TSABARI

The Art of Leaving

The Best Place on Earth

SONGS for the BROKEN ~ HEARTED

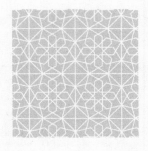

SONGS
for the
BROKEN~
HEARTED

A NOVEL

AYELET TSABARI

RANDOM HOUSE

New York

Published in the United States by Random House, an imprint and division of Penguin Random House LLC, New York.

RANDOM HOUSE and the HOUSE colophon are registered trademarks of Penguin Random House LLC.

Published simultaneously in Canada by HarperCollins Canada

The quotes on pages 131–132 are taken from Ella Shohat's essay "Dislocated Identities: Reflections of an Arab Jew," (*Movement Research: Performance Journal 1991–1992*) and from "Sephardim in Israel: Zionism from the Standpoint of Its Jewish Victims" (*Social Text,* No. 19/20, 1988, Duke University Press).

Grateful acknowledgment is made to the following for permission to reprint previously published material:

Hakibbutz Hameuchad and the Estate of Nathan Alterman: Excerpt from "Shir Hateymaniot" (The Yemenite Women Song), written for the stage in 1934 by Nathan Alterman and published in *Pizmonim and Shirey Zemer* (Tel Aviv: Hakibbutz Hameuchad, 1979). Translated by Ayelet Tsabari. Used by permission of Hakibbutz Hameuchad and the Estate of Nathan Alterman.

Hakibbutz Hameuchad and Ido Kalir: Excerpt from "Tirzah vehaolam hagadol" ("Tirzah and the Wide World") by Dahlia Ravikovitch, originally published in Hebrew in *Kol Mishbarekha Ve-galekha* (*All Your Crises and Waves*) (Tel Aviv: Hakibbutz Hameuchad, 1972). Excerpt from "Tyota" ("Draft") by Dahlia Ravikovitch, originally published in Hebrew in *Ahava Amitit* (*True Love*) (Tel Aviv: Hakibbutz Hameuchad, 1987). Translated by Ayelet Tsabari. Used by permission of Hakibbutz Hameuchad and Ido Kalir.

W. W. Norton, Chana Kronfeld, and Ido Kalir: Excerpt from "Omed al Hakvish" ("On the road at night stands the man") by Dahlia Ravikovitch, originally published in Hebrew in *Ahavat Tapuach Hazahav* (*Love of an Orange*) (Tel Aviv: Sifriate Poalim Publishing House, 1959). English translation from *Hovering at a Low Altitude: The Collected Poetry of Dahlia Ravikovitch* by Dahlia Ravikovitch, translated by Chana Bloch and Chana Kronfeld, translation copyright © 2009 by Chana Bloch and Chana Kronfeld; compilation copyright © 2009 by Chana Bloch, Chana Kronfeld, and Ido Kalir. Reprinted by permission of W. W. Norton, Chana Kronfeld, and Ido Kalir.

Amichai Serri-Menkes: Epigraph from "When I Sing" from *Edna* by Bracha Serri (Jerusalem: Hao Haganuz, 2005). Translated by Ayelet Tsabari and used by permission of Amichai Serri-Menkes.

Schocken Books, an imprint of the Knopf Doubleday Publishing Group, a division of Penguin Random House LLC: Excerpt from *Simple Story* by Shmuel Yosef Agnon, translated by Hillel Halkin, copyright © 1970 by Schocken Books Inc. Translation copyright © 1985 by Penguin Random House LLC. Reprinted by permission of Schocken Books, an imprint of the Knopf Doubleday Publishing Group, a division of Penguin Random House LLC.

Joshua Sobol: Excerpt from *The Night of the Twentieth* by Joshua Sobol, written in Hebrew for the stage in 1976. Translated by Ayelet Tsabari. Used by permission of Joshua Sobol.

Hardback ISBN 9780812989007
Ebook ISBN 9780812989021

Printed in the United States of America on acid-free paper

randomhousebooks.com

2 4 6 8 9 7 5 3 1

First U.S. Edition

Book design by Debbie Glasserman

For the women of my family
strong, brave, fierce, and passionate

When I sang in my youth
The neighboring women knew my deepest thoughts
and heard the secrets of my suffering.

. . .

When I sang on the roof of a lover
stars danced to my tune
and the skies folded their expanse
and knelt at my feet.

—BRACHA SERRI, "When I Began to Sing"

There's really no such thing as the "voiceless." There are only
the deliberately silenced, or the preferably unheard.

—ARUNDHATI ROY

SONGS for the BROKEN~ HEARTED

YAQUB

Immigrant Camp, Mahane Olim Rosh HaAyin, 1950

YEARS LATER, WHEN they are old, sitting on a porch somewhere overlooking the sea, someone would ask them how it all started, and he'd say, as soon as he saw her on the other side of the drinking fountain at the immigrant camp, he knew.

The air smelled of citrus, a sweet, tangy scent Yaqub had, until then, associated with Israel because when they got off the planes, it flooded his nostrils. But from that moment on, it was her it evoked. He was washing his hands before dinner. She was scrubbing dishes, using sand in lieu of dish soap, her face round and open, her eyes long lashed and lined with kohl. She was dressed in a buttoned floral dress and a red cardigan—in the camp they were all given used winter clothes that looked nothing like the traditional clothing they had left behind in Yemen. Shoes, too, which they slipped onto their calloused, untrained feet, feet accustomed to cracked earth and soft sand and rugged rocks.

They looked up at the same time and their eyes met. And it was as though his heart stopped. Or he was struck by lightning. Or some other terrible cliché he'd feel embarrassed by as soon as it crossed his lips. He'd try to rewrite it and fail, because, of course, rewriting only works on paper. Still, he'd do his best: he'd gaze up at the sky, eyes squinted in concentration to the delight of their listeners on the porch, and he'd say it was like everyone else vanished from the camp, and all the other smells that permeated the air—sewage and sweat and mildew and rotten garbage—evaporated, and all that was left was the scent of oranges and the two of them, looking at each other over a two-sided, rusty water fountain. She blushed and looked away. Someone behind Yaqub nudged him, urging him to stop hogging the tap, and he walked away from her gaze and her smile. When he looked back, so did she.

"No, I didn't," Saida would argue. "I would never." But this is how he remembered it.

The first time they spoke, she was sitting by the river. He'd tell them of her singing. He'd tell them of the snake. But he wouldn't tell them she was crying. He wouldn't mention she confessed she hated all of it. The stench and the crowdedness, the tent with its muddy, slippery ground for a floor, the scratchy blankets and the metal beds, the god-awful food—soggy bread, white oily spread—and never enough of it. She missed her home in the village in North Yemen, the fresh mountain air, the sweet, earthy incense that perfumed their mud houses, strong basil and lemony shadhab; how it was always spring there, never this cold, never this damp. Maybe her Muslim friends were right, and this was a terrible idea. And Yaqub had said, "Don't say that. This is the place for us. This is the promised land we dreamt about. It will get better. You'll see."

He said it like he believed it. Someone had to.

She was a poetess, and he was a storyteller. They both came from Haidan in North Yemen, both orphans, and so young. He was just a boy. She was just a girl. They met at an all-Yemeni immigrant camp in Rosh HaAyin, once a British air force base and now a large tent city, in a new country born of hope and despair, built on the dreams of some and the catastrophe of others, on an ancient land, soaked with blood. All around the country, other camps like theirs were being constructed in haste, one after the other, to accommodate Jewish migrants—hundreds of thousands of them—from Poland, Russia, Bulgaria, Iraq, Iran, Morocco. More were still coming. Some were chased by persecution and fear, others driven by ideology or faith, by messianic zeal, all astounded by the new turn their lives had taken, the future ahead unwritten, so blank it was not even terrifying. Maybe, for some, it was even thrilling.

On the banks of the Yarkon River, she sang (like an angel. No, like bells. No, like clear water drawn from a deep well) and he wrote. And in the midst of all this chaos and uncertainty, at the start of a decade in the middle of a century, they fell in love.

They weren't supposed to fall in love.

This is how their story began.

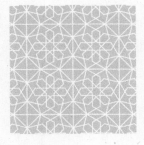

PART ONE

AUGUST
1995

I went to the wadi to search
for happy people
but all I found were my kin—
the brokenhearted

UNKNOWN YEMENI POETESS

CHAPTER 1

ZOHARA

IT WAS MY sister, Lizzie, who told me. Her voice—transmitted through telephone lines that ran underneath seas and borders from Sha'ariya, our Yemeni neighborhood at the edge of a suburb east of Tel Aviv, to this guesthouse counter in the Thai island of Ko Pha-ngan—echoed faintly.

"Zohara," she said. Not Zorki, I noted. "You have to come home." *You have to come home,* a tinny version of her repeated.

"What happened?" I said, but I already knew. I'd known as soon as I opened the bungalow door to find the guesthouse attendant, eyes shifting as he told me the Israeli embassy in Bangkok was looking for me. "Zohara Haddad," said the man on the other line without fanfare. "Yuval from the embassy. I'm putting your sister on the line."

Lizzie told me, and then told me again, that our mother was dead, that she'd collapsed in her kitchen while cleaning (I pictured an overturned bucket of diluted bleach solution, remembered how I used to joke—a joke!—that I wished someone would love me as much as my mom loved bleach), that her heart just stopped. That she died instantly, painlessly (but how did they know, really?).

My mind was slow to process the information, but my body reacted immediately, as though it recognized the loss in its bones—the final cut, the last stage of separation between us. I heard myself gasp, felt my hand pressing over my mouth, as if to stop the sounds from coming. With my other hand, I clutched the edge of the counter to steady myself. I felt hollowed out, as though my insides had been sucked out of my body and the shell might crumble to the ground like a heap of empty clothes. In the cavity that gaped, something dropped and crashed.

The South China Sea was a glassy, turquoise blue. I half-expected the idyllic image to disintegrate in front of me, to shatter into pieces or at least darken up a notch. Like the first time I ate dairy and meat together, in high school, carefully wrapping cheese in a slice of pastrami into one sinful bite. Or the first time I broke Shabbat by listening to Janis Joplin on my Walkman while lying in bed, heart pounding. But just like in those times, nothing happened. The sea remained picture-perfect. A high-pitched ringing in my ears grew, then thinned and faded. On the beach, two Japanese backpackers I had met yesterday spread out their colorful sarongs. A blond woman took off her summer dress and ran into the sea. I felt this nagging, desperate wish for a cigarette, even though I had quit years ago, after getting together with Zack.

Lizzie began to wail. Her husband, Motti, grabbed the phone and said, "How soon can you get here?"

ON THE PLANE, I sank into my seat, heavily sedated from smoking all my remaining pot before leaving. A ferry, a bus, an airport. Sand coating my skin, stuck between my toes, sea salt hardened into my curls.

A cheery El Al stewardess handed out Hebrew papers. Images from the most recent August heat wave—children running through city fountains, bikini-clad women under beach umbrellas—shared the front page with a picture of Yasser Arafat, chairman of the Palestinian Liberation Organization, a keffiyeh wrapped over his head, and Israeli foreign minister Shimon Peres emerging bleary-eyed from all-night talks toward a groundbreaking peace agreement between Israel and the PLO. The first part of the agreement had been festively signed in Washington two years ago, after lengthy secret negotiations had taken place in Oslo, the city that gave the peace process its name. Just seeing the two men together in the same frame felt like a miracle. For years, like estranged cousins, as

Arabs and Jews were commonly described, neither side was willing to even acknowledge each other.

When I first moved to New York five years ago, I tensed up whenever I caught a glimpse of my country on TV, expecting terrible news. Terror. Wars. Bloodshed. But then, Oslo happened, and a year after that, Israeli Prime Minister Yitzhak Rabin and Jordan's King Hussein signed a historical peace agreement. I was watching from a laundromat in New York, folding one of Zack's button-up shirts—all light blue, because I had said it brought out his eyes—as the leaders of these two warring nations shook hands on the White House lawns, President Bill Clinton looking on like a proud father. It was a big deal: only the second peace treaty between Israel and an Arab country after the first one (in itself, a miracle) was signed with Egypt in 1979. Through the laundromat window, New Yorkers enjoyed a warm July day as though nothing momentous was happening.

I called my mother in Israel, which wasn't something I did often. In my defense, she rarely called either. The phone remained a bit of a mystery to her, and she was unnerved by my answering machine, my recorded voice on it, speaking in English, foreign and incomprehensible to her. "Halo?" she'd yell. "Zohara? You there?" In our sporadic, short conversations, she relayed inconsequential information about people I hardly knew, neighbors who died, babies born, marriages and divorces. I never shared anything of substance, just empty assurances that everything was fine, even when it wasn't, even when things were falling apart.

"Can you believe it?" she said when I called that day. "We can go to Petra now!" And then she did something unexpected. She sang the chorus of "The Red Rock," a Hebrew song about the ancient Jordanian city of Petra the radio had banned in the fifties to discourage people from stealing across the border, a trip from which many had not returned. I laughed when she sang, out of discomfort or surprise; it had been so long since I heard her sing.

We weren't close, my mother and I. "A daddy's girl," she called me in a caustic, accusatory tone. As though she had nothing to do with how distant we were, as though she didn't make me feel like I could never live up to my missing brother, hadn't sent me away the first chance she had.

She often told me her pregnancy with me was her most difficult one, as if that, too, was my fault. Everything hurt! she announced, throwing her arms up with an exaggerated dramatic flair. Her feet, swollen beyond recognition, no longer fit into her slippers. Eating even the smallest bites gave her violent reflux that sent her retching. Breathing was strenuous; my feet kept kicking and pressing on her diaphragm. At night she'd be woken up from indigestion, from back spasms, from leg cramps, from bad dreams. She knew I had to be a girl. Boys were good to their mothers, aiming to please. Only a girl would put her mother through such misery. Especially one born a decade after her sister, when my mother—dispirited and drained after years of trying in vain—thought she couldn't have another. Especially when my mother wanted, more than anything, a boy. A male heir to replace the one she had lost.

She labored at home for two days before her friend Bruria took her to the hospital, where she gave birth without fuss. "In Yemen, women didn't cry and yell at birth like they do here, where the whole world hears you." She clucked her tongue in disapproval. "Giving birth was a private business. If you had to yell, you yelled quietly."

I was the only one of her three children to be born in a hospital. The only one, she claimed, who didn't like the taste of her milk, who flailed and thrashed when being held, needing space. "And every time I sang to you, you cried!" she said, raising her eyebrows as if, of all my transgressions, this was the most offensive of all.

My mother was a beautiful singer, blessed with one of these rare voices that give people chills. Silky, deep and lucid, it was the voice of a bigger woman. With her exceptional range and control, she could easily have been a professional had she chosen to, like her sister Shuli. But my mother wasn't interested in a music career. She was too shy to perform. Or maybe it was the God thing. Judaism regarded women's voices as obscene, immodest. The sound of women singing could lead men to have impure thoughts. Although my mother's religious observance was not of the strict, uncompromising kind. "We, the Yemenis," she used to say, "our religion is the best. It's easygoing, not fanatic."

When I was little, she sang along with the radio, often while cleaning (but not while cooking, a task she had approached joylessly and doggedly). Sometimes, she hummed melodies I didn't recognize, strung together Arabic words I didn't know. Still, I could feel the sorrow, the longing for other times, other places.

Was she singing about Rafael, my missing brother?

Later, in high school, I began to roll my eyes at her singing, cringed at the way her voice trilled and undulated. It sounded foreign, Arabic, and utterly uncool, nothing like the popular music sung by Ashkenazi singers on the radio, or the Russian-sounding nationalistic songs we had been taught in the school choir (melodies that were, in fact, often borrowed from Russian tunes). And the depth of emotion in her voice, the earnestness—it made me uncomfortable.

It wasn't just her singing. I became ashamed of many things during my time at Schneider, an elite boarding school for gifted children in Jerusalem I was sent to at fourteen. I didn't want to go. I didn't care about the scholarship, wasn't pleased by the honor, having been handpicked along with other Mizrahi teens—whose parents, like mine, immigrated to Israel from Middle Eastern and North African Arab countries—to enroll in a school my family could have never afforded. Sure, I was dying to get out of the house, but on my own terms and not yet. Her sending me off at that age, so soon after my father had died, felt like an abandonment, a betrayal.

Later, I wondered if my mom would have sent me to Schneider had she known of the price, how it would make me reject my heritage, my past. Her. It was there that I became embarrassed by her accent, the guttural *het* and *ayin* consonants, the rolling *resh*. Her Arabic name (why couldn't she Hebraize it, like everyone else?). Mortified by the fact that she was illiterate, that I had to read the dosage on her medicine for her. Her faith, her superstitions. The unfashionable flowery headscarf she covered her hair with, in accordance with Jewish law. ("If men find female hair so tantalizing," I announced, "they should cover their own eyes!") The tang of spicy fenugreek emanating from her skin, the stains of turmeric that lingered on her hands. "Does your mom make lung soup?" an Ashkenazi girl asked me one day when we talked of our mothers' food. Another girl turned to me in shock and disgust, pretending to gag. "That's not a thing, is it?" Whenever I was home from school, I became repulsed by the way she ate, how she sucked on the bones, dug into the back of chicken thighs, not wasting a morsel.

Once, she surprised me at school—she had been in Jerusalem for a shiva—and when I saw her small figure stomping down the hall, with her headscarf, her shapeless dress, a basket filled with food in each hand, my heart fell. I dragged her toward the dormitories and closed the door. "You can't show up like this," I said, my voice shrill. "Other mothers don't just show up." Her face crumpled, wounded.

The plane was quiet now and dimmed. The young backpacker in the seat next to me, dressed in fisherman pants and a frayed sleeveless shirt, shifted in his sleep. He was likely returning home from his after-the-army trip, back to start university, his life. I folded the newspaper and stuffed it in the seat pocket and stared out, telling myself most teenage daughters reject their moms. I was not special.

I flagged the flight attendant. With her red lipstick and her black, shiny hair tightly coiled into a bun, she looked like a commercial for El Al. "Can I have a glass of wine? Red?"

She nodded and turned to leave.

"Wait," I said. "Do you have whiskey?"

The effect of the pot was starting to wear off. I needed something stronger.

THE PLANE LANDED and the passengers clapped, applauding the safe return and waking me with a start. Outside was a typical Israeli summer-burnt day, everything bleached-out and withered. I got my passport stamped, hauled my backpack from the conveyor belt and slung it over my shoulder. My mom would want to wash its entire contents immediately, including the bag itself, I thought, and my heart plummeted into my stomach. I wished I could follow suit, collapse onto the terminal floor and lie there.

Outside the terminal, the heat was a white beast, the slap of humidity on my face like a hot mop.

The taxi driver took me in through the window—my loose, faded sirwal pants, my tie-dye shirt, my unwashed curls—and grinned, gold showing in his teeth. "Welcome home! Let me guess: Thailand? India?"

"Yeah," I said. He looked pleased. I shoved my backpack into the back seat and slid in after it. "Segula Cemetery."

The grin left his face. He turned his torso to look at me, as if to assess whether it was a sick joke.

The sunlight was harsh, making my eyes water. The tears hadn't come yet. They hadn't come when I first heard, nor when I explained to the airline's representative why I was asking for a bereavement fare, the words out of my mouth so unfathomable they sounded nonsensical.

My whole life I had thought myself an expert at grief, took strange pride in it, as if it somehow granted me wisdom or spiritual superiority. After all, I had been born into the pit my brother's death or kidnapping— depending on which one of my parents you asked—had left in our lives. Born out of the hope that I might alleviate some of that pain, light up a house steeped in darkness. Then, when I was eleven, my father died, and whatever light I had been able to offer went out.

My mom was the one who broke the news to me then. She returned from the hospital with Bruria, the two of them red-eyed and somber. We were sitting in the front room. Our small house wasn't arranged like my friends' houses. The front room was my dad's, and the back room, the largest in the house, was my mom's, where she slept on a single bed in the corner, but also where we dined and watched TV, where people vis- ited when it was too cold to sit outside. Then, there was the tiny room I had once shared with Lizzie, and an even tinier kitchen. In the back, at the end of a stone trail, we had a small shed with a kitchen and a bath- room that my father had built as a rental unit, a source of income.

When my mom told me my father had died, sobbing shook me, vio- lent and uninhibited. It was the opposite of how I felt now: grief was bursting out of me then, pushed against my skin, oozing out of my pores. For most of my adolescence, I had allowed grief to become what defined me. Like my mother, I had set up my home in sorrow, which, due in part to the hormonal turmoil of puberty, had often manifested in rage.

My father was old when he died. Ever since I could remember, strangers had asked whether he was my grandfather. Perhaps his curly, white beard had something to do with it. Like a grandfather, he had spoiled me rotten. It was his tikkun, Lizzie had said, a way to make amends for how he had raised her.

He was sick for only a few months. Lung cancer. He never smoked cigarettes, but he loved his mada'a, his prized water pipe. Its round body—made of blue glass and filled with water—slimmed into a finely curved brass top, spotlessly polished and attached to a long hose. A ceramic tobacco holder rested as a crown on its head, covered with burning coals that crackled when he smoked. Some nights, friends would join him after dinner, sprawling lazily on the couch, puffing fruity tobacco and chewing gat, one cheek swollen with a bundle of bitter leaves.

I loved the smell of tobacco and the haze of smoke that lingered in his room. That was before my mom demanded he do it outside; she'd heard it was bad for us, the girls. On nights when he didn't have company, I sat with him, brought out my doll and built a house for her from mud and sticks, the way my father told me they did in Yemen. I loved his stories of Yemen; he told me about his dad, who was a blacksmith (Haddad means blacksmith in Arabic) and about his mother, who was strong-minded and resourceful—"Eshet hayil," he said, using the biblical term to describe a woman of valor—who brewed arak from grapes, hung meat to dry on the roof, dehydrated grapes to make raisins. In their village in North Yemen (the wild north, they called it) Muslims and Jews lived together, children walked around barefoot and Jewish men made beautiful and intricate silver jewelry, which was lost, along with their precious, ancient Torah books, taken by the people they had trusted them with as they boarded the planes to Israel.

My father was my biggest champion. I was his smart little girl who could do anything she put her mind to. I could become a nurse, or a teacher, be the first in our family to go to university. His eyes would light up with such pride when he said that. It never occurred me to ask why he didn't think Lizzie could. This was years before I learned from Lizzie that there were other sides to him, secrets I hadn't known about.

The taxi driver clicked his tongue at something on the news. Sleep was weighing on my eyelids. I tried closing them, but my lids fluttered restlessly. When I opened my eyes, I was struck by the strangeness of everything, the brightness of this place, the ugliness of it—we were driving through industrial areas, gray, derelict buildings, shops with overflowing merchandise, scorching concrete sidewalks with no shading trees. I was home. I was heading to my mother's funeral. Every time— a jolt of disbelief, like an ice cube sliding down the front of my shirt. The taxi driver glanced at me through the mirror; I was squeezing my eyes shut and opening them, again and again, as though trying to readjust the image.

We were nearing the cemetery at the edge of Petah Tikva, the suburban city I had grown up in. I recognized the surrounding brick wall. Although it'd been a while since I last visited, I knew the way to my father's plot in the maze of graves. I directed the driver through the narrow paths that intersected the cemetery, until I spotted my family congregating. I pulled out a sarong from my backpack to cover my shoulders, the same sarong I had sashayed in along the beach just yesterday, now too pink against the grim backdrop, smelling of salt and fire.

I hugged my sister, Lizzie, and her husband, Motti, my seventeen-year-old nephew, Yoni, my aunt Shuli, a string of sobbing, limp, sweaty bodies. We stood in a clump around the hole in the earth, a gash on dry skin. Rows of shiny marble slabs spread out in front of us, blending into the pale skies. The sun glared off the stones. My mother's small body, covered in a white sheet, was lowered into the earth, next to her husband, whose grave, for years, had claimed her burial space with wild bushes she had never weeded growing over it. In the absence of a living male heir, Yoni had to say the kaddish, standing tall and willowy at the grave, his voice breaking, his shoulders quivering.

It had been twenty-four hours since that knock on my bungalow door that changed everything. Last time I was home, more than two years ago, I was still married to Zack, working on my doctorate at NYU, living in New York.

Nothing in the world could fix this jet lag.

YAQUB

Immigrant Camp, Mahane Olim Rosh HaAyin, 1950

THE FIRST TIME he heard her sing, he was walking from the camp to his usual spot by the Yarkon River. Her voice grew louder, drowning the sound of the water. "Galbi malan, yauma, ala man ashki?" she sang. *My heart is full, Mother, who will I cry to?*

Yaqub slowed down. His skin broke into chills. The girl's voice was rich and warm, at once robust and silky soft. He slunk along the trees until he could steal a glimpse of her sitting on the ground, leaning against a large rock, her eyes shut, her face gleaming wet. The girl from the water fountain. As though he had summoned her. Just when he began to wonder if he had dreamt her up.

"My heart is full of rain. If it bursts, it might flood the whole town," she went on.

Yaqub closed his eyes, mesmerized, moved. Her singing lifted and carried him away from the misery, the filth, the poverty of this place.

When they first arrived in Israel, they had been assured that the immigrant camp was a temporary solution. There were so many people and nowhere to house them. A tall barbwire fence enclosed the overcrowded rows of tents, like a prison. There was no drainage, and in the heat, the stench was nauseating. In the cold—and that winter was a particularly bitter one, the native-born Jews, the sabras, had told them—frost gathered in thin, brittle sheets on the tents and cracked under their feet on the muddy ground, rain pooled in giant, murky puddles, and the chill penetrated the layers of foreign clothes they had been given, settling in their bones.

Yaqub thought of his uncle, who'd passed away on the journey, never to fulfill his dream of ascending to the Holy Land. Like Moses, who made it as far as Mount Nebo, only to be turned away. His uncle had believed, as all Yemeni Jews, that in the Holy Land, the homeland they had yearned for while in exile for generations, the streets would be paved with gold and they would be welcomed like long-lost sons.

He couldn't have imagined this. No one could. The hunger, the desolation, the secularism rampant in such a holy place. But even as the Yemeni Jews watched their dreams shatter in front of their eyes, they didn't protest. How can one complain after consummating their historic, communal dream of return? How can one express disappointment at redemption?

Yaqub discovered the river one day, as he wandered away from the camp, past the last row of tents, the small buildings that had been abandoned by the British and repurposed as a clinic and a nursery, through a patch of weeds as tall as his waist, along a cluster of eucalyptus trees with peeling bark, over the fence where it had been trampled by a coyote or a swamp cat, and through the marshy grass lining the bank.

The Yarkon River—Al-Auja, the local Arabs called it, *the meandering*—was wider and more vigorous than the stream they had running through their village back home. He'd been told some of the sabras bathed in its green waters, and in Tel Aviv, where it spilled into the sea, they had sailed it in boats. It was a small, lushly green oasis surrounded by willows and eucalyptuses. The only sounds were the soft trickle of water and the steady croak of frogs. Water lilies floated on the surface, their heart-shaped leaves bluish and delicate.

The river became his refuge. He began going there daily, just to be alone with his books. Books he was not supposed to read: love stories, tales of adventure and mystery. Leib, the Polish guy who worked in the kitchen, had lent them to him, after Yaqub had noticed him reading on a milk crate behind the kitchen during his smoke break. The poor excuse for a cultural center, once a British ammunition shed, was sparsely stocked with old newspapers and hardly any books worth reading. But Leib, who borrowed his from the library in Petah Tikva, kindly shared. As Yaqub read, his grasp of modern Hebrew improved and his world expanded far beyond the confines of the camp.

Leib was different than the Ashkenazi people Yaqub had met upon landing, who regarded them with pity or disgust or, worse, ignored them altogether. Leib was quiet and waiflike, with eyes that appeared hollow, like Yaqub might tumble into them if he stared for too long. He was also the first Jew Yaqub had ever met who admitted to not believing in God. He revealed that casually, saying, "What God?" after Yaqub once said, "God willing."

Stunned, Yaqub watched nothing happening as a result. "Why are you here, then?" he asked. "If you don't believe this land was given to us by God?"

"Where else would I go?" Leib said simply. "I may not believe in God, but I believe this is the only safe place for Jews."

How could someone live without faith? Yaqub wondered. What an unfeeling, joyless existence it must be.

Daud Sanani, who knew everything that went on in the camp (and whom Yaqub detested for being a shameless gossip and a condescending prick. "Better a radish seller in Sana'a than a village rabbi," he said to him once) had told him Leib's entire family had been murdered in Poland. "The Holocaust," he whispered as though it were a swear word.

Inspired by the books he was reading, Yaqub began scribbling lines—descriptions, observations, recollections—on random pieces of paper he found, discarded newspapers and used cardboard boxes, until he scrounged some money for a plain school notebook he began carrying around. No one knew about his writing. Not even his cousin Saleh, who was the only family Yaqub had left. Yemenis did not think much of prose writing, found journaling frivolous. Poetry was highly regarded: the devotional men's songs, of course, mostly written by the seventeenth-century poet Rabbi Shalom Shabazi, liturgical poems about exile and redemption and the pining for Zion. Not the women's songs, which dealt with earthly things, with love and betrayal and heartache, and were sung in Arabic. These were the songs Yaqub loved hearing his own mother and aunts sing growing up. The songs the girl by the river was singing.

When he was a young boy in Haidan, as the men gathered to sing songs from the Diwan, he asked his uncle who Shabazi wrote his songs for. They sounded like love songs to him. "Ayelet Hen," for example. *Doe of grace who supports me in exile, whose lap I lie on at night.* "Good question, ibni." His uncle patted his head. "To the Shekhinah of course! The divine spirit!"

Even as a child, Yaqub was not convinced.

FOR A FEW days, he watched her from a safe distance and listened. Until one evening, he saw a black snake slithering on the earth beside her. Yaqub stepped from behind the tree and cried, "Watch out!"

The girl sprung up, hand to her heart. She watched the serpent, motionless, her chest rising as she panted. Her green handkerchief slid down the back of her head, revealing shiny black curls.

"Take small steps back," he said. "No quick movements. It won't attack unless provoked."

The snake slinked away along the riverbank. The girl slowly retreated until she stood near him, close enough that he could imagine the warmth emanating from her body. Close enough that it felt forbidden.

She glanced quickly into his eyes. "Thank you."

He reached into his pocket and offered her a date, pinched between his thumb and forefinger. He had kept that date in his pocket for days, for when the hunger was too much to bear. Sharing it with her was generous. She knew that.

The girl rearranged the scarf over her hair and looked at him askance. "Do you think it's proper for a girl to take sweets from a strange boy she just met?"

He stammered, taken aback by her candor.

She stretched out her arm and grinned. "I could use some sweetness after such fright."

He placed the date in her palm carefully as to not touch her, and she bit into its meaty center, eyes closed, chewing slowly and deliberately, relishing every bite. Yaqub became aware of his staring and looked away.

This date was in his pocket moments ago. It was still warm from his body, and now it was in her mouth. This might be the closest they would ever get.

Encouraged by her frankness, he dared to say, "You sing beautifully."

"You listened to me sing?" She giggled, covering her mouth, and even that sounded like music, cascaded like water down a fall. She grew serious. "Singing is the one thing that keeps me sane in this place. Since we came here, it's like we forgot how to sing. I miss the way we sang in Yemen, all the women together." She motioned at the notebook in his hand. "What is that for?"

"I write, sometimes."

"What do you write?"

"My feelings, I guess." He tucked his other hand into his pocket and could feel the sticky residue from the date.

"Read me something."

He fidgeted. "It's private."

"You've been listening to my singing. It only seems fair."

"It's in Hebrew." In this new land everything was to be in Hebrew. A holy language meant for prayer, brought down to earth. But of course, the women didn't speak Hebrew, didn't know it from praying like the men. Even when the Yemeni men spoke it, accentuating everything in their unique pronunciation, sometimes people couldn't understand them, barking, "Hebrew!" at them.

"Translate for me," she said.

So he opened his notebook and read to her, translating into their Judeo-Arabic dialect what he wrote the day he first heard her. "He listened to a girl sing by the river today. Her voice was sad and haunting, as though she was giving voice to all of his sorrows."

Her face broadened in wonder. "You wrote about me?" she said. Then, thoughtfully, she added, "Why did you write it like that? Like it happened to someone else?"

"I don't know." He shrugged. "It comes naturally."

She considered it. "Maybe it helps you understand better, to see yourself from the outside. It's you but not you."

He was astounded by her insight and wisdom. This from a woman who couldn't read or write.

She sat up, glanced at the direction of the camp as if she heard something and rushed to leave.

"Wait!" he called after her. "What is your name?"

"Saida!" she cried as she ran back.

"SHE IS MARRIED, you know," his cousin Saleh said to him a few days later. Yaqub's heart sank. He had spotted her waiting for food outside the dining room and nodded at her, so slightly his chin barely moved. Her face flushed and she looked away. Saleh saw the exchange. He saw the way Yaqub's face brightened at the sight of her. In Yemen, women's traditional clothing and headdress signaled their marital status: Did she have a black sudyah over her head and under the chin, or did she still have her pointy gargush on? Here, dressed in their foreign clothing, their fashionable donated headscarves, one couldn't tell. Yaqub knew, of course, she was of a married age, but around camp she was always accompanied by women, by her sister and her friend Rumia. And would a married woman be so bold as to go to the river on her own? Talk to him as she did? He had decided she must be a widow.

A few days later he saw her outside the nursery, crowding the windows with the other mothers, all waiting to breastfeed their children. A nurse shooed them away. And then another day, as he headed to the river, he saw her sitting on the curb in a row of mothers and babies. She was cradling a plump boy, round cheeked and curly haired, who was laughing as she buried her face in his belly, over and over again. When she noticed Yaqub, a half smile flickered on her lips. His heartbeat quickened.

He kept going to the river. What else was there to do? There was no work, no prospects, no idea when they would be leaving this place. He went and he hoped. He went and he waited. Some evenings she came. Some, she didn't. Sometimes they talked. Other times they were silent. She would sing quietly as though to herself (it was immodest to sing for a man, of course) and he would write. They sat on two rocks, distant enough so they could fool themselves into believing it was harmless, grateful for the canopy of trees, the tall grass separating them from the camp.

Soon, he was consumed by thoughts of her, longing for—living for—their encounters. It became a constant, persistent ache. He woke up with it like a fever, and at night, it replaced the rumble in his stomach he had often fallen asleep with. It wasn't proper for them to fraternize. Unrelated men and women were not to spend time alone as they did. Maybe it was this new place, being away from the village where everyone knew him, or the unfamiliar attire they had on, that made Yaqub feel like the rules have changed. Maybe it was the stories he read that made him dare to wish for more than what had once been permissible. "You're reading too many secular books," Saleh scolded when he confided in him. "They are giving you strange ideas."

As days passed and evenings set earlier, the frequency of her visits grew, and their conversations deepened. "Where did you learn to do this?" Saida asked one time after he translated his writing for her. "Write stories like that?"

"From reading books."

"What's in these books?" she asked. And he described the tales from start to finish, omitting inappropriate parts, of course. And she listened, resting against the tree bark, fiddling with strands of grass. Once, when he was reading *A Simple Story* by Agnon, he recited a quote for her he had scribbled into his notebook: "No matter how black your life may be, you can always find a better one in books."

"Beautiful," she said. "What is the book about?"

He told her. He had been enthralled by the story of an impossible love between married Hirshl and his cousin, the orphan Blume. There were lines in that book that resonated so powerfully that he trembled, like this one: "A skillful artist had sketched her portrait in his mind, and her beauty was always on display there."

It was as though Agnon had opened a window into his own heart and described what he saw there.

Saida lowered her gaze, thoughtful. "Sad. So many stories about unfulfilled love." She reddened at once and so did he. The mere mention of love enough to make them feel implicated.

"Just like the women's songs," he said, quietly.

She nodded, withdrawn. They fell silent. After a while, Saida said, "None of these books tell our stories. Read to me about Yemen. It will feel like visiting."

And so, he read to her about his mother, the sound of her singing as she embroidered and wove baskets with her sisters, the deep, comforting taste of her spicy soup, the sweetness of her aseed porridge with fresh sheep milk and samna—that smoky clarified butter that made everything tastier. He read about the Muslim tribesmen who provided fierce, tribal protection to the Jews, the dhimmah, and who needed the Jews—their services and craft—like salt to their food.

He read about the day he found out about the riots that broke in Aden in 1947 once the UN partition plan for Palestine was announced, and many Jews were murdered. And though his village was far away in the north, echoes of the atrocities traveled by merchants, and a feeling of disquiet settled over the Jews, reminding them that as dhimmah, they would always be second-class citizens, the Muslims would always be in a superior position.

He read to her about Hashed Camp, that hellhole in the desert near Aden where Jews from all over Yemen gathered with the hope that they would soon be redeemed, lifted up on big planes, like on the wings of the eagles, as it said in the Bible, and be brought to the land of Israel. How dozens of people died there daily, from hunger and disease, including his uncle, Saleh's father, and his little cousin, Saleh's brother. So many dead that the bodies were lined up on the ground, and they had to bury them in the desert. To spare Saleh the pain, Yaqub had volunteered to bury them himself, sobbing as he dug in the earth.

He choked up, paused from reading, and when he looked up, he saw Saida's face glimmering wet in the light of the moon. She wiped her tears and said, "Why don't you put your stories in a book? You write beautifully. And these stories must be told."

Without thinking, Yaqub reached for her hand. It was soft and delicate, and he felt it pulsating, fluttering like a baby bird. Saida froze. Then her eyes grew red and wet again. She snatched her hand away from his and darted back to the camp, the tail of her loosened headscarf flapping behind her until it was swallowed by the night.

CHAPTER 2

ZOHARA

LIZZIE'S KITCHEN WAS buzzing with women—neighbors, friends
and relatives—pouring tea and washing dishes and assembling food
platters with nuts and seeds and dried fruit. Lizzie's husband, Motti,
lugged in a big aluminum water heater for tea and bags full of snacks
and store-bought cookies. I spotted my aunt Shuli arranging pastries on
a tray and beelined to her.

Shuli was my mother's younger sister and everything my mother
wasn't: secular, modern, happy. She lived alone in the southern city of
Eilat, and sang at weddings, hotels and bars along the Red Sea shore. She
even toured in Europe once, a trip sponsored by some rich French Jew
who was probably in love with her like the rest of them. Every time I
went to Eilat or Sinai, I'd stop by her little apartment in a dilapidated
housing project, an apartment that was as crowded as our home was
bare. On the living room wall, she had pictures of herself with celebrities
like Mike Brant and politicians like David Levy, framed yellowing articles in which she was featured, and glamorous old headshots, her hair
coiled in perfect ringlets or rolled into a bun with two loose curls on the
sides, her skin dark and glowing, her lips glossy and her eyes smoky.
While my mother was petite and slender, Shuli was voluptuous, larger

than life and mesmerizing to watch on stage, with her loose, embroidered, vaguely Yemeni dresses, her theatrical gestures, her untamed curls.

Shuli was the one who taught me how to play poker, who assured me it was okay to be in love with more than one person when I called her, tortured over my crush on both Kobi and Erez, who cheered on when Mika and I formed a rock band in eighth grade, inspired by our mutual love of Janis Joplin, and who told me singing was not impure, not obscene, but godly, a portal to the heavens.

"Zorki, ayuni." *My eyes.* Shuli squeezed me, literally, pressing the flesh of my arms, feeling me up as though checking for changes and clutching me to her breasts. She pushed me an arm's length to get a better look, which was a chance for me to do the same. Her face had aged, yet somehow her beauty deepened. She had a vibrancy about her of a much younger woman. "Why so dark?" She clucked her tongue. "You should stay out of the sun."

I glowered at her. "Really? I'd expect this kind of bullshit from my mom. Not you." This was hardly the time to comment on the prevalence of shadism in our culture or the fact that, for me, spending the past few months carelessly bathing in the Thai sun was an exercise in freeing myself from this messed-up doctrine. I knew, of course, I should be applying sunscreen, for health reasons, but after a lifetime of being warned of tanning, allowing my brown skin to naturally darken felt like a revolutionary act.

Shuli held my face in her palm and her eyes filled with tears. I knew she was seeing my mother. A perfect replica, everyone said, which they meant as a compliment, of course—my mother had been beautiful in her days ("If only she wasn't so dark," I once heard my uncle's wife say)— even if it hadn't felt like one to a teenage girl hell-bent on being nothing like her mom. Resemblance ran deep in our family; we all looked like a variation of each other: younger, older, thinner, fairer, but all cut from the same mold. Shuli glanced at the room. "Where's Zack?"

"Ima didn't tell you? We split up."

Her face twisted in sympathy. "Oh, Zorki. I had no idea."

Typical. My mother wasn't close with her sister, but surely they had spoken over the past few months. Of course, she neglected to mention *that.*

"Come visit me," Shuli said. "You'll be here a while, no?"

Someone was asking Shuli about serving utensils and she turned to
them before I had a chance to answer. Truth was, I had no plans beyond
the week of the shiva. Before this happened, I had only a vague notion
of what I wanted to do after Thailand. I was making some profit from
subletting my East Village apartment (for which I was paying Zack rent)
to two sisters from Kentucky. I was on leave from my PhD program at
NYU until the end of the year, but the longer I was away, the less I
wanted to go back. My friends in academia assured me this was normal.
"I can't count the number of times I told my advisor I was quitting," my
friend Evelyn had said.

I could see my two nieces grabbing cookies from the tray and hur-
rying back into their room. I remembered myself during my father's
shiva, our house hijacked by sad-faced grown-ups, escaping outside to
play with my cousins.

I put a hand on my aunt's fleshy arm. "Have you seen Yoni?"

Shuli sighed. "He's in his room. Poor baby."

"Yeah, Ima practically raised him."

Shuli stared at me. "You don't know?"

"Know what?"

"Yoni's the one who found her."

I raised a hand to my mouth. "Oh my God."

Shuli told me my nephew came to visit my mother—"Tata," he
called her—as he did almost daily, to help her with the groceries or read
her the paper. Even after decades in Israel, my mom could barely read
past the headlines. That day, he found her dead on the floor.

I made my way through the living room, trying, unsuccessfully, to
avoid eye contact with visitors. There were many familiar faces from the
neighborhood, from the synagogue, from the community center, co-
workers from the cafeteria at Beit Ora, the geriatric hospital where my
mother worked three times a week. Everyone nodded at me, held my
hand, muttering words of condolences, some in Arabic ("Allah yerhama," *may God have mercy on her*) and some in Hebrew ("titnahmu
mehashamyaim," *may you be consoled by the skies*).

When I made it to Yoni's room at the end of the hallway, I knocked,
lightly at first, then louder. "Yoni." I raised my voice. "It's Zohara."

I heard shuffling from the other side. My nephew opened the door.

He was so much taller than me now that I had to look up. He was wearing a kippah and had stubble on his chin. His shirt collar was torn as per tradition. He looked like hozer betshuva, someone on his way to becoming Orthodox. Or was he just in mourning? He hugged me limply.

"Are you okay?" Dumb question.

He half-shrugged.

"I mean, it's okay not to be okay."

"I know."

I peeked inside—a single bed with crumpled sheets, a pile of textbooks for the new school year on his desk, the stuffy, sour smell of a teenage boy's room. I had the sudden urge—channeling my mom?—to make the bed, crack open a window and air the place out. "Feel like talking?"

He closed the door a tad. "Maybe later."

"Can I do anything for you?"

"Actually, yeah," he said, alert. "Someone needs to take care of Tata's house. You know, we should have sat shiva there. That's where her spirit lingers. I told Ima but she wouldn't listen."

"I guess it's easier for her to have it here. With the girls and everything. And there's more room." It was definitely more convenient for me: it meant I had a quiet place to go to at the end of the day. I wondered if he thought that was improper too. Traditionally, the family of the deceased had to stay at the same house for the entire week.

"We should have had it there," he repeated.

I said nothing.

"So the people from the organization said . . ."

"What organization?"

"They help with the shiva and stuff."

"Like, a religious organization?" Maybe he *was* turning religious. Lizzie never mentioned that. But I guess it's been a while since we spoke. I calculated in my head: since before Thailand? Was it possible? I was a rotten sister.

Yoni nodded. "They said, according to tradition, the house has to be cleaned and aired, and the food needs to be discarded so it doesn't go bad. Stuff like that. And I just . . ." He rearranged the kippah on his thick black hair. "I can't." He looked drained.

"I can do that," I said.

He stood there a moment longer. "Yeah?"

"I'll take care of it. I promise."

Finally. A plan.

MY NIECES WERE watching TV on their parents' bed. Ortal got up and gave me a distant hug. Lilach regarded me with a vacant look. "What do you say we get out of here?" I said.

They looked up hopefully.

"I'm taking Ortal and Lilach to the makolet," I told Lizzie on the way out. She was sitting with some of her old high school friends whom I hadn't seen in years; all had aged into clichés with their giant hair clips, their drawn faces, their cracked lipsticks, their mom jeans. They muttered condolences.

"Wait, why?" Lizzie said, eyes narrowed.

I couldn't read the objection. I rarely got Lizzie's cues. It was exhausting trying to communicate with her. "Why not? Do you need me here?"

"I don't *need* you. But people expect you here. They come to pay their respects."

"Let her," Motti said. "The girls could use a break." He mouthed thank you behind her back.

My feet led us to Eli's Makolet, though there may have been a closer one. Lizzie lived in an apartment building a few blocks away from my mom's, in one of the newer developments that sprouted at the edge of Sha'ariya, steps away from the neighborhood soccer field. The afternoon was scorching, probably too hot to be out; there was a reason my mother napped every day between two and four. We walked along the bush hedges, seeking shade. Lilach held my hand, despite, I'm pretty sure, barely remembering me. She had to be five now, and I hadn't been home in two years. I had been gone from Israel for most of their lives. I wondered if it was my resemblance to my mom that made her at ease with me. Ortal trailed behind, kicking stones. At eight she was taller than I thought she'd be, and so much more of a person than last time I saw her.

"It's weird, having all these people in your house, isn't it?" I said.

Lilach said, "They came because Savta went to heaven." As she walked, her two pigtails swung from side to side.

Ortal snorted. I noticed her wavy hair was unbrushed and knotted in the back, her bangs falling over her eyes. When did she become such a teenager?

Eli's grocery store was located a block from my mom's house, at the end of Michal Street and opposite the synagogue. In my childhood it was dim and cramped, with dusty products overflowing the shelves. Over the years, it expanded, took over the hardware store next door, and brightened. When we walked in, the coolness of air conditioning welcomed us. I exhaled with relief and headed to the cooler to grab a couple of water bottles.

Eli wasn't behind the counter, with a half-pencil shoved behind his ear to add up numbers. As a child, going to the makolet was my favorite errand to run for my mom, mostly because of Eli, who had kind eyes and a sincere smile, who asked me about school and sometimes gave me free candy.

A young guy in faded jeans and a blue T-shirt stocked cigarette packs behind the counter. He looked in his late twenties, with short black curls and a scruffy face. He was good-looking in the way some of the young Yemeni guys in the neighborhood were, the ones who wore their shirts too tight, worked out too much, listened to Mizrahi music too loudly and ogled every woman who walked by. He greeted us cheerfully, "Hey girls!" Ortal broke into a smile, raising her hand shyly. They must have been coming with my mother. I gave him a courteous smile.

"Do you want anything?" I said to the girls. Lilach's eyes lit up; she circled the ice cream freezer, selecting and abandoning different bars. Ortal browsed through an issue of *Ma'ariv Lanoar* at the entrance, a picture of a teen heartthrob I didn't know on the cover.

I stood by the counter, waiting for them to decide. The guy locked the cigarette case. "Sorry about your mom," he said. "What a loss."

"Thank you," I said. Lilach ran to me waving an ice cream sandwich. "Grab one for me," I said and then gestured to the magazine Ortal was browsing through. "I'll take that too."

"You don't remember me, do you?" He eyed me sideways as he punched the numbers on his till.

I cocked my head.

He placed a hand on his heart in mock offense.

"I'm sorry, I just flew back, and with everything going on, my mind isn't here."

"That's fair. Nir. Nir Ozeri," he said. "We went to elementary school together." He jerked his chin in the general direction of our neighborhood school.

Eager to end the conversation, I let my frown melt. "Right!"

He shook his head with a laugh. "That's super convincing."

"I'm sorry. My memory is terrible."

"That's okay," he said. "I guess I wasn't as memorable as others."

I opened my wallet to find a bunch of wrinkled bhats and a one-dollar note. "Shit."

"Don't worry about it." He waved his hand. "Pay me later."

"Really?"

"Yes, really. Your mom had a tab here."

"Wow, thank you. I'm so sorry."

"Relax." He laughed. "That's a lot of pleasantries. How very American of you."

When we got home, the men were finishing up a prayer. Ortal walked straight into the room with her magazine and shut the door. I wished I could do the same. "They already had ice cream today," Lizzie said. "I suppose they didn't tell you." She turned to Lilach. "Did you say thank you?"

Lilach nodded and looked up at me with a shy smile. We both knew she hadn't.

CHAPTER 3

YONI

HE COULD BARELY remember anything from that moment. Mid-August and the heat was stifling. By the time he got to Tata's house, he was dripping sweat, his deodorant already ineffective, his body emitting a sharp, sour odor.

He must have knocked. He usually did. He must have then opened the door. If he called her from the outside, as he did sometimes, he couldn't remember.

"That's perfectly normal," Dvora, the school counselor, said softly. "It's common amongst people who've experienced traumatic situations, like combat shock."

Yoni sat a little taller in his chair.

It wasn't his idea to go see the counselor; his teacher and his mom had arranged it behind his back. School hadn't started yet, but when Dvora called and asked him to come, he thought they must have called all seniors. When he realized why he was there, he felt tricked.

He stared out the window at the shocking pink blossom of the bougainvillea, almost obscene in its brilliance. Anger rose in his chest, misplaced. Since Tata died, it happened a lot, his anger, like a stray dog, lost and roaming, searching for an outlet. He was angry at drivers and angry at pedestrians and angry at store clerks and angry at his best friend, Shlomi. He was angry at his mom who didn't know how to talk to him and angry at his father for leaving them and at everyone at the shiva with their whispered condolences and their stupid, long faces. The bougainvillea. The heat. The sharp smell of his body.

But most of all, he was angry at himself: had he come earlier, he could have saved her. What did he do that morning? Watch TV? Masturbate?

Truth was, he did remember some things: the sound he made, a long intake of air that sounded like a whistle, a voice—his voice—screaming. Later, he would hear it replayed in his mind every time the image of his grandmother lying on the floor came to him. Her head sideways as though she were taking a nap. A pool of soapy water. A bottle of window cleaner. Crumpled newspapers. Her dress rolled up and he saw more of her legs than he wanted.

Other details eluded him. Did he get Mr. Hason and Goreni, or did they come from the sound of his scream? And which one of them was performing CPR? Why didn't he? Did he, Yoni, hug her? He suspected he didn't and that broke his heart. He should have given his beloved Tata one last hug. Tata who raised him, who sang to him, who told him stories, who loved him like the boy she had once lost.

Someone was wailing. Or it was the sirens, getting close. An ambulance squeezed through on the narrow, unpaved Michal Street, and it was the abrupt ceasing of the siren outside her house, the steady orange blinking illuminating the dim hallway, that made it real. Paramedics burst in. Where did he go? Did he stand in the hallway, folded against the wall with the pictures of his missing uncle? Did he step outside into the yard and stand in the sun and heat of the cruelest month, wishing, like always, for rain? How he hated July and August. The oppressive heat, the relentless humidity, the rage bubbling in the streets.

"I don't even know why I'm here," he said to Dvora.

BACK AT THE house, a new batch of people were coming to pay their respects, the afternoon crowd. He wished he could bar the door, turn them away, as though by keeping them out he could make her death unhappen. Like when he first saw the black-squared notice of her death hung in the staircase and thought, Who died? He almost ripped the notice off.

Motti walked in with new supplies, and Yoni jumped on his feet to assist, running downstairs to the car to lug stacks of plastic chairs and boxes of food. His body, which had transformed over the summer into a man's, was good for lifting things. "Here, let me," he said to the procession of neighbors who came carrying pots, chicken tzli with potatoes, fragrant beef soup with hilba, steaming saluf and freshly ground schug. He was grateful for the strength and function of this new body, and at that moment, even for its unfamiliarity.

If it wasn't really him, then maybe this wasn't happening.

He stepped out of the kitchen just as his friend Shlomi walked in with a few kids from class. Too late to hide. They surrounded him, closing in, tapped him on the shoulder, murmured condolences. Shlomi gave him a quick, bony hug. "May you know no further sorrow," he said, unable to look him in the eye. "If you ever want to talk." Yoni mumbled something and walked away, toward his room.

He closed the door and lay on his unmade bed, arms in triangles under his head. Why did everyone want him to talk? What was the point? He was never much of a talker. At eighteen months, when he still hadn't said a word, his mom took him to doctors and specialists who checked his hearing, his vocal cords, his motor skills. Everything was in order. They could not find a reason for his speech delay.

When he finally started speaking, his first word was *Tata*. Tata for Savta: Grandmother. *Ima,* Mother, came second. His grandmother loved the name he'd given her. Maybe because she was never just a savta to him. Yoni and his mom lived with her after his father left, and Tata watched him while his mom worked. He spent more time with her than with anybody. In a sense, she was both a mother and a grandmother. That deserved its own word.

At the age of six, before starting school, he developed chronic hoarseness. His mom took him to an ear, nose and throat specialist on Rothschild Street. The doctor did some tests and asked questions. Did he yell a lot? Cry often? But Yoni was a quiet boy. Maybe cheering in school? "Do you like watching sports?" the doctor insisted. Yoni kept shaking his head, buried his face in his mom's lap. The doctor recommended a speech therapist.

The speech therapist was a young, soft-spoken religious woman with her hair wrapped in a colorful turban. Yoni heard her explaining to his mom that he had a voice disorder, but they could initiate some behavioral changes that would help his vocal cords heal. She taught him to take deep belly breaths and relax the muscles in his throat before speaking. It was important to stay hydrated. No Coca-Cola or caffeinated beverages.

When they came home, Tata listened with a skeptical expression. "Maybe he's nervous about first grade," she said. "It's a big change. He's smart. He'll figure it out." But these words, *voice disorder,* stayed with him. And the effort to speak clearly and slowly made him want to talk less and less.

"Not everyone has to be a talker," Tata said. "Look at politicians. They talk and talk and say nothing. Some of the smartest people I know are quiet. They don't feel the need to prove themselves. Me? I'm not that smart. I talk talk talk." Her hand mimicked a mouth opening and closing.

"I love when you talk," he said.

She grabbed him, as she often did, as if overtaken by an uncontrolled burst of love, hugging him too hard, kissing the top of his head repeatedly, showering him with endearments. Ayuni, galbi, hayati. *My eyes, my heart, my life.* He laughed when she did that, delighted.

Other grandmothers read books to their grandsons before bed. His told him stories. Tata's Yemen sounded like a fairy tale, a thrilling and terrifying place. There were wild barrels of monkeys in the hills, wolves and tigers. And some springs, locust swarms blackened the sky. The men caught them by the jarfuls and brought them home to their wives. The wives snapped off the insects' heads, legs and wings, boiled the crispy bodies in water and salt, and sautéed them in a pan. Sometimes they roasted them in the tabun and snacked on them, like crispy nuts.

"Ew! You ate bugs?" He twisted his face.

Tata laughed. "Locusts are kosher! And a delicacy. Rich in protein and fat. You would have liked them."

In Yemen, there were demons and spirits, and the walls of one's house came alive at night with the sounds of the jinns, the Jiran il Beit. "I could hear them every night as I went to sleep," she said in a whisper, enunciating to enhance the tension. The family of spirits would be living their lives, grinding wheat, drawing water, dancing and singing and eating meals too bland for a human stomach, for spices and salt upset the spirits' constitution. "You had to be kind to the Jiran il Beit," Tata said, "leave food and water out for them before bed so they wouldn't harm your family." In Israel, whenever she mentioned the jinns, people curled their eyebrows up, bewildered and amused. Tata mimicked their expression in an exaggerated way. "Spirits?" they said. "In the walls?"

The queen of demons, Lilith, was so powerful she could shape-shift into a sheep or a tiger and ambush nomads and little children by water sources. Lilith was known to attack new mothers and their babies who were left alone, inflicting them with diseases and driving them to madness. A new mother was never left unattended, and for the first forty days, women stayed by her bed, hung amulets in her room to repel Lilith and tended to her every need. And Umm al-Subyan, who seduced lone travelers and kidnapped children, lived in deep wells and her legs were the legs of a donkey. She walked around naked, and her breasts were so large she flung them over her shoulder. "If you see her, you say 'Shema Israel' and make a lot of noise. It scares her into leaving."

She told him her mother was so beautiful that she had to hide her face when she walked in the market from fear of the evil eye. "Once, at a wedding, some woman looked at her funny, you know, like she was jealous, and the next day, my mom had an infection in her eye!" The curse of the evil eye, Tata explained, came from people's thoughts, not from their hearts. It fed on dissatisfaction, greed and self-pity, and overtook them against their better judgment. "That's why when you were a baby, I covered the crib whenever I walked with you in the street, so people didn't see how beautiful you were."

In Yemen they stuffed knives in babies' cribs because the metal warded off the spirits. But in Israel there was so much metal everywhere, cars and machines and whatnot. "That's why we don't have jinns here," Tata explained.

"Stop filling his head with nonsense," his mother said. "He doesn't need more anxiety in his life."

"It's not nonsense," Tata said, offended.

He knew she hadn't told any of these stories to her daughters growing up. "They were busy with other things," she said, waving her hand. But a cloud passed over her eyes. Later, there were other stories, other secrets, she told no one. No one but him.

"Yoni." His mom opened the door without knocking, poking her head in. "Your friends are leaving."

He got up, stood at the door for a moment, steeling himself before he returned to that room, back to the chatter and noise, to the empty condolences and sad glances, to his family, whom he often felt adjacent to. Back to the inconceivable reality of Tata's death.

CHAPTER 4

ZOHARA

IN THE EVENING, Motti dropped me and my backpack off at my mother's house. I stood at the door and watched him drive away, the dust rising from the unpaved road turning golden from the glow of the streetlights.

Then, it was quiet.

After years of living in Manhattan, where the sound of taxis and traffic and trucks beeping in reverse became the soundtrack to my life, I forgot how quiet Sha'ariya got in the evenings. A sleepy Yemeni neighborhood, it stayed behind, while Petah Tikva grew up and around it, cranes littering its sky. In Sha'ariya, there were dirt roads and small houses, chicks and roosters calling at dawn and the kind of startling quietness that was only disturbed by crickets chirping in a steady two-beat song, the electrical hum of appliances and the hissing of cars on their way to the airport from highway 40 nearby.

I unlatched the gate, orange with rust, predicting its familiar creak, and walked the paved path, past the names Lizzie and I had engraved in the fresh concrete when it was repaved a few years in. The laundry lines in the front yard were empty, but for a single hardened cleaning cloth, a faded yellow stain against the whiteness of the house. To the right, my mother's garden was wilting in the heat.

It was a relatively new thing, gardening. On my last visit, I was pleased to see petunias blooming in bright pink and deep purple, red geraniums, clumps of cilantro and mint, and my mother kneeling between the flowerbeds, finding joy in something other than cleaning. A miracle. Her planting things, watching them grow, felt intrinsically optimistic. Gardening added color to her cheeks, smoothed the wrinkles in her forehead. For the first time in years, she looked happy.

I glanced at the shed in the back, where Mr. Hason, my mother's most recent tenant, lived. The door was closed, the shutters drawn. I could hear faint Arabic music playing from the inside. The rental unit was a modest source of income for my parents. A few people in the neighborhood had built them back in the day as an extra unit for their children or as a rental. My mom's closest friend, Bruria, lived there first, and after she moved to a bigger place the next street down, Lizzie occupied it for a few years. When she got married, Mrs. Matalon, my favorite tenant, moved in. Mrs. Matalon spoke three languages, Hebrew, French and Egyptian Arabic, which was her mother tongue. She loved to knit, often sitting outside with her impressive updo, her eyes painted with kohl like a movie star. When she moved out to live with her daughter in a moshav by Jerusalem, a spry, elderly Persian widower moved in, who fed the neighborhood's cats and played cards with my mom. Then, I moved away and lost track.

I reached for the key over the doorframe, feeling the familiar grit of dirt before my fingers found it. I hesitated before opening the door.

Inside, it stank of unaired spices, of soup and detergent, the sharpness of bleach and citrus. Every time I came for a visit, I left with a suitcase drenched in that blend. The clean was a little faded, covered in a thin layer of dust. It would have driven her crazy.

I stopped to look at the framed pictures in the hallway that had haunted me my entire life, a modest shrine to my brother. It was the first thing you saw when you walked in the house; you couldn't miss it. There weren't many photos taken in those days; these two were all she had: one was from their immigration papers, reproduced and enlarged to a four-by-six, which made it blurry. In it, my mother appeared shell-shocked, stunned by the magic of photography and exhausted from the arduous journey. Baby Rafael was laughing in her lap, doughy-cheeked and fair against my mother's dark complexion.

The other photo was a candid black and white taken in the immigrant camp, outside their tent; I'm not sure who took it or how my family got hold of it. My mom was kneeling, dressed in an oversized coat, her headscarf tied at the chin, and smiling up at Rafael. My brother was dressed in a woolly vest, his one hand pointing at something far ahead. I turned the hallway light on, a naked bulb dangling from the ceiling, and the photo revealed my own reflection, the ghost of me, hovering over my young mother's face, smiling like I had never seen her smile.

My brother, Rafael, disappeared from the immigrant camp in Rosh HaAyin a few months after my family landed in Israel in 1949. They told me he was an easygoing, good-natured and healthy baby. When they arrived in the camp, they were instructed to house all infants at a nursery. It was better for the babies, the nurses had said. The tents were unhygienic. At first the Yemeni mothers rebelled, sneaking in to steal their own babies back, until the camp tightened security. My mother had gone to the nursery several times a day to nurse Rafael. In the evenings she would take him out, bathe him and play with him before bringing him back.

One morning my mother went to the nursery and Rafael wasn't there. The nurses informed her my brother had developed a cold, so they sent him to the hospital in Tel Aviv overnight. My father was away at the time, working up north. My mother took a bus to visit Rafael, but when she arrived, she was told by a receptionist that Rafael had died.

Every time I imagine that moment: my young mother, a teenager really, receiving the news that would alter her life forever, I feel like I can't breathe from the magnitude of inherited grief. My mom collapsed on the floor of the hospital screaming and crying. Her boy had died. Except he was completely healthy and vital the day before. Except they wouldn't give her a death certificate or show her a body or a grave. "You're still young," a nurse told her. "You'll have other kids."

Over the following weeks, stories of other babies, other deaths, other disappearances were circulated around the camp. Later, it became clear that many babies had gone missing the same way during those years, most of them Yemeni, the rest Mizrahi and Balkan, and even the odd Ashkenazi child. Some people, like Yosef Radai from the neighboring tent, didn't believe the nurses; he searched through the hospital in a blinding rage and found his girl. Undead. Rumors spread of wealthy American Jews coming to choose children to adopt, children who had been dressed for the occasion in clothes that weren't theirs, displayed like cattle. After all, Yemeni immigrants had many children, *too many* children, and no awareness of hygiene. They lacked parenting skills. And they were foreign looking, so unlike the European Jews, so easily othered it seemed okay to take their children away from them, move them to a different location, or not keep track of them. Years later, in New York, my friend Shoshi showed me some of the quotes she had found in her research into the affair: one head nurse who had been interviewed by the committee said, "Maybe we did them a favor." Another referred to the children as packages. "I would have been happy to know my kids received better education," she said.

When I was five or six, my mother took me to kindergarten one morning and found the gate locked. I remember her looking over the fence, calling the teachers' names, growing increasingly distressed. A woman who walked by told us the teachers were on strike. "Didn't you hear?" she said, critique in her voice. "They've been threatening to shut down all week."

My mother didn't take me home. We walked through the streets of Sha'ariya until we reached a bus stop. I didn't notice she was wearing a backpack, didn't think it was odd she had brought food and water. I was excited she decided to do something special with me. My mother wasn't fun or spontaneous. She never—not once—took me to the movies or to a café. I didn't know that I was a distraction, that the teachers' strike was a dent in her plans.

On the bus, I sat by the window and talked, aware that I had my mom's undivided attention. At home, she was always cleaning or cooking, always impatient, distracted. Now, she let me play with her bracelets and sang Hanukkah songs with me.

We got off at a busy bus station and followed throngs of people in army uniform to a fenced building with a guarded gate. We sat on a bench outside, under a ficus tree with dark green leaves. My mother closely watched the soldiers coming in and out. I didn't wonder why my mother had taken me to this strange place to watch boys walking out of a building. I climbed the bench and followed the tangled bark with my fingertips. I lay down with my head on my mom's thighs and looked up: the sunlight filtering through the leaves cast dappled shadows on my body. After a while, I grew impatient, tired, hungry. My mother kept saying, "Just a little longer, ayuni." She promised to buy me candy afterwards. She gave me her backpack to riffle through.

When a group of boys came out, tapping each other on the shoulder, yelling, "Mazal tov" and "Good luck in civil life!" my mom straightened in her seat at once. I watched them too, fascinated. They were beautiful in their enthusiasm and vitality. When the group dispersed, she stood up quickly. "Wait here," she ordered without looking at me. She called one of them, a gangly Yemeni boy, and he hesitantly turned to her. She asked him where he was born, who his parents were. I could tell he didn't want to talk to her. When we walked away, she was crying. "Why are you crying, Ima?" I asked, and she said, "Nothing, hayati." She wrapped her arm around me, and we walked like that until the bus station.

On the way home, she asked me not to tell my father about our trip. "It will be our little secret," she said. But over dinner I got too excited and whispered to my sister that Ima had taken me to a place with soldiers today. Lizzie's face changed to alarm. My father stopped eating. "Now you get Zohara involved? This is madness. You have to stop."

THE DOOR TO my childhood bedroom was open. It remained the same, a dusty, rundown version of it—the walls peeling, slats missing in the old wooden shutters. One side of it was used as storage now, the boxes piled high against the wall next to a broken ventilator and a couple garbage bags full of things my mother probably planned on donating. My teenage twin bed was still there, my desk carved with hearts and names of boys I had long forgotten, the bookshelf carrying the idols of my youth, Yehuda Amichai, Amos Oz, Dvora Omer, the Hebrew translation of *Anne of Green Gables,* and of course my beloved Dahlia Ravikovitch, her poetry volumes worn and well-read. I picked *A Hard Winter* from the shelf, her second book, found "Tirzah and The Whole Wide World" and read:

Take me to the north end,
Take me to the Atlantic Ocean,
Place me among other people,
whom I had never met before.

The metal hinges of my shutters creaked and resisted, until I managed to push them out against the overgrown guava tree branches, the fruit's pungent smell immediately in my nostrils, a gut punch of memories. How I loved that window, loved sitting on its sill with the shutters open wide, smoking into the night.

I kicked my flip-flops off, lay on the unmade bed and fell into a dreamless sleep.

WHEN I WOKE up, the morning heat had slithered through the shutters I left open and lay over me heavily, tangled in my sheets like a lover's sweaty body. For a split second I couldn't remember where I was, the stickiness much like the one I would wake to in my beach bungalow.

I shuffled to my mother's small, squared kitchen. Built back before open concept, before kitchens were acknowledged and celebrated as the center of the house, my mom's kitchen was a room for one master, everything an arm's length away.

At the entrance I stopped, expecting some evidence to the tragedy that took place here, a shadow of her body on the pristine floor. But it was clean. Untouched.

There was Turkish coffee in the cupboard, thank God. Ground beans from the coffee guy in the market stored inside an empty pickle jar. I dumped a hefty spoonful into a small glass cup, added a generous heap of white sugar, boiled water on the gas stove and in the meantime opened the fridge absentmindedly. The inside of it—full of things she had purchased—knocked me cold. A half-eaten tub of cottage cheese. A couple of waxy green apples, apples my mother had selected from a towering pile at the market, turning to inspect them for blemishes and bruises before dropping them in her cart. In the bottom drawer, something green wilted like seaweed. I shut the door and leaned against it, breathing.

The kettle shrieked and I poured boiling water into my cup, didn't wait for the coffee grounds to settle and stepped outside.

In the front yard, I sat squinting against the sunlight. I hadn't called Iggy or Mika yet. After five years away, they were the only friends I had left in Israel. It was inevitable, of course, but somehow it still hurt, like leaving the house without telling anybody, and returning to see that no one had called, no one came looking.

Mika's machine picked up, her voice sunny, assured. *You've reached Mika and Avner.* Avner, a down-to-earth yoga teacher she had met at a class he'd taught in Tel Aviv, owned a successful studio, cooked delicious vegetarian meals, baked braided challahs on Fridays and worshipped Mika like the goddess she was. After their wedding in Havat Ronit she had moved with him to a moshav by the airport and never looked back. "Mika, motek." I halted. "I'm in Israel." Another pause. "My mother is dead."

It was disconcerting hearing those words coming out of my mouth. Just as it was being in her house without her. I kept expecting her to walk in from the store, call me from the kitchen, to hear her TV playing, always too loudly, as if this were just another one of my visits.

Only after I moved to New York had we reached a quiet, dignified truce. During my trips back home, we existed amicably. I kept my room clean, helped with the shopping and the laundry. In the evenings, we sat in the yard and watched the neighborhood go by, the kids playing on the road, the dull echo of their dribbling ball, the elderly women strolling and stopping to chat over the chicken-wire fence, the men nodding as they returned from prayer. Our best times were during those visits.

And now I was back. I finally made it home again and she wasn't here.

I tried to remember when I last saw my mother, racking my brain, face crumpled with effort, as if having a clear sense of narrative would bring me comfort. I wanted it so bad that I summoned a made-up memory of our last embrace in this very yard, a cab to the airport idling by the gate. But the details kept shifting. Was it daytime? Night? Did she slip out of her bed to give me a hug?

Then I remembered. It wasn't here at all. The last time we saw each

other was actually in New York, during the one visit my mom had paid
me. She had started going on organized trips with seniors from Sha'ariya
a few years back. At first, they toured Israel, dipped their toes in the
Banias, walked the Old City in Akko, hiked Ein Gedi and rubbed me-
dicinal mud on their skin in the Dead Sea. Then they ventured farther,
to Turkey and Greece, on a tour of classical Europe. She even made it to
Petra, like she'd always wanted. She would come back with the most
awful, kitschy souvenirs as gifts: she bought my sister a T-shirt that said,
My mother went to Athens and all she got me was this lousy T-shirt. A
snow globe of Santa Claus in a carriage from Switzerland. An ashtray
made to look like a Dutch clog from Holland. A miniature Eiffel Tower
from Paris.

I loved that my mother traveled, was relieved to see her doing something new, showing interest in the world. Like gardening, it changed
something in her, reversed her aging. I had often worried about how
small her life was and felt guilty for thinking that. My sister was entertained by our mom's newfound wanderlust, at first, but later, I could
sense her absences were becoming an inconvenience. "She's going for
the week again." She'd sigh. "I have to leave work early or find someone
to pick up the girls from day care."

A year and a half ago, my mother called to tell me they were coming
to the US. America was how she called it. It was the big one. The group
hadn't gone that far before. She asked how cold it would be. Would she
need to buy a heavier coat or would the wool one she'd bought at the
Shekem department store suffice? How about boots? She wasn't sure
hers were waterproof. She was excited to see the Christmas decorations.
She'd heard it was festive. "It is," I said, although I struggled to see the
beauty of the season in those days. Zack and I were not in a good place,
which was easy to hide from her when phone calls were costly and she
was half a world away but would be harder to pull off in person.

In the end, she was only in the city for three days before heading to
Florida, to Disney World. On her first evening, I picked her up at the
hotel for a brief visit in my apartment, which I had scrubbed for days
before, going as far as buying a new bathroom rug and fluffy, colorful
pillowcases, removing all the dishes from the cupboards, lining the
shelves with checkered adhesive liners.

"It's tiny." My mother scrunched her nose when she walked in. "Isn't it too cramped for the two of you?"

"It's a good thing we like each other," I said too cheerfully, which fortunately she missed. She scanned the room with a critical glare.

"But it's clean," I said, despite myself. "Right?"

My mother smiled, pleased I sought her approval. "It's clean."

THE NEXT DAY I joined her group on their exploration of the city. We met outside Penn Station, near their hotel. When I saw the gaggle of women clustered on the sidewalk by the tour bus, women I knew from childhood, the grocery store, the hair salon, planted into my new life in New York, I felt the odd, disorienting sensation of worlds colliding. They took too much space, laughing and speaking too loudly, their gestures too large and out of place. I stiffened, as if their presence threatened everything I had worked so hard to accomplish, the anonymity and freedom I had gained in this foreign city.

Resolving to shed my ego, I decided to play tourist, pretend for a day I was still living in Sha'ariya, had never left, that these were my people, this was my life. For one day, I slipped into the skin of that other Zohara, the one who stayed behind, the Zohara I could have been if things were different.

At the end of the day, we stood on the roof of the Empire State Building. The weather was mild for the season, but my mother and her friends were all bundled up, unaccustomed to East Coast temperatures. Since my arrival in New York, I hadn't been up here. And now, the sky was darkening, turning deep indigo, a richness of blue it only attained in winter. The city was covered in patches of white, the night pulsating and flickering with tiny lights. A gust of strong wind thrust my mother toward me, her headscarf sliding back onto her neck, revealing her salt and pepper curls, much whiter than I remembered them. She laughed, adjusted her scarf, grabbed my elbow and hooked her arm through it, pressing her small frame against my body. I froze, thrown off by the physical closeness. There was something different about her. Had I been away for too long? Was it the new settings? Or was it me? I watched her closely, as if seeing her for the first time. She tucked a curl behind her ear. She was, I realized, beautiful.

"Cold?" I asked.

My mom nodded, her body softening toward mine. We stood there a moment. When the group was called in, we walked with our arms hooked together for a few seconds, but it was awkward, uncoordinated. She let go of my arm and stepped away.

Or was it me who let her go first?

CHAPTER 5

ZOHARA

BY EVENING, LIZZIE'S house was packed with after-work visitors, women stirring large pots in the kitchen, serving steaming Yemeni soup, tossing salads. As a mourner, I was not supposed to do any chores, but I wanted to. Most people don't know how to talk to a grieving family, which left me feeling as though I had to make it easy for them, help them through this. I had to remind myself to stop.

I almost missed Mika standing at the door, dressed in a wide gray dress, her brown curls full and bouncy. Her face was rounder, flushed. It took me a second to grasp what I was seeing. "Holy shit," I said, hugging her and then cupping her belly in my palms.

"I didn't know how to get ahold of you," she said. "I really wanted to tell you."

And it was there, standing at the door with my best friend, her belly carrying life, that I found myself crying for the first time.

"Oh, honey," Mika said, crying too.

We took the elevator down, sat perched against the stone fence outside for a while without speaking. I leaned my head on her shoulder, and Mika stroked it softly. Mika and I used to sleep together spooned like lovers, often kissed on the mouth when we met. It was an uncomplicated intimacy—never sexual, never awkward—I hadn't experienced with any other women, hadn't known with my sister or mother, whose bodies were always a bit stiff, unreachable.

Mika and I met at Schneider. The school aimed to integrate mostly affluent Ashkenazi Jerusalemite kids who returned home daily, who spent vacations abroad and owned several pairs of Levi's, with boarders— Mizrahi children on scholarships from development towns and impoverished neighborhoods. I guess Sha'ariya was technically considered one, although in all honesty, it didn't feel as disadvantaged as some. A traditional, working-class neighborhood, it consisted of small single-story homes and some public housing complexes, the kind that looked the same everywhere, long, yellowing row houses with multiple entrances, laundry sagging on strung lines suspended from service balconies, and backyards strewn with broken furniture and overgrown with weeds. Yes, we had our resident junkie in Sha'ariya too, Eddi, who knocked on doors begging for money. My mom always opened because she knew his parents, but only gave him food. We had drunks too, who sat on the benches outside the clinic or the basketball court, their smell preceding them. But mostly, it was a safe, family-oriented, traditional neighborhood. And I knew we fared better than some of my classmates, who came from rough areas known for crime, unemployment and extreme poverty.

Mika was from one such neighborhood. To get to her house, you walked for thirty minutes east from mine, across the highway and past the army base; a row of eucalyptus trees with shedding bark lined the potholed road. She lived with her mother and three brothers in one of these public housing complexes, which made up most of their neighborhood. The first time I went to visit her, there was a man passed out in the middle of the sidewalk. "That's Moshiko," Mika said as she took my hand and guided me around him. "Don't worry about him." At the street corner a few men loitered, a couple of them exchanged something furtively. The building she was living in had a Yemeni family next door, a Cochini family below, a Russian family above and one, recently arrived, from Ethiopia. We went downstairs at some point, to have some privacy, and saw a bunch of men smoking something that smelled funny. One of them whistled at us and did a thrusting motion with his crotch, to which Mika replied, "Fuck off, pervert." From another building I heard a man and a woman screaming at each other and a baby crying.

Before I met Mika, I sat through classes with my arms folded and a sulk on my face, refusing to admit I was impressed and a little intimidated by the teachers, the activities and the facilities. I went into my shared dorm room and cried into my pillow. I called my mom from the pay phone begging to come home. She said, "Give it a chance, binti. It will be good for you." So, I stopped calling, growing angry and indignant.

On our first weekend back, I noticed Mika on the bus and was surprised when she got off at the same stop. I hadn't known there was a student who lived nearby. After the weekend, she was waiting at the same pickup stop. We started talking. Mika was thrilled about school, about being away from home, on her own. "I share a room with my disgusting brothers," she said. She couldn't understand why I was upset about being sent to Schneider. "Are you close with your mom?" she asked. "Did you love your school?"

Mika wore loose sirwal pants and long, sweeping skirts, dangling feathery earrings and large beaded necklaces. She owned a real silk shirt and a furry vest she had bought at the flea market in Jaffa. "Five shekels each!" She loved Janis Joplin too and dressed like her for Purim once. She frequently walked barefoot in the hallways. She wore two different-colored Converse shoes, played guitar and sang. She wanted to be an actress and sometimes launched into an unprompted rehearsed monologue. I might say, "Shit, sorry," about something trivial, like eating the last wafer in the package, and she would transform into Miriam from Sobol's *The Night of the Twentieth* and profess passionately, "Do you want me to forgive you? Sure . . . I can forgive you if you find it necessary." But unlike other aspiring actors I knew, she was also gifted by a calming presence and a generous spirit. When I talked, she was absorbed in my words, her doe eyes large and intent. Maybe that's why she ended up becoming a psychologist in the end, not an actress.

Eventually, Mika moved into my room and the two of us slept in one bunk bed, chatting in whispers at night until the other girls yelled at us to shut the hell up. We worked together too, cleaning homes in an affluent neighborhood in Jerusalem a walking distance from school for extra cash. The houses had sprawling lawns, overflowing bookshelves, canvases on walls, vases and sculptures on shelves. My own home was almost austere in its simplicity and functionality. The concept of knick-knacks was entirely foreign to my parents. In my mom's mind, beauty was expressed through hygiene and order. "Cleanliness is the diamonds of the poor," she said.

My mom had cleaned houses for most of her life before she got the job at Beit Ora. Yet, as Mika and I soon found out, cleanliness was not an inherent skill. Living with my mom, I never had to be good at it. Or maybe I rejected it because it was "her thing." At one house, I had burnt our employer's skirt when she asked me to iron it. She kindly agreed to give us another chance, and after that, Mika ordered me to wash dishes, sweep and tidy, while she did the heavy-duty stuff. With the money we earned, we shopped at the Old City or the flea market in Jaffa, browsed for records in Piccadilly, bought books of poetry (me) and plays (Mika) at Dani Books. Once, we went to Eilat for a weekend, slept in sleeping bags on the beach and subsisted on burgers and chips at Burger Ranch.

Outside Lizzie's building, we caught up. Mika was due in November. Everything was going smoothly, *tfu tfu tfu*. I gave her a quick rundown of my time in Thailand. Last time we spoke I was still in New York, just got divorced. I never even told her what happened, exactly. I hadn't told anyone back home.

A scooter stopped beside us, its beam blinding us, then turning off. The rider pulled the helmet off his bald head. Iggy. Like with Mika, it always surprised me that I went on living without him near me. No matter how long I'd been gone, how long we hadn't spoken or written, every time we saw each other, we were back where we left off.

"Haddad," he said, calling me by my last name, the way we used to do in the army base where we met. I fell into his arms, buried my face in his angular chest.

He held me by the shoulders, looked me over. "You look terrible."

I wiped my tears and laughed. "Thanks, asshole."

He kissed me hard on the cheek. "I brought you something." He reached into his leather jacket pocket and pulled out a joint.

"You're a lifesaver."

"Guess I shouldn't offer you some?" He gestured at Mika. "Mazal tov, motek." He leaned over to kiss her.

Mika glanced at her watch. "I'm going up to see your family but then I have to run. Doctor appointment." She rubbed her belly. "But I'll see you tomorrow, okay?"

Iggy and I walked the darkening streets filled with children on bikes and young parents pushing strollers. As we walked toward the heart of Sha'ariya, the apartment buildings gave way to smaller houses, sleepy, quiet streets permanently drenched in the aroma of Yemeni soup. We turned into a small park, dimly lit, sat on a wooden bench etched with hearts and names. Iggy lit the joint and passed it to me. I inhaled deeply and coughed; it tasted rough, sandy. The pot started to blur the edges, cushioning corners, softening my vision. I leaned back.

Iggy pulled out a small plastic bag from his pocket and planted it in my palm. "I went through my dealer on the way."

I leaned into him sideways, inhaling his smell, the same sharp aftershave he'd been using for years. Sometimes on the subway or while walking down East Village, I'd catch a whiff of it off someone and be stabbed by a bout of longing.

"Poor Saida," he said. "She had such a hard life."

I looked at the houses across the lane, their floating orange windows. "I genuinely thought she was going to be around forever, you know?"

"I know what you mean. I kind of feel that way about my parents."

"Like, haven't we paid our dues already?"

He laughed, exhaling smoke. "Exactly."

"I should probably go back," I said. "Or Lizzie will have a fit."

"I'll come with you," he said.

When Iggy and I met, this was one thing we had in common; his brother was killed in the army when Iggy was around the same age I was when my dad died. It was an exclusive club: we were the only ones allowed to make inappropriate jokes about dead family members, the only ones who knew what to say to others who lost someone close.

We fell in love during long night shifts in an army operation room by the Jordanian border, a border that had little activity to report, mostly a feral dog or a shepherd's lost sheep. We were both sick of the army.

Iggy had transferred into our base after dropping out of the air force, where he was expected to follow in the footsteps of his hero brother. But then the Lebanon war started, and he watched as soldiers kept senselessly dying and wanted nothing to do with "this fucked-up badge of honor" of bereavement he was carrying around.

I had joined feeling enthusiastic and patriotic, believing in the importance of "contributing." Growing up in a place with mandatory service, where the narrative they drilled into us in school positioned us as victims in need of defense, I didn't question it. By the time Iggy came along, I'd lost my zeal, even before I developed strong political views, somewhere between the inherent misogyny and being told what to do by officers I despised, including the one who publicly asked me about my preferences in bed because "you know what they say about Yemeni girls."

AN HOUR LATER, I walked Iggy downstairs. Any excuse to get away from the shiva, even if just for a few moments. We hugged goodbye. "Come by anytime," he said. "You can stay over for as long as you like."

I thought about my mother's house. I promised Yoni to be there. But when I thought of Tel Aviv, the beach, the bars, the parties, it felt light, unburdened, full of life. "I might take you up on that."

"I promise I'll keep my hands to myself."

"What?" I gaped at him. "You told me once you'd never say no to me."

It was a running joke between us, but this time, his laughter sounded off-tune. He strapped his helmet on and swung his leg over the scooter seat. I leaned against the fence and waved at him, then lit a roach I had found in the baggie.

The truth was, for a quick moment there, I considered it. Sex with Iggy. We'd done it before. Post-breakup, I mean. And I never stopped finding him attractive. Iggy was objectively hot by any standards: deep brown eyes, an angular jaw and cheekbones, a slender physique with wide, bony shoulders. Since the last time I saw him, he'd only grown sexier, become better with age.

. . .

WHEN I CAME back upstairs, the shiva was winding down. Three men I vaguely recognized from the neighborhood were having a heated conversation about the peace process and about whether Rabin "was handing the country to the Arabs." Goreni the widower shushed them. "This is a shiva. Can we not?"

A small man turned to me. It took me a second. Mr. Hason. "May you be consoled by the skies," he said, cupping my hands warmly. I thanked him and went to the kitchen to sample snacks and spend time with the women. Leah the hairdresser, our next-door neighbor and one of the neighborhood's most notorious gossips, nudged me. "Your boyfriend?"

"Ex," Shuli, washing dishes at the sink, answered for me.

"My niece just married an Ashkenazi," Leah said, as if this was relevant. "She's over the moon. Ashkenazi men know how to respect women."

"Your mom loved Iggy, you know," Shuli said.

I grabbed a ka'adid cookie from a tray. It wasn't entirely accurate. My mom didn't approve of Iggy at first, but then again, she didn't approve of anything I did back then. I think she never came to terms with us moving in together, which we did as soon as we finished the service, found a tiny bachelor on the fourth floor of a weathered walk-up on Shabazi Street in Neve Tzedek, an old, picturesque neighborhood by the sea, inhabited by young people. The apartment was small and square, so we were never apart, our bed, like a centerpiece, in the middle of it. And we were happy. Happy when we woke up and when we fell asleep; happy when we fought and cried and stormed out; happy when the city was draped in rain, the windows covered in condensation and the ceiling leaking during storms, and we placed buckets and pots and fell asleep to the maddening, dripping sound; happy cooking omelets and pastas in tomato sauce on a camping stove, our small fridge filled with beer, cheese, olives and chocolate. I often wished I had known then what I knew now—that I might never love like this again.

Another neighbor walked in with a tray of dirty cups. "Who's your friend?"

"Iggy?"

"No, the pregnant one."

"Oh, Mika."

"What is she, Moroccan?"

I nodded. That need of my parents' generation to label everyone by their ethnicity and where they came from was the kind of thing that would have never flown in New York. My mother had a friend we had known as "Yochi the Iraqi." The fish seller at the market was "the Tunisian."

"First child?" she continued, placing the cups in the sink.

"Yeah."

"Besha'a tova. What about you? The clock is ticking, you know."

Another thing I couldn't picture happening back in New York. Only here could people use these clichéd terms and get away with it. Until now, it was subtle hints at weddings and brits. Now, maybe because my mom was gone, they were stepping it up. The hum in the kitchen quieted.

"What happened with the American?" Leah asked. "Weren't you married? How old are you anyway?"

I gave her an icy glare, but she wasn't fazed.

"Thirty-three?"

I swallowed the insult. "Thirty-one."

"That's right! I'm a year older than you," my cousin Danit said, breastfeeding her second child in the corner.

"You mom would have loved to see you settled down," Leah said. "She worried about you."

Everyone hummed in agreement. I grabbed a plate of sliced fruit and carried it outside. On the way, I caught Bruria's sympathetic glance. I knew she couldn't say anything in my defense. Not because things had been weird between us, but because she was an example of what I should not become, a cautionary tale.

CHAPTER 6

ZOHARA

ITZIK, THE SALESMAN at the gravestone store adjacent to Segula Cemetery, had a black kippah positioned in the center of his bald spot. The lowest button of his white shirt was undone over his bulging belly, revealing a white tank underneath. "May you know no further sorrow," he said as we sat down.

Against my better judgment, I sighed. Every time someone said it during the shiva, I internally bristled. Were they wishing for me to not live long enough to know more sorrow? And this guy was in the business of sorrow. Doesn't he know better?

In his prefab office, Itzik wiped his glowing forehead with a handkerchief. A ceiling fan stirred the hot air. Lizzie flipped through a glossy catalog while I stared outside the door at the rows of blank marble leaning against the fence. For people who hadn't died yet, the bleak thought went through my head.

"What do you think?" Lizzie nudged me.

I awoke from my daze to glance at the pictures, rectangular body-length tombstones with a little slab at the top, like a pillow. God, this was a terrible catalog. "How much is this?" I pointed at a simple square marble.

"Rega, rega." Itzik raised his hands. "Wasting no time, ha? Let me give you the tour."

Lizzie glared at me. "Somewhere you need to be?"

I shook my head silently.

I had nowhere to be. Nothing to do. I had woken up this morning with an almost hangover headache. My body felt heavy, filled with dread; it came rushing into the hollowness. Turned out grief was lurking in my mother's house, waiting for me to be alone so it could lodge its dirty claws into me. The shiva had ended. The fresh mound was already dried from the heat, and the flowers someone had placed there had lost their petals.

It was over.

There were times during the shiva when I actually enjoyed myself, forgot the reason we had gathered there. As if my mother was just away on one of her trips and would soon return. I understood the custom that brought people together for seven days, forced them to take a break from everyday life to mourn together, providing them with company, distraction, purpose. I couldn't remember the last time I'd had that much family around me.

Shuli told stories about my mom from their childhood in Yemen, some of which I had never heard, like the time my mom hurled a stone at an older boy who was chasing Shuli. When blood started pouring from his forehead, he ran away, sobbing. "She protected me," Shuli said proudly. "No one messed with me after that."

"I never knew my mom to be that bold," I said quietly.

Shuli squinted at me. "Where do you think you got your gutsiness from? Your mom was a badass."

Almost once a day someone spoke of her singing voice. "What a singer," they said. "She could have been Shoshana Damari or Ofra Haza!"

Where did they hear her sing? I didn't say much, feeling increasingly like I hadn't known my mother at all.

Itzik walked us through the lot, pointing at different stones. "This one here"—he motioned at a black slab—"is our most popular. Elegant basalt stone quarried in the Lower Galilee region."

He pointed at a gray stone beside it. "Turkish marble. Durable, strong and easy to polish. Comes in shades of blue, gray and cream. Touch it," he commanded.

Lizzie ran her finger along the stone. She looked at me. I reluctantly followed suit.

"Granite is also popular." He gestured at a pile of stones in the corner. "We have gray, black and even pink."

"What about something simple?" I said.

He stopped, glanced at Lizzie, clearly recognizing who was in charge. "Hebron stone is a good choice. It's light, easy to polish and it's our cheapest option. I just want you to see everything so you can make an informed decision. It is, after all, her final resting place." He stopped to wipe his forehead. I wondered how his kippah stayed on his slick head.

"It doesn't hurt to look," Lizzie agreed.

"What for?" I whispered as we followed Itzik. "You know Mom would have wanted the simplest stone. Look at Dad's."

Obviously, I was not quiet enough, because Itzik turned to me and asked, "Oh, is this a double spot? Because we could also replace your father's gravestone with a double stone. Many children choose to do that for their parents. It's a lovely gesture."

"That won't be necessary," I said. "It's bad enough they have to lie together for eternity."

"Zohara!" Lizzie said in her mommy voice, the one that reminded me of the generation gap between us.

"What? You know it's true."

She ignored me and turned to Itzik. "How much is this?" She pointed at the Hebron stone.

"Two thousand. Twenty-five hundred for the black one."

Two thousand?

"Fine," she said. "We'll take it."

"Would you like it sculpted into a certain shape or . . . ?"

"A square would do," she said.

Heading back to the office, I grabbed Lizzie's elbow. "Holy shit," I whispered. "I had no idea how expensive it is to die nowadays."

Lizzie raised a tired look. "I don't assume you can contribute?"

I stopped. Lizzie paused a pace ahead and looked back. "Why do you say it like that?" I said.

"Because you didn't offer to contribute to the funeral or any of the shiva expenses."

A classic youngest child syndrome, my friend Shoshi, who was the eldest of five, once said about me. We had gone camping together, and I stood dumbfounded in front of the camping stove, crying for help. "You're such a little sister," she said lovingly. "Shit," I said to Lizzie now. "I'm sorry. I didn't realize . . ."

"Nothing is free," she said patronizingly.

"I guess I assumed Ima left some money. It's not like she spent much."

"Maybe she did. We haven't dealt with any of that yet. But you could have asked."

She kept walking, righteous and indignant. I followed her into the office. The fan ruffled the papers stacked on the table. I searched through my purse and pulled out my credit card, slid it across the table. "Why don't I get this one," I said, as if it were my turn at the bar. "We'll sort it out later." I had some reserves—not much after this—from subletting my apartment in New York, money I meant to spend on drinks with umbrellas and rent for a beach bungalow.

As we stepped out of the office, Lizzie marched toward the car. I capped my eyes with my palm, looking over the cemetery. "Do you ever wonder if Rafael might be buried here somewhere?"

Lizzie frowned. "What are you talking about? Why would he be?"

"I don't know. It's possible, no? I thought the most recent commission of inquiry said some of the missing kids were buried here."

"Commission of inquiry." Lizzie snorted. "You know they announced a third one in January? After the whole Meshulam thing?"

Last April, when news that Rabbi Uzi Meshulam and his armed followers had barricaded themselves in his home in Yehud made it to the US, Shoshi called me, breathless. "Turn on your TV." I saw a small house surrounded by a tall hedge and guarded by armed, bearded men. The ticker in the bottom read *Rabbi demanding an investigation into the disappearance of hundreds of Yemeni, Mizrahi and Balkan babies in Israel.* The camera panned to a shaded area by a lemon tree, where a group of Yemeni women stood eager to talk. "My daughter Warda was taken at ten months," said a woman wearing a mustard headscarf. "She was healthy when I last saw her." My heart was pounding. I had never seen anything that close to home on American TV. Or on Israeli TV for that matter. For a moment, I could swear I recognized my mother's face there, standing in the shadow, but when the camera panned back, she was gone. Could she have been there?

For the next forty-five days, I watched the drama unfold on the news until the police broke into the house and arrested Meshulam and his followers, killing one of his disciples at the shootout.

"Why do you think Ima didn't report to the commissions?" I asked Lizzie.

"She reported to the first one," Lizzie said.

"She did?"

"After Rafael got the draft notice from the army, her hope was renewed. This was what led to the commission in the first place, some of these supposedly dead children receiving letters from the army. She even spoke at the commission, without Aba's knowledge." Lizzie sighed. "Poor Mom, she was so hopeful. But they came up with nothing, of course. The same old narrative of 'most of the children died and you're all crazy' and 'there was chaos in the camps. Sorry we misplaced your child.' She didn't bother with the second. It didn't help that Aba shot down the conversation whenever it came up." She kept walking. "But also, Rafael was one of the seventy, eighty cases they couldn't track down. There was nothing in the records."

"I didn't know that." We walked in silence for a moment, just the sound of our sandals crushing gravel. Lizzie beeped at her car. When we got in, the AC vents blew hot air. I stared out the window as Lizzie drove us out of the cemetery.

"Do you remember the day she took me to the army induction base?" I said. The car finally cooled down to un-sauna-like temperatures. We were stopped at a red light in the city center: graying apartment buildings with smog-stained shutters, storefronts with cheap merchandise piled in disarray on the sidewalks, the familiar Pizza USA sign, the A broken so only a triangle was left, crooked. "Wait, where are we going?"

"Getting some veggies at the market. You need anything?"

"I don't know. Maybe."

"Of course I remember." Lizzie turned onto a small street. "It would have been Rafael's release date from the army had he gone."

"That makes sense."

"You know, I found the first letter in the mailbox myself. I'll never forget it. The words: 'to Rafael Haddad.' I hid it for days before I showed it to Aba."

"Why?"

"I wanted to protect her."

"What did Aba say?"

"He said he was going to take care of it. That it was a mistake. But the letters kept coming. Then the army police came to our door."

My jaw dropped. "They came to our door?"

"Yeah. Knocking like crazy. Scared us half to death. Aba opened and they pushed him away, demanding to see Rafael. It was awful. You started crying, Ima started crying. Aba kept saying, our son is dead. Our son is dead. They were rude, saying, Where is he hiding? They told Aba and Ima they were going to arrest them. Poor Ima."

"Wow."

"She started going to the base. Every day for a month, maybe two, sitting outside and waiting for Rafael to show up for his call. Then again after three years, when it was time for his release."

"And she never told Aba?"

"At first she wanted him to come along. They fought about it endlessly."

My parents disagreed on the matter, as they did on many things. Like doctors, for example. Ima never trusted them again after Rafael. The Yemenis had herbal remedies and curses for everything, from anemia, to gas, to dandruff, to anxiety. Lizzie told me that when she suffered from night terrors as a kid, our mom took her to an old lady who performed something called fashta: she took a razor to her upper back and scratched her close to the spine and then poured ice-cold water over it. I was horrified. When it came to cold and flu, there was nothing a spicy Yemeni soup and a hot tea with ginger, lemon and honey couldn't solve. Once, when my fever wouldn't come down, my father took me against her wishes to the clinic. It turned out I had pneumonia and needed antibiotics.

Lizzie parked the car at a makeshift parking lot by the outdoor veg-
etable market. I followed her reluctantly, as I did my mother in childhood. They even had the same determined gait. She dragged a checkered
cart behind her. We entered the market from its rear end, slipping in
between two stalls and finding ourselves smack in the middle of it. The
market overwhelmed me. Always had. The yelling merchants, the
crowds, the ripe smell of fruit. I saw a coffee stall at the far entrance with
milk crates for seats on the sidewalk. "I'll wait for you there." I pointed.
"I can't deal with this right now."

"Suit yourself."

As a little kid, Rafael was my imaginary friend. Despite him being
fifteen years older than me, in my mind he remained a child, a playmate
who understood me better than anybody.

When did the cracks start to form? Maybe it was when I first told
the story to my sixth-grade teacher, Dalit Neufeld. How I loved that
teacher, a tiny blonde who took a liking to me, recommended books for
me to read, and in Purim, when I did not receive mishloach manot, a
basket filled with candy, like the rest of the kids (because whoever I was
assigned to in the raffle dropped the ball), she had gone and bought me
a prewrapped one in the kiosk across the street. At my father's shiva, she
came, sat in the corner, out of place and clearly uncomfortable. But she
came. No one else had Dalit come to their house.

One day, we were talking in class about the founding of Israel, about
the immigrant camps and the ma'abarot, the makeshift settlements that
followed the dismantling of the camps. The ma'abarot were meant to be
transitionary, but some immigrants, mostly Mizrahi, remained there for
many years.

Our textbooks described that time as this magical coming together
of Jews from around the world, skipped over the hardships, the hunger,
the losses, the discrimination. And of course, there was little mention of
the Palestinian tragedy. The Arabs, the story went, fled en masse. A sad
but uncomplicated history, palatable for children. "Anyone here had
parents who were in immigrant camps or in the ma'abara and would like
to share some of their stories?" Dalit asked, and I, along with many in
my class, raised my hand.

Everyone had a story to tell, anecdotes from their parents' childhood, their first encounter with other Jews, with different traditions. When Dalit called on me, I said, "My older brother went missing in Rosh HaAyin camp. My mother says they took Yemeni babies and gave them for adoption." I was pleased to be contributing something new to the conversation, but Dalit tensed up.

"My grandmother saw the daughter they took from her at a doctor's office in Ramat Gan a few years later," Kobi Meoded said. "The girl was sitting with an Ashkenazi woman. And the woman got scared because my grandmother was staring, so she picked her child up and left! Before the doctor even called their name!"

Kids gasped.

"Anyone else?" Dalit said abruptly.

"They liked the Yemeni children because they were beautiful," one girl said without raising her hand. "My neighbor had twins, one was white and one was dark, so they took the white one."

Kobi Meoded scoffed. "They didn't *like* them. They thought their parents couldn't take care of them and there were Holocaust survivors who couldn't have babies—"

Dalit's face hardened. "Quiet in the classroom!" When the room settled down, she said, "It was chaotic in those first days. Imagine how many Jews came all at once. Many babies died of curable diseases back then. Today we are lucky. We have vaccines . . ."

"But my brother was healthy the night before—" I started.

"No talking without raising hands!" Dalit gave me a stern look. "Let's move on."

Was Dalit angry at me? Until then, I was her star pupil.

That day I started to doubt my mother, to see her obsession as an inability to cope with the loss. My mother believed all kind of things. Like jinns in the walls, and the evil eye, and God. She went to holy men's graves to pray for Rafael's return, for husbands for her daughters; she wore amulets and spread them around the house, including in my room, stuffed plants under my mattress, hung garlic bulbs over my head; there were eye-shaped amulets with blue stones and hamsas everywhere. I began to see the story about my brother as yet another superstition. I couldn't understand why she had to make up such nonsense about kidnapping. Why couldn't she let go, like my father had? And I was angry at her for giving me hope, for making me wait for a brother who was never coming back.

The mustached man behind the coffee stall counter turned up the radio and leaned in, eyebrows knitted. "What happened?" I asked.

"Pigua an hour ago," he said. "Number 26 bus in Jerusalem."

The reporter's voice was grave and urgent as he described the burnt carcass of the bus that had been bombed. They already identified all the bodies except for one, a woman. They suspected she may have been the Palestinian suicide bomber. They noted, for some reason, the blue nail polish she had on.

Lizzie waved at me from the market. I downed my coffee, paid, and rushed to her. "There was a pigua in Jerusalem," I said.

"How many?"

"Not sure."

"I almost don't want to know," Lizzie said. "I can't handle more bad news."

WE STOPPED BY my mom's house. Lizzie gazed at it through the car window, her eyes reddening. I noticed her grays were starting to show, the humidity curling her straightened hair. "We need to deal with her things," she said.

I released my safety belt, leaned over and hugged her. "I'll do it. I promised Yoni I would."

"Yoni?"

"Yes, he said something about her spirit lingering. Is he, like, turning religious?"

"I think he finds comfort in it. If it helps him . . . I mean, it's not like he's talking to me."

"Maybe he needs to talk to a professional," I said. "I remember reading somewhere that men who didn't have a strong father figure growing up are likelier to become religious. You know, God as a father kind of thing."

She frowned. "Yoni had a father figure."

"Right. I meant . . . You know what I mean."

From Lizzie's face, it was clear she didn't. I didn't push.

. . .

WHEN I WALKED in, the house was dark and cool. The fridge hummed loudly. Taking a deep breath, I turned on the radio, tinkered with the dial until I found music and grabbed the cleaning supplies from under the sink.

I started with the living room. That's what my father's room became after he died, although none of us ever spent any time there. In fact, it was the room that had the least living in it. I cracked the shutters open and bright sunlight burst in, illuminating twirling rays of dust. When I turned, I was spooked by the sight of the coat rack in the corner, loaded with jackets and scarves and a purse.

Oh my God. Her purse.

My mom's black purse dangled, crooked, from one of the hooks, its unzipped mouth yawning like some strange animal's maw. I could visualize it slinging from her shoulder. She'd had it for so long that the vinyl was cracked and peeling.

I sat on the single armchair in the corner and riffled through it with shaky fingers. There wasn't much: a nondescript hand cream. A couple of crumpled receipts. A silver pack of lozenges with only one remaining. A hair elastic with some of her hairs tangled in it. And her wallet, square and flat. My mom didn't own credit cards, only ever used cash. I unfastened it: a few coins, a twenty-shekel bill, a couple of business cards and her ID in its soft, blue plastic case. She was young in the photo, her smile forced, the strands of hair peeking from under the headscarf still black. Under her birthdate, it listed the year (an approximation, since she did not know her exact age) and the numbers 0000 in lieu of the day and month.

Moving my finger over the faded image, I felt a bump. A small piece of folded paper was wedged behind the card. Gingerly, I released it and unfolded it on my lap. It was a dateless newspaper image, grainy and yellowing. A group of Yemeni men posing by a large tent. It must have been taken at the camps. It reminded me of the photo of my mom and Rafael that hung in the hallway.

I examined the faces in the image, searching for a familiar one but found none.

Why did my mom save this photo of strange men in her ID card? It had to be important if she stuffed it there, where it wouldn't be lost, where it would always be with her. But also, it was hidden, out of sight. What did that mean?

No one answered at Lizzie's. I placed the card back in the wallet, the purse back on the hanger and got to work.

CHAPTER 7

YONI

YONI WAS ON his way to the falafel place to grab lunch when he saw Shlomi sitting slouched on the barricades in front of the stand with a group of popular boys from school. One of them, a buff guy in a tight tank top, lit a smoke. Another spat onto the road. Yoni slowed down his pace, debating his next moves.

Up until last year, he and Shlomi were inseparable. As children, they went to synagogue together, studied for their bar mitzvah, played soccer on the same team. Neither had ever hung out with the cool kids. Both were too nerdy, studious, not athletic enough. Shlomi was short and wiry, and a severe bout of acne in junior high had left him with facial scarring. Tata once called him haba soda, the black nigella seed that dotted her ka'adid cookies. "Tiny and black and with a powerful, strong flavor," she said, pleased with herself for the joke. Shlomi laughed. You could always count on him to appreciate a good joke, even one at his expense. It was his humor and comedy skills that made the popular kids notice him suddenly. Shlomi contorted his face in funny ways, acted out different characters and could imitate all the teachers. The guys started surrounding him at recess, cheering him on. Like he was some kind of clown, Yoni thought but didn't say. Shlomi had tried to get him in with the crowd, calling him to join, but Yoni felt awkward, out of place.

The guys bellowed in laughter now, and Shlomi grinned, pleased at their reaction. He was still the shortest one there. A typical petite Yemeni. More than a head shorter than Yoni. Yoni wasn't sure where he got his own stature from, though Tata had told him northern Yemenis were known to be taller and bigger. Over the last few months, he had grown a few centimeters seemingly overnight, his body bulked, his shoulders broadened, his voice changed. He almost resented his body for growing so fast at a time when he wished to be less visible, to hide. It was too much, losing Tata and his child body at the same time.

At that moment Shlomi looked up from across the street and saw him, raising his hand in a hesitant wave. Yoni turned sharply right, walking away. He could grab a shawarma at the shipudia across the street, out of sight. He pushed the darkened glass door and walked in. The place was busy; men sat biting into pitas bursting with grilled meat, tahini and hot sauce dripping onto their plates. He scanned the prices listed over the counter, realized he couldn't afford it and turned to walk out. "Yoni," Yuda called after him from behind the counter. "What do you want? How much do you have?"

He walked gratefully toward the counter, waiting while Yuda helped another customer. He knew Yuda from synagogue. After the shiva ended, Yoni started attending shacharit prayer almost every morning. Eventually, he started going in the evenings too, channeling his grief toward praying, toward reciting the kaddish daily, asking that Tata's soul ascend and find peace, his entire body clenched with intention. He started to lay tefillin in the mornings too. Tata had bought him a set for his bar mitzvah, smelling of stiff leather, of little use. At first he worried he wouldn't remember how to use it, and the old anger at his absent father swelled in him at once. But as soon as he placed the cool box against his bicep, his body memory was activated. He recited the blessing and wrapped the leather strap on his muscle and forearm, finding comfort in the repetitive circular motions, in taking part in an ancient ritual.

As a kid, he'd watched the other Yemeni boys with their fathers in the synagogue. Some shuffled their feet, slumped in their seats, wishing they were elsewhere. At Tata's request, Shlomi's father had taken Yoni

under his wing and taught him to read the Torah in the Yemeni intona-
tion, guiding him in the correct diction and melodies alongside Shlomi,
encouraging him to use his voice, to project it farther, louder.

He especially loved going on Shabbat, adored the ceremony of
bringing in the scrolls, opening them, and listening to the succession of
men reading the Torah. The tallit felt light on his shoulders and clean.
He took great pleasure in singing along with the psalms, *Yigdal Elohim
chai veyishtabach,* hearing his small voice joining the voices of men and
knowing Tata was watching from the women's section. "You know you
got your singing voice from me," she said.

"Yes, Tata," he said. "It's all from you."

She laughed, delighted.

The guy before him paid and turned. "Oh, hi!" he said, and Yoni
nodded at him hesitantly. Did he know him? He was dressed in black
and white, like a yeshiva student.

Yuda took Yoni's money without a word and even threw in a can of
Coke for free. He shaved the meat off the rotating shawarma machine
into a gaping pita and loaded it with salads. Yoni looked over the restaurant. The tables were all occupied. The young guy from the line waved
him over and Yoni reluctantly joined him.

"Best shawarma in town," the guy said, mouth full.

Yoni nodded, tilting his head and biting into his pita.

"Baruch." The guy wiped his hand on a napkin before extending it.
"From the synagogue."

Right. Yoni swallowed. "Yoni," he said, shaking his hand. Most men
in the synagogue were older, neighbors he knew by name or at least by
face, but this guy was clearly not from the neighborhood, and Yoni was
pretty sure he wasn't Yemeni. He wondered what he was doing there,
why he chose to pray in a Yemeni synagogue.

"You live around here?"

Yoni nodded again.

"Not much of a talker, ha?"

"No," he said.

Baruch chortled.

The television screen that hung diagonally over the counter showed
footage from a violent demonstration against the Oslo peace talks with

the Palestinians; a nationalist group called Zo Artzeinu—this is our land—blocked several major intersections. Baruch looked up and nodded in approval. They cut to people lounging at Tel Aviv beach, women suntanning in bikinis, and Baruch averted his eyes. The ticker read *Twenty-one people have drowned in the sea since the season began.*

Leaning on his left sit bone, Baruch reached into his back pocket and pulled out a flyer, slapping it on the table in front of Yoni. "There's a students' Shabbat in Jerusalem this weekend. You should come."

"What's a students' Shabbat?"

Baruch stared at him for a moment. "How old are you?"

"Eighteen," Yoni said, even though he had six more months to go. Lately people kept thinking him older. Maybe it was his facial hair, which he had grown in mourning, the black kippah he had not taken off. His own reflection pleased him. He looked like someone with purpose.

Baruch laughed. "I see. I thought you had already finished the army. Where do you go to school?"

"Brenner."

"Not a religious school?"

Yoni shook his head no.

"Well, that's okay." Baruch crumpled the shawarma wrapper into a ball. "You can still come if you want. It's nothing formal. Just some university students who meet and talk about the situation. Good folks who want to make a change. Who don't agree with how things are going."

Yoni ate a bit faster, eager to leave.

Baruch eyed him. "How do you feel about the peace process?"

Yoni shrugged his shoulders uncertainly. His politics were not entirely formed yet. And he was too young to vote. But he knew what was going on in the country. He read the papers. At least sometimes. He heard people talking. He understood why many were angry at the government. When the Number 5 bus exploded in Tel Aviv and all those people died, he saw the gory picture of the dead driver on the front page before his mother snatched it away from him. He watched Binyamin Netanyahu, chairman of the Likud party and leader of the opposition, pointing a finger on TV and yelling, "This nation is much stronger than this government!" He saw Likud member Ariel Sharon calling the Labor government, led by Rabin, weak, fearful, pathetic and defeatist. And after the Number 26 exploded in Jerusalem, when Sharon went on a hunger strike outside Rabin's office, calling for the government to resign and for elections to be held earlier, Yoni admired his commitment.

Yoni loved this country. He loved it simply, unequivocally, the way one loves a mother. His heart burst with pride at Remembrance Day ceremonies and on Independence Day, pride for what this little country had achieved against all odds, for its resilience and resourcefulness and strength, pride for what the Jewish people had accomplished after being persecuted and killed throughout history.

"Let me put it another way." Baruch's tone shifted, gained a performative quality, as though he were standing in front of a crowd. "Do you believe this land was given to us by God?"

"Yes?" He didn't mean for it to sound like a question.

"And do you believe Judea and Samaria and Gaza are a part of this land?" Two men at the table beside theirs raised their eyes to look, which egged Baruch on.

"Yes," Yoni said more confidently this time.

"And do you see how the Oslo Accords are at odds with this belief? How Rabin is betraying us all by giving back land that is rightfully ours?"

Yoni nodded contemplatively. It all sounded straightforward to him.

"Then you should definitely come." Baruch grinned and spread his arms in a theatrical welcome gesture. "Meet like-minded people who care about this country and want to make a change."

Yoni considered it. School was about to start, which would keep him busy. But without his daily visits to Tata, his afternoons felt vacant. He rarely saw Shlomi, and he didn't feel like hanging out with anyone from school anyway.

"I'll think about it." Yoni wiped his mouth with a napkin. Shlomi and the guys were probably gone by now. He got up and called to Yuda. "I'll pay you back." Yuda waved his hand dismissively.

CHAPTER 8

ZOHARA

MY MOTHER DID leave some money. That was the first discovery I made when I started going through the house. After finding the inexplicable newspaper image in her ID card, that is.

I started with the bookcase in the living room. The wooden case was sparsely populated: holy books were stacked on the top shelf. On the bottom shelf, a colorful hand-woven Yemeni basket was filled with unsorted stuff: mail, receipts, unidentified keys and cables. The bank statements and bills were in the top drawer of the bookcase, thankfully organized in a manner I could follow. The latest bank statement showed a decent amount in my mother's saving account and a smaller one in her checking. My mother rarely shopped, and until she started traveling in recent years, showed no appreciation for recreational activities. It appeared she had saved some of the money she made over the years working for pennies at Beit Ora. It was more than enough to pay for the funeral, the gravestone.

The drawer below was filled with loose pictures. I picked up a few from the top: my mom with a few women against the backdrop of the Colosseum, her smile genuine, cheeky almost, as if someone had said something funny. The rest of the photos displayed a similar exuberance in them. Traveling was good for her.

I couldn't bear to deal with the kitchen. There was so much of her in it, even though my mom wasn't passionate about cooking, was driven merely by obligation. In my earliest memories from that kitchen, Bruria was often cooking alongside my mom, the two standing by the counter with their backs to the door, my mother petite, Bruria taller and big boned. My mom was insecure about her kitchen skills. Her own mom had died during my aunt Shuli's birth, so she was never properly taught. And Bruria was living in the shed back then and was frequently around. She often had lunch with us, coffee outside with my mother in the mornings. I remembered my mother asking Bruria questions as she cooked. "Is it ready?" "Did I burn it?" "Why did it not turn out like yours?" But I also remembered them being happy there, together. I remembered laughter, easy conversations, a sisterly intimacy.

After Bruria moved one street down, the soup became watery, the chicken overdone, the kitchen turned joyless in her absence. My mom went to visit Bruria almost daily, returning with sweet date squares dusted with sugar, savory ka'adid cookies dotted with nigella seeds, which I could always tell were Bruria's: my mom's were as hard as rock while Bruria's were perfectly crumbly. Sometimes she brought back pots of fragrant Yemeni soup, and when she warmed them up, the whole house was bathed in its soothing incense of turmeric, cardamom and cumin. My father would come back from the butcher shop and his eyes would shine; he devoured the soup, every morsel of it, bringing the bowl to his lips to drain the yellow liquid into his mouth, and then leaned in his seat, satisfied, and complimented my mom on her improvement. My mom never said a word.

HERE ARE SOME things you may find yourself doing when your mom, the clean freak, dies. You polish the windows with vinegar and used newspapers. Saida never read the paper but always had some random sheets in the cleaning supplies closet for that purpose.

Striving for perfection, you clean the window again, so well that by the end of it, your ghostly reflection stares back at you, and you realize *you* are the ghost, an apparition, a spirit of the house, planted here from the past or from a different world.

When you wipe the counters and surfaces, a peculiar set of thoughts compete in your mind:

Thought 1: You're removing her fingerprints, eradicating her mark in the world, diminishing her presence (and also, how sad that this is how she left her mark).

Thought 2: She'd be so proud when she came home and saw how well you cleaned. She'll quickly glide her finger over the surfaces when she thinks you're not looking, the way you saw her do once at your aunt's house, checking for dust. But this time, she'll be pleased. You passed the test!

WHEN I STARTED cleaning, it was out of duty and a need for a distraction, but after a while, my thoughts quieted down, my movements slowed, my whole being relaxed, focused on the task at hand. It became more than a diversion; it was meditative, even pleasant. The mundanity of cleaning gave me a sense of accomplishment after years of lacking just that. I was making things sparkle, attaining achievable goals.

Once, a group of us sat at the Gilman cafeteria in Tel Aviv University and bitched about the cost of tuition. When I contemplated aloud the part-time jobs I could do while studying, a moon-faced auburn-haired girl whose name I no longer remember suggested, "You should clean houses for money."

I bristled. "I can't clean. Trust me. I tried."

"I don't believe that," she said.

"That's not a bad idea," Iggy chimed in. "It's good money."

I glared at him. "You know me. I'm terrible." Iggy did most of the cleaning in our home, and he rarely complained, accepted my shortcomings. I was the kind of person who let dirty dishes pile in the sink and on the counter, who never mopped the floors, only swept and spot-cleaned when it got bad. Everything in our apartment was covered in a thin layer of dust. Was it a part of my rebellion against my mother? Or was it a protest against an unofficial tracking system that destined me, as a Yemeni woman, to a life of cleaning other people's shit?

"It's the way she said that," I later explained to Iggy, who couldn't understand why I had gotten so angry. "The insinuation that as a Yemeni, I should be able to clean." After all, Yemeni women had worked as cleaners and maids from the moment they arrived in Israel, until the word *Yemeni* in its female form became synonymous with *maid*.

In Schneider, we had studied Nathan Alterman, the great Israeli poet, and an Ashkenazi girl by the name of Smadar Horev, who never liked me (or maybe I never liked her), gave a presentation about him, in which she chose to show a clip of his "Yemenite Women Song." She claimed she had come across it at the video library at school and that she wanted to show Alterman's *range*. I had never heard this song before. Three Ashkenazi actresses dressed in loose dresses and headscarves, like my mother would wear, waved cleaning cloths in their hands and sang in an exaggerated *het* and *ayin*, imitating a Yemeni accent:

> *In my left a cloth and a bucket*
> *in my right a brush*

The Yemeni woman in the song, whose "skin is dark," whose legs are "like steel," appeared content, happy even, to be cleaning the house of the Ashkenazi missus with the "wines" and the "pralines"—all these European markers of quality and sophistication she knew nothing about. "The cloth is Yemeni, and the boss is Ashkenazi," they sang, trilling their voice poorly, bobbing their heads like idiots. The room roared in laughter. I wanted to bury myself. Of all the beautiful poetry Alterman had written, she had to pick that song? But everyone acted as though it was a random, meaningless choice, had nothing to do with me and the other Yemeni girl in class, whose face was as red as mine. Nothing to do with the fact that most Mizrahi girls at school worked in cleaning, to pay for the luxuries the Ashkenazi Jerusalemite girls took for granted.

"I honestly don't think she meant that," Iggy insisted. "The stereotype nowadays is Russian, anyway. What with the whole new mass immigration from the Soviet Union and all these immigrants unable to find jobs in their own professions."

I said nothing, feeling ashamed, frustrated at my inability to enlighten him. How could I explain to my boyfriend, whose legacy was the air force, the kibbutz, whose story was written—celebrated!—in history books, that my legacy had been branded a bucket and mop? Maybe I was still unable to explain it to myself.

Years later, in New York, when my Mizrahi awareness grew, I'd realize this is what happens when you're made to feel othered, when you experience casual racism and microaggressions so often that you can't tell when someone is being prejudiced or if something else is going on. This is what happens when the shame from being made to feel "less than" weighs on you from childhood, unspoken, unnamed, there like gravity, like the air you breathe, when your culture is unrepresented or mocked when it is, your past erased, your history dismissed, left out of history books or being rewritten to match the desired narrative. You are left wordless, unable to narrate your own experiences.

As a child, I sometimes joined my mother at work, in spacious homes crowded with books, sparsely decorated apartments with large, white tiles and dark wood furniture, airy villas at the edge of our city, bordering the orchards, with many floors and echoing living rooms. I wasn't allowed to touch anything, only to sit and watch TV or read a book, but I'd peek into children's rooms with their unbelievable amount of toys, or teenagers' rooms painted pink and covered with posters, or large parents' suites with their own bathrooms, smelling stale, of unaired linen.

Sometimes, I met the women who hired her: the broad-shouldered, white-haired professor who kept regifting to her the gift baskets from her job at the university; the bohemian in her silk house coat, who waved us in with her hair unkempt, sleep in her eyes, smelling sour, and, I think now, like wine; the one with the long braid who hugged her when she came in and always apologized for the mess and sometimes joined my mother in wiping counters, working beside her and talking. Once, her daughter was there, a girl my age who asked if I wanted to play. She had a trampoline—I'd never met anyone who had a trampoline, and when she jumped, her light blond hair bounced, framing her face like a mad, beautiful crown. I didn't want to be her friend; I wanted to be her. I wanted her room, her name—Millie, Lily or Nili, short and sweet (unlike the cumbersome Zohara)—her pale skin, which turned rosy after jumping, her freckles—she must have had freckles—and her sweet, kind mom.

By the time I started university, even without considering my failed stint as a maid during high school, I knew there was no way in hell I was ever going to work as a cleaner again. No way I would ever be cleaning rich people's shit. I didn't want to learn how to clean better. I didn't want this to be my inheritance. Instead, I went to work as a barista at a trendy espresso bar on Yehuda Maccabi Street. And still, I had to clean, mop the bar floors every night after the shift, polish the large glass doors, pour yellow bleach powder into toilet bowls. The owner once joked to a friend of his who sat on the bar at the end of the shift, drinking a pint while I mopped, "This is Zohara. I imported her directly from Sana'a," and I giggled in response.

I fucking giggled.

THE NEXT FEW days stuck together, beginningless and endless. I slept more hours than I had in years, ten, eleven, like a teenager, waking up dreamless and sweaty to the kind of stuffy heat I remembered from childhood summers: when I slept in late and watched TV in front of an exhausted oscillating fan, took the bus to the city pool with my friends, spent the whole day there until our palms were wrinkled and the smell of chlorine clung to our skin so hard that even soap couldn't get it off. Unlike New York, where the end of August often offered some reprieve, a hint to the impending end of summer, in Israel the heat only intensified, like summer would never let up and we would never be able to breathe properly again.

In the days, I deep-cleaned, packed stuff away and rested periodically, rereading books from my youth on my bed through a new, critical lens. Why were they so few women on my bookshelf? What was up with the stereotypical depiction of Mizrahi and Palestinians in some of these books I used to love?

By the end of the week the house was immaculate. There was only one room left.

I stood in front of my mother's bedroom, inhaling and exhaling deeply before opening the door. It took a second for my eyes to adjust to the dark, make out the bed, the bedside table with her toiletries, all generic and smelling sickly sweet. The heavy oak wardrobe. The dining table in the middle. The room smelled dusty and thick, like sleep.

I unlatched the windows, snapped the shutters open. The room sprung to life, flushed with sunlight. The sight of her made bed, emptied of her body, knifed me. A cluster of family photos hung over it. Lizzie's wedding to Motti. A photo of me from the army, kneeling on the concrete with a gun, smiling as if it were a toy and not a killing machine. My two nieces posing at a photography studio with their best dresses on. Lizzie again, holding Yoni after his birth, her face illuminated. Yoni in his school uniform, long and awkward with a shadow of a mustache already coloring his upper lip.

Lizzie married Yoni's father young. Everyone deemed him a good match for her, handsome, from a good family. I wish I could say I saw it coming but I didn't. Like everyone, I found him charming. Then, Lizzie started stumbling back to my mother, crying and bruised. One day, pregnant with Yoni, she showed up at our door, limping, black-eyed, face puffy from crying, a suitcase in hand. He called a few times. Lizzie wouldn't talk to him. My mother threatened to call the police. Finally, he stopped.

I was happy to have Lizzie back, and happier when Yoni was born. When my father died, I had been on the brink of adolescence. Within a year, my sister had married and moved away, and it was only my mother and me in a house that suddenly felt too big, me bursting with grief and rage, my mother silent and obsessively cleaning. I missed my father, resented my mother for being the one who stayed.

I didn't know how to channel my anger: I kicked cans while walking down the street, punched holes in corrugated walls by construction sites. I didn't wash my hair, walked around barefoot, the scorching pavement burning a layer on the soles of my feet. At home we fought spectacularly. Unassisted by my father's natural authority, my mother tried to assert her role and told me to come home at certain times, not wear makeup, dress properly, stop listening to this horrible music. This all worked with Lizzie, who was a model adolescent, a dutiful girl, whereas I screamed from the top of my lungs and told her I hated her. She yelled back just as loudly, telling me I was ungrateful. Sometimes she looked at me like she didn't know me, like she couldn't believe I had come from her loins.

I began dreaming of elsewhere, fascinated by the world, the endless possibilities it offered, New York, Scandinavia, India, Paris, Guatemala. I taped pictures on my wall I had cut out from travel magazines my mother got from Leah the hairdresser—high-rises, fjords, mountain ranges—the way other teens hung posters of rock stars.

As soon as I could, I spent most of my days outside the house, satisfying my travel bug in small doses, riding buses to the other side of town, thrilled by the unknown views unfurling outside the smeared window. At twelve I would take the bus to Tel Aviv after school—my mother was working late, anyway—and wander along the seashore, order hot chocolate at windswept cafés with coins I had stolen from her wallet.

After Yoni was born, things got better. My mother was transformed; I had never seen her that happy. Yoni was the child that answered her prayers, the one who would fill the hole in her heart, her second chance. For a while, there was harmony in the house, the three of us pampering the newborn child, taking turns tending to him at night, a united front.

A few months later, when my mom sat me down in the living room, where we never sat, and told me I had been accepted to a prestigious boarding school in Jerusalem on a full scholarship and would be moving there by the end of summer, I was confused, at first, then stunned and wounded.

"But I don't want to go," I said.

"Why not?" my mother said. "You always wanted to travel, see the world. This is an exclusive program. It will give you a start in life." She handed me a glossy brochure with stock pictures of teens smiling on green lawns.

"What are you doing?" Lizzie said to me later, after my mom had obviously called for her help. "I thought you'd be thrilled!"

"Easy for you to say," I said. "She'd never dream of sending you away. She learned to drive after you moved out, just so she could visit you in Nes Ziona." Or maybe once it was only the two of us in the house, she needed to get away as much as I did.

"This is a great opportunity," Lizzie said. "It's one of the best schools in the country and they picked you."

But all I thought was, My mother hates me so much she is getting rid of me. Now that she has Yoni, there's no room for me anymore. Had my father been alive, he would have never let her send me. He'd want me there, beside him.

. . .

INSIDE HER CLOSET, my mother's dresses hung like ghostly figures. How they used to embarrass me. Other Yemeni mothers in the neighborhood, younger ones, wore fashionable jeans and pencil skirts, blow-dried their curls in waves like Ofra Haza, highlighted their locks and wore makeup. Why did she have to look so diasporic? Now I held one out and looked at myself in the mirror. We had a similar figure, wide hipped and pear shaped. The dress hadn't been as shapeless as I remembered it. In fact, it was cinched in the waist. I could wear it with a wide belt and boots.

I hesitated for a minute, then pulled out two bright-colored dresses and one maroon cardigan to wear around the house and stuffed the rest in a black garbage bag. Fast, without stopping to smell them.

The front gate creaked. I peeked through the shutters. Mr. Hason strode by in his determined, energetic way. Short and lean, he was stylish in a way I rarely saw on old Yemeni men, dressed in long pants, even in the summer, always with a flat cap.

I didn't know Mr. Hason well. He had moved into my mother's rental unit so he could be close to his wife in Beit Ora, the geriatric hospital where my mother worked. He never came out when I was around, but once he dropped off the rent check and mentioned a broken thing he immediately offered to fix. Sometimes I'd forget he was there and be surprised by the sound of his music, the smell of his coffee. Every time, I was reassured. He made me feel as though my mom wasn't completely alone. As though I wasn't completely alone.

"Mr. Hason!" I called from the window and immediately regretted it.

He stopped, startled, squinted to look.

I slid the sticky shutters wide open.

"Zohara, shalom." He smiled warmly. "How are you?"

"Cleaning up," I said, waving my gloved hands.

"Yeah?" I detected a worry. "What are you doing with everything?"

"Donating, I guess. There isn't much. Why, do you want anything?" Why did I say that? He wasn't family. There was something heartbreaking about him: his smallness, the slight tremor in his hands, his face pocked with age.

"Oh, no." He waved his hand, but his forehead was still wrinkled. "But if I can help with anything . . ." He suddenly looked crestfallen. "And how's Yoni? The poor boy."

"He's . . . okay." Was he?

"The poor boy," he repeated.

"Mr. Hason," I said, realizing what troubled him. "We're not selling yet or anything. So don't worry. We'll let you know well in advance."

"Oh," he said, visibly relieved. "I started looking for another place too, but that's good of you, Zohara, thank you."

BY THE AFTERNOON my mother's closet was empty. The only thing of interest was a purple plastic bag packed with old documents and some letters sent from Yemen to my father in archaic language I could barely understand.

The room was beginning to be clear of her presence.

I sat on her bed, unscrewed her tub of Nivea hand cream imprinted with her fingerprints and inhaled its scent, sweet and old-lady-like. Her bedside drawer was alive with birthday cards from her grandchildren, hair ties, a tiny book of psalms, a few notes with names and phone numbers in her timid, childlike handwriting.

In the shelf below, I found a shoebox. Arranged neatly in it were tapes, stacked in two levels. Maybe fifty or more. A few were by Yemeni artists my mother had loved, their covers photocopied. You couldn't find Mizrahi artists who sang Mizrahi-style music—whether it was pop or traditional—in regular music shops. They didn't play them on the radio or in the charts. Those who loved Mizrahi music, and many did, had to buy pirated tapes at the cassette market in Tel Aviv's central bus station, as though they were illegal substances.

In my ignorance and my wish to belong, I had mimicked the music industry's bias and lumped traditional Yemeni music with low-brow Mizrahi pop and Arabic legends like Umm Kulthum, Fairuz and Farid al-Atrash, rejected all equally.

I remembered my professor Abe playing Fairuz to me one evening in his office in NYU, while snowflakes swirled outside the window. I could feel the pain, the depth of emotion, even without understanding the lyrics. Away from home, in a different context, I could hear Arabic music for the first time without judgment. Knowing Fairuz was a star in Lebanon, I thought of our own stars, the kind of music we labeled as good in Israel, and the kind we deemed inferior. I remembered how in the eighties, when Ofra Haza released an album of remixed Yemeni songs, Israeli radio ignored it. She had swept Europe by storm before Israel caught on. We were so removed from our surroundings, so stubborn in resisting Arabness.

Most tapes were plain, some had dates written on their spine. They were from the sixties, seventies, eighties. A few recent ones too. Did my mother record music from the radio? What for?

I spotted a tape recorder on the dining room table and shoved a cassette into it. There was a rush of white noise, muffled sounds of the street outside, a chirping bird, then my mother's distinct voice filled the room, unaccompanied, sounding deep and young and clear. My skin broke out in goosebumps. My dead mother was singing in Yemeni to me. What was she saying? I remembered what Yoni had said about her spirit lingering. Was my mother communicating with me through the tape recorder?

This was madness. I must have inhaled too much bleach fumes.

I hit stop.

Dizziness set in. At once, I was famished. I found a bag of peanuts from the flight in my purse and ate those in a few bites.

The phone rang and I hurried to pick it up. "Haddad."

"Iggy." What a relief.

He must have heard it my voice. "You don't sound so good."

"I just found a tape with my mom singing in Yemeni."

"Drop everything," he said. "We're going to the beach."

Grateful, I threw some things in a bag, spent a minute deciding which summer dress from my limited packed-for-Thailand wardrobe to wear over my black bikini and settled on the red one I had bought in Bangkok, feeling foolish and guilty for caring. My curls, unwashed, were tangled and frizzy and too long. I sprayed them with water and squished them in my palm. Good enough. I found the keys to my mother's silver Subaru hanging on a hook by the entrance. She had used it to drive to work, the shuk, and that's pretty much it.

The car coughed a little. I patted the wheel and whispered, "Good little car."

Still hungry, I turned onto the main street and parked in front of the makolet. The guy behind the counter looked up from the newspaper he was hunched over. "Dr. Haddad!"

I frowned. "Doctor?"

"Your mother was bragging. Naturally."

Looked like my mother gave people—the grocery store guy!—an edited version of my life in which I was still on PhD track, still married to Zack.

"I'm not a doctor."

"Not yet."

I missed everything with sudden intensity, my mom, my dad, Eli, who knew the brand of tobacco my father preferred for his mada'a without me having to ask, who saved challah for my mother behind the counter on Fridays, who reprimanded me when I bought too many candies on credit. Was this guy his son or was the store sold? On the counter I placed a banana and a bag of Bamba—the beloved puffed peanut butter snack I used to crave in New York. I grabbed a chocolate bar from the boxes lining the shelf.

While he scanned my groceries, I quickly perused the headlines in today's paper. The unidentified woman from the bus was no longer thought to be the bomber, but a German tourist. Prime Minister Rabin was advised not to visit the scene of the pigua for fear of protestors' outrage: many on the right blamed him and the peace process for the attack. In one demonstration, a man taught his five-year-old daughter, a sweet girl with bangs and a polka-dot dress, to yell, "Rabin is a murderer!" Hamas took responsibility for the bombing and released a message calling Rabin a terrorist who had declared war on Islam. "Ha," I said aloud, without looking up from the paper. "So Rabin is both a traitor against Jews *and* the enemy of Islam."

He huffed. "Wouldn't want to be in his shoes right now."

I pushed away the paper and dug through my wallet for cash.

"How are you doing?" He leaned on the counter looking at me, genuinely interested.

"I'm okay."

He eyed me. "You really don't remember me at all, do you?"

"I'm bad with names," I said. "And faces."

He laughed.

I studied him. He had thick eyebrows, unusually long eyelashes. He wore a sandalwood necklace around his neck. Maybe he wasn't the kind of guy I had pegged him to be that first day. His shirt wasn't particularly tight; he wasn't particularly buff. His curly hair wasn't gelled; in fact, it looked soft to the touch. Once again, I was confronted with the failure of my memory, with my prejudgment. "Are you Eli's son?"

"Eli was my dad."

Was? Did he pass away? That was exactly the kind of news my mother would have shared with me whenever I called home. I must have known that.

"It's Nir," he said, feigning exasperation. "For the millionth time."

"Nir. Sorry. But you only told me once, didn't you?"

"We've been through this before," he said. "When you were home a couple of years ago."

I resisted apologizing again. "Bye, Nir!" I waved goodbye as I walked out. "This is me remembering."

When I looked back, he was grinning.

CHAPTER 9

ZOHARA

JABOTINSKY ROAD, WHICH led to Tel Aviv, was congested as always, flanked on both sides by crowded apartment buildings, three and four stories high, their shutters shut and grimy with exhaust fumes. A large billboard atop one building announced *The Nation Is with the Golan*, and a few cars had matching stickers on their back windows. I had not seen those on my last visit. They sprouted as soon as Rabin began talking about retreating from the Golan Heights as an exchange for peace with Syria. It was one more thing right-wing voters held against him and peacenik left-wing voters were rooting for.

As I got closer to Tel Aviv, the view transformed and became more festive, more colorful. People were young, beautiful, worriless: girls with bikini straps under T-shirts, guys in shorts, towels slung over their shoulders, surfers in wet suits carrying boards, balconies alive with plants and flowers, sidewalk cafés bustling with people, families licking ice cream cones on shaded boulevards.

The world kept going.

The world kept going without her in it. I knew it did and still I was stunned by it.

We were meeting at the concession stand. Once a wooden shack where you could buy popsicles, chips and murky coffee in Styrofoam cups, it had become a little café since I last visited, equipped with an espresso machine and rows of plastic chairs and low tables planted in the plot of sand in front. A wooden sign announced *Mango Beach*. Iggy sat on a bar stool sipping a cappuccino and chatting with a tattooed guy behind the counter. We hugged.

"Cute!" I said, scanning the place.

"I know. They opened a month ago."

The owner—a thirtysomething man, whose skin showed the effects of his hours in the sun—stretched his hand over the bar and shook mine firmly, introducing himself as Shalom.

Iggy and I trudged through the sand toward the water, found a gazebo occupied by a few people. I spread my sarong on the sand and sat on it for a moment, inhaling deeply. "I missed this."

Iggy slipped off his shirt; he had gotten more muscular, but also too thin. "Weren't you living on a beach for the past few months?"

"Your point?" I gave him an inquisitive look. "Besides, I'll always miss *my* sea." I remembered the first time I took the F train to Coney Island, my disappointment at the uninviting frigidness of the Atlantic Ocean. Even in Thailand, where the sea was warm and beautiful, it didn't feel like the real thing. A pale imitation. No more than a holiday fling.

I took off my dress. Unlike Iggy, my body had grown curvier these past few months, from eating rich, delicious Thai food. My hips had always been wide, but now my belly, too, had changed, becoming rounder for the first time. "Making room for a baby," Evelyn had teased when I complained. She said it happened to her, too, around the time she turned thirty.

We ran to the water. It was warm, smooth. My body relaxed into it, feeling more fluid, softer. When the sea floor slipped from under our feet, we started treading water. "I should do this every day," I said.

"Why don't you? I meant what I said, you know. You can stay with me for a while."

"I appreciate it." I weighed my words. "I don't know what I'm doing right now."

"Have you talked to Zack?"

The mention of his name threw me off. What did it say about me that I hadn't even thought of calling Zack? I called Evelyn and Shoshi. But not Zack. Our breakup was so final. We were on two different islands now and the bridges were completely burnt. It actually didn't hurt as much as I thought it would. I had told people it was his choice to not stay friends, but if I were honest, I had no interest in friendship either. In fact, we had stopped being friends while we were together. First, we became roommates who had sex, until sex felt too intimate an act for how distant we were, and we became acquaintances who passed each other in the hallways and nodded politely. How could someone I'd been in love with seem like such a stranger? How could I not care? And how could I explain it to Iggy? Our breakup only brought us closer.

"I don't talk to Zack," I said. "He's moved on."

"Ouch," Iggy said. "Sorry."

"It's fine. I'm the one who broke it off." I regretted it as soon as I said it. It wasn't even completely true.

Iggy looked away. "Of course you did."

I sprayed him with water. "What is that supposed to mean?"

"That you fuck up your relationships because you're afraid of getting hurt. Come on, it's textbook abandonment issues. Dead father, missing brother, absent mother and all that. You're the one who told me that."

"Maybe some people are not meant to be in relationships."

"Okay, now you're just feeling sorry for yourself."

"What's your excuse? Last I checked, you didn't have a glowing record."

"Well, you're not the only one with textbook abandonment issues." He gazed at the horizon, beyond the wave breaker. "Did I tell you I'm gonna be an uncle?"

"No, you didn't! That's amazing, Iggy."

"It made me think." He was quiet for a moment. "Maybe I could actually do it."

"*It?*"

"The whole family and kids thing. Growing up. Maybe I'm ready."

I let my jaw drop in an exaggerated gesture, confounded by the stinging ache in the pit of my stomach.

Now it was his turn to spray me. "Don't tell anyone. It would ruin my reputation."

. . .

BACK AT IGGY'S place, I showered, changed, then napped on his couch while he worked, his face squished in concentration in front of two small monitors where a pretty brunette with red lipstick, a black dress and high-heeled boots sang on a darkly lit stage.

I woke up once and overheard him whispering on the phone. By the time I woke up again it was dark out, and he was gone. A note on the coffee table read, "Out to get dinner."

On his balcony with a joint, I watched the sultry Tel Aviv evening glittering with lights, inhaled the salty whiff of the sea. Down in the narrow street, young people walked on the road, as there was no room for more than one person on the sidewalk. They carried bags of groceries, walked bikes and dogs. Three twentysomething girlfriends were laughing hysterically, pushing each other, one saying repeatedly, "I'm dying. Stop." Again, I was struck by the nonchalance of living. Something in the world wasn't as it should be. These people didn't know it, but something was majorly fucked.

Right.

I looked back up, traced the crowded city roofs, spotted our first apartment, only a few blocks away. This could have been my life had I stayed, I thought. This street. This neighborhood. This city that never sleeps. Iggy.

But no, it wouldn't have been. Even if I'd stayed. Iggy and I broke up, eventually, when I got accepted to NYU. It was inevitable, but I only understood it truly when I met Zack. What were Iggy and I supposed to do? Marry and have children? We were too young: we needed to live more, do more things, have sex with other people, experience heartbreak and fall in love again. It was bound to end. We must have known it already then, so we lived every day like it was going to slip out of our hands. It's why we fought so hard and fucked so hard and held on to each other so desperately at night. I once told him I wished we had met later in life, like, at twenty-seven, so we could've just married and gotten it over with. He laughed shortly, and a shadow clouded his eyes, like I broke the spell by speaking about it.

Fortunately, we ended up with something better. We had been best friends ever since.

Then why that twinge in my stomach?

Maybe it had nothing to do with Iggy and everything to do with me feeling like I'd fallen behind. Mika had moved on, got married and moved to a moshav, was having a child. Now Iggy was talking about settling down, while I selfishly needed him to keep me company in this existential crisis, a crisis that far preceded my mom's death. And now that I was on leave from academia, I couldn't even blame my lagging in life markers on my pursuit of a PhD.

In Israel, I'd loved university, was convinced I had found my calling. Maybe a part of it was my father and what he had instilled in me, or maybe it was Schneider that paved the way. I was smart, disciplined, good at studying, and I loved that I found a place to challenge myself. But my first year in New York was the loneliest I'd ever had. I constantly felt not good enough, not smart enough, my English not fluent enough. A fraud. Then it was winter, and I was stupefied by the cold, depressed by the grayness and flat broke. I felt out of my element, less certain about my path, less inspired about my work, filled with dread and anxiety on an almost daily basis.

Everything at NYU was hard, much harder than I had expected. The competition was fierce: there was never enough room at the table, and, as it became increasingly clear, never enough jobs upon completion. Later, I realized a part of the challenge for me was how white everything was, how Ashkenazi, including my own research, which would explain, in retrospect, why I felt so disenchanted with it. But during the first couple of years, I didn't know it, couldn't name it. And so, I dismissed my doubts, drowned those voices out. I stuck it out and felt like a hero for it. Maybe it was inertia: I had been committed to it for so long I couldn't envision a different life, couldn't picture what else I could possibly do. My sense of self was so entwined with academia that imagining a life outside of it induced panic.

Looking down from the balcony in Neve Tzedek, I saw Iggy emerging from the grocery store two blocks down. He was hunched over some guy's lighter with a cigarette, face lit up. He sauntered down the street, looking confident, happy. I enjoyed watching him like that, clandestinely. The boy I had loved had turned into such a fine man; grew into the self he was meant to be. I was filled with pride, as if I had something to do with it. He looked up at that moment and beamed, raised his bag of groceries and announced, "Shakshuka!"

"Yum!" I yelled back.

I STAYED AT Iggy's that night and the next day. He was working at home, while I sat on the balcony reading. It was the calmest I'd felt in days. The next evening we ordered takeout Italian and watched *The Princess Bride* for the millionth time. I fell asleep in his lap, and when I woke up, he was sleeping too, his head back against the wall, mouth slightly open. He didn't want to wake me. I sat up and watched him for a moment, his supple lips, his perfectly straight nose, the hair that had started to grow unevenly on his shaved head. Gently, I touched his cheek with my palm, and he stirred awake. "Hey," he whispered, lips closing into a smile, and the affability of that smile defused the moment—or what it could have been. He stretched loudly. "I'm going to bed," he said. "You got everything you need?"

"Yeah, I'm good."

I watched him go into the bedroom and threw myself back on the couch. It was only midnight. Would Mika be up?

Mika sounded drowsy. "Zorki?"

"Did I wake you?"

Suddenly she was alert. "Mami, where are you?"

"At Iggy's."

"Didn't you get my message?"

The answering machine was blinking. Iggy never checked it. "I didn't. What happened?"

"Your sister has been worried sick about you. You didn't answer the phone at your mom's, and she came over and you weren't there. The tenant said he hasn't seen you for a couple of days. We didn't know what to think."

It occurred to me I forgot how to do this, forgot what it's like to have family around, people who kept tabs on your whereabouts.

"You don't have to stay at your mother's, you know. If it's too hard. You can stay with us."

"No, I want to. I think." As soon as I said it, I wondered if it was true.

Why stay there? What's wrong with staying with friends? With Iggy? Away from all this grief?

IN THE MORNING, Iggy was gone. A blue sticky note on the kitchen counter said, "Out for errands." In the phone book I found my sister's work number at a bank on Rothschild Street. Her voice was formal. "Hi, Lizzie," I said.

"Zohara," she whispered loudly. "Where the hell are you?"

"At Iggy's. What's going on? What happened? Everyone okay?" I overreacted on purpose; maybe she'd see how ridiculous she was being.

"Nothing happened," she said tersely. "It's common decency to tell your family where you are."

"Well, Iggy said I can stay here for as long as I like."

"What about the house?"

"I'm almost finished. I'll get it done."

"How are you going to get it done from Tel Aviv?"

"I'll get it done."

"Do whatever you want," she said, just like my mother whenever she wanted to show her resigned disapproval. I didn't feel like arguing anymore. Especially when I had no idea what I was being accused of. I grabbed a quick shower, cleaned up the remnants of dinner and wrote on the same note, "Went home to get some things sorted. Be back later." I drew a wonky heart under it.

BY THE TIME I returned, with a small backpack stuffed with some clothes and toiletries, it was around lunchtime. I knocked on Iggy's door a few times. Could he have not returned yet? I didn't think to take a key. Finally, I heard shuffling from the other side. He opened the door to a crack. "Hey." His face brightened but then he looked behind his shoulder and lowered his voice. "Sorry, motek. It's actually not a good time."

"Oh?" It took me a moment. "Oh!" I peeked inside, surprised by the pinch of jealousy. "Okay." I turned, grateful he hadn't noticed the backpack.

"Can you come back? In, like an hour?"

"Yeah, maybe."

I skipped down the stairs and walked toward my car. Of course he had a girl there. Why wouldn't he? Did I expect him to be completely absorbed with me and my dead mother and my lack of direction?

On the seat next to me was a bag with a few unmarked tapes. I had grabbed them before coming here to listen on the drive but ended up turning on the radio instead. Now, I shoved one into the tape player. My mother's singing filled the car. I removed it, inserted another one. My mother again, her voice heartfelt, longing. Were all the tapes of her singing? I clutched the wheel with both fists.

After my father died, an old woman showed up at our house and half cried, half sang in Yemeni. She threw a handkerchief over her face and kept choking as if overcome by emotion. Who was that woman? She didn't know him. Why was she crying? The theatrics embarrassed me, angered me. But no one else seemed perturbed by the performance. Later, my aunt Shuli explained she was a professional wailer, a mekonenet. They were older women who'd suffered losses, who knew pain, women whose "heart was burnt with sorrow." Her wailing was meant to inspire mourning, to unlatch the sadness in people's hearts. "The same way that putting on a smile can make you feel good." I remember thinking it was strange that people needed help to feel.

My mother's voice was like the voice of the wailer, the sorrow and longing releasing my own tears. I didn't think I needed the help, but here I was, sobbing. Was it possible for someone to be a wailer for their own death?

I inserted another tape, forwarded and rewound it. Then another and another. It was all her. Hours upon hours of her singing. Why did my mother record dozens of tapes of her own singing? What did the songs mean? And why were they so sad?

I ejected the tape, turned on the radio and put the gear into drive.

YAQUB

Immigrant Camp, Mahane Olim Rosh HaAyin, 1950

SAIDA HADN'T RETURNED to the river after Yaqub grabbed her hand. He did not see her at the camp, either. Once he had seen her friend Rumia, who eyed him and blushed. Did Saida tell her what had happened?

The camp was growing even more crowded, estimated at thirty thousand people. The lines for food and showers grew longer, the toilets and sewage smelling even fouler.

The weather wasn't accommodating either. It was dreadfully cold, the kind that paralyzed, invaded the bones. Yaqub had only ever felt such chill on that unusually freezing winter his father had died, when the ground in Haidan was covered with white pellets and his family slept by the fire, cuddling to keep warm. When he sat alone by the river, bundled up in layers, staring forlornly at the water, his breath came out in little clouds.

He was grateful that work at the orchards came through after months of unemployment. The farmers expected the Yemeni men to be naturally good at manual work and were surprised to learn that in Yemen, they had all worked as artisans and craftsmen, their hands better at fashioning filigree jewelry than lifting heavy weight, but Yaqub was young and healthy and eager to learn.

While he was picking oranges, he had time to contemplate what happened with Saida, consider what he'd done wrong and how he should atone for it, but instead, he couldn't stop replaying every moment they had spent together, wishing her back.

One morning, they woke up to find workers from Petah Tikva had blocked the camp's exits in protest, shouting, "We want work! We won't be replaced!" Turned out the Yemeni immigrants were being paid seven hundred lira a day at the orchards for the same job the workers had done for twice as much. Of course, the Yemenis didn't know any of that. They just wanted to work. They woke up earlier so they could slip out unnoticed, but the workers began camping outside at night.

Yaqub tried speaking to one of the protestors once, to appeal to his heart, and the man replied, nostrils flaring, "We brought you here from your shitholes in the desert, gave you room and food, and now you want our jobs? What's next? Do you want to sleep with my wife, too?"

EVENTUALLY, ONE CLEAR evening, as he walked toward the river, he could hear her singing, and his heart thrummed.

Saida was perched on a rock facing the water in a long purple dress that showed glimpses of her curves under an oversized coat. The dress rode up, exposing her pants, the traditional, striped embroidery on the calves. "Habibi baka ala eini, wakam rah lu vakhalani," she sang. *My lover made my eyes tear, he got up and left me.*

He stepped on a dry leaf and the crunching sound startled her. She looked up and immediately away. But in the split second their gaze met, he saw her eyes light up.

"New dress?" he asked, shy and awkward all over again. Over the days of her absence, he had decided that if all he could have was this—listening to her, speaking with her from a distance—then this was what he'd settle for. This was enough.

"A new delivery arrived," she said. "It smells nice, too. The lady had a nice perfume." She laughed, hiding her mouth.

"What does it smell like?"

She closed her eyes, breathed in deeply. "Mmm, like flowers but . . . not exactly." She opened her eyes. "I can't describe it. You're the writer."

"And you're a poetess."

She laughed. "I just sing what's in my heart." They locked eyes again. This time she boldly held his gaze a moment longer before casting her eyes down. She wanted him to smell it, he realized, astonished. He looked across the river at the row of drapey willow trees. Saida tightened the coat over her body. Yaqub pulled a napkin with few raisins out of his pocket and presented it to her, his brows curled up in question.

She nodded but didn't make a step forward, forcing him to come closer, and when he held the napkin open in the palm of his hand, he bowed ever so slightly and sniffed her from a safe distance, but close enough and audibly enough that she trembled. She grabbed a couple of raisins. "So?"

He sat on the other rock. "Like . . . flowers after the rain."

"Yes!" she exclaimed. "That's it!"

But also, he thought, like her. Faint, sweet sweat, rosewater and fenugreek. What would it have felt like to bury his nose in the nape of her neck and inhale deeply?

"Have you written anything recently?" she asked. "Any inspiration amongst the oranges?"

He shook his head. "Too busy." The previous week, he'd spent the nights at the farmer's barn to avoid the closures on the camp. Finally, police intervened to break the strike.

She wrinkled her brow. "My songs don't care how busy I am. Sometimes they appear at the most inconvenient times, like when I'm doing housework or visiting my boy."

"Just like that?"

"Like a bird crossing the sky." She sliced the air over her head with her arm theatrically. "And you'd either hang on its wing or be left behind."

He swallowed. "That's beautiful."

"Sometimes I worry people can see it on my face. You are never more vulnerable than when a song strikes you. One has to be open to the heavens. To God."

He envied her, for he had to labor at writing, teasing words into existence. But that night, when he returned to his tent, he discovered her words inspired him. He lay on his mattress and wrote until his neighbors were fast asleep and all he could hear was light snoring and shuffling, and finally, birds, signaling to him that soon it would be time to wake up for work.

THE NEWSPAPERS WERE talking about the camps' imminent closures. The government was building ma'abarot: semipermanent transition camps where immigrants would have more freedom and space. But meanwhile, people were still arriving. One morning, a rich family from Sana'a arrived, dressed in their finest garments. The man collapsed crying when he was shown the tent he'd be sharing with other families. "I left a five-story house in Sana'a for this?" he said.

"I would want to live by the sea," Saida said that evening to Yaqub, her eyes dreamy. They were imagining life after the camp, skirting the fact they might never see each other again. "My father used to travel a lot for work. He always came back bearing gifts—large silver coins from Saudi Arabia he laid into a necklace for my mother, a weird spiky fruit from Aden that tasted sweeter than anything you ever tried."

Yaqub leaned back on his palms, listening.

"I felt like I was getting to travel through his stories. I couldn't imagine I'd ever get to do it myself; you know?" She laughed shortly. "He told us about Sana'a, where they had towers built of mud and the brides wore cone hats of gold, and about the green, mountainous city of Taiz, where Rabbi Shalom Shabazi was buried. But Aden was my favorite. Whenever he returned from there, he had a special scent." She inhaled deeply, as if reliving the moment. "A salty, airy smell. I kept asking him about the sea. And he tried to explain, but . . . how does one describe the sea to a mountain girl? The idea of water everywhere, with no end. And then, when I saw it, in Aden, it was . . ." Her face was stretched in awe. "More beautiful than I could have imagined. I cried. I did! I was so moved. And sad my dad hadn't lived to see it with me. And after we landed in Israel, we drove along the shore to Atlit, to the absorption camp, and I was glued to the window, watching the road curving, catching glimpses of the Mediterranean, the fishermen on the rocks with their rods. And the smell. It will forever remind me of my dad."

He watched a family of ducks drifting down the stream. When they first arrived, he and his cousin Saleh had their sights set on Jerusalem. They had dreamt of the holy city their whole lives, until it became synonymous with the country. They had not come here to live in Rosh HaAyin or Tel Aviv. He had yet to see Jerusalem, but he no longer yearned for it in the same way. Something happened to him in Israel. Something unexpected. The last few months had made him wish for a different life. A life less holy.

In Haidan, his uncle had received a letter from a relative who'd been in Palestine a while. Don't come, he forewarned. There is no work, the living conditions are dreadful, and worst of all is the spiritual bankruptcy of the Jews in this place, who do not believe in God and take pride in their secularism, who shave their simonim—the sidelocks that distinguished them from the Muslims—and their beards. The women prance around with their arms and legs bare, their skin and hair exposed, God have mercy! Yaqub gaped at Saleh, the cousins barely able to contain their excitement. They were so used to women being covered from head to toe that they had become experts at guessing, tracing their contours through the oversized fabric. Even a belt was frowned upon because it accentuated a woman's figure. And to find out that in the Holy Land, women's skin was showing! It truly was the promised land.

"I like the Kinneret," he said.

"You've been there?"

"A few months ago, before you came, they sent a few of us to work at Kibbutz Ginosar. A beautiful place. On the shores of the lake. The water was so blue I was almost tempted to take off my clothes and jump in."

She giggled.

"I loved the landscape, and I loved the work, scaling palm trees for dates and picking grapes off the vines. But it's not like I could ever move there. Everyone was Ashkenazi there. Socialist Zionist youth who built the place when they arrived from Europe in the thirties. But I could see myself there."

When they took them to the kibbutz dining hall for lunch, the other Yemeni workers protested. They couldn't possibly eat there! It wasn't kosher! Yaqub secretly wondered how was it possible they couldn't eat food made by other Jews? After all, despite their restrictions, they ate at their Muslim neighbors' homes in Yemen. And once a year, when the

Jews were required to pay the jizya head tax by working the fields for the village sheikh, they gratefully ate the delicious meal he provided. That day was the first time he realized he was different than his fellow Yemenis. What they resisted, he wished to embrace.

"I would love to see the Kinneret one day," Saida said.

"Maybe I can take you," he dared to say. "We'll start our own kibbutz."

She laughed again, flushed. "You're such a fool."

WHILE THE CONFLICT outside the camp was resolved, inside the camp, tensions abounded. The Yemeni parents didn't approve of boys and girls studying together, spending time together. Everything was pritsut to them. Immoral. Sinful. They demanded segregated religious education. One of them, a rabbi from Dhamar, had even written a letter to Prime Minister Ben-Gurion. "They are trying to undo our religion and teach our children secular ways," they complained. "We are just teaching them to dance the hora," one doe-eyed instructor said in a pleading tone.

But then, a few boys returned from school crying, after the barber had forcibly cut their simonim, telling them, "You don't need those anymore. Here everyone is Jewish." As though cutting their sidelocks would somehow nudge them toward a more secular life, rather than make them feel humiliated and violated. For a while, the classrooms remained empty.

One evening, the Ashkenazi instructors arranged for a movie screening at the youth club. Somehow, the event slipped through the cracks. And yes, there was kissing on screen. Wonderful, illicit, immoral kissing. Yaqub stared, heart pounding, a pleasant tickling rising from his toes to his groin. The other teens were astounded. Some gasped. Some averted their eyes. Some giggled. Others left in protest. The parents were livid. Saida wasn't there—he hadn't seen her for a few days—but she must have heard about it.

The following evening he found her sitting at the riverbank, tossing stones into the water, her gaze distant. When she finally spoke, she said, "What do you think about Pnina?"

He hesitated. Was that a trick question? Pnina was a Yemeni instructor, a sabra. Her family migrated in the first wave of immigration from Yemen in 1881. Her face was Yemeni, her skin was Yemeni, but she wore shorts and boots, like the Ashkenazi women, her curly hair wild and uncovered. And she spoke differently, had a confidence about her he'd never seen on a Yemeni woman, not even Saida, who was the boldest woman he'd known. "Why do you ask?" he said.

"The women talk about her. How shamefully she behaves and dresses. But—" Saida hesitated. "I think she's a good person. She helped me talk to the nurses when my sister was sick. And she's kind. All they see is how her hair is exposed and her pants are short, and that she talks to men. That's all they care about."

"And you?"

Saida looked down. "You know she told me there is a Yemeni woman in Mapai? The Workers' Party? She said in Israel, women can do things they couldn't in Yemen. She asked me, 'What do *you* want to do, Saida? If you could choose to do anything, what would you do?' I didn't even know how to answer her." Her voice caught.

He understood. Yaqub knew he was living proof the Yemeni parents were right to worry; he was drawn to this new, secular way of life, fascinated by the way the men and women fraternized, touching casually, laughing, the way their mouths said one thing, but their eyes said another. He closely observed the laid-back way in which they communicated. Their women weren't afraid to talk to men, like that one Ashkenazi instructor who used to casually chat with the Yemeni men while they smoked their mada'a, like there was nothing to it. The Yemeni women quietly muttered insults as they walked by her.

"The other day, Rumia and I saw Pnina talking to an instructor in the dining room," Saida said. "She rested her arm over his shoulder. In public! Can you imagine?" She laughed awkwardly.

"You talk to me," he said. "You would have never done that back in Yemen, would you?"

Saida's alarmed look made him instantly regret his words. She straightened. "Are you scolding me? Trying to make me feel bad?"

"No, of course not," he stammered. "I was saying . . . I was *trying* to say, aren't we already different than the way we were in Yemen? This place has changed us."

She nodded slowly. They were quiet for a moment. He leaned down to collect stones and toss them one by one into the water.

"But we're not the same, me and you," Saida said quietly. "You're a man. You're unmarried. You can do anything."

For a moment, they sat dejected and glum, looking at the river. When he glanced at her, he saw she was crying.

"My husband came back from work for a couple of days," she said, almost whispering. "That's why I stayed away."

He stiffened, flinging stone after stone with a jerk of his elbow.

"I'm supposed to be happy we're here, finally, in the Holy Land. This was our dream. Wasn't it? Everything we ever wanted! But I'm not happy. Is it awful? I'm not happy being away from my child. The only times I'm happy—" She stopped and peeked at him, tears streaming.

His heart pounded. She didn't need to say anything else. Without thinking, he reached over and grabbed her hand, and this time she let him. They sat there, holding hands, trembling with the gravity of their situation, while the Yarkon River gushed toward the Mediterranean Sea.

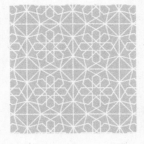

PART TWO

SEPTEMBER 1995

If I were yours
And you were mine
If I were a rain cloud
I'd quench your thirst
If I were a bird with a curly wing
I'd shelter you from the hot sun
If I were grapes strung on a vine
I'd squeeze the flesh of my fruit
and pour juice into your mouth

UNKNOWN YEMENI POETESS

CHAPTER 10

ZOHARA

SEPTEMBER ROLLED IN with no fanfare, offering more of the same punishing heat of Israeli summers. But with the children back in school, the restless energy of summer holidays receded. The beach was quieter, even the waves had calmed: August was notoriously stormy; too many cases of drowning, too many black flags.

I trudged through the sand to the first row of seats at Mango Beach, propped my sandy feet on the opposite chair and ordered a cappuccino and a croissant from a bored waiter. I spread open the newspaper I had bought across the street with the thought of perusing the classifieds, looking for something that would pay the bills as I contemplated my next moves.

The front page announced that security on Rabin and Peres had been tightened following the recent violent demonstrations. I turned to the classifieds: a nursery was looking for a sales representative with knowledge of plants. An import-export company was seeking a sales representative with experience in the food business. A small boutique was looking for salespersons. Experience a must.

I folded the paper, drew a rolled joint from my purse and lit it. A shirtless runner passed by with a dog on their heels. An older, sun-crusted man planted a folding beach chair by the water. I inhaled. Exhaled. For a moment I forgot about everything. My life, elsewhere, unsorted. The jobs I wasn't qualified, or maybe overqualified, for. My mother.

In the early afternoon I drove back to Sha'ariya to do some more work around the house. I was hoping to finish cleaning it before the end of the shloshim, the first thirty-day mourning period, which concluded with the unveiling ceremony of the headstone. It was an arbitrary deadline. There was nothing awaiting me on the other side of it. I still didn't know what I was going to do next. Everything seemed pointless, colored by her absence, by the finality of death.

I hadn't gone back to Iggy since that day, and it was probably a good thing. I needed to be here. Despite everything, this house remained the only real home I knew. Eventually we would have to sell it, rent it, strip it of whatever made it ours. I needed to say goodbye to it properly, goodbye to her.

The piles of storage my mom had kept in my bedroom turned out to be mostly mine: school notebooks she had saved, art projects, letters from pen pals I had in elementary school, which I sat and read for the entire afternoon, seeking mentions of my own letters to them, echoes of my own childhood. ("I am sorry to hear your father passed away," Shlomit from Dimona wrote. "At least you know he's in heaven now.") There were some old albums with photos from school trips—me and my elementary school girlfriends, blowing kisses, climbing a rope ladder in a nature reserve in Judean Desert, posing by palm trees in Eilat.

When I looked up, I saw the light had seeped out of the room, the sky in the west turned strikingly peach, almost unnatural in its luminosity. I stepped outside and plucked a half-smoked joint from the copper ashtray. My lighter sparked idly, so I decided to go get a new one; I needed some groceries, anyway.

Nir was sweeping outside the makolet. I walked in, made a scene of choosing a lighter, hungry for conversation.

"How's it going?" he said when I settled on the red one and placed it on the counter.

"Okay," I said as I walked toward the dairy fridge. "I've been dealing with my mother's stuff."

"Do you need help moving anything? Furniture?"

"Actually, I think I might stick around for a bit."

"Walla? The prodigal daughter returns?"

"Just for a while."

He nodded resolutely. "Good. You shouldn't do anything impulsive when you're grieving. This is not the time for big decisions."

I placed milk, sliced yellow cheese and a bag of plump, fresh pitas on the counter.

"So you're donating most of the stuff?"

"Yeah. Well, there are some tapes I'm not sure what to do with. Yemeni music." I didn't tell him about the ones with my mother's singing. It felt private somehow. I hadn't told anyone about it yet, walked around with the secret tucked in my pocket as though I was keeping a small part of her memory for myself, refusing to share. Maybe I was afraid of what I might discover if I told my family. Maybe I didn't feel like talking to Lizzie.

On the other hand, I hadn't been able to play them again either, couldn't bear to hear her voice.

He stared at me. "What do you mean? Keep them!"

"I just . . . I don't listen to that kind of music."

He opened the till with a ding to drop the coins inside. "Of course you don't." His patronizing tone annoyed me, though he wasn't entirely off. In high school, I announced in distaste that "I hated Mizrahi music," so that everyone knew I wasn't *that* kind of Mizrahi girl. I was evolved.

"I mean, I wouldn't *mind* listening to it. I just don't know what's good."

"You listen, and if you like it, then it's good."

He was right, of course, which made him even more annoying.

"Or you bring it here and I'll tell you what's good." He grinned.

"Maybe I will."

I stepped outside and he followed, bringing in boxes. The sky had calmed down a bit now, the sunset colors deeper and more subdued. On the front step, I lit the half-smoked joint, exhaled the gritty smoke and waved it in his direction. He wiped his hands on the back of his jeans, took one quick puff and passed it back to me. "So is your husband going to join you soon?"

I laughed, shaking my head.

"What's funny?"

"There's no husband. Not anymore."

He studied me but didn't ask anything further, which was a relief.

What happened with Zack had been the question on everyone's minds. My mom, my sister, Iggy, Mika. The only time Zack and I had come to Israel together, the only time my friends and family met him, we were in the glow of the honeymoon phase, which, in our case, preceded the actual marriage. And although it had been almost a year since we separated, I was reluctant to talk about it. It was partly that in the light of losing my mom, the story didn't seem as dramatic as it had once felt. Or maybe I still couldn't shake off the tremendous guilt. Let's face it; this story didn't make me look good.

I had given my friends and family the same rehearsed account: Zack and I had moved too fast. We'd realized we weren't compatible. But my mom wasn't buying it. I could tell she presumed it was my fault. Which, granted, it was, but still it hurt that she hadn't considered the alternative. She seemed cross with me, as if I was guilty of getting her attached to all these nice, young men, first Iggy, then Zack, and ripping them away from her. As if I, too, took men, potential sons, away from her.

I handed Nir the joint, but he declined, piled some boxes and carried them in. I watched him. "Nir, right?"

He laughed. "Right."

"I'll see you tomorrow," I said.

Zack and I had met in a jewish meetup I had been invited to by Kate, another PhD candidate at the department. I wasn't sure how I felt about going at first. The name of the group, Havura, called to mind an American Jewish summer camp, the kind I had seen in movies. I didn't think I'd fit in.

"It's more Jewish than Israeli." Kate spoke quietly, her tone perpetually apologetic. I expected that; I was the only Israeli PhD candidate in my year. "But it's nice. We do holidays together. Once a month we do

Shabbat," she continued before carefully adding, "It's not very diverse," which I realized to mean it was mostly Ashkenazi, but I was used to that in our department, too. At that time in my life, I chose not to see such things. I wanted to believe it didn't matter. I wasn't attached to my Yemeni-ness. I had spent so long distancing myself from it, and the surgery worked. If you asked, I'd define myself as Israeli first, Jewish second. That was it.

Zack was standing with Renee, a blond, dreadlocked girl from Portland who was studying film at CUNY. In her last short film, she peed on a brightly lit stage for a long time; she must have held it a while. When I first met her, she exclaimed, "I love your curls! They're so . . ." She searched for a word and somehow landed on "exotic!"

Renee, whose parents were hippies, had not been raised Jewish, knew little about Israel or Judaism. She wished to learn more about her heritage, she had said to me overenthusiastically the first time we met. That's why she started coming to the gatherings.

She waved me over urgently. "This is the Yemeni girl I told you about." When I raised my brow, she added, "Oh, I was just telling Zack here how you don't look Jewish at all."

I laughed uncomfortably at the introduction. "Um, what does Jewish look like?"

Renee blushed. "Sorry. You know what I mean. Not like the typical American Jew." She threw her hands up. "But what do I know about Jews? I didn't know Jews of color existed before I met you and Blake!" Blake was a student at Columbia Business School and the only Black Jewish student who attended the meetings.

Zack smiled into his beer with his mouth closed.

"Shit, I'm sorry." Renee put a moist hand on my arm. "Was that offensive? We were talking about Ofra Haza, do you know her? Isn't she amazing?"

"Yeah, of course," I said. Zack's smile grew.

Renee slapped her forehead, her face now bright red. "What am I saying! Of course you know her! Anyway, you came up . . . because of the whole Yemeni thing. It's not like I go around telling people, Look at this brown Jew!" She erupted in huge, sloppy laughter. I clued in; she was utterly drunk.

Zack smiled and stretched his hand toward me. "Nice to meet you, Zohara." He was tall and broad shouldered, with longish, messy, light brown curls, big blue eyes. He was built like an athlete, but scruffy looking, unshaved, which is why I hadn't noticed the all-American look behind that until later.

We ended up sitting on the balcony and talking for most of the evening. Zack was a law student. He asked many questions about my life, my family. When I told him about my dad, he said sincerely, "I am so sorry," making eye contact, touching my hand; it was the kind of American earnestness that usually made me uneasy, uncloaked in cynicism, but in Zack, I found it refreshing, as I did his politeness and chivalry: he kept bringing me red wine, offered to hold my purse when I went to pee.

At some point, I raided the dessert table—that display was one of the reasons I came back to these events—and returned with an assortment of cakes and pastries. I took a bite of one cake, scrunched my nose, tried another, all while sitting cross-legged on my chair, shoes off. "Do you want some?" I gestured at the plate. "The cheesecake is really good."

"I'm not a sweets guy."

I stared at him in faux astonishment, then made as if to get up. "Okay, bye."

He laughed.

"Whatever, more for me." I licked my fingers. He was watching me closely.

Zack was the first American I really got to know. I mean, know *well*. My closest friend at the time was Evelyn, and she had come to the US from the Philippines as a child; we met when we worked as teaching assistants together. Evelyn was writing about the history of Jews in the Philippines and the community of Holocaust survivors that had found refuge there, which is a story no one, including me, had ever heard about. She was one of few graduate students in the department who had no ties to Israel or Judaism. I found myself annexed to her big family in Queens on holidays and some weekends. There was something comforting about the noise in her home, her honesty and directness in the face of American politeness. Perhaps we both found a semblance of our home country in each other.

Before I met Zack, I hadn't had the time or mental space to explore and enjoy what the city had to offer; social outings were limited to campus events at NYU, mingling while munching on cheese platters and drinking cheap wine. Falling in love with Zack was falling in love with New York and with America and with Americanness. With the promise of another life.

Zack's family lived in Long Island. The Rosses were the kind of Jews I'd only ever seen in movies, the kind who went to synagogue (shul, they called it) on High Holidays dressed in fancy clothes, who lived in a huge house with a fireplace and manicured backyard, who knew which fork to use when. My own parents hadn't used cutlery before coming to Israel.

The first time I met his mother, Diane, a petite blonde, she hugged me tightly, pecking me on both cheeks. She wore a turquoise cashmere sweater and pearls and matching, teardrop-shaped earrings. I was taken aback for a moment. Although Zack was affectionate, I imagined his American, Ashkenazi family would be reserved, would shake my hand curtly. When I admitted it to him later, Zack flinched. "That's a bit racist," he said. "Don't you think?"

"Tell me how to pronounce your name," Diane insisted, holding my hand in both her palms.

"It's Zo-ha-ra," I enunciated.

"Beautiful!" his mother exclaimed. "How do people call you for short?"

"I call her Zo," Zack said. Zack and Zo. I loved it, had even bought him, ironically of course, a cheesy set of house robes for Hanukkah that year—we weren't doing gifts—with the names Zack and Zo engraved.

"Zoe!" His mom had misheard. "I love that name. Would it be okay if I call you that too?"

I didn't have the heart to correct her.

"Are you sure you don't mind?" Zack whispered as we walked behind his parents toward the dining table. "I can tell her. It's no big deal."

"Let her," I said. "I love the name Zoe."

After that, she introduced me to people in their family, to friends of hers, as Zoe. At the same time, Zack began introducing me as Zo. I got a thrill from the newness. When I was Zo or Zoe, I could do anything, be anyone. I was lighter, new, unburdened. And even more severed from my origins. In school I was Zohara. But with the exception of the few Israelis in the program, it was pronounced a little off, with the *ha* like *hair* rather than *ha!* like laughter.

Mispronunciation by mispronunciation, I was losing myself. But doesn't everyone lose themselves a little in a new relationship?

I remember the first time, at a party with Zack's friends from school, when I introduced myself as Zo. The strong sense of alienation and self-betrayal that followed.

In Israel I tried to be more Ashkenazi. In New York I wanted to be a New Yorker. You'd think being an immigrant (however temporary my position was) would make me understand my mother, relate to her more. After all, upon arriving in Israel, the authorities tried to change her name too, to Simcha—Saida meant *happy* in Arabic—but she resisted. If anything, my experience of migration made me feel superior to her. I was a better immigrant than she ever was. I didn't hold on to the past like she did, I assimilated better.

In my second year of the program, I was no longer eligible for subsidized housing and was sharing an apartment off campus with four other PhD students on Houston Street. It was cramped, unclean, the kitchen smelling like compost, and even still, too expensive. I subsisted on white rice doused with hot sauce. When Zack suggested I move into his one-bedroom apartment in East Village, I agreed immediately. We knew it was quick but justified it by telling each other how busy we'd been with our studies; too busy to see each other some weeks, only briefly checking in by phone. That way, at least we'd get to sleep together in the same bed. At least we could share a pot of coffee from time to time.

Zack's place was on the third floor of a redbrick walk-up with a zigzag black iron fire escape and a galley kitchen that suited us fine, since neither of us cooked. The living room window framed a red maple tree.

That summer we flew to Israel for two weeks. Zack had been once, as a child. His memories were vague: the sea that was as warm as bathwater, the bleached sky, the surprising sweetness of halva. His parents weren't the kind of Jews who *needed* to visit Israel, he said. It was too hot, too Levantine. If they chose to travel that far, surely they would do better in Italy or France.

Before our trip, I drew a family tree, so he would be able to tell my relatives apart. He memorized the names. "Your brother who died when he was a baby?" He pointed at Rafael's name. It was time to tell him. He couldn't meet my family without knowing the whole story.

It'd been so long since I told anyone about it, and it came out hurried and convoluted. I used the word *disappeared* first, and when his face betrayed his confusion, I added that he was likely given away for adoption, but, of course, nothing's been proven. There were other unsolved cases like that. Hundreds. The stories have been silenced, dismissed as "wild, oriental imagination." The two committees of inquiry both resulted in nothing, the equivalent of a shrug. They concluded that the children had all died. Well, not everyone. They admitted they couldn't trace some children, but compared to the hundreds of cases reported, it seemed negligible. Some of the materials in the archives mysteriously disappeared. Others were closed to the public. The authorities had not been forthcoming.

"Wow," he said. And, "Your poor mother." And, "I don't understand. Who would do that?"

My mom had been reluctant to point fingers when I asked her the same question. There was a strong dissonance she couldn't settle. There was Israel, the land of her dreams, and there was the government, the establishment, that never helped find her son. And still, she loved this place. Considered herself lucky to have made it here, to have raised her daughters here.

WE GOT MARRIED for the most prosaic reasons, similar to how we moved in together. Zack always dreamt of teaching English in Thailand. Now was his chance, before he had to study for the bar exams. There was nothing I wanted more than to go to Thailand. But I was on a student visa. I couldn't just leave.

One evening, in bed, he turned on his side, leaned on his palm and looked at me, a glint in his eyes. "What if we got married?"

I looked up from my book, stunned. "What?"

"For the green card," he hastened to add.

"Seriously?"

"And, I mean, we're in love, right? I'm not going anywhere. Are you?"

With my family history, I didn't have a high opinion on the institution of marriage. I never dreamt of a proposal or a big wedding. Maybe this was as good a reason to get married as any.

My mom was delighted by the news, but quiet and crestfallen when I said we'd be doing it at city hall.

"It's more of a formality. No one is coming."

"Does it mean you're staying for good?"

"Not necessarily," I said, slowly. It dawned on me that Zack and I never spoke about this, not really. Perhaps because we got married for the sake of convenience, we managed to sidestep that entire conversation. When I first moved to New York, I imagined I'd go back to Israel, eventually, but as time passed, I became comfortable, intoxicated with the possibility of a new life. I could just stay. Never return. But even if I did, the question was more complicated than that. I knew how hard it was to find jobs in academia, especially if you weren't willing to live in small town United States, and I knew Zack was planning on staying in New York, to work for his dad. I remembered Evelyn telling me about a brilliant guy she knew from the department who ended up abandoning academia and teaching at a private high school in order to stay in New York, where his wife had a career and a family. Was that what my future held now that I was marrying Zack? Shouldn't we have at least discussed it?

Later, Lizzie called to tell me my mom was hurt I hadn't invited her to the wedding. I called her back and suggested we plan a party for next time we're there. This appeased her.

At the wedding ceremony, Zack looked handsome in a suit that complemented his athletic physique; I wore an off-white strapless dress I got on sale at Zara. It was a cold day in March, and I was freezing, so Zack lent me his suit jacket. Evelyn and Zack's best friend, Dean, were our witnesses. His parents surprised us at city hall and took us to a fancy dinner at a French restaurant in Tribeca, with tables covered in white cloths and dishes that looked more like art than food. "It's a shame your mother couldn't be here," Diane said, and I was filled with remorse. But when I tried to imagine her there, I couldn't. I was so far away from her, from my previous life in Sha'ariya.

In the pictures from that day, we stand smiling, leaning our heads toward each other. Zack and Zo. Husband and wife. When we got back to our apartment, we had wild sex, strangely turned on by matrimony, as if we were role playing, like that time he pretended to be a cop arresting me for speeding.

YAQUB

Immigrant Camp, Mahane Olim Rosh HaAyin, 1950

FOR A FEW days, the rain hadn't ceased. Families huddled in their tents, which kept them mostly dry, but the ground was so mucky that many chose to remove their sodden shoes and walk around barefoot. The men, Yaqub amongst them, dug irrigation canals around the camp.

Then, the storm hit. Wind shook the tents, the sheets loudly flapping. Rain slashed sideways, ferociously and abundantly. The canals they had dug overflowed, and muddy torrents raged between the rows. Tents came apart, ropes loosened, household items drifted away. Yaqub hurried over to Saida's tent, where she stayed with her sister and with Rumia. Her husband was still away, working up north. Her face was flushed with gratitude. He helped her carry her luggage, tied in fabric, chased a bundle that sailed down the slope. The water was up to his calves, his only coat soaked. She mouthed, "Thank you."

That night the staff laid mattresses on the cold floors of the shack they had used as a synagogue. A single oil lamp lit the entire space, painting everything warm amber, casting long, swaying shadows on the walls. Above their heads, the rain pounded on the roof; the wind shrieked, angry sounding. When the room filled with light snores and rhythmic breathing, he sat up and looked for her. There were hundreds of bodies in that small, cramped space but he had boldly placed his mattress close enough that he could almost smell her. At that moment she looked up, too, and smiled, then quickly scanned the room to make sure no one saw the exchange. The tension in his body was almost intolerable.

He went to sleep deliriously happy that night.

THE NEXT MORNING, a brilliant sun illuminated the destruction. Collapsed tents, strewn tree branches, soaked mattresses. The air was so crisp it felt brittle. Women bundled up with their families, while the men worked to restore the camp.

In the afternoon, two men in suits came by the camp. The taller, bespectacled one carried a notebook and a recording device, while the other lugged around a heavy camera. The rumors spread quickly: they were writing a story about the camp for the newspaper. The tall one frantically scribbled notes as he spoke to Shoshana, the staff member in charge of supplying them with warm clothes. They visited the cultural center, the makeshift school, the dining hall, snapped photos all around the camp, including a group photo Yaqub ended up posing for. The kids followed them everywhere, curious, giggling, the men trailing a few steps behind.

On Friday morning, Daud Sanani ran down the main path with a pile of freshly inked newspapers in hand. The men gathered, jostling to get a better look. Yaqub managed to grab one of the copies. He scanned the grainy black-and-white images; one showed a group of men picking oranges at the orchard, another was of the men cleaning up after the storm. He found himself in the third picture: a group of smiling men, some crouching, some standing, some dressed traditionally and others— he amongst them—in pants, shirts and caps.

The men were delighted by their own images. But when Yaqub skimmed the article, he saw them described as "emaciated people who came from darkness, from extreme poverty, walking in herds, behaving strangely and in awe about everything they see, the cars, the radio, the telephone."

He carefully ripped the picture, folded it and slid it into his pocket.

. . .

A FEW DAYS passed before he could resume his visits to the riverbank. During the storm, the river had flooded the surrounding fields, and even after the water receded, the path was too swampy to cross. As soon as the mud and puddles dried off, he went back, waited a few days, but to no avail. Saida didn't show.

Then, one day, he heard her faint singing as he got near, and his heart swelled.

"I was worried," he said. "Is everyone okay?"

She nodded. "My sister started asking questions. I couldn't get away."

They stood staring at each other. This was the first time they had plainly admitted that they were waiting for each other, that this was something one needed to get away for, something others may ask questions about. And as if the severity of their circumstance dawned on Saida at that moment, she sunk to the rock, shoulders slumped.

He touched her shoulder, lightly.

She jerked away from his hand. "Don't."

He withdrew, said nothing.

"Why do you do this?" Her eyes blazed. "Talk to me? Touch me like this? Do you think so poorly of me?"

He spluttered, "Of course not!"

She turned her head away from him, but her back, her shoulders, quivered.

He sat on the rock beside her. Saida wiped tears with her sleeve. "I remember my mother telling me as a little girl, beware of men. They will always want something from you. She even said"—she snickered bitterly—"even if he gives you sweets, don't go with him."

His chest felt heavy, his windpipes constricted.

"There were always stories going around. Stories about girls who ran away with men, sometimes even Muslim men. You must have heard these stories too. Every village had them. Girls who disappeared one day to a different life. My sister and I eavesdropped while the women whispered, pretending to mind our own business. I don't know why I loved these stories so much. I was fascinated by them. They were like the books you read, you know? So far removed from our lives. It could never happen to us. We were good girls, from good homes. We did the right thing. Unlike those wicked girls, who were shamed and shunned. They could never come back to the village. Their lives were over." Her voice broke. "And now, I am no different than these girls." She sobbed into her hands. He knew not to touch her, as much as it pained him. "Everything I do is wrong. I speak too much. I want too much. And I try! My God, I try. I try to be different. I try so hard to *feel* differently." She wiped her face again. "As God is my witness, I tried to love him. I did. I tried to make him love me."

Yaqub had no concept of love except for what he felt for her, and what she said sounded wrong to him. His love for her took him over and he was defenseless against it. It overpowered him, like the deluge that devastated their camp. It required no effort.

"My aunt used to say to me, men, you don't need to love them," Saida said. "You just need to get along. It's not like in the songs. She said I was lucky Hassan agreed to marry me. An orphan, and so dark."

"Shehora ani venava," he dared to quote from the Song of Solomon. *I am black and beautiful.* She snickered. An awkward silence fell between them.

"I know he loves *her*," she said quietly. "I can see it in his eyes. Sometimes I feel sorry for her. Here, take him, I want to say. You can have him! Some days, I think, if I left, they wouldn't even notice. And I would be free!" She folded herself onto her knees and broke into sobs again. "What am I going to do?"

He could no longer bear to watch her without doing anything. He lowered himself to the ground beside her and wrapped her in his arms, crying with her.

They remained embraced like this, and then her sobs subsided, and still they were locked in a hug, her body was warm, alive and smelling of rosewater. As if he had forgotten everything she was just saying, everything he was telling himself, everything he knew about what was proper and right, he placed a light finger under her chin, raised her face toward him and kissed her. The touch of her soft lips on his. The warmth that spread over his entire body like a rash. Was there ever a feeling better than this?

In his memory, the moment lasted a while, time stretched, elastic.

But in reality, it must have been quick. Saida gasped, pushed him with both hands, and he stumbled backward onto his palms. She stared at him, wounded. And then she slapped him. An untrained slap, landing dully on his cheek.

She picked up her skirt, bunched the tail of it inside her fist, revealing the embroidered hem of her pants, and ran, sobbing. Yaqub placed his muddy hand on his warm, stinging cheek. A sick feeling stirred in his gut.

What had he done?

CHAPTER 11

ZOHARA

NIR WAS ARRANGING tins on a high shelf when I walked into the makolet with the tapes. He climbed down the ladder, wiped his hands on the rag stuffed in the back pocket of his jeans and leaned on the counter. "What can I get you, Doctor Haddad? Chocolate bars? Bread? Yellow cheese? How about some vegetables for a change? You're going to get scurvy eating like that."

"Thanks, Mom," I said, and my smile faded. "You know nobody gets scurvy anymore."

I pushed the shoebox toward him on the counter. He removed the lid and flicked through the tapes with one finger. "Yeah, there's some classics in here, Bracha Cohen, Zion Golan. It's a great place to start if you're serious about learning."

Watching his face, I tried to decide if he was being critical or helpful. I caught a glimpse of old newspapers piled behind the counter. The ones my mom had kept for cleaning were all finished. "Hey, mind if I take some of those?"

He glanced back. "Yeah, sure." He placed a stack on the counter. Last week's weekend magazine had a picture of the woman who died in the pigua on its cover, finally identified as a forty-five-year-old religious divorcée, a mother of two. *The Mystery of Her Life and Death,* the headline read. I quickly skimmed the article. No one knew where she had been that day on the bus, or what she'd done for a living since the divorce. For days, this woman's identity kept shifting, slipping, and now that she had been identified, the mystery remained. A picture showed her smiling with her two adult daughters. They were fooling around, making funny faces. How come no one noticed she was missing? How come no one knew her schedule, her routine, what buses she frequently took? I thought of my mother and how little I knew of her life. Would I have known to tell the press about her day-to-day activities?

Nir inserted a cassette into a bulky tape player behind him. "I love this one. 'Miskin Ya Nas.' Bracha Cohen is this amazing singer no one outside of the Yemeni community had ever heard of."

The beat was fast, catchy. Nir started bobbing his head, grinning in a way that showed all his teeth and singing along. He had a warm, lovely voice. The sound of tin drums awoke something in me. I started bobbing my head too. "It sounds like every family wedding I've ever been to."

"Doesn't it make you instantly want to dance?"

I laughed. "It really does."

He turned the music up, rounded the counter and grabbed my hand, launching into a Yemeni step. "You can't do the Yemeni step alone," he said. "It's against the rules." I gave in and sprung into it. The dance was in me, indelible, like riding a bike. My feet didn't falter. Nir jiggled his shoulders up and down. We bounced right and left in unison, advanced and retreated.

"What is the song about?" I asked, breathless and flushed, when it ended.

"What most of these songs are about. Love." He rewound the tape, leaned in to listen. "It goes something like, 'People, look at this poor guy, his beloved got married to another.'"

Something clicked. "Miskin. Poor guy. Like misken in Hebrew."

"Exactly." He listened, eyes narrowed. "I love this line: 'I wish I were a bird, and my feathery wings were like a warm bed for you.'"

"Who wrote it?"

He riffled through the box. "It's one of the women's songs."

"What's that?"

He gave me a quick look. "You know, the songs the women wrote?"

There it was. Judgment. Just when I was starting to warm up to him.

"Right," I said.

He picked another tape, turning to read the list of songs on the back. "Your mom never listened to those tapes at home?"

"I was away for high school."

"And before that? Or when you were home, like on summer holidays?"

"Sometimes."

"And your dad?"

"When he chewed gat with his friends, there was always music, yes. But you know, I was a kid. It wasn't my scene."

He laughed. "Yeah, gat and music go hand in hand. What are these?" He held up one of the numbered tapes I had left there by mistake.

"Oh. Turns out my mother recorded herself singing."

He gaped at me. "Oh, wow."

"I wish I understood why she recorded them, like, what's the story behind it."

"Maybe we can ask my mother."

"Your mother?"

"Yeah, you know, they were in the singing group together."

"A singing group? Like a choir?"

"You didn't know about the singing group?"

I tensed up. You're not better than me, I wanted to say. For staying in the neighborhood, working in your father's store, knowing your mom, speaking the language.

"They meet at the community center to sing from the women's songs. I can ask her when they're meeting next. Maybe they could help." He opened the fridge behind him and poured us cold water from a jug.

I chugged the water. "How do you know Yemeni?"

"My parents came to Israel later than most, in the sixties. So they spoke it at home. Then, I studied Arabic in high school, first Fusha, like Modern Standard Arabic, but then I made a point of studying the local dialect, which was easy for me because I had the foundation from home. A totally different dialect, obviously, but still. And in the army, I was in intelligence."

"Oh?"

"You seem surprised."

"No," I lied. "Impressed."

"What, that they took a Yemeni boy from Sha'ariya for intelligence?"

"No. That you're so fluent. I envy that." For a moment a memory of my professor in New York, Abe, whispering Arabic hotly in my ear flashed through my head. "Honestly, I didn't like the sound of Arabic growing up. I guess I associated it with negative things. Like, my parents on one hand and the enemy on the other."

"Yeah, they did a number on us," he said. "They made us believe that to be Israeli, you had to reject your heritage, especially Mizrahi. It's fucked. And sad. I mean, look at you. You know so little about where you came from."

I flinched. "That's not true."

"I mean, it's not your fault," he hurried to add. "But I can imagine it wasn't easy, spending your formative years away from home in a place that idealized Ashkenazi culture. No?"

An older lady came in and nodded at me. I said hello. She grabbed milk and asked Nir to add it to her tab. "No problem, Mrs. Tassa," he said to her. As he opened his book, he said, "Don't get me wrong. They did a number on me too. They tried to send me to technical high school. The advisor at school told my parents, 'Oh, he'll suffer in a regular school.' I mean, I was a bit of a troublemaker, sure, and my grades weren't great, but still. And of course, if you look at technical schools, most of the students there are Mizrahi. The tracking system is real. My dad fought them over it. If he hadn't, who knows where I'd be today?"

The guy was working at his parents' grocery store. I said nothing, nodded in agreement.

I was about to leave when he said, "Maybe she recorded the songs for safekeeping. It's a lost art, you know. Maybe she wanted you to have them."

"Me?"

"Traditionally, the songs were passed from mother to daughter."

"Right." I didn't ask any more.

. . .

ON THE WAY home, I thought, What is it about Nir that gets to me? He was being nice, helpful even. Something about our dynamics felt familiar: that sense of inadequacy I had around him, that feeling of not being Yemeni enough. I spent half my life trying to fit in amongst Ashkenazi, and now I was trying to do the same with my own people. Like in that book *The Painted Bird* by Jerzy Kosiński, when a bird catcher paints one of his birds a different color and releases it back into the wild, to search for its kin. Its flock mates no longer recognize it as one of their own and attack it.

Then, I remembered. This was how I felt the first time I met Shoshi.

WHEN SHOSHI AND I MET, ZACK AND I HAD JUST RETURNED from Thailand. Evelyn, my closest friend in New York, had accepted a tenure-track position at a college in Vermont and left me friendless. I spent hours at the library while Zack was studying for the bar and apprenticing with his dad. After two and a half years together, our life felt deadened, mirroring the frosty grayness outside our windows. The new Zack wore a suit, had short hair and worked long hours, only vaguely resembling the fun, barhopping guy I had married. He returned home when I was already sleeping, quietly sneaking into the bed beside me. By morning, he was already gone.

When I grew bored of my research, I found myself browsing the newspapers in the library, searching for news from Israel, which I had rarely done before, preferring to distance myself from it, protect my bubble. Things seemed to be getting better since Rabin was elected prime minister in 1992. The first phase of Oslo, the peace agreement with the PLO, had been signed that fall, and there were hopeful discussions toward peace with Jordan. Tel Aviv was becoming known as a new party capital in the world, its beaches and clubs covered and celebrated in international media. I felt a tug, for the first time since I'd left, to return. Even during my first year in New York, when things were objectively hard, I hadn't felt that way.

That's when I met Shoshi. I continued going to Havura meetings because I craved human interaction, a reminder of home. Zack rarely joined. It was meant for grad students, he said, but really it was another indication of how far apart we'd grown. Shoshi had a head full of tightly wound curls and a contagious energy. She wore an oversized green sweater over tights. Holding both my hands in hers, she said, "I am so excited to meet you. A fellow Yemeni in New York!"

She had her doubts about the Havura meeting. "I've had it with Jews," she said. "I came to New York to meet other people." She'd resisted for a few months, but Kate, who invited her, was insistent.

Shoshi was doing her PhD in journalism at Columbia. "I wanted to go to CUNY so I could take a class with Ella Shohat. But CUNY doesn't offer doctorate studies in journalism."

When she saw my polite smile, her eyes widened. "You know Professor Shohat, right?"

"I've heard of her."

Shoshi's eyes grew as if I had said the strangest thing. "*Heard of her?* She's my hero! Have you not read her essay 'Dislocated Identities: Reflections of an Arab Jew'?"

I shook my head, body stiffening.

"Oh my God. Mind blown. You absolutely must! It's brilliant! She disrupts and challenges the binary between Arabs and Jews, that whole Eurocentric way of thinking. And she wrote a great book about Israeli cinema and the politics of representation, which was groundbreaking when it came out in Hebrew. She writes about the whole macho sabra image"—Shoshi's stance changed and her voice thickened to match her words—"as opposed to the weak, diasporic Jew, and how Zionism used cinema to reinforce it. Know what I mean?"

A tall, slim woman in jeans and a blazer with a V-neck underneath wrapped her arm around Shoshi's waist. Shoshi introduced her as Yasmin, her partner.

Before coming to New York, Shoshi worked at *The Punch*, a social justice left-leaning magazine I hadn't heard about. "The punch," she explained, "because it's like a punch in the face, but also, you know that Yehuda Amichai poem? About how the fist was an open hand once?" Yasmin whispered in her ear and moved on.

"I was starting to feel hopeless in Israel. Maybe it was of all the injustices I was exposed to in my work at the magazine," she said. "I didn't know if I could continue living there. And immigrating didn't seem far-fetched. I mean, I already felt like an immigrant in my own country."

"What do you mean?"

She leveled a look at me. "Somehow, I never felt truly at home in Israel, you know? Despite being born there. Like, to belong fully always required me to turn off a part of who I am. To pretend. Let's face it, Israeli-ness at its core is Ashkenazi. And it's no secret it's hard to succeed as a Mizrahi woman in Israel, especially in academia."

I shifted my weight. "I don't know. I didn't feel that, personally."

"You didn't?"

"Don't you think anyone can succeed if they put their mind to it?"

She laughed, but it wasn't truly a laugh, more like a loud Ha! Then she looked at me newly. "Oh, I see."

I hardened, feeling as though I was failing some test I hadn't known I was on. "I mean, obviously it was harder for our parents' generation. But I went to Schneider . . ."

"Oh my God! You went to Schneider? I went to Ma'alot!"

I raised my brow.

"Ma'alot? It's an elite ulpana for religious girls in Jerusalem . . . It's the religious equivalent of Schneider. Same idea of integrating Mizrahi children from developing towns and neighborhoods with a more afflu-ent Ashkenazi population. Molding Mizrahi kids and turning them 'modern.'" She signed air quotations. "Like, it was in the protocols of the school. Did you know? I wrote about it for *The Punch*. It said clearly that an identity crisis could be a positive thing in pushing Mizrahi students in a more Western direction. They wanted to reeducate us, distance us from our past."

I fingered the heart necklace I got from Zack for my last birthday. My mind was racing.

"You liked it there? Schneider?"

"It's complicated. I didn't want to go, but in the end, yeah, I had a great time. And it got me here, didn't it?"

She nodded empathically. "So, I *did* like it. I was dying to go. I didn't see how problematic the place was until much later. When I think back about some things that happened there, like how ashamed I became of my parents. Or, there was this Yemeni girl from a small moshav who had the thickest accent, and we made fun of her, imitating her." She shuddered. "I hate thinking about that now. That place fucked me up."

I remembered my mother walking down the hallway with her bags of food, how my heart sank at the sight of her. The girls laughing at my mother's cooking. The Alterman song. I remembered myself walking through my neighborhood like a stranger. No, not a stranger, a tourist. A patronizing, Westernized tourist.

Shoshi wasn't telling me anything new. I was so immersed in my role, in my trajectory as the excelling Mizrahi girl, that I preferred not to see. I pushed aside anything that would have forced me to face the truth, reconstruct my narrative, work toward change. I wasn't ready.

"But I think the biggest fracture for me was when I started studying the missing children," she said.

My entire body broke in chills. "Oh my God." I leaned in and placed my hand on her arm, clutching it. "Did it happen in your family?".

"My cousin. He was in Ein Shemer. One day my aunt came to see him—"

"And he wasn't there," I continued. "My brother went missing in Rosh HaAyin."

"Your brother? Oh my God, I'm so sorry."

"Me too."

"Every time I tell this story—" Shoshi exhaled audibly. "I almost can't believe it."

We looked at each other, eyes brimming, and hugged.

"You know," Shoshi said, wiping her eyes, "as a teenager, I once told my dad, I can't believe you didn't raise hell. I'm so ashamed thinking about this now. Classic victim blaming."

Shoshi was planning to write her dissertation about the affair. When she asked about mine, I answered unenthusiastically, shoulders sagging.

"So who are some of the poets you'll be writing about?"

"Dahlia Ravikovitch, Yona Wallach, Tirza Atar . . ."

"Any Mizrahi poets?"

"Like who?"

"I don't know. Bracha Serri?"

"She was writing in the eighties. I'm focusing on the fifties and sixties."

"Miri Ben-Simhon, Amira Hess—"

"Same."

"Huh." She sipped from her wine. "So there were no female Mizrahi poets working in the fifties and sixties? None?"

I shrugged, feeling like I was failing again.

A COUPLE OF weeks later I came for Shabbat dinner at their apartment in Brooklyn. Zack and I got into a fight about that, too. "You can't spring this on me," he said. "I told my mom we'd be there this weekend."

"Without consulting me?"

If we were truly communicating, I would have told him how important it was for me to make new friends in the city, now that Evelyn was gone. "She's making Yemeni soup," I said, feebly, as though trying to persuade him. But the truth was, I was relieved to be going alone.

They both cooked: Shoshi's Yemeni soup filled the house with the familiar aroma that hit me with a severe bout of longing. Yasmin made maklouba, a Palestinian dish layered with lamb and vegetables. I brought wine and chocolate and handed them to Yasmin in apology. "I'm not much of a cook."

"We won't hold it against you," Yasmin said. She had angular sharp features that matched her straight, shoulder-length black hair. A contrast to Shoshi with her curly hair and curvy figure. Even their clothes: Yasmin was smartly dressed in black jeans and a silver, silky blouse. Next to her, Shoshi was adorably frumpy and bohemian in a sweeping skirt and a flowery blouse. She wore large Yemeni silver earrings laid in with an orange stone. "Beautiful." I touched one.

"My father made it," she said, revealing a lipstick stain on her tooth. "He was a silversmith. No Zack?"

"So was my grandfather!" I exposed my teeth to point to where her lipstick stain was. "Zack had plans with his parents."

Yasmin walked by with wine glasses and laughed. "They were all silversmiths!"

Shoshi managed to get the lipstick stain off with her tongue. "I read an article from *Yemen Times* lamenting the loss of that craft in Yemen," she said, leading us to a round table at the corner of the living room. "The Jews were their artisans, and when they left, they took that knowledge with them."

Shoshi and Yasmin had met at *The Punch*: Yasmin was a photographer. "A gifted one," Shoshi said, leaning toward her with adoring eyes. They both applied for programs in the US; both got accepted in New York. Yasmin had some family here, too.

"Falling in love with Yasmin was the final straw," Shoshi said, as though continuing our conversation from the first day. "What hope did we have for our relationship in Israel?"

I stared blankly at them.

"Oh, I thought you knew. Yasmin is part Palestinian, or 'Israeli Arab'"—she air-quoted again—"as Israelis love to say."

Yasmin placed the soup bowls on the table. "Because saying you're Palestinian when you have an Israeli citizenship is so offensive to people."

"Last straw, because your families didn't approve?"

"My family was fine with it," Yasmin said. "They were already trailblazers. My mother is Jewish. My father is Muslim. They met as students at the University of Haifa."

"Wow," I said. "I can't imagine what they went through when they got married."

"Yeah." She dipped some challah in the soup. "They had it pretty rough at first. Both families threatened to disown them. But they were lucky. Their families came through. So my parents had to be fine with Shoshi."

"Though there was the lesbian thing." Shoshi placed her hand over Yasmin's on the table.

"Yeah. I had to go fall in love with a woman." Yasmin laughed.

"But my family . . . you can imagine, Zohara," Shoshi said. "I'd gone to an ulpana! My family is this super traditional Yemeni family. First, I'm gay, then, Yasmin. It was too much."

"But once they agreed to meet me—" Yasmin grinned.

"And fell in love with her!"

"—her mother decided since my mom is Jewish, I'm Jewish, and that's that."

Shoshi laughed. "We didn't get into the whole 'Muslims go by the father' thing. Whatever works."

"I love this," I said.

"But still," Shoshi said. "It's complicated for a couple like us in Israel. Here, no one bats an eye."

The walls of their tiny living room were covered with Yasmin's photographs, black-and-white pictures of city scenes, some blurry, close-up shots of things I couldn't make out. To compensate for the monochrome art, the couch was covered in a colorful spread and bright cushions. I felt more at home there than I had felt in a long time.

"And there's your work, babe," Yasmin said to Shoshi, pouring more pinot noir into my glass.

Shoshi swallowed her bite, nodding effusively in affirmation. "You tell me. Where in Israel would have I been able to do a PhD about the Yemeni children? How come no one in Israel has written a dissertation about it yet? I know someone who tried, and the university wouldn't approve it."

"No one ever talks about it there," I agreed. "And when you do, people look at you like you lost your mind."

Yasmin got up and collected our plates. "No one talks about a lot of things in Israel. Especially when it interferes with the dominant narrative. When did you actually learn about the Nakba?"

"Umm, never?"

"I remember in elementary school," Shoshi said. "There were these ruins adjacent to it. They were just there. We climbed them on the way home from school. And no one ever told us this was an Arabic village once. We called it the hirbe. Ruins. Even the word was in Arabic!"

THAT WINTER I spent more time with Shoshi and Yasmin than with anyone. The feeling of discomfort I had felt in Shoshi's presence melted away the longer I knew her. I realized it had nothing to do with her. It was all me. I read "Reflections of an Arab Jew," which started, astonishingly, with the words, "I am an Arab Jew. Or more specifically an Iraqi, Israeli woman living, writing, and teaching in the US." I felt seen, felt the truth of every word in my bones. I found and read other essays by Shohat, was astonished to discover she mentioned the missing children, bristled as I read the quotes she included from Israel's first prime minister, Ben-Gurion, who spoke of Mizrahi as "lacking the most elementary knowledge," and stressed the need to "fight the spirit against the Levant, which corrupts individuals and societies." She quoted from a series of articles published in *Haaretz* in 1949 by Arye Gelblum, who wrote this about the immigrants from Yemen and Africa: "These are a people whose primitiveness is at its peak. Their level of education borderlines complete ignorance, and worse is their inability to absorb anything intellectual. . . . What will be the face of Israel with such populations?"

"Yes, it was so blatant back then," Shoshi said when I expressed my astonishment to her. "The xenophobia, the racism." Her master's thesis had been about the way the immigration from Islamic countries had been portrayed in Israeli media, so she'd read many of the same articles. One of the most shocking things she encountered was a promotional video shot by the army in the fifties. "I wish I could show it to you," she said. "This teacher says to a group of youth, Ashkenazi battalion instructors, 'We have to raise them to our level, or we'd find ourselves at theirs.' He says that! And then they show this sweet Yemeni boy, Saadia, and this Ashkenazi female instructor, Ruthie. And the narrator says, 'Saadia is far from the light and Ruthie's job is to bring him up to her level and into the light!'" Shoshi blew air out of her puffed cheeks, making an explosion sound.

The more I reconnected with my Mizrahi identity, the further I felt from my writing. The difficulties I had with my dissertation made sense. It's like my subconscious had known it before I caught on. I shared my doubts with Shoshi. "I get it," Shoshi said. "How can one write about female poets and feminism when the definition of feminism is limited to an Ashkenazi female experience? How can one write about Hebrew literature and the canon without acknowledging its glaring absence of other voices? It starts in high school, you know, they teach us certain poets, so these are the poets we end up admiring and writing dissertations about."

I remembered how I fell in love with Ravikovitch when I read her first book, *The Love of an Orange*. How my heart cracked open at fifteen when I read, "On the road at night there stands the man who once upon

a time was my father." How I related to her insurmountable grief, her
wanderlust, her desire to be away. Women are not meant to dream of
adventure and of leaving. This was a man's role. Was her desire to travel
an unconscious wish to find her father? I often felt the two correlated in
my own life. As a glum teenager, I had colored her depression in romantic terms. I felt kinship and deep admiration toward her, admiration that
grew when later she dared to speak her mind in the protest poems she
wrote after the Israeli invasion of Lebanon in 1982, becoming a prominent voice in opposing the government and critiquing Israeli society, as
she pointed out the responsibility we all bear when we stay silent.

I never stopped loving her, never stopped being moved by her poetry. But I couldn't help but wonder what would have happened if I was
taught other poets? What would've happened if other writers were allowed into the canon? Into the school curriculum?

And most importantly, how could I write an entire dissertation that
supports the same system that excludes Mizrahi voices?

I tried talking to my advisor about it. What if I changed it, I asked, and
instead of focusing on father-daughter relationships and limiting the time-
frame to the Statehood Generation, shift it to write about power relations
and gender in feminist Israeli poetry, which would allow me to include
Mizrahi poets like Bracha Serri and write a critique of the literary canon,
and the power imbalance inherent in the hegemony, into the dissertation.

Professor Segalovich leaned back in her leather chair, staring at me
narrowly and inhaling from her cigarette. I wished I had thought my
plea through before bringing it up to her. Even I wasn't convinced by it.
"How familiar are you with Bracha Serri's work?"

"A little," I lied. "It's bold. Subversive. She was way ahead of her
time—"

"This is a terrible idea," she said and burst into a coughing fit. "At
this point in the game, you want to introduce a poet you've only started
reading? You're so close. If you still feel passionate about this after you're
done, you can do it in postdoc." She cleared her throat loudly. "You're
making this more complicated than it has to be. Remember, a good dissertation is a finished dissertation."

She picked up the phone and started dialing, signaling the conversation was over.

CHAPTER 12

ZOHARA

MY NEIGHBORHOOD'S COMMUNITY center was in a washed-out building a walking distance from my mother's house, by a rusty playground in dire need of updating and a basketball court where teenage boys played hoops. Inside, a fluorescent-lit hall was buzzing with women chatting in a disorganized circle.

I peeked in, feeling shy. A woman in her forties, dressed in a long skirt and an airy blouse, neck and wrists laden with jewelry and hennaed curls brushed out to give her head an unfortunate pyramid shape, stood in the center of the room, talking with one of the women.

A small woman with a black felt cap covering her hair walked toward me. I recognized her from the shiva. She grabbed my shoulders, looked into my eyes. "How are you holding up, my dear?"

I nodded hesitantly.

"I was so happy when Nir told me you were coming." Of course! Nir's mom. What was her name? Why was I so bad at this? "It's so good of you to want to learn! Your mom would have been so happy." She grabbed my hand. "Come. I'll introduce you to Yael."

She led me to the younger woman in the center of the room, who was clearly running the show. When Nir's mom introduced me, Yael's face fell. "Your mother. What a loss. And her voice! My God, she could have been a professional."

"My aunt sings professionally, actually."

"Runs in the family!" Yael exclaimed. "And you? Are you a singer, too?"

"Oh, no. I mean, I used to sing in high school . . ."

"Zohara is a doctor for literature," Nir's mom said. "In America."

I shifted my weight. "Actually, I haven't completed my PhD yet." But no one was listening.

"We're going to start now." Yael touched my wrist lightly. "You're welcome to join us."

"Oh, I'm just here to watch," I said as she walked away.

"Girls, girls," she unironically shouted at the group of seniors, who shuffled toward their seats. "Let's begin. Some of you know Zohara, Saida's daughter. She will be joining us today."

I waved and gave an exaggerated smile.

"Shall we start with 'Yuma and Yaba'?" Yael enunciated slowly and loudly, I guess to make sure some harder-of-hearing women understood. "Something easy Zohara probably knows." She straddled a copper darbuka and accompanied the women as they sang, swaying with the beat. The song was, in fact, familiar. My fingers drummed along on my jeans.

Yael looked up at me when the song ended. "Did you understand some of the words?"

One woman scoffed. "Her generation doesn't understand Yemeni."

"It's a song they used to sing at the henna ceremony," Yael said. "The young bride says, 'Mother and Father, why did you sell me?' You know, in Yemen, it was common for the groom to pay a bride price to the family. She sings, 'Why didn't you have mercy on me? Sell the cattle, sell the sheep and goat instead.'"

"Sad," I said.

"That's how it was," one woman said. "Most of us didn't want to get married. We were just girls."

"I was nine!" another said. "I just wanted to jump rope all day."

"My God. A child!" Yael cried. Other women clucked their tongues and sighed.

I tried to conceal my shock. And here I thought my mom had married young.

"It was a different time," Nir's mom said. "We didn't know any different."

They moved on to another song.

MY MOTHER MARRIED around the age of thirteen. Or so she estimated. They didn't keep dates in Yemen, and she never knew her birthday. She told me she had been married off to my father to circumvent the orphan decree, which had the Muslim authorities convert Jewish orphans to Islam. Regardless of the decree, child marriages were common practice. My mother didn't want to marry my father. "He was old," she said, laughing. But she was an orphan, which meant she had little value or say. Her uncle arranged the marriage and her aunt convinced her she was lucky, my father was a good man, and at the end, my mother acquiesced. It's not like she had many options.

As a child, I had made it sound romantic to myself. My father "saved" my mother from the authorities, agreed to marry her even though she was poor and had no family. But as I grew older, their story made me more and more uncomfortable. I didn't like to think about being born not just from a loveless marriage but of a union that was forced on my mother, at an age when I was crushing on David Bowie and Omer Zehavi from the eighth grade.

There were no pictures from their wedding. No pictures from Yemen at all. No documents or artifacts. Our past was a blur. In my mind, Yemen was a dusty place, in shades of brown and beige, like Eilat but lacking the glamour and appeal of a vacation spot, houses made of mud bricks, narrow wadis fringed with shrubs. "I cried and cried." She chuckled when she told me about her wedding, trying to lighten her tragedy. "But in Yemen all girls cried when they married."

At the community center, the song ended, and Yael retrieved a folder from her briefcase and leafed through it. "I just remembered I have this." She handed me a sheet with the lyrics for the song "Galbi," *my heart,* the Arabic transliterated in Hebrew letters and the translation of the song written beside it. "You know this one, right?"

"Of course." "Galbi" was a major hit in European clubs in the eighties when Ofra Haza gave it a disco remix. Eventually, Israeli radio followed suit and started giving it airtime.

She sat back down. "Next time I'll bring more lyrics for you. How does that sound?"

"Great," I said. *Next time?*

"The Yemeni women's lives were hard," Yael said and everyone nodded. I realized she was speaking to me. "They were not allowed the freedoms men had. They were told to be submissive, silent. I remember the poet Bracha Serri saying there was no greater insult for a Yemeni woman than to be considered unquiet. They couldn't celebrate their loves. They couldn't be passionate." Women murmured agreement. "The songs were their way of speaking their heart, having a voice."

"We didn't talk so we sang," a woman with a squeaky voice said. Tziona. I remembered her. She used to clean at our school.

"What do you mean?"

"We didn't talk about our problems," Tziona said. "You know, we got married and we didn't know what to expect from the first night. You didn't talk about such things." The women laughed with a note of discomfort.

"Only the day before the wedding, my mom told me," Tziona said. "It's going to hurt but it only takes a minute and you'll be okay."

"Even about pregnancy!" another woman, her curly hair dyed jet-black, chimed in. "We knew nothing! We were so naive."

"And it wasn't like here, where everyone prances around pregnant. Pregnant women didn't go outside much," Tziona said.

"Why?"

"From the shame."

"Shame?"

"The pregnancy was proof the marital relationship happened," Yael explained.

I tried to keep a neutral expression. I couldn't wrap my head around this kind of thinking.

"Not like here!" Tziona said. "Here, they take pictures with their bellies half naked and hang them on the wall!" She mimicked a pose, holding her belly in one hand and her head leaning back in the other. Everyone burst out laughing.

"It's better like this," one woman said. "Why be ashamed?"

Some women murmured in concurrence, but another said, "No, not better. Now we went to the other extreme. They could learn some modesty from us."

I was fascinated by the conversation, which felt like a secret glimpse into my mother's world. When they started singing, I followed the lyrics and joined in. It was energizing, singing in unison with other women. When I closed my eyes, I could imagine this was a field recording in some "world music" record, the kind I used to get when I signed up for a service in New York that delivered them to my mailbox. This strange, disorienting sense of defamiliarization on my home turf, amongst my own kind, had happened to me before. At times it made me feel guilty, as if I was exoticizing my own culture. But now, it felt like I belonged here, singing with these women. I was the next generation, a rightful successor. I was home.

On the way out of the community center, I stopped by Yael's table. A few other women were chatting with her as she packed her things and started heading out. I followed until we stood at the entrance under a lone streetlight. Yael was holding her car keys.

"My mom left some tapes behind," I said. "Of her singing."

Yael's eyes lit up. "Oh, that's wonderful! What a gift!"

"I wondered if you could maybe tell me what's on them? I brought a couple."

She glanced at her watch. "I have to get home to my kids, but why don't you play me one or two songs right now?" She pointed at a Fiat parked by the curb, two car seats strapped in the back.

In her car, I shoved a tape into the deck. Soon, my mother's voice filled up the small space. Yael stared at the tape deck. "It sounds familiar. I recognize a line here and there."

"What do you mean?"

"You know the women were illiterate, so the songs were passed on orally and were constantly being rewritten as they were sung. With the exception of the ceremonial songs, like, for henna, which were usually more fixed. So the poetess—"

"The poetess?"

"The one who traditionally wrote the lyrics, usually to one of many existing melodies. Once she sang them, they were out of her hands, so to speak, and other women were free to change and alter them. Some gifted poetesses could make up a verse on the spot! It's very cool. So there are many variations. You could also find certain lines repeated in different songs, like this one." She pointed at the tape deck. "It means, my heart is thirsty and even if I drink the entire sea I won't be quenched. I've heard that line being used elsewhere."

"So the same melody could be used with different lyrics?"

"And the same lyrics could have different melodies."

"Sounds complicated."

"Not complicated," she said. "Dynamic. Collaborative."

How could I have not known of that tradition? Here I thought Shalom Shabazi, the famous seventeenth-century Jewish Yemeni poet, was my only literary heritage. I had no idea there was another tradition, running parallel, a pantheon of unnamed women poetesses whose songs weren't recorded, weren't written down. "So, the women always sang in Arabic?"

"Well, yes. They didn't know Hebrew. Only the men did. From prayer."

"So that's why Shabazi's songs were in Hebrew."

"Actually, Shabazi sometimes mixed Arabic and Aramaic into his songs. He created a language that mixed all three, in a way. It was very innovative."

We listened a little longer. Yael placed her hand on her heart. "Hearing her voice gives me chills. You know, most of the women in our group are not singers. I mean, they can sing well enough, but they are not there for the art. They come for the companionship, for their spirit, for their health." She caught my quizzical look. "Yes! Singing together is good for you! And of course, it's our way of keeping the tradition alive. But your mom was different. Her voice sounded louder than the rest. She didn't want to draw attention, but when she sang, it's like she couldn't help herself. Like she reached some . . . I don't know, another plane, when she sang. She became a different person. Or, maybe the opposite. Maybe she was more herself, truly herself. We all felt it. It was a privilege to sing with her."

I remembered the one time I saw my mom singing at a family henna. I was about four, and when she started singing, I burst into tears, frightened, terrified of the intensity of her emotions. When she sang, she was unrecognizable to me.

"Were there many songs?" I said.

"Hundreds. Not all survived. Maybe this one is from a specific region? Your mother was from Haidan, no?"

I nodded.

"My family came from Sana'a. The community in Sana'a was more segregated. In rural areas Muslims and Jews mixed more and so did their songs." She was quiet for a moment, listening with her eyes closed. "It's sad."

"What is it about?"

"It's a love song to a lover who went away." She opened her eyes. "It's hard for me to translate. I don't actually know the language well. I was born here. I mean, I know specific words and expressions. And I know the songs and their meaning, so I can catch a word or a phrase. Do you know someone who's fluent?"

"Maybe," I said.

"I don't know, maybe your mom wrote it," she said casually. And before I had a chance to respond to this wild idea, she glanced at the clock. "I have to go, but I have a book you can borrow, about the tradition, if you like."

My eyes lit up. "I'd love it."

"It's the only one I know of. But we're getting into holidays now, so we won't be meeting until mid-October. Here." She reached into her purse and pulled out a business card. "Call me if you want to borrow it."

NIR'S STORE WAS busy. He caught my eye when I came in and smiled warmly. I walked around, selecting random items. Pasta. I could make pasta. And salad greens. I hadn't been eating well. Or at all. My clothes had started to feel looser.

When the store emptied, I brought my groceries over. Nir glanced at them. "Branching out, I see."

I smiled.

"My mom told me you went to their group." He rang the items. "Found the answers you were looking for?"

"Some. I was thinking, can you translate a song for me?" I pulled the tape out of my purse. "Even the gist."

"Sure." He slid it into the deck, rewound for a while until we got to the beginning. When she started singing, Nir gave me a quick look. "Wow. That's your mom?"

I nodded.

He closed his eyes to listen. "Oh, I love this one. 'Ya Raytani Lak.' It means if I were yours."

"You know it?"

"Sure—" He stopped. "Oh, wait. Different lyrics."

"That's what Yael said about another song."

He nodded to the music. "That's common. The first line is the same. 'If I were yours and you were mine.' And one of my favorite lines is in there too. 'If I were a bird with a curly wing, I'd shelter you from the hot sun.'" He repeated the line in Arabic. It sounded natural and beautiful in his mouth.

"So what's different?"

He concentrated. "Okay, this. Interesting."

"Why?"

"It says, 'If I were grapes strung on a vine, I'd squeeze the flesh of my fruit and pour juice into your mouth' . . . Or something like that."

"Okay?"

"It's a bit . . ." He laughed a little coyly, a dimple cleaved in his right cheek. "Explicit for the women's songs."

"Explicit?" My cheeks tingled. My mother? Singing unsavory lyrics? Possibly *writing* unsavory lyrics?

"Squeezing flesh, mixing bodily fluids . . ." He met my eyes and chuckled. "I don't know. The women's songs were usually more subtle, only hinting. But I suppose it could mean something else." He was in thought for a moment. "You know, Shabazi has a poem, it became a popular wedding song, 'Ayelet Hen.' Do you know it?" He didn't wait for an answer and broke into song. He had such a warm, deep voice, and his guttural *het* and *ayin* were more pronounced when he sang. "So there's a verse that says, 'To her wine glass I am always welcome, and we will mix, her wine yearns for my wine.' Now, it was written three-hundred-odd years ago, but it sounds pretty suggestive to me. Some people consider it to be racy and too carnal for Shabazi. But others say it's symbolic, that Shabazi's lyrics should never be understood simply. So maybe the poetess here is making a reference to Shabazi?" He was thinking aloud. "But that's also unusual. Shabazi was considered highbrow, almost holy, untouchable. The women's songs were considered foolish and earthly. There was no allusion from one to the other that I know of." He shrugged. "But I'm no expert."

"So, let me get it straight." I raised an eyebrow. "The women's songs were always foolish, even when they were totally innocent and Shabazi's songs were always highbrow even when they were obviously about sex."

He laughed. "Don't say this aloud. People in the community would be outraged."

"So, you're saying this line would be considered, what, vulgar?"

"I wouldn't say vulgar. It's poetic. At least in my opinion. But it's unusual."

"Huh."

"Why don't you ask your aunt Shuli? Wasn't she a henna singer? She would know all the songs. And she knows your mother."

"That's not a bad idea."

An elderly man with a kippah came in for groceries, leaning on his cane. Nir asked after his knee and if he needed help with the groceries. Two children brought candies to the counter, counting their coins. I stepped off to the side for a moment.

"How do you know all this stuff?" I asked when they left.

"I heard my mom sing when I was little. I wanted to understand what she was singing about." He ejected the tape and handed it to me. "If you want to leave a couple of tapes with me, I'll translate them for you."

"Yeah? You don't mind?" I randomly pulled a couple of tapes and handed them to him.

"I'd be honored," he said.

LIZZIE, WHEN I finally called her, sounded unimpressed with my discovery. "Yeah, I saw Ima recording herself."

"What for?"

"No idea." I heard her inhaling smoke. "You know Ima loved singing. She always sang."

I was quiet for a minute. "I remember she sang a bit."

"Yeah, she didn't do it so much when you were around."

"Why?"

"Why?" She snorted caustically. "You were adamantly against it."

"I wasn't adamant."

"Once she had Yemeni music playing and she was singing along, and you turned on your own radio super loud to compete, playing some Europop shit. So she listened to her music when you weren't around."

I fell into silence.

"Whatever, Zorki, you were a kid. Kids are assholes."

I laughed. She didn't join me.

"Also, I found a photo in her ID case of some men. Looks like it's from the immigrant camp. Something she cut from a newspaper."

"Huh. Interesting," she said in a way that countered her words.

"It reminded me of the photo of her and Rafael from the immigration camp," I said. "I looked inside the frame. There was nothing there. Do you know how she got that photo?"

She was quiet for a minute. "Yes, actually. I was with her when we ran into the photographer in Tel Aviv. By Habima Square, I think. He didn't remember her; he took many photos that day. It was for an article, but her photo wasn't published."

"Maybe it was the same article."

"Maybe. She told him her son went missing and she didn't have a photo of him. I think it helped that his wife was there. Anyway, he gave her his phone number and promised to help, and he did. He sent her the photo."

"Do you remember his name?"

"You're pushing it," she said. "Anyway, why does it matter?"

Maybe she was right. Maybe it didn't.

"How is the house coming along? Did you get it packed?"

"Most of it."

She was quiet for a moment. "What are you doing all day?"

"I don't know. Figuring shit out."

"Like what?"

"I don't know. Stuff. Looking for a job."

"So you're staying?" I couldn't read her voice. Was she happy?

"Maybe. For now, anyways."

"Come over for dinner Friday."

"Okay," I said. "I will."

CHAPTER 13

YONI

THE DAY OF Tata's stone reveal, he came home from the cemetery to find a thin brown envelope in the mailbox, marked with the distinct triangular army stamp. He stuffed it in his pocket so his mother, shuffling a few steps behind him, wouldn't see it.

In his room, he tore it open. A draft notice from the Israeli Defense Force for July 31. Less than a year away. He thought of the letter his uncle had received seventeen years after he supposedly died. And then he thought of how Tata would react when he told her, before remembering he couldn't.

This kept happening. Every day he woke up and plunged into the same pit of loss that could never be fixed, faced again with his failure to save her, with his powerlessness, with the infuriating impossibility of turning back time. Seeing the stone over Tata's grave, engraved with her name, should have made it real. She had told him once that the Yemenis did not place tombstones on their graves, so the soul could ascend more easily. She also told him not to visit at her grave. "I'm not there."

"Don't talk like this," he had said. "You have a long life ahead."

His mother was struggling, too. There was something fragile and panicky about her since Tata died, her movements jerky, fretful. When she washed dishes, he expected them to shatter. The other day, as she drove him to the stationery store for school supplies, a cheesy ballad came up on the radio, and he caught her eyes in the mirror and saw they were filled with tears.

Somehow, his aunt Zohara appeared more together than his mother. Maybe it was her newly acquired Americanness that made her more restrained, more polite in her expression. Like on American TV, where people barely cried at funerals, held it all inside.

The other day, he heard her talk about him to his mother. "He needs help," she said. "I can't imagine what he's going through." His mom lit a match. She had gone back to smoking. He felt a flicker of contempt for her weakness. His mom said something with an air of annoyance, which seemed to accompany much of their exchanges, their communication laced with accusation. *You left. You weren't there for me. You didn't protect me. You think you're better than me.* "Would you like me to check with Mika?" his aunt said. "She's a certified child psychologist now. It's probably unethical for her to treat him but maybe she can recommend someone?"

He was irritated at being labeled a child.

THAT EVENING, BARUCH waited for him after the prayer ended. He slapped his shoulder familiarly. "How's it going, my brother?"

Yoni nodded and started toward his house.

"Listen." Baruch stumped his cigarette butt with his heel and caught up with him. "Me and the guys are planning a protest against the Oslo Accords. It's big. We're meeting to talk about it this week. Would you like to come? It will take your mind off things, and I can give you a ride there and back. It's in Ramat Gan."

Yoni stared at his sneakers: size 43. Sometimes they looked like monster feet to him.

"It's good guys, students, activists. We're trying to inspire change. Exercising our democratic right to protest, you know."

Yoni liked the sound of these words: *Inspire change. Democratic right to protest.*

"Whenever I go through hard times, it helps me focus my attention elsewhere," Baruch said. "Know what I mean? I felt that way after my grandpa died last year."

Yoni looked up at him in surprise.

"Someone at the synagogue mentioned it. May you know no further sorrow."

Yoni stole a glance at Baruch. There was something about this guy he liked. Something honest. Something real. He talked more than Yoni was used to, but he used words smartly. Didn't waste them, like some people. His mom, for example, who chatted on the phone with her friends, spewing stupid, unnecessary words. His sisters with their fights. Motti, talking over dinner about his job, about soccer. Words, words, words. They all wanted him to engage in that stupid habit, too. Like something was wrong with him if he didn't. Except for Tata. She understood the power of words, knew how carelessly some people emitted them, oblivious to the consequences. The evil eye, for example, could be cast by way of speech, like calling a baby beautiful or commenting on something insincerely.

That's why he liked going to synagogue. Because the words had already been measured. Reciting, singing, praying was easier, safer, than forming one's own words.

"So?" Baruch said.

"Yes," Yoni said. "I'll come."

THE MEETING WAS HELD IN A BASEMENT SUITE IN RAMAT Gan. A row of small windows just below the ceiling displayed the feet of passersby on the street. A couple dozen young men and a few women socialized by a folding table arranged with pop in plastic bottles and bowls of chips. Most of the men wore kippahs. The women wore long skirts and some had headscarves. Almost everyone appeared older than him. He reminded himself that most people would never guess his real age.

Baruch had picked him up in his dusty white Beetle. He drove erratically, switching gears and changing lanes frequently in the jammed

Jabotinsky Street. The second gear often slipped into fourth by accident, which made the car rumble. As he drove, he told Yoni about the movement: it started out as a religious political student group but had grown bigger and more inclusive since. He glanced at Yoni. "What does your family vote, Likud?"

Yoni nodded. It seemed like everyone in the neighborhood voted for the center-right party, at least judging by the signs hanging on porches at the last election.

"Of course they did," Baruch said. "I'm telling you, the left in Israel, they forgot what it means to be Jews." He swerved his car, yelling at a driver. "Moron! Who taught you how to drive?"

At the meeting, Baruch stood up and cleared his throat. The room fell silent. People found seats on couches and plastic chairs. "Last week was two years since the signing of the catastrophe called the Oslo Accords," he started dramatically. "Instead of peace, we've seen more terror, more Israeli deaths, which Arafat, despite his promises, has done nothing to stop. Rabin and his Labor government are ignoring what the people want, at least those who live outside of Tel Aviv state." He said those last three words in derision, almost spitting. "Now Rabin intends to cede more of our land, putting all of us, including those in Tel Aviv, in danger and completely ignoring our biblical birthright. Who is he representing? Is it us or the PLO? The Jewish people lived here for two thousand years before the Arabs came. We have a total and absolute right to this place!" Yoni recognized that performative quality he had seen in Baruch that day at the shipudia. "As Likud member Ariel Sharon eloquently said, 'What's the difference between the Jewish leadership in the ghetto and this government? There, they were forced to collaborate. Here they do it willingly.'" The people clapped and cheered.

A small, fair-skinned man in his forties spoke next. He wore glasses, had a shadow of facial hair, and his clothes were rumpled. "This is Yair, one of the founders," Baruch whispered as he sat next to Yoni. Yair's voice was deeper and louder than his appearance suggested. He reminded people of the weekly protests in front of Prime Minister Rabin's residence in North Tel Aviv, listed demonstrations planned in major junctions. Buses would be picking up protestors at certain times and assigned spots. "There are still spaces for the protest outside Rabin's residence on Friday. Remember, we are limited to fifty people, or we'd need a permit.

"One more thing." Yair raised his hand to indicate he wasn't done. "I'd like to clarify a point that was brought up in our last meeting. We are not and will never be associated with Kahane and the Kach movement. Why? Because we work within the law and Kach is a terrorist organization. That isn't what we're about."

Yoni felt reassured by Yair's comment. Last year, when a gun-toting Kahanist walked into the Cave of the Patriarchs in Hebron and murdered twenty-nine Palestinian worshippers, it shook him to the core. It was the first time he had seen a Jew committing such an awful act in the name of God. Terror was something that happened on the other side, used by Palestinians against Jews. After the massacre, the Israeli government declared the far-right movement that had been founded by Meir Kahane to be a terror organization.

Someone was watching him. He turned and caught the eyes of a girl about his age, her light brown hair tied in a ponytail on her back. She dropped her gaze. He looked away quickly. When he glanced at her again, she was listening to Yair, leaning forward on her fist, her other arm folded over her long denim skirt.

"Let's get out on the streets and make our voices heard!" Yair said. "Use our anger as fuel for action!"

The room erupted in clapping and whistles. Yoni's heart pounded with resonance. Over the past month, his grief had transformed into a beast, writhing and ugly and hard to contain. Some days he walked into his mother's kitchen and imagined smashing every cup and every plate with a bat. Some days he imagined punching Shlomi in the face, relished in the image of his blood dripping.

But now he was being offered a legitimate reason to be angry, a target at which to release his rage. He was comforted by the idea that his anger could be channeled into positive energy, fuel for action, like Yair said.

When they stepped out into a cooler evening, Baruch was bouncy, buzzing with adrenaline. "So? What did you think?"

The girl in the jean skirt passed them by. He watched her go, willing her to turn; she didn't. A grin spread on Baruch's lips. "That's Hodaya. Nice girl."

Yoni shrugged as though he had no opinion on the matter.

"So you're in?" Baruch said. "Shall I pick you up Friday for the protest?"

"I'm in," Yoni said.

"Good." Baruch grinned. "Because I already signed you up."

HE SPENT THE next few days learning as much as he could about Oslo, reading the papers from start to finish. He sat next to Motti as he watched the news every night. "I don't trust him," Motti muttered once, jerking his chin at Arafat. "He's up to something. He won't give up the dream of a Greater Palestine so easily."

"And Rabin?" Yoni asked.

Motti glanced at him, surprised at his interest, or maybe pleased to see him initiate conversation. "I didn't vote for him, that's for sure. I'm Likudnik, always have been, always will be."

"So am I." His mom came from the kitchen with a cup of tea. "But the Likud also made peace with the Arabs, let's not forget that. Menachem Begin signed a peace agreement with Egypt when he was in power. He gave back the Sinai Peninsula, and you voted for him. If Rabin brings peace, I'm all for it. Maybe you won't have to go to the army," she said to Yoni as she sat beside him.

That seemed a little naive, even for her. He'd heard that before, of course. Generations of Israelis kept telling their children that one day the conflict would end and they wouldn't have to go to the army. But didn't she know how old he was? Lately, he'd been wondering what would happen if he changed course, chose to study Torah in a yeshiva instead, get an exemption on a religious basis. Had Baruch gone to the army? How religious did you have to be? Then he thought of Tata and was filled with shame. He could hear her reproaching him that everyone had to do their part.

Tata rarely spoke about politics with him. He doubted she ever voted. She disliked all politicians equally, except for Menachem Begin, who was the only leader who saw Mizrahi voters, she said. The rest were "all snakes and liars." Still, she never spoke ill of this country, even after what had been done to her. But Yoni knew it was the Labor Party, or its earlier version, Mapai, who was in power when his uncle went missing, and he was angry on her behalf. The only time he had seen her glued to the screen for something other than the Friday night Arabic movie was last year, when Rabbi Uzi Meshulam bunkered in Yehud, demanding an inquiry committee for the disappearance of the Yemeni, Mizrahi and Balkan children. Tata sat in front of the screen and cried. She had never seen anyone speaking about this so publicly before, she said. God bless him. But of course, the media had portrayed him as a madman. Nothing changed after the police arrested him and his followers. And for a few days, the light in Tata's eyes had gone out. She stared outside, picking at the fringes of her sweater, and didn't speak.

YONI'S HEART FLIPPED WHEN HE SAW HODAYA IN THE GROUP of protestors gathered outside Rabin's residence. Rabin's apartment was on the top floor of an average-looking building in a shaded, residential street in North Tel Aviv. It did not look like a prime minister's home: a palm tree and a fruitless banana tree in front, a short stone fence covered by an overgrown hibiscus bush, a blue number 5 affixed on the left corner and a row of metal mailboxes on the right, much like the ones in Yoni's building. Children rode their bikes, and two elderly women with puffy hair chatted on a wooden bench across the street, glancing at them from time to time. No security in sight.

Baruch walked resolutely over to Hodaya, and Yoni followed. "This is Yoni. You're the same age," Baruch said and left, winking at Yoni. Fortunately, Hodaya spoke first, asked where he was from and how long he'd been involved in the movement. And then she kept talking.

Hodaya was beautiful in all clichéd ways, the kind of beautiful that was way out of his league, that normally wouldn't give him the time of day, and yet, for some inexplicable reason, she did. She had a constellation of freckles on her nose. When she smiled, all her teeth showed, and he was relieved to see the top ones were a little crooked, a flaw that made her all the more endearing. She came from a family of reputable rabbis in Jerusalem, and she would probably marry a fancy yeshiva guy one day, certainly not a Yemeni boy from Sha'ariya whose family didn't even observe the Shabbat, who had only started wearing a kippah and laying tefillin because his grandma had died. She was a few months older, already doing her national service. She knew she wouldn't go to the army—it was no place for religious girls—but she wanted to give something back. The men in her family had all gone to the army. Her father believed serving was a mitzvah and an obligation, even for religious boys. He was also the one who inspired her activism. "Two years ago, when Rabin signed with Arafat the first time, we watched it on TV together, and I felt so angry to see this and so worried. And he said, 'Then do something. We live in a democratic society. Fight for what you believe in.'"

"You're a good listener," she said at some point. "That's a rare quality in men." She laughed. "Sorry, I have a lot of brothers."

"I only have sisters," he said. "I grew up with women."

"That explains it."

When he went home that evening, he felt elated, energized from the protest, from his conversation with Hodaya. At dinner he chatted with Ortal about school, helped his mother serve food. And that night, for the first time in a long time, he went to sleep feeling almost hopeful.

CHAPTER 14

ZOHARA

ON FRIDAY, I woke up with an urge to write, to document everything Yael and Nir had shared with me about the women's songs. For the first time in forever, I felt inspired by something. The idea of oral poetry that was created and disseminated by a community of women fascinated me, the fluidity of it, the riffing and rewriting and borrowing, which stood against the idea of authorship as it was known and celebrated in the West. There was so much more I wished to know.

I made coffee and pulled out my journal, a blank notebook with a paisley cover. The last entry was from months ago, soon after I'd arrived in Thailand.

In the afternoon, when it got hot, as though summer had changed its mind and decided to stick around a bit longer, I drove to the beach. As expected from a summery Friday afternoon, the café was hopping, people in minimal clothing were waiting in line for a table, and loud dance music was playing from speakers. It felt like a party.

I swam to the wave breakers and back a few times, and at one point climbed up on the rocks and faced the sun as it dipped into a layer of smog. I dove back in, floated on my back and watched a flickering lone star and a plane slicing through the purple-orange glow.

When I heard my name, I jerked and straightened. The buildings on Herbert Samuel were already illuminated. The skinny figure calling my name was haloed, backlit by the spotlight on the beach. Iggy. I walked out, taking my time.

Iggy opened his arms. "How long were you in there? I started to worry."

"I'm wet." I recoiled. "How did you know I was here?"

"I don't mind. I'll get dry in a minute." He pulled me into an embrace and gestured toward the tattooed guy who owned the place. "Shalom mentioned he saw you at the café."

I grabbed my towel from my bag and wrapped myself in it.

"You never came back that day. I called a few times. Are you checking your messages?"

I cocked my head to one side to release water from my ear. "Yeah, sorry. I've been busy. Cleaning the house. Sorting through my mom's stuff." I could hear the discordant, defensive note in my voice.

We sat at the restaurant, ordered beer and hummus. Iggy leaned forward in his seat. "Listen, I have time these days. They're reshooting some stuff for the music video, so I'm free until they send me the footage. Let me help. I can come over and we can finish it up together. Whatever you need."

I took a swig from my beer and licked the foam off my lips. I *could* use the help, or at least the company. Iggy was my friend. And I missed him. Why was I being so weird? So I told him about the tapes, about the women's songs, about the singing group.

Iggy leaned back. "Wow. I never even knew your mom sang."

"It was kind of a private thing for her."

"So, this tradition: are there recordings of it anywhere?"

"Apparently there's a book. I'm going to drive up north tomorrow to borrow it from this woman who runs the singing group." I glanced at him and blurted, "Want to come?"

"Sure. Michal is working all day tomorrow."

I looked at him sideways. "She has a name."

"Yeah. Sorry I was weird when you came." He looked down. Was he blushing? My heart squeezed. "It's all so new still. I guess I'm being protective."

"I get it." If it's new, a thought snuck up on me, maybe it's not too late.

"What did your aunt Shuli say?"

"I didn't talk to her."

"Why not?"

"I don't know. Over the phone? She's all the way in Eilat."

"Then go see her."

"That's what Nir said."

"Nir?"

"The guy from the makolet by my mom's."

"You talk to the guy from the makolet about this kind of stuff?"

"We're friends, sort of." That sounded a little sad.

Iggy glanced at his watch. "I should go. Dinner at my mom's."

"Shit." I sat up. "What time is it?"

LIZZIE OPENED THE door with her hair in a messy bun, dark bags under her eyes, a checkered towel slung over her shoulder. "You're late." She turned away. "We're already done."

"Sorry. The daylight savings throws me off." I followed her into the kitchen. She resumed washing dishes. "Where's Motti?"

"In the bedroom, resting." I couldn't read her voice. Was she angry at me? At Motti? "Where were you?"

"In Tel Aviv. With Iggy."

"Nice," she said. It didn't sound like she meant it.

"I should have found a phone and called."

She didn't answer.

I sat down at the kitchen table by the pile of weekend papers, leafed through them mechanically. I didn't know how to talk to my sister, the same way I never knew how to talk to my mother. Both spoke in codes, impossible to read. As a teen, I imagined I must have taken after my father, who was a great conversationalist, a storyteller, and who I perceived as worldlier than my mother. My naive, traditional, provincial mother who represented everything I didn't want to become.

Of course, that was before I knew everything about him.

The first time Lizzie shared her experience of growing up with him,

I was fifteen. I was back home for the summer. One day, after yet another fight with my mom, I ranted to Lizzie, accused Mom of being too rigid, unreasonable. "Dad wasn't like that," I said. Lizzie, feeding Yoni with a spoon, snorted. "You have no idea what you're talking about. You're idealizing him because he's dead."

Lizzie told me how strict he had been with her, growing up. "I wasn't allowed to hang out with boys. I wasn't allowed to wear jeans because it was immoral, or something. Once I saved money from babysitting and bought my own jeans, and I came home from school to find he had shredded them. I cried so much. Another time, I came home half an hour after curfew from a school party. He slapped me and forbade me from going to parties for two months."

I listened in horror. "Oh my God, Lizzie. I had no idea."

"You know how people are different with their grandchildren? Softer? More permissive? You were like his granddaughter. After Rafael, after me. He finally enjoyed his fatherhood. He was different with you. Like, he wanted you to study, go to university. But it took him time to get there. When I was growing up, Mom was the progressive one. You know he didn't like her working? She made more money than him, by cleaning, which was unheard of in Yemen. It bothered him. He never quite adjusted to life here. He kept lamenting how things were better in Yemen, how the youth in Israel were corrupt. Like he was morally superior, which is ridiculous, considering."

"Considering what?"

She eyed me for a moment and looked down. "Nothing."

"Obviously it's something."

"Let's just say he wasn't the best husband," she said.

My eyes widened. "Did he cheat?"

"Let it go," Lizzie said firmly. "I already said too much."

Now, I raised my eyes from the pile of newspapers and watched my sister. "Do you know about the women's songs?"

"Sure. I mean, what is there to know?"

"I don't know. I didn't know it was a thing. Separate from the men's songs. I just thought some songs were in Hebrew and some in Arabic."

"Yeah, the men sang only devotional songs in Hebrew. Shabazi mostly, from the Diwan. Remember the Diwan Aba had? It was like, three hundred years old." She turned to shoot a sharp look at me. "I hope you didn't get rid of that."

"Of course not," I said, annoyed at the accusation. The Diwan, a collection of liturgical hymns and poems, was one of my father's most prized possessions. One of the only things he managed to bring with him from Yemen.

"Ima." Lilach came marching from the living room, stomping her feet. "Ortal won't let me watch my show."

"Whose turn is it to choose?"

"It's hers but her show is longer than mine and it's not fair."

Lizzie kept scrubbing the pots furiously and turned to yell over her shoulder. "Ortal! Share with your sister!"

Ortal shuffled her feet into the kitchen. "Ima, she already watched *Tiny Toon*. It's my turn."

"What are you watching?"

"What difference does it make?"

"It has people kissing." Lilach puckered her lips, making a loud kissing noise.

"It doesn't!" Ortal yelled like someone who knew she was losing.

"Turn it off," Lizzie said.

"It's not fair!" Ortal began crying.

"Enough!" Lizzie turned to them. "Both of you." She stormed out toward the living room, grabbed the remote and turned the TV off. "If you can't agree, then no more TV." Lilach and Ortal both stared at her, Lilach in astonishment and Ortal in indignation. Ortal ran crying to her room and Lilach followed her. Lizzie threw her towel on the counter and closed her eyes.

"Why don't you take a moment?" I said. "Go sit outside. Have a glass of wine. I'll finish up here."

Lizzie looked at me dubiously.

I opened the fridge, found a bottle of white wine that had likely been there a while, looked through the cupboards for wine glasses, or any glasses, and settled on a mug. I handed it to my sister. "I got this."

Lizzie hesitated a minute before she took it, grabbed her pack of cigarettes from the table and stepped out onto the porch, sliding the door behind her.

I finished washing the pots and pans, turned on the dishwasher, swept the kitchen floor. Then I moved into the living room, where a mountain of laundry towered on the couch. I knew Motti worked late, but it didn't seem right he was taking a nap while my grieving, overwhelmed sister was left to do everything on her own.

Yoni came out of the room and grabbed an apple from the fridge. I called out to him, "Hey, Yoni!"

He spun, surprised to see me. "Oh, hey." He bit into the apple, turning to go.

"Wait," I said, tucking socks into balls. "Stay a while. Talk to me."

"Can't. Homework," he said as he walked away. Apparently, I didn't know how to talk to my nephew either.

I turned the TV back on and zapped through the channels until I found the evening news. Prime Minister Rabin was walking through an airport, waving. They cut to footage from a right-wing demonstration, held at the site of the recent pigua in Jerusalem. Protestors carried a prop coffin covered with an Israeli flag and screamed, "Rabin is a traitor!"

Motti walked into the room dressed in gray sweatpants and a white sleeveless shirt, stifling a yawn. Already a big man, more than a head taller than my sister, he had grown heavier lately. He noticed Lizzie through the glass doors reading the Shabbat magazine. "That's sweet of you, Zohara. Thank you."

"This guy." I jerked my chin toward the screen, where right-wing Knesset member Rehavam Ze'evi called the government "The Jewish Munich Government." "What does this even mean?"

Motti shrugged, yawning again.

I realized I was holding up his underwear. I folded it quickly and placed it on a pile of clothes. It felt like a good time to speak up. "Lizzie is struggling," I said.

"I know."

"I don't mean to overstep, but maybe she could use some extra help these days."

He stiffened. "I was just about to bathe the girls. I do my part."

"Maybe you could do more than usual."

"Zohara. You haven't been around. You don't know our lives."

"I'm just saying—"

"Thank you for your help," he said curtly, walking away.

My face felt hot. Motti was a sweet, gentle man. Our relationship wasn't deep, but it had always been good. Should I have not said anything? In the bathroom, Lilach and Ortal squealed as they got ready for their baths, their earlier fight forgotten. I finished folding as fast as I could.

≈

IGGY PICKED ME UP IN HIS FADED RED FIAT UNO EARLY ON Shabbat morning, before cars began piling up on the highways for their day trips. As we drove out of the neighborhood, I saw men ambling back from the synagogue in their white shirts, hands clasped behind their backs. I cowered in my seat, apologetic for disturbing the quiet and magic of the day.

Iggy had asked to listen to some tapes on the way, so I brought one, marked 1990. The year I moved to New York. We heard the clicking of the recording, a chair being dragged across the floor. I ached hearing those domestic sounds of life. Of her living.

When she started singing, Iggy turned to me with wide eyes. "Holy shit."

As if on cue, my eyes filled with tears. "Fuck."

"We don't have to listen to it."

"It's okay. I want to."

"Now I understand where you got your singing voice from."

I looked at him puzzled. "Me? I don't really sing. I sang a little at school assemblies. And I fooled around in high school."

"What are you talking about? I remember the first time I heard you sing. We were closing Shabbat in the base. That guy, Udi, brought a guitar, and we made a fire, remember? You started singing and everybody was like, 'Dude! You can sing!'"

I scoured my brain for the memory. "I don't remember that."

"How's Yoni?"

"I tried talking to him yesterday." A toddler waved at us from the back seat of the car ahead. Iggy waved back. "He was weird."

"He's a teenager. Teenagers are weird."

"He's grown so much since I last saw him. He goes to synagogue now. And he still wears his kippah, even though the thirty days of mourning are over."

"You know how it is. Some people turn to God when they're grieving."

"I guess." I had known people who became religious and estranged themselves from their entire family. There was this girl Renana I knew in the army. On night shifts we'd talk about sex. She had rich experience and she loved sharing. And what else did we have to do there in these long hours in front of the screens? Two years later, I saw her in Tel Aviv, and she was heavily pregnant and full-on Orthodox, long skirt, head covered in a knotted scarf. I was in shorts and a tank top. She pretended not to see me. What if Yoni was heading that way? And my sister wasn't paying attention?

YAEL LIVED IN a Yemeni moshav in Jezreel Valley, where it looked and felt almost tropical, lush and humid, the streets lined with slender palm trees laden with dates. We drove past dairy barns and strawberry fields and little one-story homes. Old Yemeni ladies with headscarves eyed us from their porches. Citrus, banana and apple trees grew in their yards; laundry lines were strung between them.

Yael's house smelled familiar. Underneath the freshly baked smell of warm jichnoon, I could detect the ripe aroma of hawaij, the spice mixture that gave Yemeni soup its distinct flavor, the freshness of basil and cilantro, the lingering sour-sweet scent of hilba.

A tin pot with a tight lid gleamed inside a lit oven. "Would you like some?" Yael asked.

"How can we say no to jichnoon?" I said, as if we had not stopped on the way for a cappuccino and halva Danish. Israeli pastries were a weakness of mine and I had been deprived for too long.

We sat at a kitchen table covered with a white plastic tablecloth. Yael served jichnoon with a bowl of grated tomato, a jar of green schug dotted with red chilies, and browned eggs. The rolled dough was soft, buttery, and emitted delicious, sweet-smelling steam. Iggy groaned as he bit into it. "I can't believe I had a Yemeni girlfriend for five years and this goodness was denied me." My mother made kubana, a moist Shabbat bread that was baked overnight, but never jichnoon. It wasn't traditional to her region, she said; only in Israel, all Yemenis and their traditions were lumped into one. And anyway, it was too much work.

Yael glanced at me, realizing we were not together. I wished Iggy hadn't said it.

"I'm sorry my mother didn't meet your stereotypical requirements of a Yemeni mother-in-law," I said.

Iggy laughed. "Saida was perfect just the way she was."

"That she was." Yael nodded.

Almost on instinct, I pursed my lips and raised my eyebrows ever so briefly, enough to register my disagreement. Iggy pushed my shoulder in a friendly, joking way. Then I remembered. A sharp pain in my chest.

We moved to sit under a mulberry tree outside, watching Yael's children playing at a playground across the street with the neighbors' kids; some of the boys wore kippahs and a couple had sidelocks. Yael served coffee, black for Iggy, sweet and milky for me, placed a tray with sliced watermelon and green grapes in the middle of the table. She handed me the book, an image of a young Yemeni woman in traditional garb on its cover.

Before she found the book, it was all in her head, she said. As a little girl, her mom and aunts used to sing together, and she wanted to join, be a part of the sisterhood. "I always loved to sing. You know how it is with Yemeni people. Singing is in our blood."

"Why is that, you think?" Iggy said. "It's like every Yemeni person I know can sing."

"It's true," Yael said. "Look at the Israeli singers who won the Eurovision contest. All Yemeni. You know, in Yemen, the Jews believed that in mourning for the destruction of the Second Temple, you were not allowed to use musical instruments. You could use your voice and you could have rhythm. That's why the only instruments you see Yemenis play are tin drums or copper trays. In the moshav we joke that if you need a drummer for your wedding, just grab any kid from the street."

We laughed.

"The Yemenis start to develop musicality at a young age. Most Yemeni boys go to synagogue, where their fathers encourage them to use their voices, to join in, to be heard. In our moshav, the boys start taking Torah classes with the mori when they're three. And the Yemeni prayer is very musical, melodic. There's a lot of trilling involved. In Yemeni synagogues, everyone is a cantor."

I recalled my conversation with the women, remembered how silenced they felt, how female quietness was considered a virtue. What an entirely different experience it was to be a boy in this culture.

"Singing is a day-to-day activity in Yemeni homes," Yael said. "We sing when we clean, when we cook. We sing when we're happy. We sing when we're sad. In celebrations. Even in death."

"Fascinating," Iggy said, looking truly gripped. "Before Zohara told me about the women's songs, I never knew it existed."

"Well, you must know 'Galbi,' right?" Yael said. "From the *Yemeni Songs* album by Ofra Haza? That was written in the tradition of the women's songs."

"Of course!" Iggy looked at me. "Didn't I buy you that album for a holiday, or . . . ?"

"My birthday." I sipped my coffee, glowering at him.

Iggy erupted in laughter. "She wasn't impressed."

"Why not?" Yael asked. "It's a lovely gift."

"Right? I thought it was special."

"It *was* special," I said. "Just not as special as other gifts."

"In her defense, she took me to Sinai for my birthday."

"Gifts were never his strong suit," I said.

He grinned at me. "I have other redeeming qualities."

I nodded and rubbed his knee. "That's true. He does."

Yael watched us and smiled.

WHEN WE WERE getting ready to leave, she said, "What about Bruria? Why not ask her about the tapes?"

"Bruria? I didn't know she sang with you."

"She couldn't make it last time. But she was your mother's closest friend. Surely, she can tell you more."

I nodded half-heartedly and turned to leave. But Yael grabbed my wrist and said in a low voice, "Don't let this one go."

"It's not like that." I waved my hand. "We're just friends."

"Aha." She lowered her chin, placed a finger on her cheek and pulled it down, exposing the white of her eye. "I know what I see."

I watched Iggy walking slowly toward the car, his shoulders curved over his cupped hands as he lit a cigarette. When he looked back to check where I was, my heart squeezed in my chest. Fuck. I gave Yael a quick hug. "Thank you."

"Remember what I said," she whispered in my ear.

CHAPTER 15

ZOHARA

ON THE MORNING before Rosh Hashanah, I was meeting Mika at the beach. I had promised my sister I'd help with the cooking, and this time I couldn't be late.

For the first time in years, I was home for the holidays. It was also the first time my mom wasn't around, cooking alongside my sister, who, fortunately, was a better and more enthusiastic cook, having learned some Moroccan recipes from Motti's mother to spice up the family repertoire.

I ordered a cappuccino while waiting. Every Rosh Hashanah, I took stock of the passing year and made resolutions for the one ahead. This time, when I looked forward, I saw nothing, like a snowy TV screen at the end of the broadcasting day. When I looked back, my mind was spinning; so much had happened. I couldn't believe it had only been a year.

Last Rosh Hashanah, Zack and I were at his aunt Mimi's. That Labor Day weekend, which coincided with the holidays that year, had been the coldest on record. It was depressing. The beginning of September was too early to be that miserable.

Aunt Mimi was lovely and kind, with striking blue eyes and brilliant red hair. She was the artist in the family. No one understood why she married Jim after her first husband passed away. Before I met Jim for the first time at a family wedding, Zack's sister, Simone, warned me that he could be "inappropriate and touchy-feely, if you know what I mean."

Sure enough, at the wedding, Jim had shaken my hand and held it in his moist palm for too long. He looked me up and down, and said, "Is it *shalom* or *salaam*?"

"Either is fine," I said, laughing uncomfortably and retrieving my hand. What exactly was he was asking?

At the Rosh Hashanah dinner, I was seated between Mimi and a family friend, Cheryl, who wore a pink cardigan and a matching lipstick. "Such beautiful people, the Yemenis," Cheryl gushed upon learning my heritage. "So modest. So nice."

I smiled politely, spreading a linen napkin on my lap. Mimi had seated Zack opposite me, between another set of family friends whose names I forget. "Whenever we are in Israel, Maury and I go to a Yemeni silversmith in Old Jaffa to buy jewelry," Cheryl continued, and Maury, seated next to her, nodded. "We just love Israel."

On my other side, Mimi was talking to an older man with a fake, orangey tan.

"Diane says you are quite the success story!" Cheryl said.

"Me?" I raised my brow while buttering a chunky piece of challah.

"She mentioned you're the first in your family to go to university. Your parents must be so proud."

"Oh, yes. They are." I bit into my bread.

"I watched a story a while ago, on the news." Maury spoke loudly so the entire table turned to listen. "About this eccentric Yemenite rabbi who bunkered himself in his house in Tel Aviv . . ."

"Yehud," I said quietly, immediately on edge.

"You saw it! He and his followers made outrageous claims about Yemeni children going missing in the immigrant camps after Israel was founded. Thousands, according to this guy . . ." He snorted.

"What do you mean *missing*?" Mimi asked.

"There was chaos in the camps, and the infant mortality amongst Yemenis was high, so I guess children died and some were misplaced . . ."

"How does one misplace so many children?" I said.

Zack looked up at me from across the table, alarmed.

Maury paused. "Right. I guess most died."

"Some died. Some might have been given to adoption," I said.

"Adoption?" Maury said. "Is there evidence to that?"

The blood rushed to my brain. "Like you said, there was chaos. Some archives have been conveniently lost or burnt. Some files are unavailable to the public for some reason, and one can't help but wonder why. But, yes, some nurses said they saw people coming to choose babies."

"Why would they do such a thing?" Maury twisted his face. "Are you suggesting they maliciously . . ."

"I didn't say that," I interjected. "Maybe they couldn't find the parents. Maybe they didn't try hard enough. I just know the parents' stories are all eerily similar: the children were healthy or had a cold, and then they were dead. No bodies, no death certificates, no graves."

The table was rapt now, the room still. I caught a glimpse of Diane's face; it was horrified, mouth slightly open.

Maury furrowed his brow. "But stories are not evidence. How can we believe some random stories? Or someone as crazy as Meshulam?"

"You think the parents are lying?"

"It's a holiday dinner," Diane said with a saccharine smile. "Let's leave politics for another day."

"It's not politics," I said. "It's people's lives."

"It's people's stories," Maury said.

"Are Holocaust survivors' testimonials just stories?"

Zack gave me a hard, icy glare.

"Are you comparing this to the Holocaust?" Maury looked at me incredulously, his face red. "These are actual testimonials." Cheryl placed her hand on his lap.

"Of course I'm not comparing this to the Holocaust. But what makes one a story and the other a testimonial?" I looked at Zack, but he was staring down at his plate. "If we're only relying on written history, what stories do we miss? What happens to the stories of people who were illiterate? To marginalized communities? Whose stories are written in history books? And who decides which stories to include?"

"She's right," Mimi said, kindly. "Sometimes all we have are people's stories. Oral history has value, too. Do you know any children who went missing, sweetheart?"

I nodded, but then asked to be excused, pushed my chair back and rushed into the guest bathroom. There, I broke down in sobs. Zack knocked after a few minutes, but I didn't open the door, furious at him for not defending me, for abandoning me. Furious Mimi had to do it. How could he not see how alone I felt?

I came back to the table eventually, ate quietly, spoke to no one. On the train ride home, I stared out the window and refused to talk with him. Later I thought: Was that one of the things that pushed me into Abe's arms? Or was I making excuses for myself?

MIKA SANK INTO the seat with a sigh. "I may never be able to get out of it."

"Well, you look"—I tried to avoid the cliché but couldn't—"glowing."

"Shut up."

"Having dinner at Silvy's tonight?"

"My mom has lost it. She's gone into full grandma mode."

"Silvy? I can't imagine that."

"Well, she doesn't want to be called grandma, if that's what you mean."

In high school, Silvy was the mom I wished I had. Her hair was highlighted blond and blow-dried and her eyes were smoky. She owned an arsenal of makeup, a million bottles of nail polish and perfumes lining her vanity table, and a closet filled with dresses and stiletto heels she let us try on freely. And you could talk to her about everything. Sex. Drugs. You name it.

Shalom walked by carrying a stack of chairs and flashed a toothy smile at me.

"Who's that?" Mika followed him with her eyes. "Cute."

"Oh, Shalom. He owns the place."

"How do you know him?"

"I've been coming here a lot. Just to get out of the house. I swim. Check the classifieds for jobs."

A young waitress in jean shorts and a pierced belly button took our coffee order.

"Wait, you're looking for a job?" Mika frowned. "How would that work with school?"

"I'm still on leave," I said, feeling the tightness in my throat that came about every time I thought of my academic future. "Right now, I need to make some money and be busy."

"Why don't you ask Shalom for a job?"

I watched our waitress picking up dirty dishes from a table, dropping the bills into her apron. I didn't have waitressing experience, but I worked as a barista in my early twenties. How hard could it be?

"He'll give you a job all right," Mika said, voice full of innuendo.

I laughed.

"Sorry. I've never been so horny in my life. I see sex everywhere."

Shalom passed by with another stack of chairs. I eyed him, considering. "Actually, I've been kind of thinking about Iggy."

"What about Iggy?" Mika was perusing the menu. "Shall we order breakfast?"

"Sex."

She looked at me and down at the menu. "Oh."

"Oh?"

"Isn't he seeing someone?"

"I don't think it's serious." He didn't even mention her when we went to Yael. Not once. We ended up hanging out that entire day. He came over and we made dinner. He fixed a loose knob on the bathroom door and helped me clear some of the bags I wanted to donate. We got stoned on the front porch and talked. It was easy, fun, comfortable.

"Avner ran into him on Shenkin a couple of weeks ago. Said it looked serious."

The waitress dropped our cappuccinos. I sat up, mixed sugar into my coffee. "Serious how?"

"They were holding hands. He said they looked really into each other."

I sipped from my coffee.

"Honestly, I don't think it's a good idea anyway."

"Why? We've had casual sex before."

"Are you sure it was casual?"

"Sure."

"For him, too?"

"I think so."

"I don't know," Mika said. "I always thought Iggy never quite got over you."

I inhaled. The sun hid behind a single cloud, and for a moment it felt like fall. "What if it isn't casual?"

Mika stared at me. "What do you mean?"

"I don't know," I said, sounding more defensive than I'd intended.

Mika gawked at me. "You want to get back together with Iggy?"

"People get back together."

"Mami, are you sure it's not the grief talking?"

"What if it is? What if losing my mom made me see what I really want?"

Mika leaned over and placed her hand on my wrist. "Mami, I love you. But you're going through a hard time right now, and Iggy feels safe and familiar, and he loves you. He'll probably always love you. It's easy to get confused. It will pass."

What if I don't want it to pass? I thought but didn't say. What if I was meant to come back here and be reunited with Iggy? I found solace in the idea that everything I had gone through—my time away, my marriage to Zack, my affair with Abe—were all stops I had to hit on my way back to Iggy. This was a story I could live with. If that wasn't true, I wasn't sure about anything.

Mika waved the waitress over and ordered us a couple's breakfast platter, which sounded like way too much food, but I wasn't going to argue with a pregnant woman.

"Okay." Mika grabbed her coffee with both hands and stared at me intently. "I think we both know you owe me a story."

I leaned back and breathed in deeply. "We're doing this? Now?"

"It's been months since you and Zack broke up. And soon I won't have time to sit on the beach and drink coffee with you."

I exhaled audibly. Rosh Hashanah eve may be the perfect time to recap the year that began with the ill-fated dinner at Zack's aunt's and ended with me sitting on the beach in Tel Aviv, divorced and orphaned.

"Fine," I said. "But I hope you don't have plans today because this may take a while."

≈

SHOSHI WAS THE ONE WHO REMINDED ME OF ABE. "PROFESsor Al-Masri," she said, her eyes dreamy. "I'm dying to take courses with him. He's brilliant. Have you met him?"

I had, in fact. Back when I used to smoke, before I got together with health-conscious Zack, I noticed Abe smoking outside. The Middle Eastern department shared a wall with Judaic Studies, but they rarely interacted. Typical.

One day, he asked for a lighter and we got to talking.

"Zahra." Abe repeated my name, pronouncing it the way my mother did, omitting the *o*, breathing out the *h*, rolling the *r*. "Beautiful name. Arabic name."

"Hebrew too. It derives from glow."

"Blossom in Arabic."

"And Abe?"

"Ibrahim."

He was handsome, but not in an intimidating way: tall and broad shouldered, but with a slightly crooked nose and permanent stubble. But he had sex appeal by the oodles, effortless and inexplicable. Every time we talked, there was a wordless moment in which he looked at me appreciatively, and I cocked my face or licked my lips, the space between us brimming with visceral attraction. But there was a ring on his finger. And then I met Zack. Whenever I saw Abe outside, I nodded, and he nodded back. Sometimes we chatted briefly. Whenever I walked away from him, I knew he was watching, and I liked knowing that. The way he looked at me was almost illicit, but somehow not dirty.

By the end of my fourth year, driven by my newfound interest in my own Arabness, I wrote Abe an email and asked to audit the course he was teaching in Middle Eastern literature. I said it was related to my field of research, that I was interested in seeing Israeli literature and culture within a larger geographical and cultural context.

He answered right away. "Ahlan wa Sahlan, you are most welcome," he wrote, as if he knew I'd recognize the words in Arabic. Which I did, even with my limited grasp.

I wish I could say writing to him was entirely innocent, strictly professional. Truth was, taking a course with him was the first thing I'd felt excited about in a long while. Once Shoshi had mentioned him, he was back on my radar, and I craved to feel his eyes on me again. I wanted something to splinter my life open because I couldn't do it myself, because I felt paralyzed. And Abe was there, handsome, brilliant and different from everything I knew, and yet, familiar. From the edge of that cliff he had unwittingly offered, I opened my arms and I leapt.

Abe was a charismatic lecturer, funny and interesting. He had the class rapt; the women leaned forward in their chairs, faces open and attentive. They all wanted to jump his bones. When he made eye contact with me, I felt chosen, special. Did they all feel that way?

Our second class fell on Yom Kippur. Zack was only mildly baffled by my choice to attend class that morning. I promised to be back in time for us to take the train to his parents' for breakfast. It had only been ten days since the dinner at Mimi's and things were tense between us. As I walked out after class, Abe called to me. "Zahra, I'm surprised to see you here on your holiday." He perched on the table behind him, folded his arms across his chest. Even dressed in a gray sweater and trousers, I could tell he worked out.

"I'm not observant," I said. "For me, Yom Kippur was always more fun than atonement."

"Fun? Isn't it a day of fasting?"

"Not for me, but even if you don't fast, there's something special in the air. The whole country shuts down. Stores close. No cars . . ."

"No cars?"

"Can you imagine? For a whole day! No TV or music, either. Everything is really quiet."

"Wow. Sounds amazing."

"Right? As kids, we waited for it all year. It was the one day you got to ride your bike everywhere, like, even on the highway! But here, it's just"—I shrugged—"whatever."

He gazed into the distance. "Can you imagine Manhattan with no cars for a day? We should make Yom Kippur a civic holiday."

We spent a moment imagining the city, people walking in the middle of the highway, bikes everywhere.

He collected his papers. "It's always good to have you, but if you need to take time off for your holidays, I understand. You're auditing, anyway. Just come see me, let me know."

Come see me. Couldn't I just email him?

"Come see me after class," he said at the end of another class, supposedly to discuss my paper. I wasn't required to submit any papers, but I chose to, not like I was having much luck progressing in my dissertation, anyway. Whenever I came by his office, we talked a little about course stuff but mostly about other things. Our conversations grew deeper, the tension thicker. I was highly conscious of my body, how my hands moved, the way I moistened my lips, tucked a curl behind my ear. The sense of danger was palpable. The door was open to a crack.

One day, the class was going to a reading by a young Syrian American poet in SoHo. Afterwards, a few went for a drink. I didn't know most people, was feeling shy. "I can't stay long, either," Abe said. "We'll have one drink and walk to the subway together."

I sat next to him in a smoky, narrow, high-ceilinged bar, legs accidentally touching, then, increasingly, staying pressed against each other, growing warm. He disregarded me entirely, speaking in Arabic to Tara, an enthusiastic white student who'd lived in the Middle East for a few years. I envied her fluency, though I could hear her American accent clearly coloring her words. I was chatting with Aziz, a half-Egyptian student who, like me, couldn't speak the language, though he was trying to learn now. All he wanted to talk about was Israel. How was life there? How were people reacting to Oslo? Did I believe peace was possible? We didn't get a chance to delve into it before Abe finished his whiskey and turned to me for the first time since we sat down. "Ready to go?" I downed my beer and stood up.

We stepped out into a cool October evening. I pulled a pink woolly scarf from my backpack and wrapped it around my neck. Abe rounded his shoulders over his chest, rubbed his hands together and breathed into them. "Do you have a lot to walk after this?"

"I might walk the whole way. It's only twenty minutes."

"It's too cold!" he said. "Why don't I take a taxi and drop you off on the way uptown?"

In the cab we sat looking out at opposite directions. I was aware of his hand on the seat beside mine, the proximity of his pinky finger to my own. The city lights glittered outside the window, beaded with rain. "Zahra, Zahra, Zahra," he said, so quietly, it was like I imagined it. "What am I going to do with you?"

I swallowed, chuckled awkwardly. "I don't know."

"This is a terrible idea," he said, his finger finally touching mine, shooting an electric current through my body, making me tremble.

My breath shallowed. "The worst."

"What are we going to do about it?"

"We really shouldn't," I said, as if I didn't know there was no bigger turn-on than these words.

He looked at me then, leaned over and kissed me. Soft at first, then more assertively, with the right amount of pressure, the right amount of tongue. And at that moment, it felt as if the source of all my troubles had been that Abe hadn't kissed me yet, and now everything was going to be okay. As if I'd never wanted anything like I had wanted this kiss, never that intensely, that desperately. That kiss felt like redemption. Like the answer to everything.

We kissed for the remaining five-minute taxi ride without stopping. Then the cab was idling outside my apartment building and the turban-wearing driver was rudely knocking on the glass between us. The sight of our familiar rundown redbrick building sobered me up. My apartment. With Zack in it. My husband. Whom I had not had sex with for weeks. I scrambled for my wallet, hands clammy, fingers shaking.

"Please." Abe touched my hand. A shot of electricity again. "I got this."

All through the next week, the memory of our kiss struck me at unexpected times, while washing dishes, riding the subway, teaching, and sent shivers down my body that were part pleasure, part anguish. And when I saw him in class the following week, I was breathless, hot and instantly turned on. I packed my things up slowly so I could catch him after class, but of course Tara was there, chatty as always, and eventually I had no choice but to walk down the stairs toward the exit. He caught my eyes and interrupted her. "Tara, excuse me. Zahra, do you have a minute?"

We had sex that day for the first time, me sitting on the desk in his office, leaning back on my palms, him standing, face buried in my shoulder. He smelled like coffee and a sharp, minty aftershave.

The following two and a half months were a series of furtive encounters in his office. Later, in hotel rooms. Never, of course, in either of our places. We never called each other at home, only at our work numbers. Two and a half months of rarely seeing Zack: different hours, too much work. Of not thinking about my dissertation. Of not thinking about the string of bad news from Israel, suicide attack after suicide attack, not thinking of anything but when I would see Abe next, when we would have sex again. I was alive in a way I'd forgotten I could be.

In November, as Christmas lights draped over trees and in display windows, I joined Abe for a conference in Seattle. I told Zack I was presenting a paper and would only be gone for two nights. There, in the bed we shared, after waking up snuggled into his body for the first time, I told Abe about Rafael. His face contorted with sorrow. "I never knew that happened in Israel. How awful." Things like that happened in other parts of the world, he said. It happened in Australia to children of Aboriginal descent. It happened in Canada with the Sixties Scoop, where they forcibly removed Indigenous children from their communities and placed them for adoption. "It's a method of the dominant group to reeducate a community they believe is backward and primitive, by cutting off the link to their origin."

I was so grateful for his words I teared up. I thought of how Zack didn't defend me in front of his family. Then, I thought of Schneider. Wasn't that also reeducating? A cutting off from my family and origin?

THE AFFAIR ENDED sensationally, like a scene in one of these Egyptian movies my mother used to watch religiously: Abe's beautiful, blond, American wife, Amy, screaming at me in the hallway, "You little slut," and slapping me so hard I covered my cheek with both hands, tears leaping into my eyes and crimson red blooming on my skin from the impact. Abe rushed outside from his room to the sounds of the commotion, his face whitening, and when he realized Amy hadn't seen him yet, backed away, straight into his room, as if he could close the door on it, on us.

As I walked away, my cheek stinging, my entire body shaking, I wondered if there was any way Zack might not find out about it. And then, if that was what I wanted.

When I came home and saw Zack sitting in the dark living room, staring out the window, I knew he knew. "Your professor's wife called."

"I'm sorry, Zack," I said, sincerely, tears in my eyes. On the coffee table I saw a bottle of whiskey, an empty glass. I gazed down. A piece of dried fusilli was tangled in the carpet.

We'll work on it, we said. We'll go to counseling. We'll fix it. But even as we said that, I had a sneaking suspicion we wouldn't. That it was over. Zack must have felt the same because only a week later, I woke up to him staring at the ceiling. "I think we should break up," he said, his voice hollow.

It was a good time to ask for a leave of absence. The therapist at the wellness center agreed to recommend it. Along with the grief, the heartache, the shame, I felt enormous relief.

I FLEW TO Thailand because I needed to be away and alone somewhere warm. The last time I had been in Thailand, working with Zack, I looked down on backpackers, judged them for their privilege and lack of awareness. Now I was one of them. I rented a beach bungalow in Ko Pha-ngan, where I spent hours walking, swimming, sleeping and replaying everything that happened, trying to understand what wrong turn had gotten me there.

There was so much I didn't understand, but I knew that I had been more in love with the idea of Zack than I was with Zack: we were both attracted to how different we were, to what we symbolized, and once that faded, which it was bound to, there was nothing holding us together. I knew that some days I missed Iggy and what it was like to be in love with your best friend, someone who knew you in and out. And that I had become bored, with the planned trajectory of my life, with school, with sex, and Abe was an antidote, a quick fix. And like many quick fixes, it was really a form of self-sabotage.

But I also knew that in my American exile and my quest to belong,

Abe felt more familiar than Zack had ever been, which made sense, considering our homes were only two hundred kilometers apart. And while Lebanese had little in common with Yemenis, still, there was the Arabness. When our bodies were entwined, I sometimes looked as if from the outside and marveled at the aesthetic harmony. The sound of his words, the musicality; it was the sound of my mother and father.

I desperately missed home, missed myself, and I confused Abe for an answer.

CHAPTER 16

YONI

NIR AND BARUCH were leaning on the checkout counter, staring up at the television set suspended in the corner, when Yoni walked into the store. Israeli prime minister Yitzhak Rabin and PLO chief Yasser Arafat were striding purposefully against a scorched desert background. *New Year, New Agreement,* the caption announced festively.

Nir glanced at him. "Hey, Yoni."

Baruch turned and hollered. "Yoni, my brother! Shana tova!"

"How do you know Yoni?" Nir frowned.

"From the synagogue." Baruch gave Yoni a friendly slap on the shoulder.

Yoni grabbed a newspaper from the counter and skimmed the principles of the interim agreement. The West Bank would be divided into three areas and the Palestinian Authority would be given some power and responsibilities in two areas. Unless a miracle happened, the agreement would be formally signed in Washington on Thursday.

Arafat's smug face appeared on the screen now. He wished Israelis a happy new year, and added a message to Palestinian prisoners, "I assure them the dawn of freedom is coming."

"Did you hear it?" Baruch pointed at the screen. "They're going to release poisoners with blood on their hands. They are giving up most of

Hebron, too. Apparently, Arafat stormed out in the middle of the night, so they caved. Like little girls."

"It's a negotiation," Nir said while ringing Mrs. Radai's groceries. "Both sides compromise. Israel still controls most of Hebron. There are only four hundred Jews living there . . ."

"It's not about four hundred Jews. It's about four thousand years of connection to the land of Israel."

Nir, ayuni," Nir's mother pled as she bagged Mrs. Radai's groceries. "The store is full. It's Rosh Hashanah eve."

Yoni turned the page and saw an opinion column stating, "The Dream of a Greater Eretz Israel Is Over." He tossed the paper into his basket. Walking around the store with his mother's barely legible note, he grabbed a warm challah, two bags of milk, yogurt, yellow cheese and Milky.

On the screen Rabin and Arafat shook hands. Baruch sneered, pretending to spit. "*Tfu.* Shaking hands with the devil."

"I'm not a fan either," Nir said. "But—"

"Not a fan?" Baruch stared at him. "The man is behind some of the most atrocious, deadly terror attacks of the century."

"As Rabin said," Nir said, "peace you make with enemies. Better than no peace, no? Things can't stay as they are."

"This? No," Baruch said. "This isn't better. They won't stop until they throw us all in the sea."

"Are you serious?" Nir raised one eyebrow.

Baruch turned to Yoni. "What do you think?"

"Leave him alone," Nir said. "He's a kid."

"A kid? He's bigger than you."

Yoni's cheeks flushed.

THE QUIET AT Rosh Hashanah dinner was deafening. The holiday season used to be his favorite time of year. The excitement and renewal of fall, the opening of the gates of heavens, a chance for a new start.

This year, everywhere he looked, all he saw was Tata's absence. He tasted it in his mother's food, a watered-down version of the dishes she used to make when Tata was around. Even the apples his aunt had sliced for dipping in honey were yellowed, their texture sandy. Motti rushed through the blessings; you could tell his heart wasn't in it. Ortal sulked in the corner of the table, bangs hiding her eyes.

Tata used to pick up his sisters from school and make them lunch three times a week, whenever his mom worked late. Somehow, he felt like his time with her was more meaningful than the time she had spent with his sisters, which he considered babysitting. But what did he know? Maybe Tata made them feel as special as she did him.

Lilach was the only one around the dinner table who appeared to be excited about the holiday, everything like new to her, experienced for the first time. She kept demonstrating her knowledge of the holiday, announcing, "We eat honey so our year will be sweet!"

"That's right," Motti said, brightened by her energy. "As sweet as you."

She must have not remembered last year's dinner. Would she remember her grandma at all?

"How's school, Yoni?" Zohara asked as they were eating fish. "So we will be a head and not a tail!" Lilach announced.

He shrugged. "School."

"It must be an exciting time," she said. "Do they talk about it at all?"

He looked at her quizzically. His aunt appeared tanned and refreshed, like she spent time at the beach.

"The peace talks!"

"Oh. Not really."

"I started high school the year they signed the peace agreement with Egypt. There was so much hope. Everyone wanted to go see the pyramids and take a bus to Cairo . . . There was a bus, eventually, wasn't there? The Number 100? What ever happened to that?"

"Doesn't seem as hopeful this time around." Motti scooped rice onto Lilach's plate.

"I think it's hopeful," Zohara said. "Since I was a little kid, all I heard was one day we'll have peace. One day the conflict will end. All the songs we sang growing up were about peace. Now we finally have a chance."

"Yeah, but at what price?" Motti said. "People feel abandoned by the government. Have you seen the demonstrations?"

"A bunch of lunatics," Zohara dismissed. "Kahanists and fanatics."

Yoni scoffed, quietly.

Zohara glanced at him. "What?"

"Not only."

"How would you know?" His aunt, so direct, so in-your-face, so sure of herself. Even after reading about the situation, educating himself, her conviction rattled him. He crushed a small piece of challah between his fingers. "I'm not happy about it, and I'm not a Kahanist."

"You're not happy?" She looked at him in disbelief.

"You are?" he said, gaining confidence as he went on. "You're happy we're giving our country to the Palestinians?"

She snickered. "That's not what's happening. The agreement gives Palestinians in the West Bank more rights. That's a good thing. We've had enough bloodshed."

He scoffed again. "So why do we still have terror attacks? Just last month they blew up a bus in Jerusalem. In July they blew one in Ramat Gan. Last year was awful. Tata stopped taking the bus entirely."

"You can't expect immediate results. That's just childish. Why don't you blame Baruch Goldstein, who committed the massacre in Hebron? Before he went and killed all these innocent people, there was peace and quiet. That's what led to Hamas's string of suicide bombings. Not the peace process."

He felt the blood rushing to his head, all the way to the tips of his ears. "They were killing us long before the massacre, since before I was born. And what do you know about this, anyway? You don't live here, and even when you're here, you can't see beyond Tel Aviv. You live in a bubble."

"Yoni!" his mom said sternly. Everyone was staring at him. His family wasn't used to him being that argumentative, that vocal. Damn, it felt good.

Zohara gawked at him. She turned to his mom. "Where does he get these ideas from?"

"I'm not a child." His vocal cords were being stretched. "I'm going to the army in July. I think I'm capable of forming my own views."

His mom looked up as if stung. "July? When did you get the draft notice?"

"The other day."

"Why didn't you tell me?"

"I forgot."

His mom stared at the plate. Her lips quivered.

"It's no big deal."

His mom put down her fork. "Then why didn't you tell me?"

"Come on. It's not like you didn't know it was coming," he raised his voice.

His mom pushed her chair back, got up and left the room. Motti left after her.

Zohara stared at him for a moment, as though she were seeing him for the first time. "We'll keep talking about this another time," she said. "I know I can knock some sense into you."

He filled his mouth with rice and didn't answer.

HIS MOM ONCE told him that for the first few months of his life, all the Haddad women were at home with him. His mother, his grandmother, and his aunt, all doting on him. They took turns changing and feeding him. The four of them would be lying on a blanket spread in the middle of Tata's room. It was the last time all three women were living together. But of course, he had no memory of that. For most of his early years, Zohara was in a boarding school. Then she was off to the army, far away in the south.

There was a brief period when Zohara and Iggy babysat him for a few hours in the evenings, when his mom and Motti started dating. His best memories of Zohara were from those times. They took him to the beach, where he would swim on Iggy's back, hands wrapped around his neck; they ate ice cream at Yotvata Café on the seashore. One time, after they brought him back to Sha'ariya, he overheard his mom saying on the phone that watching Yoni was good practice for Zohara and Iggy. But then Zohara "had to go and screw it up" with Iggy. She took off to the US and Yoni rarely saw her after that.

He was angry when she left. When she called, he didn't want to talk, and he never wrote to her, even though his mom had asked. "He doesn't do well with goodbyes," his mom apologetically told his second-grade teacher Daphna, his favorite, when he refused to hug her goodbye at the end of the year, burying his face in his mother's skirt. It didn't take a detective to figure out what it was about.

After his mother married Motti, the three of them moved into a new apartment and suddenly there was a man in their home. The bathroom messier, the fridge full of foods they hadn't eaten before—salami, matbuha, pickled carrots. His mom learned to cook Moroccan dishes Yoni had refused at first, as if out of spite. She was saddened by his resistance. In her mind, Motti was a solution to the problem, not an additional challenge. When she introduced him to Yoni, her face beamed like she was presenting him with a gift.

When his sisters were born, and he saw how present and involved Motti was with them, and later, as Yoni attended bar mitzvah ceremonies of his classmates with their proud fathers standing beside them, his wound opened and stung anew. He was not a kid anymore, about to become a man and was ready to hear whatever his mother had to say. By then, he knew men could do horrible things; popular media had introduced him to cheating and domestic abuse. But his mom was stingy with details. Even Tata wouldn't say more. "The only good thing he'd done in your life is you."

His questions remained. What kind of man just leaves? What kind of man doesn't want to know anything about his son?

"Be kind to your mother," Tata often said to him. She didn't say, because *she* stayed, but it was implied. He left and she stayed. She struggled to raise him, alone, working two jobs, cleaning houses. This is why he'd been left with Tata so often until she had felt like a mother to him.

And still, sometimes, when he was feeling lonely in his own home, an outsider in his own family, he daydreamt about his father's return. He imagined him knocking, dressed in pressed pants and a white button-up shirt, smelling manly, of aftershave, his black hair jelled back, like an actor in the Egyptian films he had watched with Tata, a specific one, in fact. My son, he would say, and open his arms to embrace him. He would ask for forgiveness; tell him he had turned his life around.

Tata, in the rare moments when she spoke about Rafael, described a similar scenario to him. A knock on the door, a young man, well-dressed, achingly familiar, tears in his eyes. "Mother," he would cry. "I am back." Maybe that's why the two of them felt so connected. Both waiting, both missing an integral part of themselves, the constant ache in their bodies throbbing like a phantom limb.

YAQUB

Immigrant Camp, Mahane Olim Rosh HaAyin, 1950

BY THE TIME Yaqub walked back to the camp, the night was so dark he had to concentrate on every step, the stars offering a faded glow, not enough to guide him. And for the next few days, he walked as if still led by that faint light, dazed and listless. At times, the memory of their kiss stirred him awake, fleetingly breathed life into him, but then the guilt and shame washed over him, deflating him.

What had he done?

He went to work, picked oranges, dropped them into the crate, surprised when he saw it was full, as if someone else was doing the work all along. He hardly ate, slept fitfully, didn't write. Couldn't write. Saleh asked if he might be coming down with something. Maybe he should visit the clinic.

After a few days, he saw Saida before dinner with Rumia. She stared hard at a spot deliberately away from him. Rumia gave him a severe look. His stomach churned.

Eventually, he returned to the riverbank. For a few days he sat there with a book Leib had given him, still unable to write. Then one day, she was there. Saida. Drawing circles in the sand with a long stick. He was so stunned by the sight of her, he stopped in his tracks.

She looked up at him. Neither of them said a word.

He moved slowly, breathing shallow, as if she were a wild animal he was afraid to disturb, the way he'd been taught to do as a child wandering the wadis in Haidan. He perched on the tall rock, opened his book and pretended to be reading. Then he shut the book and paced back and forth. He opened his mouth to speak, but then thought better of it, folded the unsaid sentence back into his mouth. A few moments later, he tried again. "Saida," he said earnestly, "I'm sorry. I am so, *so* sorry. I want you to know I respect you and . . ."

"What are you reading?" she interrupted him.

He paused, hands in midair.

"Is it a love story?"

He nodded.

"Forbidden love."

He swallowed. "Yes."

"Tell me more."

SPRING HAD FINALLY arrived, and the camp was transformed. Some days, lifted by the blue in the sky and the warmth of sun on his skin, Yaqub found it almost beautiful. Grass grew tall and wild between the tents, yellow flowers coiled around the chicken-wire fence. By the river margins, the papyrus bloomed like a fountain, radiantly green, and the sun glinted off the translucent tree leaves. Everything was vibrant. Renewed. Alive.

As the weather changed and the days lengthened, more people from the camp discovered the river. Eventually, someone tore down the trodden fence, the last barrier that had kept the place somewhat inaccessible. It was no longer their secret spot. During the days, children skipped stones into the water and chased turtles. A couple of times Yaqub found Saida speaking with women from the camp who had gone for a stroll and ran into her, and she glanced at him quickly, apologetically. They started sneaking in later, in the dark, which made it feel more illicit. Yaqub knew her husband's work contract would terminate at the end of spring, and then what?

They rarely spoke about the future. They continued talking about books and stories and inspiration. From time to time, when he felt courageous, he gently removed a curl from her face, his hand briefly brushing her cheek, and she would close her eyes and tremble.

He never kissed her again.

It was like walking around with a constant fire stoking inside him.

AS THE CAMPS reached maximum capacity, Daud Sanani and a couple of his friends called for a hunger strike: the food they were given, they said, was subpar, and the rationing for bread was insufficient considering it was the Yemenis' main source of nutrition.

The representatives of the Jewish Agency arrived to negotiate by the following day. Shortly after, Daud came out of the dining hall and announced their demands had been met. The rationing would be raised. Everyone cheered. "There's more," he said, grinning. "The camp will close down this summer! They are building a permanent town." People cheered again.

Yaqub's heart dropped.

That evening when Saida sang, leaning against the tree trunk, her face appeared to be beaming with hope. Her blue scarf was tied back neatly and knotted over her head, revealing her long neck. It was a new style the young women at the camp were experimenting with.

"Did you hear the news?" he asked, sullen by her joy.

She nodded eagerly. "Yes! Finally, I'll be able to live with my son. Be with him day and night. Feed him when I want to. Cradle him when I want to. Like a mother should." She sighed. "It's a dream!"

Her words sobered him up. Saida would go back to living in her own home with her husband, her family. She would forget all about him. Their story—this fantasy—could never withstand the real world, and he was a fool to believe otherwise. He took a step toward the river, stuffed his hands into his pockets and stared at the roots of the paper reeds swaying underwater.

"This is life, Yaqub," Saida said softly.

He said nothing; a stone was lodged in his throat.

"I wish we could both have everything we want."

He turned. "Why can't we?" He could hear the desperation in his voice. How quickly he forgot the promises he made himself. He walked over to her and grabbed her hands. "Why can't we make our own lives? This is a new world. Everything is possible. You said it yourself. Women can be in the government. Women can talk to men in public. Why must we hold on to the way things were in the old world? What was so great about the past?"

She looked away from him, shaking her head repeatedly. "You don't know what you're saying."

There was nothing to lose. He grabbed her by the waist and he kissed her, and she didn't turn away from him this time. She didn't slap him. She kissed him back.

She kissed him back.

For the next few days, while it was still fresh in his mind, he'd replay that moment in a loop—the tenderness of that kiss, the way her body softened toward his—wishing to cement it in his memory so he could summon it at any given time. Like a book he could grab from the library, immerse himself in, escape to.

Then, they heard voices.

Saida moved away first, stumbling for a moment, and Yaqub extended his arm to steady her, but she didn't take it. Her eyes were fixed on the shadows approaching them, their gait fast and steady and menacing.

She gave Yaqub one last look. That, unfortunately, he will never forget. It was frightened, devastated, or was it pleading? What was she trying to communicate? Did he do the wrong thing? Should he have taken her hand and run?

The two men barreling down the path were big, bigger than him. One of them grabbed Yaqub by the collar of his shirt, the other struck him clumsily across his face, but strong enough that Yaqub dropped to the ground. Behind the men, Saida's young sister and Rumia came running, breathless, both crying, begging them to stop. Rumia was pulling on one of the men's sleeves. Others came, too. Yaqub's face was in the mud, the taste of wet earth in his mouth. Someone kicked his ribs. "You bastard," he muttered, teeth clenched. He heard Saida's stifled sobs. He didn't look up. He didn't want her to see him like that.

The commotion quieted. All he heard was his breathing, the croaking of frogs growing louder, a rustle in the bushes. A swamp cat. A jackal. He wasn't afraid. It didn't matter.

Moments later, his cousin Saleh was pulling him up, supporting him back to the camp. The other family who shared their tent looked away as Saleh urgently helped Yaqub pack his belongings. "He better not find you here tomorrow morning," he said. Before he packed his notebook, Yaqub browsed through it quickly, then ripped a page out and folded it, handing it to Saleh pleadingly.

Saleh shook his head. "I'll do anything for you, you know that. But don't ask me to do this."

Saleh was right. He couldn't get anyone else involved in this. He stuffed the paper in his pocket. Then, he remembered the picture he had cut from the newspaper article, which he had tucked into his notebook. He folded the two together.

As Yaqub hoisted his bundle over his shoulder, Saleh handed him a small hand-sewn maroon pouch. From its weight, Yaqub knew it was precious. Inside, he found an intricately made silver bracelet, once belonging to Saleh's mom. Saleh was one of the lucky few who managed to sneak jewelry from Yemen. The women wore theirs to board the planes, so the Jewish Agency emissaries made them take it off. It was too heavy, they had said. The planes wouldn't take off. They never saw their jewelry again. Saleh had his stacked in his pockets, and he marched past their watchful eyes, unnoticed.

"No, Saleh," Yaqub whispered. "I can't."

"What's mine is yours," Saleh said, embracing him. "I'll be enlisting in three weeks anyway."

The camp was asleep as Yaqub walked toward the nursery. He circled it a few times, watching the sleeping babies through the windows. A nurse paced between the cribs, covering one child, rocking another. She picked up a crying baby, speaking to him in a language Yaqub didn't understand. Then she walked out of the room with the baby in her arms.

This was his chance. The front door was unlocked, and he pushed it in. He hadn't expected to see Rafael awake: the boy had Saida's dark eyes set in his cherubic round face, his father's light complexion, two dimples in his cheeks. Without thinking, Yaqub placed a finger to his own lips, which amused Rafael, who giggled and flapped his hands. For a moment, Yaqub thought to pick him up, hold his small body against his chest for comfort. He caressed Rafael's cheek, and Rafael clamped his fist around Yaqub's finger and held on to it. Tears leapt into Yaqub's eyes.

There were times when he imagined this was his child, when he rewrote history to conceive one in which theirs was a legitimate love story. The two of them married. Rafael, their child, born of love and passion. Footsteps echoed in the hallway. Yaqub awoke from his fantasy, stuffed the folded papers on the side of the crib and placed his palm on the boy's chest, feeling the flutter of his beating heart. "Goodbye, beautiful boy," he whispered.

"What are you doing here?" A tall, blond nurse stood at the entrance to the room.

He picked up his bundle and ran out, past the nurse. He kept running until he reached the hole in the fence and slid out through it.

By morning he'd made it to Petah Tikva's bus station, sat on a bench and considered his options. He ate one of the dates Saleh had packed for him and counted his coins, hoping for inspiration as to what he should do. Like a sign from the heavens, a soldier walked by, lugging his kitbag. He looked so young. Too young to be in uniform. He stopped by to read the timetable, then crouched, smoking a cigarette.

A couple of hours later, at the army absorption base in Jaffa, Yaqub told a female soldier with a red, curly ponytail that he came to inquire about his draft notice since he was already eighteen and had not received one yet. Of course, they had no birthdate on record for him. As with most Yemenis, his real age had been a guess. Seventeen, eighteen, what did it matter? She took his name and ID number and promised to send a new one to the camp.

"Please, miss," he pled. "I can't go back there. If I don't enlist today, I'll be sleeping in the street." She took pity on him. Maybe it was the visible bruises on his face. They enlisted him right away to the infantry corps.

By the end of the day, he was dressed in khakis, his feet clad in black boots. The army barber gave him a close cut and Yaqub tucked his simonim behind his ears. He caught sight of his reflection at a window. He looked like a sabra now. A new man. One who could be anything. Do anything. As he walked toward the bus that would take him to the new base, his new life, a young female soldier eyed him appreciatively.

If only Saida could see him now.

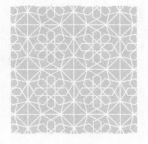

PART THREE

OCTOBER
1995

Oh, my love, my love
How do I hold on to you?
If I place you on my crown
the wind might take you
If I place you over my eyes
my tears may blind you
If I fasten you around my waist
the yetser hara may test you
So, I keep you buried in my heart
and pretend to forget you

UNKNOWN YEMENI POETESS

CHAPTER 17

ZOHARA

BY OCTOBER, THE weather had changed, cooling as soon as the sun went down. At night, I closed the windows and replaced the sheet I used as cover with a light blanket. When I woke up, the tile floor pierced my feet. I found my old slippers and placed them by the bed, started turning the boiler on to shower.

My mom's house was mostly packed and pristinely clean. Iggy came over again to help me clear bags. Like my mother, I became obsessed with keeping it that way, so the smell of bleach lingered on furniture and fabric, welcomed you when you walked in. My whole life, I thought about her cleaning as a response to trauma, a way of maintaining control. But I could never make sense of her love of bleach. Surely, they had not used it in Yemen. "You know it's bad for you," I used to tell her. Was that her way of purifying? From what? Dirt was a part of life; was life itself. Bleach was a whitening agent. What color was she trying to remove?

Maybe I was channeling her now, or wishing to appease her lingering spirit, but I somehow began associating the sharp tang of bleach with cleanliness. I discovered that cleaning made me feel quiet, focused, satisfied. One day, while polishing the window with old newspapers and vinegar, I caught my reflection as the light outside dimmed and was startled by the image of her. I froze in mid action, afraid it would revert into my own face.

Cleaning, like singing, became a way to be with her.

NIR'S MOM AMBUSHED me outside the makolet. "Zohara, will we see you at our meeting tonight?"

"Oh, I don't know." I squirmed. "I don't know the songs."

"It's easy, we repeat every line twice," she said. "In Yemen, the poetess would sing, and the women would answer. And didn't Yael say she'd bring the lyrics for you?"

Inside, Nir was bent over a newspaper with a pen, his usual pose. He tipped his head toward me with a smile. I hadn't seen him in a few days. Mika was right; Shalom had gladly offered me some shifts at Mango Beach, and I'd spent the last week working my ass off. She may have also been right about him liking me, since he forgave my many mistakes, the forgotten orders, the uncleared tables, the misplaced bills. Turned out waitressing was a lot harder than I thought.

"Come, Zohara," Nir's mom pleaded. "We never get young women like you anymore. We need some fresh blood around here."

WHEN I WALKED in later that evening, the women welcomed me with cheers. A stocky woman with a bright pink headdress went through the trouble of pulling a chair from a stack in the corner and planting it on the floor. "We talked about it and decided you must sing with us," she said. "You're your mother's daughter, so we know you can sing."

"Have you met a Yemeni who can't sing?" Geula from the spice shop said.

"I have! My husband!" another exclaimed, and everyone laughed.

Bruria sat in the corner, strands of silver hair poking out from her headscarf. She smiled at me, and I waved.

Yael handed me a sheet with the Yemeni words written in the Hebrew transliteration, and the translation handwritten beside it. It was titled "Sa'at Rahman." *This is the time of grace, and the demons are far.* "It is sung at the zaffah, so it has the pace of walking," Yael explained, and I nodded to indicate I understood she was referring to the wedding procession. I had been learning, immersed in the book she'd given me. I started thinking of the women's songs, that insistence to be heard, as subversive, audacious, feminist even. I liked the idea of the women using their creative expression as a form of protest. It made me see my mother in a whole new light.

When the meeting was over, I waited for Bruria at the door, and we walked out together. I hated that it was still awkward between us. Of course, it was all me. Bruria hadn't changed. The love in her eyes whenever she looked at me, spoke to me, hadn't diminished. "It's good you came."

"I've been meaning to ask you something," I said. "I found tapes with my mother singing on them. Do you know anything about that?"

Bruria nodded. "It was her way of saving her songs. She didn't write so she recorded them."

I stopped walking. Yael had been right. "She wrote them?"

"Of course. Your mom wrote beautiful songs."

I stared at her, mouth agape. My mom wrote songs, love songs. To whom?

"Why didn't she do anything with it?"

"Your mother was very private," Bruria said. "The songs were personal."

I looked at Bruria's round, honest face. I hadn't had a real conversation with her in what felt like ages. I wanted to ask so many questions, about my mom, about my dad, about all the things I hadn't wanted to know growing up. How would I even start this conversation?

Like she heard the words I hadn't spoken, Bruria said, "Come by sometime," and placed a light hand on my shoulder. That slight touch made me want to crumble into her arms. "I'll make you ka'adid."

"Who's rumia?" I asked Lizzie when I was sixteen. At school, we were doing a roots project, tracing family histories and interviewing parents and grandparents. While I was home from Schneider for the weekend, I dug through my parents' closets for materials. Amongst the receipts and warranties, I found a thin, folded document from Hashed Camp in Aden, from where they'd been airlifted to Israel. I studied the flimsy, yellowing paper, ripping at the creases. Written in English were the following names:

Hassan Haddad, 35

Rumia Haddad, 25, wife

Saida Haddad, 18, wife

Rafael Haddad, 2 months, son

I read the list again. Something didn't add up. Who was Rumia? And where was her husband? And how come she had our last name?

My mom was out. Lizzie was living in the shack with Yoni. I knocked on her door and showed her the document. "I found this registration form from Aden," I said. "Who's Rumia?"

"Oh," Lizzie said, eyes downcast. "That."

It dawned on me at once. There was no other explanation. I knew they practiced plural marriages in Yemen. Still, the idea of polygamy had been so far from my life I had never considered it.

I sat on Lizzie's small love seat and shook my head again and again. "I can't believe it. Why didn't you tell me?"

"What difference would it make? By the time you were old enough to understand, it didn't seem relevant."

"Who was she?"

Lizzie bit the inside of her cheek repeatedly.

"Who?"

"It's Bruria. Rumia was her Yemeni name."

I gasped loudly. "*Bruria?* But she's Mom's best friend!"

"They became friends, eventually."

"So, when Bruria lived here . . ." Comprehension washed over me like an ice-cold bucket. "Oh my God. Oh my God." I got up and started pacing in the tiny room, the very same one Bruria used to live in. "That's so messed up. He literally kept another woman in the back while he was living with our family in the main house. How was Mom okay with it? This is so disturbing. It's perverse."

"See? That's why Ima didn't want you to know. She knew you were going to judge."

"I'm going to be sick." Growing up she was Aunt Bruria to me, my mom's closest friend, closer to her than her own sister. As a child, I loved visiting her at the little shed in the back. Bruria's life as a single, childless woman didn't seem sad like all the movies and books told me it should be. In fact, she looked happy, happier than my own mother, who had been grumpy and grieving. Bruria and I made cookies together, played dress-up. I'd sit close to her on the hard couch she had covered in red embroidered fabric, the matching rug at our feet. Everything in Bruria's room was colorful and floral. Her little house made ours appear drab and lifeless.

After my sister moved into the shed, Bruria moved one street down, to the next unpaved road. When I visited, we watched Arabic movies together, enthralled by the drama, the betrayal, the heartbreak. Her home smelled of food and baking. The radio was on. She had pets, a ginger cat named Kinly and a fluffy poodle called Muki, at a time when few people in our neighborhood owned them. "Yemenis don't like pets," she had said. "They think the spirits can come in the shape of animals. But I don't care. They bring me joy."

Once, when we walked to the makolet together, she stayed out with Muki while I walked in to get milk. When I was by the fridge, I heard Miriam Mashraki saying quietly to Shula Aharoni, "She thinks these animals are her kids."

"How did you find out?" I asked Lizzie.

Lizzie shifted in her seat. "I saw him coming out of the shed one morning. I was a little older than you are now, old enough to understand what I saw. I'll never forget the look in his eyes."

The thought of my father, sneaking there after we fell asleep to do whatever married couples did was too much to bear. "Ewww." I was overwhelmed by another wave of nausea. "I can't."

"Imagine how I felt!"

"Did you confront him?"

"As if. You don't remember him that way, but to me, he was terrifying. If I misbehaved, he pulled out the belt. There's a reason why I was such a good girl."

"Oh, Lizzie."

"I came to Ima. I tried talking around the subject. Asking where they knew Bruria from and why she lived there, why she didn't have a

husband or a family of her own, but eventually, she saw what I was getting at. She sat me down and told me. She said everyone knew; it wasn't
a secret. It was common in Yemen. But in Israel people looked at them
funny, so they decided not to talk about it for our sake. The next day Ima
told me they thought I was old enough to have my own space. That's
when Bruria moved out."

"And he stopped seeing her?"

"Of course not," she said. "They stayed together till he died. They
just added some distance for appearances' sake. And obviously Ima and
her are still best friends."

This was more than I ever wanted to know about my parents. I
couldn't think of anything more mortifying, more humiliating. More
primitive. And wasn't it how Yemenis were seen anyway? I imagined the
kind of reactions my classmates at Schneider would have to such a
scoop. No one could ever know. No one.

I wished *I* didn't know.

I AM NOT proud of what happened after that. Like my mom and Lizzie
had predicted, I judged her. For allowing this to happen, for not throwing him out. And I was angry at him, my dead father, who'd been my
hero up until then, for being greedy, a cheater. I was mad at Bruria, too,
for ruining our family, even though we hadn't been an ideal one, even
though my parents didn't get along. Mostly I resented her for making
me love her, for lying to me.

And for coming first.

Because Bruria being the first wife meant that if anyone was illegiti-
mate, it was us: my mother, Lizzie, me. I begrudged being made a part
of it. Everything about my family history, even my memories, felt
tainted.

For the longest time, I kept this part of our story hidden from people. I had told Mika right away, on the bus to Schneider the next day. But
no one at the school. No one until Iggy, and even with Iggy, I played it
down, as if it was something that happened in Yemen and ended in Israel, an interesting anecdote from the past.

Later, in New York, I began throwing it around in parties, out of nowhere, relishing in the shock and disbelief. I was already an outsider, already exoticized. My mom is a second wife, I'd say if someone mentioned polygamy, or Mormons, or Saudi sheikhs. "Yemeni Jews did it too." Maybe I enjoyed the attention. Maybe I liked shattering their preconceptions about Jews, about what kind of people were born to second wives. Maybe I wanted to reclaim this history without shame.

And yet, my relationship with Bruria never recovered. After I found out, I stopped coming by. Knowing that my father had kept visiting there all those years changed everything for me. I couldn't even look her in the eye. After high school, I moved home for a few weeks before the army. "I'm going to Bruria," my mom would say almost every afternoon, "would you like to come?" And I'd say, "No," without looking up from my book, the TV screen. As if by maintaining a relationship with her, I was somehow complicit in their sordid arrangement. If my mom knew the reason for my sudden change of heart, she never let it show.

Once, I came home drunk from a party, and walked absentmindedly onto Bruria's road instead of ours, stumbled halfway down the way to where my mother's house would have been, turned and found Bruria's instead. That parallelism in their lives struck me as poetic. Even from the outside, with the greenery, the well-maintained balcony facing the street, it looked more inviting than our bare, concrete front yard. Warm, soft light glowed from the inside. I wanted, more than anything, to go in, but I didn't.

YAQUB

Beer Sheva, 1955

YAQUB WAS HEADING back to his dorms in the College for Village Teachers in Beer Sheva when he saw Rumia and froze. Tel Aviv's central station was bustling with people in a haste, jostling against each other, lugging suitcases and knapsacks and dragging small children. Rumia was squinting up at a bus stop sign, trying to read the numbers.

His heart pounded. Should he approach her? What would he say?

By the time he awoke from his shock, Rumia was gone. The station was alive; the throngs of people had swallowed her whole.

He shuffled to his stop, boarded the bus and sat by the window feeling defeated and dejected. He knew of polygamous couples who hadn't stayed together after a few years in Israel. He remembered Saida telling him, "I know he loves *her*." What if Saida was free now and he didn't know how to find her? What if speaking to Rumia was his only way?

In the camp, he used to accompany his cousin once a week on the hour-long journey to Petah Tikva to buy a lottery ticket for twenty-five agorot. On the way there, Saleh daydreamt aloud about what he would do with the winnings. A house, of course. Maybe an automobile. Once, as they walked back, Yaqub gushed about Saida. How beautiful she was, and how smart. How alike they were, the two of them, both orphans, both interested in stories and books in a way most Yemenis were not. How unfair it was they couldn't be together. "You should hear her sing, Saleh," he said, dreamingly. "There is no way she sings like this for her husband."

Saleh sighed heavily a few times. Finally, he yelled, "Enough! She is married. You need to stop with this fantasy."

"This from the guy who spends his hard-earned money on lottery tickets!"

"My fantasy is harmless. What exactly do you think is going to happen with her?"

"He already has one wife," Yaqub said. "Polygamy is frowned upon here. So maybe . . ."

Saleh stared at him incredulously. "That's your plan? You think he's going to hand you one of his wives because he has a spare? Are you even listening to yourself?"

The bus drove into a tunnel, and Yaqub's own reflection floated in the dark window. Would Rumia have even recognized him? Often, as he searched for Saida's face in the crowds, he wondered that same thing. In the army he cut off his simonim. At first, he felt naked without the sidelocks framing his face, kept absentmindedly wanting to twirl them around his finger, but then he felt liberated, new. He no longer needed those markers to distinguish him as a Jew, as he did in Yemen. Unimaginably, almost everyone around him was Jewish. And unlike Saida, his relationship with God was not as intimate. He used to envy her for how steadfast her faith was, and in the best kind of way; her faith was about peace and kindness, not about arbitrary rules, the way he often felt it was for his family. As a boy, the mori he was studying the Torah with told his uncle, "Yaqub is asking many questions and disrupting the class. Who knows where he gets all these strange ideas in his head."

He had been a curious child, often pestering his uncle with questions: What did it mean to be a dhimmi, a non-Muslim in a Muslim country? Why did the Jews need protection? Why couldn't they carry the jambiya, the short dagger all Muslim men wore? And if Yemen was their home, then why did they dream and pray of the Holy Land?

He continued seeing unanswered questions everywhere. During his time in the army, he saw them in the abandoned villages and beautiful ancient stone homes where Arabs had once lived. What happened to them? Did they leave of their own accord? Were they driven out? "It was war. They lost," his sergeant answered, irked. "They could have agreed to the partition plan the UN had suggested, but they chose not to. I, for one, am grateful we finally returned to our ancestral homeland. Grateful we are safe after living in exile for so long. Think of the refugees and the Holocaust survivors who had nowhere to go."

But looking at these homes Yaqub felt the pain radiating from them, like throbbing, severed stumps. He saw the grief, the lives brutally uprooted. He felt it in his bones, the same way he could feel Saida's sorrow when she sang.

At the college, he found a kindred spirit; his roommate Sami Moallem saw things the way he did. A lanky boy from Baghdad with a thin mustache and curly hair, Sami was an aspiring writer who wrote in Arabic and was reluctant to abandon his mother tongue. Sami had decided to apply to the program—made up entirely of immigrants, mostly Mizrahi, and founded to address the shortage of teachers in the camps and immigrant towns—after he saw the way the teachers in the ma'abara treated them. "They patronized us," he told Yaqub. "They looked disgusted by everything, not wanting the mud to stain their fancy shoes. I saw them and thought, I can do better."

In Baghdad, Sami had been a member of the communist movement. "Not a Zionist," he clarified. He'd been a boy of about eleven during the Farhud, the pogroms in which almost two hundred Iraqi Jews were killed. A few days before, the doors of Jews had been marked with a red palm print. It was the first time their sense of safety and belonging was shaken.

After the declaration of Israel, and even during the months leading to the partition plan, things got worse. Jews were persecuted, fired from their jobs, harassed and driven to destitution. Even Jews who had no affinity to Zionism. They were not allowed to leave, so they fled, leaving everything behind.

"Stories like that remind me how fortunate we are to have this country," Yaqub said.

"But can we live here in peace knowing so many of the Arabs were displaced?" Sami countered. Sami maintained that as Jews from Arab lands, they had more in common with the local Arabs than with the Ashkenazi, who thought their culture was inferior, who saw their "Arabness" as a problem to be solved. "Ben-Gurion himself had said the Yemeni Jew is primitive, two thousand years behind the Ashkenazi. He called the Iraqi Jews human dust," he said. "These kinds of quotes are what make Mizrahi align themselves with the political right."

No, Saida wouldn't have recognized him. He'd changed so much, not just physically—he gained some weight and muscle during his service—but mentally. He was growing stronger, more resilient, more confident. He was no longer the inexperienced, insecure boy Saida had known. He even dated women. One of them, Rina, was a Hungarian immigrant whose skin was so pale he could trace the veins on it with his finger. They were watching Raj Kapoor almost kissing the gorgeous Narjis at Cinema Mugrabi when Rina placed her hand on his thigh and his heart forgot how to pump blood.

And still, even after he had known other women, had experienced the pleasures of the body, when he closed his eyes and summoned the memory of Saida taking the date in her mouth, warmed from the heat of his thighs, he was instantly stirred.

He pulled out his notebook from his backpack and began writing. Maybe by writing their story he could write her, write them, back into existence.

CHAPTER 18

YONI

THE DAY WAS cool, but the basement suite felt hot and airless, permeated by the faint odor of sweat. Hodaya sat in the row ahead, smelling,
as always, laundry clean. Yoni furtively sniffed his own armpit, relieved
to find the new deodorant his mom had bought him, which promised
twenty-four-hour protection in bold letters, worked.

In the front of the room, Yair was riled up. "Just yesterday, less
than twenty-four hours after the ceremony in Washington, a rabbi was
stabbed in the Old City in Jerusalem. So far, 164 people have been murdered since the blood government signed the Oslo Accords in September 1993. This is a security nightmare."

They had to step up the resistance, Yair continued. The Knesset was
going to vote on the interim agreement on the West Bank and the Gaza
Strip after Yom Kippur, which confused Yoni. Why would they vote
after the agreement had already been signed? Not once, but twice, first
the handshake in Taba, then the official ceremony in Washington. But
he was too shy to ask. Daily demonstrations were planned. Most importantly, a large protest was scheduled in Zion Square in Jerusalem on the
day of the vote. Several Knesset members from the opposition were
going to speak. "If you come to anything, come to this," Yair said. "We
must show our strength. Show them our numbers."

"Are you going to the protest in Ashkelon tomorrow?" Hodaya asked as they were heading out.

"Sure."

"Cool, me too."

She was wearing a blue button-up shirt that made her eyes appear bluer. Small Star of David earrings hung from her lobes. As they stepped out, she hugged her purple sweatshirt around her chest. "Always wanted to try this falafel stand." She nodded across the street at a small hut with a red awning and a few plastic chairs and tables scattered in front.

"Me too," he said.

They were both silent. He glanced at Baruch. He was his ride, but Yoni could find his own way home. Hodaya lowered her gaze.

"Do you maybe want to go now?" he finally said.

As soon as they walked into the stand, it started drizzling. "First rain?" Hodaya looked up in anticipation.

"First drizzle at least," he said, to which she chuckled. He was praying it would turn into rain, stranding them in there for a while. He always longed for rain. Every fall he felt himself growing impatient. The first rain washed the world clean, offered a fresh start, a softer, kinder touch after the violence of summer. In Yemen, Tata had told him, the Muslims believed the Jews could bring on the rain. In times of drought, they'd ask the Jews to pray for it. He considered telling Hodaya about that.

At the counter, he realized he did not have enough money for both the bus and a falafel. Hodaya was already stuffing her pita pocket with salads, drizzling tahini on top, while he frantically counted his coins, searching his pockets for more. "What do you have for three shekels?" he asked. "I can get you Nescafé," the guy said wearily. Yoni placed the coins on the metal counter. The coffee came in a small Styrofoam cup and was so bitter he had to add way too much sugar to make it drinkable.

"Not hungry?" Hodaya asked when he sat down with his cup.

"Just remembered we had dinner plans at home."

"Well, this is embarrassing." She laughed. "I was counting on us both eating. There is really no graceful way to eat a falafel."

Yoni choked a smile. "You're doing fine."

He asked about her national service. She loved working at the nursing home, talking to old people, listening to their stories. "These people built up this nation!" It was sad, how quickly people forgot the old.

"My grandma worked at a nursing home for years," he said. "And now—"

"What?"

"I was going to say now she's old herself, but . . ." he trailed away. He turned to look at the street. It was already dry, no sign of rain. When he looked back at her face, he saw she understood.

"When did it happen?"

"In August."

"I am so sorry. Were you close?"

He nodded, practically clenching his teeth now to avoid crying, aware of the quivering in his lips.

"May you know no further sorrow," she said, softly. And as much as he'd hated that saying when it was uttered by other people, from Hoda-ya's lips, it sounded sincere, and for a moment, even plausible.

AT THE PROTEST the next day, Hodaya held a sign that read, simply, elegantly, *This Is Not Peace,* written in her neat, rounded handwriting. "Do you want me to hold it for you?" he thought to offer after a while.

Her face brightened. "Thank you. It's heavier than I thought." He felt chivalrous for offering, proud to be waving her sign for her, to be clearly associated with her in the eyes of everyone.

As they walked back to the bus, she said, "To be honest, I was a little worried about coming today."

"Why?"

"I heard someone at the meeting yesterday saying there was a din rodef on Rabin."

Din rodef? The law of the pursuer? It sounded like something from the Talmud. He stared at her blankly, not wanting to betray his igno-rance, but she mistook the source of his confusion and continued, "I know. It's ridiculous. That guy explained that if a Jew puts the state of Israel at risk, din rodef applies, because it's the same as if Rabin was pursuing someone with the intent to kill him. So basically, it means you're allowed to kill Rabin, I guess, to save everyone else?" She shook her head.

"Who was he?"

"I don't know his name. He was quoting a rabbi who claimed saving an entire nation trumps 'Do Not Murder.' I talked to my dad about it, and he said giving away land absolutely doesn't fall under din rodef. It's taking it too far."

"I agree."

"This is not what protesting is about for me. I see protest as a kind of prayer. We instill it with our intention."

He swallowed. "That's beautiful."

She beamed. Was she blushing?

On the way back, she fell asleep against her backpack. He watched her, followed the delicate line of her neck, the shape of her lips, the slight upward tilt in the corner of her mouth. He imagined what it would feel like to kiss her, the suppleness of her lips. Closing his eyes, he tried to shake away the image, ashamed by the intensity with which he wanted her, by the bulge in his pants.

Outside the window, the cluster of crowded cities that constituted Gush Dan—Tel Aviv, Ramat Gan, Petah Tikva—unfolded in all its urban ugliness, the buildings stained by moisture and blackened by exhaust, miserably leaning against each other. It felt rotting to him, crumbling, Godless. For a moment, he allowed himself to conceive a different path for himself. What if he never took off the kippah? After the army, he could move to Jerusalem, study in yeshiva so he would be worthy of her. Jerusalem, a city surrounded by thick forests and rolling hills, where the air was fresh and cool, where everything was ancient, biblical, suffused with meaning. Was it so wrong to dream of a different life? What was holding him here, anyway? Now that Tata was gone?

CHAPTER 19

ZOHARA

THE YOM KIPPUR prayer at the local synagogue concluded, and people strolled back to their homes, nodding at me as they passed by the yard, greeting me with "Gmar hatima tova." *May you be written in the book of life.*

For the first time in years, I was in Israel for Yom Kippur, and I was spending it alone. When Iggy called the day before, I was hopeful, but he didn't invite me over, which meant he was probably with her.

I wasn't fasting, not since Schneider, where I first encountered students who hadn't observed the holiday and weren't shy about it. It was also the first time I came across the idea that secularity equaled modernity, that having faith was primitive, naive, especially the kind of faith our Mizrahi parents practiced, laced with mysticism and superstition.

"Gmar hatima tova," another person said. I looked up from my book. Nir was walking by with his mother and a young, bearded man in a black kippah and a suit. The man eyed me. I returned the greeting.

"I'll catch up," Nir said to them. He leaned against the metal gate, his face gleaming in the streetlight. He cleaned up nicely for the holiday, freshly shaven, a white button-up shirt tucked into dark blue jeans. "Fasting?"

"Nah. You?"

"Yeah. A habit, I guess. Listen, I got some of the songs translated. I can bring them over later if you like."

I perked up. "Thank you. That would be great."

An hour later, he returned with a stack of papers, grabbed a plastic chair and planted it next to mine. The naked lightbulb above us swarmed with bugs. I raised the papers closer to the light and skimmed the poems; his handwriting was impressively arty, the letters sharp and slanted. My eyes immediately landed on a line that read, "I dream of you three times a night . . . Breasts like pomegranates . . ."

"Whoa," I said.

Nir leaned over to look at the line and laughed. "That's actually not unusual. There are often detailed descriptions of body parts in the women's songs. It's also not unusual to write from a male's point of view. The women would describe how they're seen through a male's gaze."

"Of course they do," I said dryly. I kept reading: "Don't deny my soul its desire . . . I've traveled far, and yet I haven't arrived . . . If I were to be jailed for my love for you . . ." It was all so intense, so full of drama and passion. What did my mother know about romantic love?

"I don't get it," I said. "Who would she write these for?"

"So, it is her songs!" Nir exclaimed. "I had a feeling."

"I don't get it," I repeated.

"She probably wrote love songs in line with the tradition, not to anyone specific," he said. "I asked my mom about that once. Knowing what we know about Yemeni women and how conservative and traditional they were, something didn't check out. And she said—it was so interesting—that love in the world of the women's songs was different than real life." He squinted, trying to articulate the thought. "Like, the women knew romantic love existed, even if they hadn't experienced it in their own marriages, so the songs were a way to feel that, metaphorically, I guess. Or express longings for it."

I stared at the pages. "That makes a lot of sense actually." My mother was singing what she wished she had known. It was sad, yes, but it also put my mind at ease. I placed the papers on the stool. "So, you go to synagogue?"

"Not regularly. My mom wanted to go. Since my father passed away, it's hard for her to go alone."

"I had no idea it was that recent."

"Two years in April."

"That's fresh. I'm sorry," I said. "You know, I loved your father when I was a kid. He was always so kind to me. I can't believe I never knew you."

He burst into laughter, shaking his head. "It stings a bit. I won't lie."

I turned my torso to face him. "Okay," I said decisively. "Let's open this up once and for all. Was there something specific I'm supposed to remember? From the store? From school?"

"Yes! We even sat together for a while."

"What?" I opened my mouth in an exaggerated shock.

"I was too rowdy, so the teacher moved me next to you to straighten me up."

"When was that?"

"Fifth grade?"

"Yeah, I don't remember a lot from that year. It was the year my father died."

"I remember."

"You do?"

"I have this clear memory . . . It must have been right after he died. You just . . . sat there and cried all day, silently. I watched you, and I felt so helpless. I didn't know what to do."

I was stunned for a moment. I looked away, blinking away tears.

He searched for my eyes. "You okay?"

I nodded but couldn't speak.

"I'm sorry. I didn't mean to upset you." He grabbed my hand and squeezed it, which was just the right amount of touch I could handle at that moment. His hand was warm. He kept it there for a moment and then removed it, for which I was also grateful.

I swallowed a couple of times before I was ready to speak. "It's weird to hear someone talk about that. Someone who was there. Who saw me."

"I can't imagine having to go through such loss as a child."

"I honestly don't know where I'd be if I hadn't gone through it at that age. Like, maybe I wouldn't have rebelled as much as I have."

"You? Rebelling?" He scoffed. "What part of being accepted to a fancy school counts as rebelling?"

"Well, I wasn't a very good daughter to my mom. We fought a lot."

"When I was fifteen, I stole my dad's car and drove it into a tree. You know the tree in front of the old movie theater?"

I gasped.

"Another time me and a bunch of high school buddies partied at his store and drank liquor he had for sale. In the morning when he opened the store, he saw Yogev—remember him?—passed out on the floor."

"Oh my God."

"And then, after the army, I went to South America for a year and came back with long hair, a piercing in my eyebrow—"

"No!"

"And an American girlfriend named Mel. Not Jewish, of course."

I placed a hand on my mouth.

"Blonde, tattoos everywhere. A full sleeve on her arm."

"Wow."

"I'm pretty sure that's what gave my dad the heart attack."

"Stop it." I hit his arm lightly.

He laughed. "I'm kidding, that was years later. But I'm surprised it didn't happen sooner with everything I put him through."

"Nir!" I leaned back in my chair, eyeing him anew. "I see you in a whole new light."

He folded his arms across his chest, grinning. "Yeah? Why? Who did you think I was?"

"I don't know, a good son, working at his parents' store, going to synagogue, living at home."

"That's how you saw me?"

"It's all true, isn't it?"

"Fair enough. Guess I'm paying my debts now. I moved back home from Jerusalem after my father died. My mom needed the help."

"What were you doing there?"

"Studying. Started out with Middle Eastern studies, then switched to law. Because that's what this country needs. Another lawyer." He rolled his eyes. "I am starting again this term, actually. But in Tel Aviv so I can stay home and help my mom with the store."

"See? You *are* a good son."

"I suppose I am." In the darkness his teeth glowed white. "You know how it is, losing a parent makes you reevaluate everything. It's a cliché, but it's true. You become super aware of mortality. And it's scary but it also makes you live life with more awareness. Gratitude even."

"Yeah, I'm not there yet."

"You're, like, in the thick of it."

An orange cat leapt out of a garbage bin, startling me.

"And it's not like I'm so enlightened," he added. "I was really angry at first. Angry he was gone. Angry my mom aged so fast after that. That I had not seen it coming. That I hadn't been around."

"After my dad died, I used to punch things, kick things," I said. "Like, I had bloody knuckles once from punching sheet metal outside a construction zone."

"And now?"

I took a moment to consider. "Not so much, no. Huh. Is that a good thing? Does it mean I've evolved?"

Nir laughed. "Sure. Let's go with that."

We said nothing for a moment. He glanced at me and smiled. "I should get going. You can get me more tapes if you like."

I walked him to the gate. He turned toward me and opened his arms. He was tall enough for me to nestle comfortably against his chest, which was wider than I'd expected and good-smelling: clean laundry soap, the kind my mother used, and something sharp and manly but not overpowering, his deodorant maybe.

Was I evolved? I kept thinking after he left, or was that another way in which I'd become more American? Anger had been an emotion that came easy to me in life. In the army, they called me "short fuse"; youthful and emotional, I was quick to spark and explode. Like my mom, who went from zero to sixty in mere seconds, at least with me.

Dr. Beth Hudson, the therapist I went to after the divorce, called me on it in our first session. She leaned forward in her seat, which made her perfectly defined chocolate brown curls bounce, and asked, "What are you so angry about?"

I stared at her in a way that may have been perceived as angry but was meant to signal surprise. "I'm not angry. I'm Israeli. We're like that."

To her credit, she smiled. "Okay, what are you, then?"

"I don't know. Sad. Guilty. Confused." I fell quiet for a moment, and she did that thing therapists do when they don't fill the silence with words. "I feel helpless, mostly," I said finally.

"Anger can be a manifestation of helplessness," she said. "It comes from a place of weakness, not strength."

Of course, Dr. Hudson was right. I *was* angry. I thought of how enraged I was at the man who placed his mat too close to me at yoga class, or at the woman on the subway who chewed too loudly, or at my student for submitting a poorly written paper. Every time, rage washed over me like a tidal wave, and I flailed along, defenseless.

After moving to New York, every time I returned to Israel, I felt on edge. As though during my years away, I had lost my buffer, the rough exterior one needed to cultivate in order to live in this country. New York was intense, yes, but Israel had a different kind of intensity, less driven by ambition, more frantic, heated. More emotional. Primal. In the US, I sometimes couldn't recognize people's anger; they masked it in sweet words or facial expressions I couldn't decipher.

Back home, everything felt tinged with rage, hot red, a pot on the brink of overflowing. People were so quick to blow up, in the bank lineup, on the road—especially on the road—and they did it in such an uninhibited fashion. An honest, unbridled and raw display of emotion.

Maybe Israeli anger was also a manifestation of helplessness, of grief. This was a nation of migrants, exiles and survivors, people who fled from genocide and persecution only to arrive at this place where wars never end, and kids join the army at eighteen, from where some never returned, or return only in body, where border towns are shelled, buses explode, malls and cafés are blown up. A country erected on the ruins of others, the oppression of others. The conflict was everywhere; you couldn't look away from it, and God knows, we tried. This was the reason we built an armor, constructed a bubble.

On bad days, I looked at the paleness of the sky, and all I could see was how deeply fucked up everything was, how much the pain radiated from the earth, fury bubbling up like hot lava underneath the surface.

Other days, mostly at the beach, I would breathe in the saturated air and be filled with gratitude. Despite everything, this was the only home I knew. Flawed, imperfect, but home. And though my sense of belonging was fractured, still I belonged here more than anywhere else. Maybe that's why I held on to this dream of peace so desperately. I needed to believe we were heading somewhere better. If peace came, maybe we would finally be able to let out the breath we'd been holding for forty-seven years, and exhale.

CHAPTER 20

YONI

ZION SQUARE IN Jerusalem was packed to the brim, the crowds spill-
ing over onto the surrounding streets that fanned out from the square
like fingers. Yoni had never seen that many people in any demonstration. Taking in the surroundings, he realized he'd been there once, on a
day trip with his family a few years back. They'd sat at a table overlooking Ron Hotel, ate ice cream and watched tourists with their maps spread
open, teenagers on skateboards scaling the stairs in front of the bank,
the Hasidic Breslovs singing and hopping in the center and a group of
young, long-haired teens in ripped jeans playing guitars on the ground.
The place felt to him like the whole world then.

Hodaya didn't come. At first Yoni was disappointed. But as he
looked around at the crowds that enfolded him, all with the same spark
in their eyes, the same lifeforce in their raised fists, his spirit soared. He
was jostled into the center, pulled sideways, as though the crowd was
one body, a living, breathing animal. It felt strangely comforting, lulling,
to be rocked along with it. A few policemen stood at the fringes, looking
bored. In a briefing the night before, they had distributed flyers with
instructions that read, "As long as a cop treats you respectfully, you must
refrain from violence. In detention do not give any details. Answer each

question with the answer, This is a political investigation." He memorized the flyer but didn't take one. If his mother found it, it would be the
end of him. Lately, she'd been asking questions. Today, he had to lie and
tell her he was hanging out with Shlomi and the guys in the park. It
seemed to satisfy her. Please her, even.

The energy shifted with each speaker who went up on the protrud-
ing balcony of Ron Hotel, a large banner below it declaring in red, *The
People Didn't Sign.* Yoni didn't always know why the crowd reacted the
way it did to each of the speakers, but he trusted the animal. He felt
the anger and derision when David Levy, a former Likud member who
had formed his own party, came up to speak, and he joined the crowd as
they booed him off. "There's an incited crowd here that could do more
damage to Israel than the biggest leftie!" Levy yelled as he stepped down.
Yoni was swept away by the excitement when Binyamin Netanyahu,
chairman of the Likud and the leader of the opposition, yelled from the
balcony, "Is there anyone in this crowd who believes Yasser Arafat?"

When Likud member Ariel Sharon spoke, the crowds went wild.
"You can't break the spirit of the Jews!" he announced in his booming,
nasal voice. "These are days of total, shameful surrender by the prime
minister and his foreign minister to the war criminal Arafat!"

Yoni booed when the crowd booed. He chanted, "Rabin is a traitor."
He yelled, "In blood and fire, we'll drive Rabin out!" until his throat
dried out. The sound of thousands of voices coming together to a single
chant, their deafening echo, was infectious, electrifying.

Yes, he heard the chant "Death to Rabin," saw the enraged crowds
jumping and screaming at the top of their lungs with such glee. Did he
join in, too? He couldn't remember. He remembered finding it catchy,
rhythmically addictive. He saw the stack of papers being passed around
with the image of Rabin dressed as an SS officer and the posters of Rabin
with a target on his face, a keffiyeh draped over his head, both his eyes
poked out; saw, somewhere to his right, protestors hurling burning
torches at policemen. There were things he barely registered, like the
bearded men next to him who lit a match to Rabin's image. And later,
when he was pulled into a dance around a fire, arms weaving around
other sweaty men he didn't know but who felt to him like brothers . . .
What was being burnt? What were they chanting?

He was awash with sweat, his body loose, his heart pounding, fist pumping up at the night sky, throat dried and hoarse. He had a voice, and he was using it. He was making a difference. And after a while, it was as if he wasn't yelling at all; he opened his mouth and the voice of the animal came roaring out of his throat, becoming his own.

Later, when the crowds migrated as one toward the Knesset, where the vote was about to be counted after a day of heated discussions, he moved along with them, and when they swarmed Rabin's car with his terrified driver inside, rocking it and trying to turn it over, throwing torches and stones at it, he cheered, a new feeling stirring inside of him, the joy of destruction. And then, he was kicking the car, the metal giving to his heel. Harder. Wishing to break it. To destroy. He saw the fear in the driver's eyes as one guy climbed on the roof and jumped on it. Another took a stick to the headlight and smashed it.

It was close to midnight when they returned to the bus. He would have no voice tomorrow; he was sure of it. Baruch was energized; he spoke fast, eyes ablaze. "Did you see that? Did you see what the people can do when they come together?"

Yoni leaned on the headrest, smiling, his body buzzing with adrenaline. He closed his eyes for a moment and slept for the entire hour-long drive back to Tel Aviv.

CHAPTER 21

ZOHARA

THE YOUNG RELIGIOUS guy I saw walking with Nir on Yom Kippur was smoking outside the makolet when I came by on Friday. He nodded at me. I nodded back. When I walked in, Nir was hunched over the counter, pen in hand. I tilted my face to look. "Crossword puzzle?"

"Cryptic."

I stretched my face, truly impressed. "Those are hard."

"Kind of the idea."

As he rang my groceries, I browsed through the paper on the counter. The Interim Agreement was approved in the Knesset late last night. A map showed how the West Bank would look at the end of the phased withdrawals. It divided the area into three: Area A included eight Palestinian cities and would be administrated by the Palestinian Authority; in Area B, the Palestinian Authority would be sharing security control with Israel; and Area C would remain under IDF control until it was gradually transferred to Palestinian jurisdiction.

Looking at the map, I was reminded how close everything was. How tiny. I placed my fingertip on Tel Aviv, walked my pinky to the Green Line. The belly of this country was in the West Bank, and it was filled with life.

The guy finished his smoke and walked in. He jerked his chin up. "A pack of Time."

Nir pulled one out from the cigarette stand above his head and tossed it to him. The guy caught the package and glanced at the paper, just as I flipped the page to a spread with images of the demonstrating crowd, their faces glossy and twisted with hate. One guy was holding a picture of Rabin as an SS officer. Another protestor giddily jumped on Rabin's car. *The Mob,* the title read. A minister whose car had been vandalized was quoted saying he felt more threatened than he had during war. "Is that from last night?" The guy leaned over to get a better look, encroaching on my space. I recoiled.

"Weren't you there?" Nir asked.

"Yeah. Great demonstration."

"Great?" I couldn't help myself. "This looks horrible."

He shrugged, pointing at the image of Rabin in the Nazi uniform. "If it looks like a duck and walks like a duck."

"You've got to be kidding me."

Nir gave me a quick no with his eyes and chin.

The guy studied me for a moment and a big smile spread on his lips. "Aren't you Yoni's aunt?"

I stared at him. "How do you know Yoni?"

"The synagogue. Good kid."

"He's a great kid."

"Isn't your brother one of the missing children?"

I narrowed my eyes.

"Who do you think was behind that?"

"Are you suggesting Rabin stole my brother?"

"His friends at the Labor Party. Or Mapai back then. Same same."

"That has nothing to do with the incitement toward Rabin. And I can't believe you're justifying it."

"Incitement." He whistled. "Big word." He grabbed a newspaper. "And everything has to do with everything." He unwrapped the pack of smokes and stepped outside.

"He doesn't pay?"

Nir sighed heavily. "This is Baruch."

"Baruch?"

"My brother-in-law."

"Wait, your sister is religious now?"

"For about four years now. Then she met this clown. And now he's family."

"They live here?"

"They're building their house in Kassif. A settlement in the West Bank. My sister is pregnant and on bed rest, so for now they're living with my mother. Which means, basically, my mom is taking care of her while Baruch is out there causing trouble."

I lowered my voice. "I don't like him hanging out with Yoni."

"He probably just sees him at synagogue."

Nir's mom walked in. "Zohara! We loved having you sing with us!"

"I had fun too."

"Where are you doing Shabbat? Why don't you come over for dinner?"

"Yeah." Nir looked up. "Come."

I hesitated for just a moment. I was supposed to go to Lizzie, but did I have to? It had been so tense there. "I'd love to. Should I bring anything?"

"Just yourself, binti." She rubbed my back.

We watched her leave. "I assumed you went to Lizzie's every week," Nir said. "I would have invited you sooner."

"Honestly, I could use the break. Are you sure I'm not imposing?"

He sighed theatrically. "Stop being so American. Should I send you a proper invite? So you can RSVP?"

MY SISTER WAS rushing to pick Lilach and Ortal up from school. I tried relaying the conversation with Baruch to her. "So, he's Racheli's husband?" she said, rummaging through her purse for the car keys. "And they're living with Yaffa?" Yaffa! That was Nir's mom's name! "He can't be that bad, then."

I almost said something about the man she had been married to once but thought better of it. "I'm just saying, keep an eye."

"Yoni seems better, actually," she said. "At least he's out, seeing friends."

"Do you know his friends? Does he bring them home?"

She glared at me. "Of course I know his friends. He and Shlomi have been best friends since first grade." She dug out the keys. "We can talk tonight."

"Actually, Yaffa invited me for dinner."

"Oh." She looked as relieved as I was. "Well, I gotta run."

And she was out.

BARUCH WASN'T AT the dinner. "He organizes students' weekends," Nir said as he diced tomatoes, cucumbers and white onion for salad. "They meet and talk shit about the government, I guess? I've never been clear about what happens there. Anyway, he's in Hebron this weekend. Probably would have been better if he took care of his wife, but whatever. At least we don't have to listen to his tirades."

"Tell me how you really feel," I said.

He laughed.

I heard my name and turned, surprised to see Racheli's slight frame at the doorway, her belly preceding her. She was wearing a gorgeous fuchsia and gold wrap over her head, two black curls framing her face.

"Racheli!" I said. "Are you allowed to move around?"

"Here and there," she said.

"So you remember my sister?" Nir said, hand on his heart in mock hurt. "Her but not me?"

"How could I forget Racheli?" I gave her a gentle hug. "She was the cutest, sitting on the counter while your father worked."

Racheli nudged Nir. "Did you hear that? How could you forget Racheli." Her voice was soft, her *het* and *ayin* more pronounced than Nir's.

The dining room table was set with a white cloth. Yaffa's sister, Malka, also a widower, covered the braided challah at the center with a white embroidered fabric. Nir recited the kiddush with the Yemeni, songlike inflection I remembered from my father, from home. It was beautiful and, to my surprise, deeply moving. I couldn't remember when I last heard it since my father's death. We all joined in Amen, Nir's mother and aunt watching him affectionately. After he sipped from the

wine in the silver kiddush glass, he passed it on to his mom and aunt,
who passed it to me. He tore pieces of challah and dipped them in salt.
Our fingers touched when he handed me one. Yaffa served bright yellow
Yemeni soup with a spongy lahuh, green foamy hilba and spicy schug.
Malka brought a beef stew. I devoured my food, barely able to hide my
pleasure at getting to eat a traditional Yemeni meal. Nir glanced at me,
entertained. "There's more. Don't be shy." I elbowed him.

After dinner, Nir and I cleaned up while Yaffa and Malka chatted by
the table, cracked sunflower seeds and drank tea. I envied their sisterly
ease.

"So where is your room?" I asked Nir as I dumped the waste from
the sink into the bin.

"I fixed up the shed in the back when I came back home." He tied
the garbage bag and pulled it out of the bin. "I'll show you."

We stepped out into the cool evening. Nir hurled the garbage into
the green bin outside and returned. Similar to ours, his unit was at the
end of a cobblestone path in the back of the house. The door was unlocked. As we stood at the entrance, he pointed to parts of the room and
announced, "Kitchen, bedroom slash office, bathroom." A blackened
stovetop espresso stood atop a two-burner gas stove. A small desk was
laden with textbooks and binders, and beside it, a wicker bookshelf
filled with books. Over the bed a framed picture of Miles Davis hung, a
cover of his album *Tutu*.

"My living room is basically outside," he said. And so, we stepped
back out and sat on an old sunken couch that forced us to lean toward
each other. Nir brought two bottles of beer and rolled us a joint, his
torso stooped over an overturned milk cart.

We drank in silence for a while. Nir lit a match to the cone-shaped
joint. He took one puff and passed it to me. I leaned my head back on
the couch, smoking and gazing up at the starry sky, then handed him
back the joint. "You never said what happened with the American girl."

He laughed, surprised. "Mel? It's not that interesting."

"Try me."

He sucked in smoke. "It was never going to last. She wouldn't have
survived here." He passed me back the joint. "Though sometimes I wonder what would have happened if I'd moved there like she wanted me to."

"Were you ever tempted?"

"Not really. I love traveling, but I like living close to my family."

"I get that," I said, though I wasn't sure I did. I held the joint up between us.

"Nah," he said. "I'm good. I don't need much."

The night darkened and cooled. I smoked the rest of the joint and put it out. Nir stifled a yawn.

"I should go," I said. I stood up too fast and got lightheaded, losing my balance for a moment. I shouldn't have finished that joint. Nir grabbed my elbow to steady me. "You okay?"

I nodded, taking a moment. Nir watched me with furrowed brow, his face close enough that I could see the stubble on his chin and a deep scar over his left eyebrow. I reached and traced it with my finger. "What's that from?"

"Nam," he said in a deeper voice, breaking into his cheeky smile.

I laughed.

His eyes stayed on me a moment too long. I felt a startling flutter in my stomach. "I should really go," I said and added, as way of explaining, "I had an exhausting week. Every part of my body aches."

"Welcome to the working class." He grinned. "I can walk you."

"I'm okay. It's barely a block."

"I'll walk you anyway," he said.

We walked home in silence. Everything was silvery-lit and lightly swimming. Nir watched as I searched for my keys, crouching by the door and rummaging through my purse, pulling items out onto the ground until I fished the keys out and exclaimed, "Ta-da!"

"Drink lots of water before bed," he said.

I fumbled with my keys as I opened the door. "Thanks for tonight."

I watched him through the slats as he walked away, his slim silhouette, hands tucked in his pockets. He whistled. When he looked back, I quickly stepped away from the window, as if he could see me.

In the living room, the machine was blinking. "Hayati," a sunny voice from far away yelled. Shoshi! "Clear your schedule! We're coming to visit!"

CHAPTER 22

ZOHARA

LIZZIE WAS INEXPLICABLY mad at me as soon as I arrived at her house for Sukkoth dinner. "You're late," she said into the dishwasher.

I peeked into the pots on the stove: chicken with potatoes, Moroccan fish with cilantro and carrots, delicious-smelling steamed rice. Everything was pretty much done. "I am? It's not even four P.M."

"I've been cooking since noon."

"Um, you could have called."

"Zorki, half the time you don't answer the phone."

"Well, I'm here now."

I sat down to slice the cauliflower into florets. How big did she want them? I was afraid to ask. Maybe it wasn't me. She seemed to be mad at everyone for everything. As often happened when Lizzie was like this, she ended up nicking her finger, this time while slicing eggplants, blood oozing out onto the white cutting board. "Shit." She brought her finger to her mouth.

I rushed to her side. "Let me see."

"I'm fine," she barked and left the room, returning with her finger wrapped in a Band-Aid. Earlier that day, I had given Shalom Lizzie's number in case he needed me that night. It was hard to predict, he said, sometimes on holiday eves, the place is dead; other times there's a rush after family dinners wrap up.

I was starting to hope he'd call.

We had a quiet, tense dinner at the communal sukkah they had erected on the yellowed lawn in front of their building: white sheets stretched taut between wooden poles; dried palm leaves strewn on top for a roof. One of the neighbors had lowered a power cable and a bulb from his living room window and dangled it from the middle beam. Lilach and Ortal had made the decorations: cellophane garlands strung across the top; glossy pomegranate mobiles swirled over our heads.

"Look!" Lilach pointed up. In the gaps between the fronds, the moon was round and brightly shining.

"Sukkoth is the one holiday that coincides with the full moon," Motti said to her. "Unlike other Jewish holidays, which fall on a new moon."

"It was Tata's favorite holiday," Yoni said quietly. Everyone looked at him.

"It was?" I said.

"She used to say it was the one holiday that was all celebration. No talk about war and destruction and victory, no repenting or asking for forgiveness."

"The moon looks like Savta Saida's lahuh," Lilach said. "With all the holes."

Everyone laughed, and the mood momentarily lightened.

AFTER DINNER, I offered to read the girls bedtime stories. Lizzie was finishing the dishes and Yoni was packing leftovers in Tupperware, while Motti reclined into the armchair in front of the television set with a chilled bottle of Goldstar.

I was wedged between Lilach and Ortal on the carpet in their room, reading them a children's book by David Grossman about Itamar who could walk on walls, when the phone rang. I sprung up to answer it. As soon as I heard Shalom's voice, I knew I had to go. I could hear yelling in the background, the loud murmur of people's conversations, the clanging of dishes piling up. "Give me a few minutes," I said. When I returned to the room to finish the story, Ortal was sitting on the rug with her back to me, playing with her Barbie dolls. "Where is Lilach?" I said. Ortal shrugged.

Lilach wasn't in the bathroom, the living room or the service balcony. She wasn't in Yoni's room, either. I didn't have time for her games. I began opening closets. "Help me look," I told Ortal, a little impatiently. She reluctantly got up, searched under beds. "Nu, Lilach, it's not funny," she said. As moments passed, dread crept in. I called her name, my movements becoming more frantic. At the entrance to the kitchen, I stopped and breathed out. "Have you seen Lilach?"

Lizzie exchanged a panicked glance with Yoni. "What do you mean? She was with you."

My voice was shaking now. "I was on the phone. They need me at work and now we can't find her."

"Lilaaaach!" Lizzie began screaming instantly, shouldering me as she raced out of the kitchen. She ran to the balcony and slid the door open, looked behind the couch, senselessly moving cushions as if Lilach could be underneath one.

Ortal stood at the entrance to her room sobbing. "I'm sorry. She was right here," she said over and over again. I dropped to my knees and collected her in my arms. "It's not your fault."

"That's right, honey," Lizzie said. She shot a firm look at me in case anyone had a doubt whose fault it was.

Motti had already leapt from his seat toward the stairs, leaving the front door open. "Stay here with Ortal," Lizzie ordered while she and Yoni followed.

Ten-fifteen minutes later, Lizzie and Motti walked back in, their energy diffused. I searched behind them with my eyes.

"She's in the sukkah with Yoni," Motti said. "She wanted to sleep there, like they used to do with Saida."

Lizzie went to the kitchen and started putting dishes away carelessly. I leaned against the doorframe and watched her. "That was scary. You okay?"

She didn't even look at me.

"I'm sorry. I was on the phone for like, one minute."

She snapped. "Didn't you say you had to go?"

I looked at Motti. He gave me a sympathetic shrug.

"What are you looking at Motti for?" Lizzie said. Her anger was over the top, disproportionate.

"I don't know. I don't get why you're so mad at me."

"My kid went missing on your watch and you can't figure out why I'm mad?"

"Lizzie—" Motti touched her shoulder, but she jerked and shook him off.

"I was on the phone for one minute. Literally."

"If you say you're with the kids, you're supposed to be with the kids. That's how it works."

"Lizzie, that's not fair. Things happen."

She let go of the metal bowl she was washing, and it bounced noisily against the sink. "*Things?* That's not things! My child went missing!"

"Okay! I get it!" My tone was no longer apologetic.

"Next time, just don't offer to help, okay? You think I don't know how to take care of my own children?"

"What are you talking about?"

"*Do you know who Yoni's friends are? Do you know who he talks to?*" She was imitating me, though it sounded nothing like me. "Like I need *you* to tell me how to help my own son?"

"That wasn't—"

"You think we needed you to come back from America and fix our lives? Like you're some authority on relationships and parenthood?"

"Wow," I said, drawing the word out. I looked at Motti, who averted his eyes. From where I was standing at the entrance, I could see Ortal peeking from her bedroom. I smiled at her reassuringly. Motti caught the exchange and walked out of the kitchen, ushering Ortal into the room and closing the door behind them.

"And you talked to Motti?" Lizzie said in a loud whisper. "You go behind my back and talk to my husband? Who gave you the right? Do you have any idea how embarrassing that was? You don't know anything about our lives. Did you even know mom was prediabetic?"

I raised my hands up in surrender and walked away, grabbing my purse from the hook by the door. "You have officially stopped making any sense."

"And the thing is, I actually could have used you. Like an idiot, I thought, Oh, I should call Zorki. She'll help! What was I thinking?" She raised her voice again, forgot to whisper. "You say you're here to help. But then you don't answer your phone. You say you'll come for dinner, then you forget. You disappear again. You don't tell us where you are. You could have been dead in some ditch or something . . ."

Wait, what? Was she referring to that one incident nearly two months ago when I stayed with Iggy? Is she for real? I laughed unkindly, raised my hand like a stop sign to signal I was no longer having this conversation. My body was growing hot and tingly.

"I was calling everyone looking for you, like a lunatic . . . In case you forgot, Zohara, I have three kids to take care of. Three grieving kids who lost their grandmother—"

"I'm grieving too!" The cry came out of me like a wail, like vomit, and I was startled by its intensity and volume. There it was: the anger, the loss of control, the helplessness. "I lost my mother!" And as I said that, the pain sliced me.

I lost my mother.

I lost my mother.

It was never *not* going to be the truth. I reached for the door, dropping my unzipped purse. I knelt down, stuffing things back into it, my whole body shaking. "You're being such an asshole right now."

"I'm an asshole? That's rich."

"Please." Motti showed up. "Ortal can hear you."

"Tell that to your wife." I opened the door. "Oh, wait, apparently I'm not allowed to talk to you."

"Yeah, walk away," Lizzie yelled as she turned back to the dishes. "You're so good at that."

I slammed the door behind me.

I don't remember getting to the car. My fingers trembled so much I could barely insert the key in the ignition. Lizzie was right about one thing, which I found infuriating, of course: my first instinct was to take off. Get on the first flight back to New York. This was my go-to response, run while wallowing in self-pity. No one needed me here. No one would miss me. My parents were dead. Iggy had moved on. It was that same corner I'd found myself pushed into since childhood; I was back to being that young girl who was sent off, who felt cast away from her family, who felt like she didn't belong.

Shalom was expecting me at work, but first, I had to stop crying. I pulled over near a pay phone in the deserted city center; everything was closed for the holiday, lit dimly by cool, bluish light. I wanted to explain what was taking me so long, give Shalom an ETA. "Oh, good," Shalom said, exhaling. "I called back, and no one answered. Everyone came at the same time, and it was over as fast as it started."

Both Iggy's and Mika's machines picked up. They were probably with their families. I sat back in the car and stared at the gleaming asphalt, cried some more. Then I drove back to Sha'ariya, parked by the synagogue and walked down the cobblestone trail to Nir's room. I knocked lightly. It was quiet inside. Feeling sheepish, I turned to walk away. His door creaked open. "Zohara?" Nir was standing, shirtless, in the lit triangle.

"Did I wake you?"

"No, no. Come in."

"Are you sure?"

"Of course I'm sure." He grabbed a shirt from the closet and slipped it on. "Coffee?" He unscrewed the stovetop espresso. I nodded, standing by the bookshelf and staring at the spines. That's when he saw my face. "What happened?"

I thought I'd stopped crying but here I was again. I wiped my face repeatedly, as if it could make the tears stop.

"Go sit." He nodded toward the door. "I'll make coffee and you can tell me all about it."

Eventually, he walked out, a steaming cup of coffee in one hand and a beer in the other. "Options," he said, raising one, then the other. I laughed and pointed at the beer.

He placed both drinks on the table, and then pulled a Pesek Zman, my favorite, hazelnut-filled chocolate bar, from his back pocket.

I gasped. "Am I that easily knowable?"

He laughed and joined me on the couch.

I took a bite from the bar. "Lilach went missing after dinner. On my watch."

He looked at me, horrified. "Is she okay?"

"She was hiding in the sukkah. But Lizzie blew up at me and accused me of, I don't know, everything wrong in the world."

"The Israeli-Palestinian conflict, the Intifada, world hunger . . ."

"Exactly."

"Shit. I'm so sorry."

"I don't know why we get on each other's nerves like that."

"Has it always been that way?"

I considered his question. "We've had better times. But it's never been easy. I mean, we're ten years apart, and we are *so* different. It's always been an effort. And now, with my mom . . ." I trailed off.

"It's hard to see other people when you grieve. When I think back to the months after my father died, I know my sister and my mother were there, but I don't remember them. It's weird. Like I lived alone."

I took a swig from my beer. "Honestly, I don't even know what I'm doing here. After tonight I just want to go back to New York."

Nir pulled a joint from his cigarette pack. "So, your PhD . . . What is it in?"

"Hebrew literature."

"Can you continue working on it here? Like, do you have to go back?"

I leaned back. "I don't know. I mean, I can write it anywhere and go back from time to time. But a part of me wants to just . . . quit." It was the first time I said it out loud. Until now, I'd been telling myself I was just taking a break, figuring it out. "But it's not that simple. I'm so deeply into it now. I have done everything but write the damn thing."

Nir passed me the joint. We smoked in silence.

"It's not just my sister," I said, suddenly. "I got into this huge argument with Yoni on Rosh Hashanah. About Oslo, of all things. I always thought it doesn't matter which side of the political map you're on, ultimately everyone wants peace. Right? Like, isn't peace more important than land?"

"Sure, but you can't reduce this conflict to land," Nir said. "It's about ideology."

I straightened and stared at him. "I thought we were on the same side!"

"We are," he said. "But I also get the trepidation some people may feel. Honestly, last year was terrifying. Racheli was having major anxiety just walking by a bus. Her best friend lost a brother on the Number 5. A seventeen-year-old boy. It destroyed the family."

"I'm so sorry."

"But obviously it's different for you."

I hardened. "Why?"

"Well, you weren't here."

It was Yoni all over again. "I grew up here. I'm still Israeli."

"Of course you are. But living away skews your perspective. For better or worse."

I stared over the fence at the row of pointy cypress trees, my body stiffening. He missed the point. I wasn't talking about Oslo. I was talking about how alone I felt. How hard it was to communicate with my family, the people who were supposed to love me no matter what. He didn't get it. Why did I think he would?

"Look, I agree with you," he said softly. "But you know we're an exception around here. Surely, this isn't a surprise to you. Traditionally, Mizrahi vote Likud."

"Are you trying to say I am mishtaknezet?" I said with a tiny smile, as if it was a joke, but I was starting to feel put on the spot. It was a term I heard thrown at me in the army, at university, as if I was trying to pass as Ashkenazi.

"I never said that. And I don't use that term."

"But you think that. You've basically told me that in other words. *You know so little about where you came from.* You said that."

"Well, you were literally taken out of your home and put in this super Ashkenazi institution. That's a fact. Not a judgment."

"It's not like I chose it. Seriously, it pisses me off when people say that—"

"What people?" he tried, but I was on a roll.

"I've had people tell me it's in how I talk. How *do* I talk? What am I supposed to sound like? Or the fact that I only date Ashkenazi men—"

"And do you?" He seemed particularly interested in that last bit of information.

"That's not the point!" I threw my hands up. Why was I mad at him?

"So what is the point?"

I thought of Iggy, my first love. Iggy Sadeh, a kibbutznik whose grandparents had been road-paving, orchard-planting, Mapai-voting pioneers. Was there anything more Ashkenazi than that? But he was also Iggy: kind, beautiful Iggy who knew me better than anyone. I didn't like reducing our relationship that way. And then I thought of Ashkenazi men I met who made cracks about how Yemeni women were spicy. Hot in bed. Once, in a bar, a man actually used it as a pickup line: "Is it true what they say about Yemeni women?" And I sipped my beer without looking at him and said, "I guess you'll never know."

I glanced at Nir. His eyes were soft, kind. He wasn't mad. He wasn't letting me drag him into an argument, despite how hard I tried.

"Okay, yes," I relented. "I guess I dated mostly Ashkenazi. I don't know. Maybe I wanted something different than what I saw at home. Like, maybe I thought an Ashkenazi guy would be more . . . liberal, or something? It's stupid." I could hear my tone; it was still defensive.

"I get that," Nir said quietly.

Out of nowhere, my eyes filled with tears. I looked away from Nir. Why did I even come here? "I'm gonna go." I got up abruptly. "Thank you. I'm sorry." Again with the thank-yous and sorrys.

"Zohara, wait," Nir called after me, but I was already walking away, tears streaming down my cheeks again.

ON THE WAY home, the street was so empty I could hear the rhythmic tapping of my footsteps, the sound of clanking dinner plates and cutlery, the chatter and song of families around the table. I felt intensely lonely. This was the longest stretch of time I'd spent in Sha'ariya since childhood, the longest I'd spent in Israel since moving to New York. If this was return, then why wasn't I healed? Why did it feel like another fracture? Another displacement? Was this what they mean when they say you can never go home again?

There were people I knew who chose to never return. Evelyn's father, for example, never set foot in the Philippines again. He was looking forward, not back. Or that guy I met at a party in Brooklyn once, Ilan, who had been out of Israel for a decade. He told me he didn't like Israel. Politically, temperamentally. He never felt at home. He couldn't stand the heat. He was estranged from his family. I was both fascinated by and suspicious of him. How can one sever ties so radically? Have such little attachment to where they are from?

And then I thought of those who could never return. I remembered Yasmin telling me about her family in New York, who fled Jaffa in 1948, while her father's family stayed behind. They left behind their home, their books, their furniture, believing they'd be back one day. Thinking about that made my own musings feel foolish, privileged.

And there was my mom. For her, Israel was the true homeland. Still, like all Jews from Arab lands, she could never return to where she came from. With their Israeli passports, they were not even permitted to visit. I asked her once if she wished she could. "I'd love to see it," she said. But the community was all gone. Everyone had left.

Maybe Evelyn's father and Ilan were on to something. Maybe leaving and never returning, never looking back, was better. Or, maybe, it was best never to have left. Stay close. To your family, your community, your source. In New York, I sometimes imagined the version of me who'd stayed, the parallel life she might have led. I thought that if I returned, I could catch up to her. Like two transparencies, one placed over the other, I could slide into the skin of that ghost Zohara who stayed, everything restored, the unlived life resurrected.

Now I felt so far from that other Zohara that I could no longer visualize her. She had dissolved. Any attempt to salvage her was futile. I thought I could reclaim my vacant seat at the table, slip into the space my departure had left, but that gap had closed. Even my attempt to learn the women's songs felt artificial now, as if it could un-sever me from my roots, help me regain an authenticity I'd lost, turn me into a better Yemeni.

There was no fixing this, no reclaiming. It was too late.

CHAPTER 23

ZOHARA

SHOSHI AND YASMIN were in Israel for one week only, for Yasmin's sister's wedding. That was all they could manage in the middle of a semester. On the way to Akko, my heart flitted every time the train skirted the shore and the sea was revealed, glittering blue.

In Haifa, a mother and daughter boarded the train and sat opposite me. The girl, her pigtails tied in red ribbons, sang Christmas songs in Arabic the whole ride to Akko, the way only kids with no concept of social codes could. Her mom smiled at me in apology. I smiled back, saddened by knowing that blissful unawareness wouldn't last. I remembered a grad student I once met in New York who told me he started singing out loud in the subway or on the street because in New York people were so unfazed by eccentric behavior that they didn't bother looking at him. What would it feel like to belt out a song whenever I felt like it?

It was the first day off I'd had in a while. Over the Sukkoth holiday, Shalom was short-staffed and I was inundated with shifts. The beach was filled with families enjoying the last opportunities to swim. The water, I discovered when I jumped in one day at the end of the shift, was getting cool.

Iggy came by the café twice. The first time, I was slammed, and we exchanged a hurried hug. The second time, he came early for coffee. Just as I stepped out of the bar to join him, a large group of tourists came in. "We'll find a time eventually," Iggy said.

Conveniently, work kept me too busy to worry about potential Friday night dinners. But also, Lizzie had not called, and I was too mad to be a bigger person.

YASMIN HAD GIVEN me directions to Hummus Said, but still, I got lost in the narrow stone alleys, at some point disoriented by the sight of a picturesque marina with fishermen casting nets and the Old City wall curving around a small beach. Women in abayas pointed me in the right direction. Finally, I recognized the restaurant's blue arched doors and Shoshi's curls from behind the glass. She squealed when I walked in. We hugged, rocking from side to side. When I sat down, she wheeled a small, weathered carry-on toward me. "I couldn't find everything you asked for. Your closet is a mess."

"You're a lifesaver," I said. "I have no winter clothes at all."

An older, mustached waiter spoke to us in Hebrew first, then switched to Arabic once Yasmin ordered for us. A colorful assortment of small mezza and a basket with plump, fresh pitas filled our table.

"When are you coming back?" Shoshi said.

"I don't know if I'm coming back," I said. "At least not yet."

"Don't say that." Shoshi reached over the table to grab my hand.

"Every time I think about going back, I'm filled with dread. That can't be good."

"It makes me sad, but I get it. I just want you to be happy."

I ripped a pita and scooped hummus with it. "How's New York?"

"Cold." Yasmin shivered as she said it. "I don't think I'll ever get used to that. I miss the sunshine."

"At least we have that working for us. Especially now that it's cooled down a bit."

"Cooled down?" Yasmin stared at me. "Take it back!"

I stuffed a pickle into my mouth. "Give me gossip. How are people?"

Yasmin and Shoshi exchanged glances.

"What?"

"Zack is dating," Shoshi said.

"Oh?"

"Remember Renee?"

"Not Renee!" Fucking Renee. To think she was the one who introduced us. Did I throw a wrench in her plans that day?

"Probably a rebound. They've been coming to the havura meetings."

"Well, I'm happy for him," I said, resolving to act maturely. "I was horrible to him, and he deserves to be happy."

"Don't be so hard on yourself," Shoshi said. "It takes two, you know. Also, I heard through the grapevine Professor Al-Masri is getting a divorce."

It was interesting how little effect the news had on me. It was all so distant now.

At the table beside us, someone was flipping through today's paper, pausing on a full-page ad for the peace rally at Kings of Israel Square in Tel Aviv. It read, *You don't make peace by sitting in your living room. Show up and make a difference.*

"Are you going?" Shoshi gestured toward the ad.

"See how I feel. There have been so many protests from the right lately. Every day there's something. A little celebration of the peace process would be nice."

"I'm still on the fence whether it's worth celebrating," Yasmin said.

"Really?"

A strand of her hair fell on her face, and she shook it away. "Is it good Israel and the PLO formally recognized one another? Sure. But what exactly are the Palestinians getting from this agreement? There is no commitment by Israel to freeze settlements. They're still building them."

"But the numbers dropped. Rabin halted construction that was underway. That's why the settlers are so pissed."

"And there have been extended closures on Gaza and the West Bank on and off for weeks now," Yasmin continued. "Even after the Goldstein massacre in Hebron, the Palestinians wanted the settlers evicted and what did they get? Another closure."

"Really? Why?"

"See, and people don't know that!" She looked at Shoshi as if responding to an earlier conversation. "It all gets lost under the bigger news." She sipped from her malt beer. "Why? Because the IDF feared retaliation and protected the Israelis. But the closures also mean tens of thousands of Palestinians who work in Israel can't get to work. Is this really making Palestinian lives better? And how come no one is talking about the Palestinian Right of Return?"

"Do we think it's practical, though?" I asked carefully. "Aren't there millions of refugees by now?"

"Maybe. But acknowledging the tragedy would be a start. And yes, I think at the very least, we can speak about compensation."

"So you don't think the agreement is a step in the right direction?"

Shoshi raised her eyes to look at Yasmin, as if she had asked the same thing before.

"I don't know." Yasmin shrugged. "I guess I'm feeling pessimistic."

The waiter brought three small cups with black coffee and a plate of baklava drizzled with syrup.

"Rabin is in New York right now." Shoshi grabbed a baklava. "For some UN thing. He has such tight security there; Mubarak didn't come because he feared for his life. It just shows you how lacking Rabin's security is."

"I don't know," I said. "I find it hard to believe anyone would hurt him."

AFTER LUNCH, SHOSHI and I went for a walk on the seawall. Yasmin stayed behind to run some errands for her sister. There was so much to cover, so little time. I snuggled up to Shoshi. She wrapped her arm around my shoulder as we walked.

"How are you, really?" Shoshi said. "New York isn't the same without you."

"As well as I can be. One day I think I'm all better and the next day it's shit again."

Shoshi nodded empathetically.

"I've discovered some new things about my mother." I told Shoshi about the songs, the tapes. She listened, rapt.

"My mom and my aunts used to sing together," she said. "And when my sister got married, we had a henna and I remember my mom translated the songs for me. I had no idea how tragic they were."

Lizzie didn't have a henna before her first wedding, because my parents couldn't afford it. And she felt it was inappropriate for a second marriage. I never thought I wanted one, but now, I indulged in the vision of me dressed in the traditional, glittery outfit, a huge, jeweled cone-shaped crown on my head, and found that I liked it. In that fantasy, without effort, Iggy was beside me, smiling goofily, happy to be dressed in a Yemeni outfit and participate in my tradition. But then again, my mother was also there, beaming and proud, leading the singers in the zaffah, Iggy and I walking slowly behind them.

"So what's going on with your dissertation?" Shoshi asked. "Have you managed to work on it at all?"

I shook my head. "Just talking about it gives me anxiety. I feel so disenchanted with it all."

"What are you going to do?"

I looked at the sea, which was calm and flat as a pool. "Since I started studying the women's songs, I've been thinking about how much more interesting it would have been if I'd studied that."

"Oh my God, yes. Absolutely. Yes." Shoshi's eyes shone.

"It's a crazy idea," I dismissed. "What, scrap everything and start with a new subject?"

"But continuing to work on something you're not interested in . . . That sounds like hell." She frowned in contemplation. "What if you renegotiate the subject? The women's songs are poetry. It's literature, if you argue that it is. So, you're staying within the general area of your thesis but shifting your research angle?"

"My advisor wasn't agreeable even when I suggested a smaller change," I said, but my mind was racing. It isn't really Israeli poetry, is it? Unless I research the way the tradition is practiced in Israel, like my mom, and her friends. Even then, they would probably peg it as folklore. "Or I could quit," I said. "And become a full-time waitress."

Shoshi smacked my arm but then her face turned serious. "The way I see it, you have three options: you can push through and finish the dissertation, which sounds like something you don't want to do, or you find a way to work on a topic that interests you, which may be a hard sell, but possible. Or, if you feel like academia is sucking the life out of you, then you could quit. And that's also okay."

My eyes filled with tears. "Is it?"

"Of course it is! Oh my God, are you crying?" Shoshi stopped and embraced me.

"No one ever said that to me," I said, part laughing.

"I know this is an unpopular opinion in our circles, but there's life outside of academia. You can still be an intelligent, brilliant, productive person. Your happiness and mental health are more important. And you can call me any time you need to hear this."

I wiped my tears. "You know I'm going to call every day, right?"

She laughed. "It's not a threat."

"Anyway, I can't make that decision right now. My brain isn't fully functioning. I'm so focused on this whole thing with my mom."

"So, what, you think there might have been another man in her past?"

"It's hard to believe," I said. "Though I did find a photo."

She stopped in her tracks. "Of a man?"

"A bunch of men. It's from a newspaper. But she kept it in her ID case, which is weird."

"What a mystery to try and solve," Shoshi said, wistful.

"It can't be solved. You know how it is with Yemenis, there's no written documents or photos. My mom never learned to write so there's no diaries or anything. There's nothing."

"But you haven't exhausted your resources," Shoshi said. "The image, for example. Maybe you can find where it is from? Go to the archives, find the article."

We leaned against the ancient wall, looking out at the sea. A few seagulls swooped into the water.

"Listen to me, I'm a journalist," Shoshi said, grabbing my wrist. "Look better. Look at places you didn't think to look, places you overlooked. Ask people who were close to her. And if you did already, ask different questions."

I thought of my aunt Shuli. It would be good for me to drive to Eilat, see her. "I'll look better," I acquiesced. "I promise."

CHAPTER 24

YONI

THE BELL RANG, marking the end of last period. His language teacher, Tsafrira, looked over the room until her eyes landed on him. "Yoni, can you stay, please?"

He lingered at his desk, collecting his things. His classmates eyed him as they hoisted their chairs up on their desks. When the echoing chatter and laughter faded, Tsafrira gestured at the chair in front of her.

"Yoni," she said softly, pushing her glasses up her nose. "How are you? How are things at home?"

"Fine," he said.

She leaned forward with both forearms on the desk. "I know you've been going through a hard time, but we are getting into matriculation exams next term. It's not like you to be late."

He raced through the options in his head. He was supposed to submit something. But what?

"Due to your extenuating circumstances, you can submit your essay by next Sunday," she said, her tightly wound blond curls bobbing as she spoke. "But next time, please talk to me, ask for an extension. It's a shame to lose marks over this."

"Yes, thank you," he said. "I'll get it done."

"By next week," she repeated as he left. "Not a day late!"

He caught up with Sigalit, a bookish girl from the neighborhood who sat across the aisle from him. The assignment was to write about someone who made an impact on the world, she said.

"Who did you do yours on?"

"Golda Meir."

AT HOME, HE swiveled on his office chair, staring at the blank page. He started doodling and found himself scribbling her name. Hodaya. He wrote it in print letters, rounded letters, punctuated.

She wasn't at the meetings lately, and she hadn't attended any of the demonstrations these past couple of weeks. Things in the country were coming to a head. The papers showed pictures of jubilant Palestinians celebrating as the civil administration offices were evicted. *Salfit Today, Jerusalem Tomorrow,* the front headline quoted the chanting crowd. Beside it, an army official was folding an Israeli flag with a somber face. It looked like defeat.

Yoni had been going at least twice a week by now, riding along with Baruch to major junctions, blocked by stacks of burning tires that smelled nauseating. Protestors, almost all men, shouted the same chants he now knew by heart, like his prayers, felt their pulse in his chest, synchronized with his heartbeat. Yoni rejoiced in this chance to let loose, push, burn, destroy. He was one with the crowd. A part of a brotherhood.

In the shower, he rubbed the multicolored bruises on his arms and legs from the pushing and shoving, pressing lightly until he felt a satisfying ache. He came to think of them as badges of honor.

He eventually mustered his courage and asked Baruch about Hodaya, but the only thing Baruch knew was her father's name, so Yoni looked it up in the phone book. When he called, a man answered, and Yoni quickly hung up. He did that twice more over the following week, hanging up every time.

He dragged the phone to his room and dialed her number. When Hodaya answered, after only two rings, he was so startled he said nothing. "Hello?" Her voice lilted.

He swallowed, heart pounding. "Hodaya?"

"Who is this?"

"It's Yoni."

She was quiet for a moment. "Yoni?" she whispered. "How did you get this number?"

"I was worried about you. I looked it up."

"One sec." He heard shuffling, imagined her dragging the phone into her room. "You shouldn't have called here."

"Are you okay?"

"My father doesn't want me involved in the movement anymore."

"Why does he have to know? My mom doesn't."

From the silence on the other end, he knew he'd said the wrong thing. "Honestly, I agree with him," she finally said. "It feels out of control."

"Why? We are exercising our democratic right to protest." He noticed he was quoting Baruch.

"Okay, yeah." She noticed too. "But I heard people say Rabin should be killed. In Zion Square, people were yelling, 'Death to Rabin.' And did you hear what happened at Wingate Institute last week? Someone tried to attack him, physically. And that Kahanist guy on the news, a young guy, the one who pulled the hood ornament off Rabin's car after the Zion Square protest . . . Did you see that? He held it up and said it proves they can get to Rabin just as easily. What does that say to you?"

He had the feeling she wasn't actually asking.

"Did you hear about the Pulsa diNura?"

"What's that?"

"It's some Kabbalistic death curse. It means 'blaze of fire' in Aramaic. Some Kahanists performed it outside of Rabin's residence, wishing for his death. Can you imagine? It's too much."

"Look, there are always extremists," he said. "But there are good guys, too, who are trying to make a difference. You can't discredit an entire movement because of some bad apples."

She didn't speak. He was encouraged. "Do you still believe Rabin is wrong? That he's taking the country in the wrong direction? Giving up parts of our land?"

"Of course I do," she said. "But this isn't the way."

"So what is?"

"I don't know. My father was appalled after the demonstration at

Zion Square, the signs of Rabin in SS uniform. Were you there? Was it as bad as it looked?"

"No, it wasn't," he said, vehemently. "People were passionate, and it was powerful. Yes, some people went overboard, but not everyone. Like you said, protesting is a kind of prayer, right? We instill our own intention into it."

"You remember." It sounded like she was smiling.

"Of course I remember." He took a breath. "Some of us are going to the peace rally on November fourth, in Tel Aviv. At Kings of Israel Square."

"I doubt my father would let me go."

"It's too bad," he said, and then, quietly, boldly, added, "I was hoping to see you again."

Hodaya was silent on the other side, so long that for a moment he thought she'd hung up.

"Are you there? Did you hear what I said?"

"Yoni," she said softly, his name so sweet in her mouth. "This could never work, you know that, right?"

"Why not?"

"I like you. But it's too complicated. We are too different."

His heart sank.

"I have to go," she said. A long, steady dial tone punctuated the end of their conversation.

Only when he'd placed the receiver back in its cradle did he realize how tight he'd been clutching it to his ear. He lifted it again, this time slamming it into the cradle repeatedly.

He picked up his Book of Psalms and read from it. But the words went lackluster, the verses sterile, empty of meaning. He heard his mom and sisters coming into the house, the sounds of his sisters bickering, his mom exasperated, yelling orders and reprimanding them. He placed a pillow over his head, hot angry tears flooding his eyes.

His mom opened his door without knocking. Why was it so hard for her to realize he needed his privacy? He removed the pillow from his head. She stared at him. "What are you doing?"

"Nothing."

"I need your help with the groceries."

He went downstairs to the car. The trunk was filled with bags of produce from the market. He used to love accompanying Tata to the market, watching her bargain with the vendors. "You have to take your time with the fruits and vegetables," she said emphatically. "Feel them. Turn them around. Smell them."

Clarity washed over him. He knew what to write his essay on.

Upstairs, he dropped the bags on the kitchen table.

"Wouldn't kill you to put them away!" his mom yelled as he dashed back to his room.

"I just remembered this essay I have to write," he hollered back.

Once he started writing, he couldn't stop. The words poured out. He wrote quickly, without editing, without judgment. He'd never found pleasure in writing before, but now it was as if he was consumed by it, losing himself in the sentences, the images, the stories. Why hadn't he thought of putting this down on paper before? Before time passed and her stories were forgotten? Maybe there was a reason Tata had chosen him to be the keeper of these stories and no one else. She confessed once that when her daughters had started asking about her migrating to Israel, for school mostly, she didn't want to tell them about the hard stuff. She made it better, revised it a bit. She told them about the big birds that came to take them from Aden. She told them a funny story about the mirror in the plane's bathroom. She told them how they fell down to their knees and kissed the earth.

It was an easier-to-digest version, the story she wished for. And she didn't mention Rafael. Not in this context. This story was meant to be all redemption and miracles.

But she told Yoni the real story. Maybe because he truly wanted to know everything about her life. Maybe because more time passed; she had better perspective.

Or maybe because he was her favorite.

MY GRANDMOTHER SAIDA
Composition Essay by Yonatan Haddad
October 26, 1995

My grandmother, Saida Haddad, made an impact on many people's lives, especially on mine. She was a great singer and songwriter, and her voice touched people deeply. She was also a skilled storyteller. Growing up I loved listening to her stories about Yemen and her immigration to Israel.

She was born in Haidan in North Yemen. Before they immigrated to Israel, she hadn't been anywhere. Only a few times she took a day trip on the back of a donkey to the market in the walled city of Sa'ada, where shopkeepers sat on sun-faded rugs selling their goods.

The Yemeni Jews dreamt about the Holy Land their entire lives, praying for it, longing for it, writing poems about it. After Israel was founded, letters arrived urging the Jews to come. The new Imam, Ahmad, who came into power after his father's murder, surprised everyone by announcing that he would allow his Jewish subjects to leave for Israel if they chose to. Word of planes that would take them to the Holy Land reached the north. Thousands of Jews packed up their lives and began the journey to Aden.

It wasn't easy saying goodbye. They cried, and their Muslim neighbors cried with them. The trip to Aden was long and difficult. Two elderly women from their group died along the way. My grandmother blessed our family's good fortune; they were big boned with some fat to burn through to keep them well. The men were the tallest in Haidan, the women the curviest. Of course, by the time they made it to Hashed Camp in Aden, they were all as emaciated as the rest of them. They also had no money left; the local tribes had set up checkpoints and demanded hefty taxes for passing.

On the plane, my grandmother was paralyzed for the first hour, convinced that at any minute, they were going to plummet down. The women in the tight, short skirts who gave them water and fruit didn't look scared. In fact, they smiled, a smile that didn't leave their faces, as though drawn on.

They were flying, like birds, through the clouds, so soft-looking my grandmother wished she could touch them. On the wings of the eagles, as it said in the Bible. The clouds parted, and down below she saw hills and puddles of sunlight, and what she thought was another tiny plane and realized was the plane's own shadow.

The plane dropped a little and the passengers gasped collectively. One flight attendant tripped over an elderly man in the aisle, who grumbled at her, and my grandmother glanced at her sister, and they stifled a laugh. No wonder, she thought. Who in their right mind would walk in such shoes? With pointed heels, like small, upside-down pyramids. The only time my grandmother wore any shoes at all was on her wedding day, when she was given leather sandals that blistered her skin.

At some point she handed her son, Rafael, to her sister and went to explore the plane. She was braver than most, who were terrified to leave their seats. She found a small door, and when she opened it, she saw what must have been a toilet. When she turned, she was startled to see a woman there. "I'm sorry," she said. And the woman said the same thing at the same time. She raised her hand, and the woman did too, but when she tried reaching out to her, she felt the touch of cold glass instead. She noticed the woman was wearing the same dress, with the same embroidered squared neckline, her favorite, and it dawned on her it was her own face reflected. "We never saw mirrors before. Can you believe it?" she told me, laughing. When she returned to her seat, she told her sister she must go to the bathroom. "But don't be scared when you see someone else in there," she said cheekily, not wanting to ruin the surprise.

When they landed, some people fell onto the blackness of the road, kissing it, tears in their eyes, even the carpenter who cheated everyone of their money, even their neighbor who almost ran off with a Muslim man when she was fifteen and caused a scandal that was talked about all the way to Sa'ada. My grandmother clutched Rafael to her breasts. The end of the tarmac disappeared into a smoky haze. There was a sudden knowing inside of her. She was as far away from home as she would ever be, and she was never going back.

In Atlit, they separated the men and the women into two rooms and sprayed them with a strong, tingly substance; its awful smell stung in her nostrils, her lungs.

The clerks wrote their names. Saida, they said, would now be

Simcha. Happiness. She rolled the name on her tongue and knew right away she'd never use it. Her sister, Salama, immediately took on a new name, Shuli, thrilled by the possibility of reinvention.

They slept in a tent with other families at first. It smelled of body odors and mildew and salt. When they arrived, a young man in a khaki outfit announced, "Welcome to the land of milk and honey!" To my grandmother, it was the land of salt. She could taste it on her lips. The taste of the sea.

They woke up from loud yells and the hum of idling buses bringing more people. They were herded to a hall for breakfast, bread with butter, jam, a white cheese. Things they never ate. Tasteless, bland things. They didn't touch the olives, which looked to them like goats' droppings. They were loaded back on the trucks on their way to the camp in Rosh HaAyin.

There were new things to adjust to all the time, like the wonder of running water, or the first time they saw the camp's washing machine and thought it was possessed. Surely, there were demons in it! Or the new winter clothes they'd been given, strange, oversized and smelling of other bodies, other places.

The hardest thing of all was having to leave her son at a nursery. A child should be with his mother; this wasn't natural. "This is how things are done here," the nurses barked, like they knew better what was best for her son. Like she didn't know how to care for him.

But the worst was yet to come. A few months after they arrived, when my grandmother went to breastfeed my uncle, the nurses told her he'd been taken to the hospital in Tel Aviv because he fell sick. When she got to the hospital, they told her he had died.

My grandmother never believed it, especially since, many years later, she got draft notices for him from the army. Until the end of her days, she believed her son was taken from her and that he was still alive.

And yet, despite all the hardships and trauma she experienced in her early days in Israel, she remained passionate about this country and its people. She believed it was the place for us, was happy we were raised here and not in Yemen. She managed to pick herself up after her terrible loss and raise an exemplary family in Israel, two daughters and three grandchildren. She worked every day of her life and never complained.

My grandmother died in August 1995, but her stories live on. As her grandson, I am honored to put them down to paper.

I hope that by doing so, I am making her proud.

CHAPTER 25

ZOHARA

IGGY FINALLY CALLED, leaving an apologetic message about "crazy work" and "time getting away from him" and invited me to a launch party for the new music video he'd been working on.

I dug out my one nice dress from the suitcase Shoshi had delivered, an A-shaped black dress Evelyn passed on to me, paired it with a jean jacket and my beloved brown leather ankle boots, smelling like winter in New York. I washed my hair, scrunched my curls with cream, even put eyeliner on.

I could hear Lizzie's disapproving voice in my head. "You're going to a party? Two months after Mom died?" I turned down the dial. It's not that I didn't get the reasoning behind a year of mourning. But also, I had to do what felt right. And going to a party—Iggy's party—felt better for my mental state than being home alone for another night. Or so I told myself.

On my way there, I drove by the makolet, and saw Nir piling boxes outside the store. What was he doing open at that hour?

I hadn't seen him in a few days, maybe a little bit on purpose, slightly embarrassed by my behavior the last time we talked. He noticed my car, so I stopped across the street and rolled down the window. "Go home!" I yelled.

"Inventory," he yelled back. He crossed the street and leaned with one arm on the window frame. He quickly gave me a once-over. He'd never seen me dressed up before. A flash of satisfaction coursed through me.

"Looking good," he said casually. "Out on the town?" I was grateful to him for not making it weird.

"A friend's party." For some reason I felt the need to add, "I know I'm not supposed to—"

He raised both his hands. "Hey, no judgment here. Have fun. Don't drink and drive." As he walked away, I checked him out in return, his jeans hanging low. He walked like he knew I was watching.

THE PARTY WAS held at the top floor of an industrial building on Salameh Street. The space was packed with bodies, moving, swaying, a thin haze of smoke hovering over their heads. The music video screened soundless in a loop on a white wall. In it, the singer, dressed in a feathery outfit and fuck-me boots, was singing on a dramatically lit stage, holding the mic in both hands and gyrating her hips.

Iggy was nowhere in sight. I found the bar but no bartender. A glamorous-looking woman in a silvery minidress and heeled sandals was waiting. She was taller than me by almost a head, her hair dyed black, contrasting her pale complexion and bright red lipstick. We glanced at each other.

I stretched my neck to look into the back room. "Hello?"

"Maybe it's free," she said.

I gave a polite snicker and eyed her. "I know you."

"Yeah?" she said, unsurprised.

"Where are you from?"

"Tel Aviv."

"No, before that."

"I grew up here."

"Huh. That's rare."

The bartender showed up and she ordered two beers. She tried to hold them in one hand and dig in her clutch for change with the other. When that didn't work, she placed the beers back on the counter.

"For you?" the bartender said.

I ordered a beer. He grabbed one from the fridge, and the woman I thought I knew now had a man's arms wrapping her waist from behind. She turned to look at him and beamed. My heart stopped.

"Zorki!" Iggy said.

"You two know each other?" The tall girl arched her painfully thin eyebrows. That's when I knew where I'd known her from. Duh. The singer from the music video.

Suddenly I needed that drink urgently. I grabbed the beer from the counter and took a mouthful. Iggy and the girl unwrapped themselves.

"So you met?" Iggy said.

"Not really." I smiled widely at her. "Zohara."

"Michal." From her face I could tell she had no idea who I was. Oh my God. He didn't tell her. I didn't know if I should feel offended or flattered.

Someone behind me screamed, "Holy shit! I'm seeing things! Zorki!" Effi, who worked with me at the bar years ago. Effi was one of those fast friends you make when you work every day together in the same place. Then, I left for New York. I was never good at staying in touch.

Effi swallowed me into a giant hug, offering me a joint, whisking me away to the balcony. I signaled to Iggy I'd be back, happy to get away from him and that freakishly tall girl whose image gyrating in the music video was stuck in my head. Did she have to be so fucking hot?

"So that was weird," Effi said after we caught up for a bit.

"What?"

"You with Iggy and Michal right now."

I exhaled slowly and shrugged.

"To be honest, I always thought you'd get back together."

"Obviously that ship has sailed."

"What, that?" She huffed. "Give me a break. There's no way this is going to last."

My heart was injected with hope. "Why do you say that?"

"I know Michal. And I know Iggy."

"Oh, I didn't realize you knew her."

"Iggy didn't tell you? I did the styling on the video. I was there when they met."

I shook my head no.

"You forgot how small Tel Aviv is, didn't you? It's not New York. Everyone knows everyone here. It's a fucking kibbutz."

"So, what is she like?"

She eyed me. "What do you want to know?"

"I don't know. Forget I asked."

"She's okay. She's nice. Very driven."

"And hot."

"If you like that kind of thing."

"You mean, supermodels?"

She grinned. "She's not you."

"Aw." I hugged her. Maybe there was a chance after all.

We reminisced about people who worked with us: who got married, who had kids, who moved back to Haifa, who started a career in television. And somehow, I never mentioned my mom. It was like I was still twenty-two, living in Tel Aviv, working at the bar, living with Iggy.

"He didn't tell me you were home," Effi said, pricking the fantasy. "We've been planning this and talking guests and he never said."

That stung.

At some point Michal took the mic, thanked people. Then they played the song with sound. Michal sang in a bored, nasal kind of way that was becoming popular these days. Like she couldn't be bothered.

Effi was flirting with some girl. It was time to go. I put on my jacket and was making my way through the crowd when Iggy stopped me. "You're leaving? We didn't get a chance to talk."

"I'm tired," I said. "Why didn't you tell me you worked with Effi?"

"Oh. I kind of forgot about that connection. Can we hang out? I have some time before the next project. Let's go hiking or something."

"Hiking?" I twisted my nose. "Who are you?"

He laughed. "It will be good for you to get out of the city."

"What about Michal? She likes the outdoors?"

"Michal is off to Paris tomorrow. Some meetings with a potential record label. But shhhh. We're not supposed to talk about it."

"Wow. Good for her." So that's how it was now? We could only hang out when Michal was away?

"You're sure you can't stay? I wanted you to get to know Michal."

"She doesn't even know who I am."

He crinkled his nose. "What? Of course she knows. She must have not associated the name to the stories. It's a big night for her. She's distracted."

I looked away, out at the view from the balcony, city roofs crowded with water heaters and solar panels. "I'll call you," I said, gave him a quick hug and left.

WHEN I GOT home, I couldn't sleep. I kept thinking of what Shoshi said. Look better. Ask the right questions. I reread the translations Nir had done, trying to analyze the poems, find patterns and hidden clues—I was a literary researcher, after all. Maybe if I read her work with a critical, distant eye, I'd discover something new.

The most aching poems, I noticed, were some of her earliest. Nir denoted each translation with the tape number and the year, if one was mentioned. I dug out the image of the men from the camp and studied their faces. Was Nir right and my mother was imagining what it might have felt like to be in love? Or was she singing to a man in that photo? Which one?

The plastic bag with the documents was at the bottom of her closet, the purple bag with the words *Geula's Purses* on it. I had briefly glanced at them when I first pulled everything out and hadn't seen anything worth scrutinizing. Now, I took my time with it, read document by document, determined not to miss a thing.

There were leases for the house. Her passport. Some hospital forms, blood test results, receipts and warranties older than me. A few letters sent from my father's family in Yemen.

Rafael's draft notices were held together by a paperclip. I had never seen them before. The wording became more urgent and threatening in the bottom ones. A letter from the Bahlul-Minkowski Inquiry Committee in response to my mother's testimony titled: "In the matter of Rafael Haddad, son of Saida and Hassan Haddad." I felt a jolt, seeing their names on an official document.

Below it the complaint was detailed as told by my mom. I read the familiar story with a stone in my throat, and the listed findings:

1. The committee located a registration of the Jewish Agency's entry into Israel, which shows Hassan Haddad and his wife Saida immigrated to Israel on December 21, 1949.
2. The child's mother reported he was taken to Hadassah hospital in Tel Aviv in July 1950.
3. The investigators conducted extensive searches in the various archives and in all sources of data available to them but were unable to find any further information about the fate of Rafael Haddad. The committee does not have any information that can indicate the cause of death, the date of death, or the place of burial.

They concluded with, "The committee is offering its sincere condolences to the family."

I knew from Shoshi that only a small number of cases were considered unresolved by the committee. In most cases, they confirmed the child had died, even though many people didn't believe it. But Rafael was one of a few dozen who were lost even in the eyes of the authorities.

My parents' immigrant cards—a little stapled booklet that had been issued upon arrival—listed the family members, their relatives in Israel and items my parents had neglected to return to the warehouse upon leaving the camp: it detailed two cups and two spoons. "Please charge Hassan Haddad 320 prutah."

They kept track of the cups and cutlery. But they couldn't track down my brother.

THIS WAS IT. There was nothing more. I lay on her bed and looked up at the cracked ceiling. The top of the wardrobe needed to be dusted. I had scrubbed this room clean but somehow, I overlooked that. My mom would have never missed it. I stared at it for a moment. Was there something there? I sat up, squinted, then jumped off and reached on my tippy-toes to retrieve it.

A large brown envelope, unmarked, stuffed with thin, neatly handwritten papers.

I propped a pillow against the wall and sat on the bed, knees bent. The papers were so thin, almost translucent, I was afraid they might rip to the touch. The top sheet looked different than the rest, like it had been folded and unfolded. There was no date or attribution. The first words said, "Years later, when they are old, sitting on a porch somewhere overlooking the sea, someone would ask them how it all started, and he'd say, as soon as he saw her on the other side of the drinking fountain at the immigrant camp, he knew."

My skin broke into goosebumps.

I quickly perused the stack with trembling fingers. Some of the other pages had years and names of places on the top of the page, like letters. But these weren't letters. This was a story. A love story. A woman named Saida. A man named Yaqub. Was he one of the men in the picture? Did he write this?

My mom couldn't read.

Why did she keep stories she couldn't read? And how did he get them to her? What if my father had found them?

I held up the first page and began to read.

YAQUB

Merhav, Northern Negev, 1957

HOW TO WRITE about Ruth? The girl he married? The girl who helped him forget Saida?

He always believed one day Saida would read this story of them. She was his one and only reader. He knew she couldn't read, but he wrote for her, to her. One day they'd be together again, and he'd read aloud to her the book she had asked him to write all those years ago by the river. The story of their youth, of their lost love and eventual reunion.

It was a foolish fantasy. But for a long time it was all he had. And he believed that if he wanted it hard enough, it would happen.

He realized how naive this sounds.

By the time he met Ruth, he was beginning to accept he might never see Saida again, and even if he did, it wouldn't change a thing. Even writing about her felt futile. His memories of the past appeared distant and hazy. The intensity of emotions had faded. He was finally living. In the present.

Maybe Ruth was where that story ended.

A new story begun.

. . .

IN COLLEGE, HIS friend Sami invited Yaqub to spend a Shabbat with his family in Or Yehuda. The family had just moved into a permanent home, a small bungalow in a newly built neighborhood where the ma'abara once stood.

When they sat down for dinner, Sami's younger sister, Ruth, placed a bowl of hearty soup with rice, chicken and tomatoes in front of him. He was engaged in conversation with Sami's father and hadn't noticed her, but he smelled the overwhelming sweetness of rosewater mixed with the sharp smell of onions she must have sliced for dinner. He looked up at her, surprised—Sami hadn't mentioned he had a sister— a slender girl with a shiny black braid on one shoulder and thick, prominent eyebrows. When she sat down to eat across from him, their eyes met.

After dinner, Yaqub offered to help. Sami's mom shooed him away, but he insisted. He had been living alone for so long that he'd had no choice but to acquire some housekeeping skills. Both women were astounded. "You make us look bad," Sami whispered light-heartedly before retiring to the yard to smoke with his father. Of course, it was an excuse to stay in the kitchen with Ruth. She cleared the table, and he scrubbed the dishes. In between they talked. She was on her military service, working as a teacher-soldier. "I'd like to be a kindergarten teacher one day," she said. In Iraq she used to play the piano; her hands were delicate and long-fingered. She liked to cook. "I love children," she said. And at that moment, Yaqub had a clear vision of his future fanning out in front of him. He could see Ruth. A family. A home.

"SO, YOU FANCY my sister," Sami said a few weeks and dinners later, on their bus ride back to Beer Sheva.

Yaqub swallowed hard and said nothing.

"I think she's smitten with you too. And I couldn't ask for a better brother-in-law." He added with a snicker, "Normally, my parents wouldn't be too thrilled with a Yemeni groom. You know, they think Yemenis are savages, uneducated, uncultured, but you are something else, Yaqub."

He wasn't sure how to respond to that remark. Sometimes he felt like Jews who came from Arab lands were in it together, facing the same prejudices, the same fate. Other times he was reminded that even amongst them, Yemenis were considered backward.

But once Sami gave his approval, Yaqub realized nothing was standing in their way. This is how it felt to be permitted to love someone.

THEY MARRIED IN the summer, on the street outside her parents' home. In the fall Ruth's stomach began rounding.

After the wedding, Ruth moved into his two-room bungalow in Merhav, a small moshav in the Northern Negev populated by Yemeni immigrants; most were farmers, growing wheat, potatoes and onions. Since his time at the college, Yaqub had grown enamored with the desert, its silence, its solidness. It reminded him of his wife, who had a quiet firmness about her, a presence that was strong and calming at the same time. A rock he could lean on.

His seventh-grade students were bright and curious. While they were born in Yemen, they were a different breed, bolder, more direct, almost sabra. One precocious student, Ofra, challenged him to find a Yemeni author to teach. "Why do we study Bialik and not Shabazi?" she asked. "Why don't we learn about the first immigration of the Yemenis in 1881, who came before the Biluim? Weren't they also pioneers?"

One day, he caught two older students kissing behind the classroom. He backed away, embarrassed, shocked, pretending not to see them.

Ruth helped with the small children at the kindergarten. Once the baby was old enough, she hoped to enroll in a teachers college, too.

He was a good husband, massaging Ruth's feet when her ankles swelled, running to the makolet to buy her favorite orange soda when she craved it, picking fresh flowers from the field outside their home for Shabbat and placing them in a jar.

How little he had known of marriage when he met Saida. He knew better now. He understood that love could grow over time.

In the evenings he sat on the front steps of his new home in the desert. It was so quiet that he could hear his own breathing, the creaking of his marital bed as his pregnant wife shifted in her sleep, the rustling of a lizard slithering on the ground. He watched the desert unfold far into the distance, the horizon indefinite, blending with the darkness of the night sky, and he brimmed with anticipation, feeling on the brink of something new and exhilarating.

One story ended. A new story began.

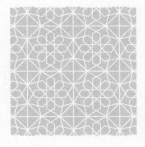

PART FOUR

NOVEMBER 1995

In the heat of my love
I went sleeping amongst the cacti
and imagined them
as rugs and cushions under my head

In the heat of my love
I walked through the wadi
like a woman alone
with no worry in this world

Oh, dark-skinned beloved
my family scolded me for loving you,
but the more they scolded,
the more my love for you grew

UNKNOWN YEMENI POETESS

CHAPTER 26

ZOHARA

JUST OUTSIDE BEER Sheva, a red warning light flashed on the dashboard. I wasn't even halfway to Eilat. A gas station beckoned a few hundred meters ahead. I drove over and parked by the pay phone, wishing, not for the first time, someone had taught me what to do when your car breaks down. If I opened the hood, nothing would make sense to me. I hated that. I looked through the glove box for a manual but didn't find one.

The sky was clouding over in the west. Great timing for the first rain to arrive, with me stranded in a gas station in an area prone to flooding, far from home and farther from my destination. For a moment I wasn't sure whom to call. Mika was too pregnant. Aunt Shuli was too far. I tried Iggy, but it went straight to his machine. Didn't he say he had some free time right now?

Riffling through my purse, I found the note crumpled in the bottom. I hadn't planned on using it. I straightened it on the metal shelf under the pay phone. It read *Tali* in Nir's neat, slanted handwriting.

"I'll come get you," Tali said, her voice raspy.

I called Iggy again, this time leaving him Tali's number.

Nir had given me her number when I went to see him at the makolet yesterday. I no longer pretended I was there to get groceries. Perched at an angle on the counter was a tray of fresh donuts for Hanukkah, plump and covered in icing sugar, a little mound of strawberry jam at their center, smelling sweet and deep-fried. I gasped dramatically. "No! Is it time already?"

"Every year about a month before the holiday." He gestured with his chin. "Come on, take one. You know you want to."

I grabbed one, bit into its greasy, doughy goodness, closed my eyes and moaned loudly. "Oh my God. *So* good."

"Shh," he admonished me in a lowered voice. "There are children in here."

I snickered. He handed me a napkin with an amused expression. My shirt was sprinkled with icing sugar.

When I told Nir about the pages I found, his eyes glinted. "Have you read them yet?"

"Just one. It was really good. But then I stopped."

"Why?"

"Maybe I'm a little scared of what I might find out. I can't imagine my mom having an actual affair."

He perched on the stool behind the counter. "Why not? We all think our aging parents never had a life before us. But they were young once, you know? People, especially young, hot people, fell in love and cheated and made bad decisions throughout history."

"But you know how traditional Yemenis were back then. I don't know. It seems impossible, somehow."

He shrugged. "People are people."

Still, I couldn't reconcile the idea of my mom as an adulteress, a woman who continued to write passionate songs to her long-lost lover. But then again, could you blame her? My father had another wife, after all.

Before I left, Nir drew out a piece of paper from the register and scribbled on it. "I have a good friend in Beer Sheva. If you need anything along the way, just call."

"Tali," I read the name on the paper and looked up. "A friend, you say?"

He looked pleased. "We used to date ages ago. On and off kind of thing. And now we're friends."

"I have one of those exes."

He studied me. "And are you on or off?"

I hesitated. Interesting that he focused on the on and off part, when I obviously meant something else. "Off."

"You don't sound sure."

"No, no. It's off."

He got up. "I should close."

WHEN THE SKY split open, I was standing with the gas station attendant, whose name tag read *Ahmad,* and looked out through the glass. The rain came down so hard you couldn't see past the first line of pumps. A man ran from the bathroom into his car holding his jacket over his head.

Living in New York, I had missed the phenomenon of first rain. I loved that we had a Hebrew word for it, *yoreh,* and for the last one, *malkosh.* When the yoreh came, it was always a wonder. After months of dry weather, it was as if we forgot it could ever rain, the sound of it on the roof alarming and unrecognizable at first. We'd run out to grab the laundry off the lines, remove cushions from garden furniture, getting wet and giddy. There was a quality to the first rain that was beyond a weather event. It washed more than the city. It invigorated and renewed. It made me feel inexplicably hopeful.

By the time Tali drove by, half an hour later, in her beaten white Opel, a chocolate brown Labrador panting in the back, the rain had stopped, and the world smelled freshened, the air cooler and easier to breathe. Ahmad and I had already spoken about my time in New York, his plans for the future (computer studies) and our shared love of Ofra Haza and Umm Kulthum. Tali was short and curvy, with wavy brown hair, dressed in low-rise black jeans and a faded black T-shirt. She looked tough and beautiful in a way that was muted and slightly intimidating, her face open and makeup free. "This is Stella," she said.

I crouched to rub Stella's chin. "Sorry you had to come in the rain."

"No worries. I live in the desert. I love the rain," Tali said. "Can you turn on the car?"

I did, waited for the light to show up.

"Yup. It's overheated."

Tali, it turned out, knew what to look for when she propped the
hood open. She peeked below the car. "How long has your oil been leaking?"

"I have no idea."

She instructed me to buy oil. She poured it in and checked for
dripping.

"It might be your head gasket. When was the last time you ser-
viced it?"

"It's my mom's car," I said. "I've only been driving it for the past
couple of months."

"All right, let's get it to Khaled's garage. Hopefully they'll manage to
fix whatever is wrong today. But if not, you can stay over for the night or
however long you need."

"Really? That's so nice."

"Of course. Any friend of Nir's."

Khaled welcomed Tali with a hug and Stella with a snack. Turns out
Tali's diagnosis was right. "I'm sorry," Khaled said. "The garage is full
today, and tomorrow we're closed. We'll do our best to get to it first thing
Sunday."

"It's okay," Tali said. "Stay the night and tomorrow you can take the
bus to Eilat and pick up the car on your way back."

TALI LIVED WITH Stella in a scarcely decorated apartment by Ben-
Gurion University, where, she said, she was teaching in the Arabic and
Middle Eastern department. She made us tea, stuffing our cups with
fresh mint.

"So you're also an Arabic speaker."

"Yeah, we met in the army. Nir didn't tell you?"

I shook my head.

She jerked her chin with a certain smile. "How do *you* know
Nir?"

"Oh, we're neighbors." I tried to deflate the insinuation. "We've
known each other since we were kids."

Tali glanced at the clock hanging over the table. "Listen, I gotta get
groceries and run some errands. Make yourself at home."

After Tali left, I sat on her corduroy couch and drew the brown en-velope out of my backpack. Through the shutters yellow light poured in. I felt a flutter of anxiety. Maybe I wanted to savor these words, because I feared once they ended, there would be nothing more of her for me to discover.

The phone rang and the machine picked up.

"Um, hi. I'm looking for Zohara . . ."

Iggy. Thank God. I turned so quickly I nearly knocked my cup over, rushed to the phone and picked it up. "Iggy, hey," I said, breathless. "Now how do I turn off this damn thing."

"You okay? What's going on?"

I pressed a few buttons on the machine. "My car broke down on the way to Eilat. It won't be ready till Sunday."

"Are you safe?"

"Yeah, I'm in Beer Sheva. At a friend of Nir's."

"The makolet guy?"

"Yeah."

"Were you driving to see Shuli? Why didn't you tell me?"

My heart skipped. "You wanted to come?"

"You don't want me to come?"

"Of course I want you to come."

I finally managed to turn off the machine.

"Okay. I'm on my way."

"Seriously? Isn't it raining? The roads are super slippery. First rain and all."

"I'll drive carefully. Can I get you anything from Tel Aviv?"

"Um . . . maybe your passport?"

"My passport?"

"I brought mine. I was thinking of going to Sinai for a night or two. It's been a rough few weeks. I could use a break."

He was quiet, considering. "I could too. But I only have a couple of days." Until Michal returns from Paris? I didn't ask.

"That sounds perfect." The car breaking down was shaping up to be a really good accident.

"Are you okay to hang out there for a couple of hours?"

I glanced at the pile of papers on the couch. "I'll be fine."

YAQUB

Merhav, Northern Negev, 1960

THEY HAD ENTERED the Days of Awe, the days of repentance following Rosh Hashanah, when Ruth found his writing.

Things between them had been strained for a while. Yaqub had hoped his wife would fall in love with the desert the way he had, but the transition to living in the moshav hadn't been easy for Ruth. She missed her family in Or Yehuda, and the summer heat and pungent smell from the barns took its toll on her in the early days of pregnancy. "Give it time," Sami said when Yaqub confided in him, but as time passed, Ruth's dislike of the place just grew. "Look around you," she said. "There's no future here. Everyone is struggling to make ends meet. Is that where you want your children to grow up?"

She was right. The men sitting outside the makolet, smoking their mada'a, chewing their gat, often complained about the injustice of being placed there, "to populate the desert" while Ashkenazi immigrants had been sent to live in cities, where there was work, opportunities, a better life. They felt let down by the Mapai government, whose socialism appeared to exclude them. "First, they took our children, our books and jewelry," they said. "Then they threw us here to work like donkeys. As if they are the true pioneers and we are their work force." The women who passed by on the way to the makolet hushed and scolded them. "This is our home. Only Eretz Israel."

It didn't help that Ruth got pregnant with their second so soon after Rami was born, before they got a chance to catch their breath. Yaqub knew Ruth had dreams and ambitions, too, and now all she did was take care of two demanding babies: breastfeeding, changing diapers, cooking, slaving over the laundry. By the time Yaqub came home, she was exhausted, resentful, would not meet his eyes. "If my mom was around, at least I'd have help," she said. "I wouldn't be so lonely."

But he felt responsibility toward these people, toward his students. He couldn't just leave.

"And what about your family?" Ruth said. "What about your responsibility to us?"

It broke his heart to see what they had become. A couple who constantly quarreled, who rarely touched. Even his reading habit enraged her. "You brought us here," she said caustically. "The least you can do is help." He tried. He washed all the dishes after dinner. He spent time with the babies after work. He took them for walks so she could catch up on sleep.

It wasn't fair to Ruth that he thought of Saida during these times. Before their relationship troubles began, he'd almost convinced himself he had forgotten about her. She was nothing more than a bittersweet memory that had no bearing on his life. But now, certain things—smells, sights, details—evoked the memory of her all over again.

The scent of oranges in bloom.

Dates. Their taste, even their sight. The other day, as his bus passed by a date grove—rows of trees lined up in an orderly fashion, lit soft amber by the fading daylight, casting long, diagonal shadows on the ground—an image struck him. A wedding in a date grove: Saida in white, like an Israeli bride, accentuating her beautiful skin, curls cascading, Yaqub in a suit he didn't own and a white kippah. (Because in his fantasies, he omitted the presence of *him* entirely.) He indulged in that image fleetingly before he was consumed by terrible guilt.

The sound of Yemeni women singing. He married a woman from Iraq, and for all her virtues, singing wasn't one of them. But sometimes, he caught sounds of a neighbor singing as she hung laundry outside, and it was like he knew all of her secrets; felt her longings and sorrows.

Every time a woman closed her eyes when she bit into something sweet and delicious.

Every time the topic of inspiration came up in conversation. "I once met a poet who said inspiration appeared to her like a bird in the sky," he told his students the other day, and it felt illicit, talking about her in public.

No. It wasn't fair. Saida wasn't real. Fantasies are, by definition, untouchable and unbeatable. He thought of the way they had pictured Israel back in Yemen, what years of yearning could do to a person. "We thought it was the coming of Messiah," the farmers outside the makolet said bitterly. "We thought angels of God would be walking the streets."

Israel was a desired woman they never stopped pining over. No wonder the reality was such a slap in the face.

He had told Ruth about Saida once. Not right away. When she first asked about his old girlfriends, during their courtship, he stumbled and blushed, and said, "There was one girl in Tel Aviv, Rina. We dated briefly."

"What happened?"

"Her ex-boyfriend came back from the army, and she forgot all about me."

Ruth studied him seriously and asked no further questions.

Why hadn't he told her about Saida then? He couldn't explain. Maybe *girlfriend* felt inaccurate to describe what she was to him. Maybe he still felt guilty.

A couple of years later, when they were already married, they ran into Rina on Dizzengoff Street. She hugged him and introduced him to her husband. They all had a pleasant conversation and went on their way.

On the bus back to Merhav, Ruth was deep in thought. Suddenly she asked, "Was there another girl in your life?"

Yaqub swallowed hard. "Why do you ask?"

"I've always thought you harbored feelings toward someone from your past. I assumed it was Rina, but now that I saw the two of you together, I know she's not the one. So who was she?"

His heart was racing. He had an unsettling sense that his deeper thoughts, his inner feelings, were written all over his face. "There was a girl in the camp," he said in a defeated way. "But I'm not harboring any feelings."

"A Yemeni girl?" She ignored his last remark.

He nodded. "I wouldn't call her an ex-girlfriend, though."

"Why not?"

He stared out the window.

"She didn't feel the same way?"

"She did."

"Then why?"

"She was married," he said.

"Yaqub!" She sounded impressed. Then she added, "I didn't think a Yemeni girl would be that . . . bold, I guess. Do they even talk to boys? Don't they lead completely separate lives?"

He shifted uncomfortably. "It depends. Women from rural areas had more freedom than women in the city. More agency. The women in my family would sell their crafts in the market. We even danced to-gether, men and women."

"Huh. I didn't know that," she said. "The Yemeni women I met in the camp were so sheltered, so naive. Covered from head to toe. I couldn't imagine . . ."

"She was different," he interjected.

Ruth stopped talking and stared at him in a new way.

"And I mean, weren't Iraqi women oppressed too?"

"Sure, but not like Yemeni women, I don't think."

He was aware suddenly that he was talking to his wife, defending *her* in front of his wife.

"Sounds like she was special," Ruth said. There was a sharp edge to her voice. "What happened?"

"We left the camp and lost touch," he said, eager to finish the con-versation.

"Just like that?"

"And then I met you." He forced a smile. "And I forgot all about her." Ruth looked away. He knew he'd hurt her somehow and didn't know how to fix it. He wished he could stuff the genie back in the bottle.

They never spoke about Saida again. Until now.

His writing was tucked inside a large book of prayers he knew she'd never look at. That evening, she was cleaning the bookshelf and the book came crashing down, the papers scattered all over the floor. She bent down to pick them up. "What's that?" she said. He was reading Rami a story on the couch and had never sprinted faster in his life.

"Nothing." He knelt beside her, urgently collecting the papers.

"Doesn't look like nothing."

"It's something I'm working on."

"Like, a book?"

He nodded.

"Why don't you want me to read it?"

"Because it's embarrassing," he said too loudly. "And it's private."

She got up and walked away, began washing dishes. He stuffed the papers in a folder on his desk.

After a moment his breathing settled. He watched her at the sink and his heart went out to her. Every year around the Days of Awe, he felt reflective, closer to God, to something bigger than him, despite his doubts and misgivings. He realized he was not being fair to Ruth by writing about Saida. He tried to convince himself it was harmless. But was it? Really? Then why was he hiding it?

Writing is powerful. It can bring back vivid memories, reignite old emotions, reopen old scabs. Every time he wrote about Saida, he was falling in love and losing her all over again. Every time, he found himself looking for her on buses, in the marketplace, on the street. And some days he did see her, except it wasn't her at all but someone who did not resemble her even remotely.

Ruth spoke little of the past, found no use in dwelling on it, and while he admired her ability to let go, envied it, he sometimes found it strange, cold. He wondered if it was her refusal to live in the past that made her forget, or if it was her flawed memory that cured her of nostalgia.

He followed her into the kitchen, apologized for overreacting, hugged her from behind. She was stiff in his arms. "I'm protective of my writing," he said. "Insecure. I promise when I'm ready, you'll be the first person to read my work."

She shut the water off but didn't turn. "What is it about?"

"My life."

"Do you write about her?" He could feel a tremor in her body.

"Some. But also about you."

"You write about me?" She finally turned to face him.

"Of course," he said. "You're my wife. My beloved. You're my every-thing."

She softened in his arms, forgave him. Then why did he feel so awful?

THAT NIGHT, AS he lay in bed beside his sleeping wife, her body curled so small she appeared to be a girl, he vowed to never write about Saida again. It was a childish and hopeless pursuit. Yet, when he tried to write something else; if he set out to write a poem, say, uninspired by her, it came out stilted and forced. Only when he sat with the pretense of writ-ing their story did the muse relent. He felt guilty thinking about her but also guilty when he forgot. As if by doing so, he was forgetting a part of himself, betraying a part of himself.

He rolled over and spooned Ruth. She shifted to accommodate him, her body warm. Tomorrow, he would start looking for a new job in the center. He would put his wife and family first.

CHAPTER 27

ZOHARA

ON THE WAY to Eilat, I caught Iggy up on everything that happened, sharing tidbits from the pages as though I was relaying the plot of a book I'd read. I talked fast, buzzing with the thrill of discovery and astonished by what I had read. Happy to know my mom had loved, had been loved, and heartbroken it was so short-lived.

Upon Iggy's request, I read to him a couple of paragraphs, but I quickly became self-conscious, as if I was barging in on a romantic moment that wasn't meant for me, catching a stolen glance between lovers.

Or maybe the act of reading a love story to Iggy felt too on the nose.

"You have to find him," Iggy said. "Was there anything on the envelope? Address? Stamp?"

"Nothing," I said. "I don't even understand how and when he sent it to her. For all we know, he could be dead, too. And I mean, all I have to work with is his first name, which was probably changed into Hebrew."

"It's good you're seeing Shuli," he said.

I stared out the window at the desert; its vast emptiness always inspired loneliness and awe in me. The road curved around soft, barren hills. Reading the pages, I sometimes had to remind myself this was my mother. That smart, courageous, creative young woman. I was mad at myself for years of not asking, sad my mom thought she couldn't tell me. Was she ashamed of the person she had been once? Then why did she keep these pages? Perhaps she didn't know what was in them. She couldn't read, after all.

Would Shuli even know? My mom and aunt weren't close. And it wasn't just the physical distance.

Growing up, Shuli was my glamorous aunt. I know now that my idea of glamour was skewed, since she lived in a tiny apartment in a run-down housing complex. When I went to see her singing at hotel bars, she'd be dressed in shimmering dresses that hugged her curves, her hair hennaed or highlighted, her lips brightly red. She was magnificent. I couldn't fathom why she wasn't a star, why she wasn't performing for thousands in the open-air Roman theater in Caesarea. She had the voice for it, the charisma, the stage presence. And I saw the way men lusted after her when she sang, especially the tourists, who waited for her afterwards, buying her drinks and lighting her cigarettes.

Somehow, Shuli's big break never came. After a few years, already divorced twice, she met an American tourist who swept her off her feet and they moved to Eilat, of all places. The American never survived the heat but she stayed. In a small apartment on the outskirts of town, facing the sea on one side and the mountains on the other, her walls covered in evidence of her past glory. From her kitchen window, you could see the shores of Aqaba sparkling across the Gulf at night, and big ships from Asian cities mooring in their port. Taba, the entry to the Sinai Peninsula in Egypt, was only a fifteen-minute drive. "I live at the intersection of three countries," she loved saying. Outside her service balcony, where she hung laundry and stored cleaning supplies, was the desert, the mountains that edged the city, red at sunset and wild and swirling black at night. It was the kind of view you could only dream of where I came from, where all you saw from the window was the guava tree and the bluish TV light streaming through the blinds of Leah the hairdresser. And the idea of wildlife was stray cats rummaging through garbage cans and the occasional hedgehog.

By the time we rolled into Eilat, the sun was bleeding red onto the mountains. Shuli swallowed me into her arms and rocked me back and forth. Iggy hugged her, too. "That's a surprise," she said, eyeing me meaningfully.

Iggy watched TV in the living room, and I stood next to Shuli in the tiny kitchen as she cooked pasta for dinner. "Iggy, huh?" she said, nudging me with her hip.

"Mika thinks it's a bad idea," I said. "He's seeing someone."

She searched my face. "And what do you think?"

"Honestly I feel like I finally know what I want."

"Well, he's here with you. Right? That must mean something," Shuli said.

After dinner, we sat together at her kitchen table, looking at the ships like giant hippos crossing the Gulf of Aqaba. Iggy had retired to bed. Shuli poured us two cups of arak, the clear substance clouded with water and ice.

"I found something in my mom's things," I said. "Stories about her time in the camps. Written by a guy named Yaqub, I guess?"

Her face lit up. "Wow. I didn't know about those."

"But you knew about Yaqub."

"I was there."

"Who was he?"

"A sweet boy from the camp. He was madly in love with her."

I dug out my mom's ID case, pulled out the flimsy photo. "Is he here?"

Shuli grabbed her reading glasses. "Oh my God, where did you find this?"

"In her purse."

Shuli's eyebrows rounded. "After all these years?" She studied the image and then pointed at the young man standing in the back, a slight smile on his face. He wore a black cap, his clothes were Western, his hands tucked in the pockets of his trousers. "That's him. That's Yaqub."

I looked at him for a long moment. There he was. The man from the songs, from the pages. My mom's true love. "So she didn't talk to you about it."

"I asked her, once." Shuli looked outside the window. "She was flushed, upset, denied everything. I was only fourteen. She was maybe seventeen? Eighteen? And you know, she was never in love before, so I could tell from her face. Something changed in her. It's no secret your mother wasn't happy with your father, and there was this young, handsome guy who fell in love with her, who admired her singing."

"You saw them together?"

"I came looking for her once. I will never forget it. She sat on one rock, singing in that angelic voice of hers, and he was watching her like he was witnessing a miracle."

"Where was my father?"

"He was working up north with my husband. They were gone weeks at a time."

"You were married already?"

She nodded slowly. "I married at twelve."

"Oh, Shuli," I said.

"You have to realize your mother was considered lucky. And she knew it. She was a poor orphan, dark-skinned, and still your father agreed to marry her."

"Why?"

"She was charming, beautiful and whip-smart. She could cook."

I snorted. "Arguable."

"Good enough, apparently. And she was fertile."

"How did he know?"

"That's what the matchmaker promised." She threw her hands up.

"And Bruria wasn't."

"That's right."

A car drove by blasting loud Middle Eastern music.

"Were you not as lucky with your husband?"

Shuli looked away; her face dimmed. From the seawall, a lit-up ball—an amusement park ride—shot up to the sky and then slowly descended back to the ground. I followed it, transfixed. "I remember when he came by to see me for the first time. I was playing marbles with my girlfriends. I didn't want to come in. I was in the middle of a game." She lit a cigarette and blew smoke out the open window. "The night of my wedding, I ran away back to my uncle's house. But after a couple of days, my uncle said I had to go back."

"You never told me about this."

She looked at me wearily. "What is there to tell? Nobody talked about these things. We didn't know anything about what it meant to be married. We didn't know about sex. You know, virginity was the woman's honor, a virtue. But no one spoke about the pain or the act itself. The first time he came to me, I didn't even have my period yet. At least your father waited. But my husband's mom wanted to see blood. I remember she took the stained sheet and hung it outside for everyone to see. It sounds crazy now, doesn't it?"

"Oh, Shuli. That's awful." I had tears in my eyes.

Shuli looked at me, laughed and reached over with her hand to rub mine. "Don't cry now, silly." Her expression turned serious. "For Yemeni women, there was nothing more important than raising a family, being a mother and a wife. This was our destiny. There was no other life. No other option. And your mother and I, we were dreamers. It wasn't considered a good thing. Because we were orphans, we had no parental authority—our uncle and aunt didn't offer much supervision—so we grew up a little unruly, I guess. Not like the other girls."

"But you eventually left your husband. She stayed."

"Your father was not like my husband. He was a good man. He respected her, he never hit her . . ."

"That's a definition of a good man!?"

"For many women of our generation, it was. Sadly."

"He was married to another woman."

"I think that suited her. It's hard to imagine because it's such a different culture nowadays. But your mom didn't mind. He had his needs filled elsewhere . . ."

"What about her needs?"

"After Yaqub, and then Rafael's disappearance, she didn't think about her needs. She felt tremendous guilt about it."

I couldn't resist. "He wrote they kissed. I don't know if it really happened or . . ."

Shuli nodded. "Honestly, I suspected something might have happened. But even if it didn't, already people were talking. Just sitting there with him, alone, that was taboo enough."

"You were there when my father found out."

Shuli puffed air out. "It was so awful. Your mother was shamed. Yaqub left the next day. He had to. *Everybody* talked. And then, a few weeks later, your brother went missing, and your mother . . ." Shuli's eyes reddened. "She was destroyed. Whatever spirit was left in her was gone. And that was it. She never saw Yaqub again. Never mentioned him. She focused on survival. I had no idea she kept this photo all these years."

I leaned my face on my hand, my eyes tearing up. "My poor mother."

"Allah yerhama."

"But he kept writing about her. All these years. I mean, obviously he knew she couldn't read it. And does it mean he found her? Gave it to her? How? There is nothing about that in the pages."

"I wish I could tell you more, but you know, your mother didn't really talk to me."

I met her eyes. "Why?"

Shuli shifted in her seat. "I loved my sister, but we're different." I thought of Lizzie. How I loved her but didn't always like her.

"Was that all?"

Shuli sipped her arak, looking out. "I think it was hard for her that I had four sons. Especially since I had Yoram soon after Rafael disappeared, and when I gave birth, I was so careful. I wouldn't let him out of my sight. I learned from her experience. It was too painful for her. She preferred to be away from us, to not inflict us with the evil eye without meaning to. And later, after I divorced from my first husband, I dated, I sang in public in front of men, I led a secular life. I used to go to haflas in the Yemenite Quarter in Tel Aviv, at night, to drink and dance. I had a blast!" She smiled, getting caught up in the memories.

"So, she judged you."

She considered. "It felt more like she resented me. Like—" She paused. "As a kid, your mother was feisty, rebellious. She had more guts than anyone. I looked up to her. Who knows what she could have become if she was born in your generation?"

"So what happened?"

"Life happened. It crushed her. You have to understand what happened with Yaqub was unheard-of. It was not something Yemeni girls do. Even single girls. And married? You were as good as dead for many people. That's why your parents didn't stay in Rosh HaAyin, where people knew them. And after all of that, your father forgave her. Which Bruria probably had something to do with. After Rafael was gone, I think she felt she was being punished. For falling in love. For dreaming. For daring."

"That's awful."

"So she devoted her life to being a good mother, a good wife, pushing all her dreams away. And then there was me, who did everything I wanted. I didn't care what people thought. Screw everyone, right? I think it was hard for her to see that, like I was a reminder of the life she hadn't lived. It wasn't fair, but life isn't fair, is it?"

I sighed. "That's so sad."

Shuli's face softened. She reached out for my hand. "I think she found peace in the last few years. She found things that made her happy."

I burst into tears again, wiping them as they came. "Thank you for saying that." Shuli pushed back her chair, walked around and held me in her arms.

It was after midnight. I got up and took our glasses to the sink.

"Come and stay with me for a weekend sometime," Shuli said. "I'll take you dancing."

"I'd love that," I said.

When I got to the room, Iggy was asleep, the book open on his chest. I placed it on his backpack, and slid into the mattress beside his, inching closer and closer until our legs touched. I could smell his minty breath, his soothing scent. He jerked awake and whispered, "Did you have a good talk?"

"Yeah," I said. "I'll tell you about it tomorrow."

"I'm glad." He turned onto his side. "Good night, Zorki."

"Good night, Iggy." I stared at the ceiling for a moment, replaying some of our conversation and thinking back to the pages I'd read. I knew what I needed to do. Where to find better answers. "I should talk to Bruria," I said into the dark room, but Iggy was already asleep.

CHAPTER 28

YONI

ONCE AGAIN, TSAFRIRA asked him to stay after class, her birdlike face severe. His essay was on the table between them, the mark hidden by her coffee mug.

"I read your essay. It was"—she weighed words—"interesting."

He looked up in anticipation.

"I didn't know you had a knack for writing."

Did he? Yoni sensed a "but" in her tone.

"But that wasn't the assignment."

"You asked us to write about someone who made an impact . . ."

"On the world."

"Well, she made an impact on me and other people. And I am a part of the world."

She sat back and folded her arms. "Okay. Let's say that's true. Where in this essay are you showing that impact?"

"By telling her story," he said, a little desperately. "It's a story of triumph. We never study stories like hers in school."

She tapped on the paper. "Where is it in the text?"

He didn't answer.

"What I read was a bunch of anecdotes, with no thought of a narrative or a thesis. In some places, it reads like a rant. Angry, personal."

"It *is* personal."

"The way you described the camps, for example. It lacked complexity, and it wasn't grounded in facts. The part about your uncle . . ."

He raised his gaze.

"It's added as an afterthought toward the end. Since you chose to refer to it, why not mention there had been inquiry committees that ruled out kidnapping? What about the other side of this?"

He stiffened. "What other side?"

"Look." Her voice softened. "I think it's great you're writing about your grandma and putting her story on the page. But at the end of the day, this does not meet the requirements." She slid the essay across the table. The mark 60% was written in red and circled on the top left-hand side. "I didn't fail you because the writing was strong. Do you read a lot?"

He shook his head no.

"Maybe you should."

HIS MOM CALLED him from the kitchen as he walked in. He kept walking, dropped his bag in his room. "I'm talking to you!" she yelled. He shuffled back and stood by the door, shoulders drooped.

"Your teacher called." She leaned against the kitchen counter with her hip, a spatula in hand, schnitzels sizzling in the pan. "Do you want to tell me what it was about?"

"What was *what* about?"

"What's with the tone?"

"I don't know what you're talking about."

She flipped the schnitzels. "She's worried about you. She said you were late to submit an essay and that it was messy . . ."

"That's her opinion."

She stared at him. "Her opinion is what counts."

"She basically told me Tata was lying."

His mom put down the spatula. "*What?*"

"She said, 'What about the other side?' when I mentioned Rafael . . ."

"You wrote about Rafael?"

"She was skeptical."

"That's news to you? People have always been skeptical about this."

"I'm entitled to write our story."

His mom sighed. "Of course you are, hayim sheli, but it's your final year and you've worked so hard."

He threw up his hands. "I don't care anymore."

"Well, I care!"

"Fine. Can I go now?"

"I need you to step it up in school, Yoni," she said firmly. "I mean it. No more staying out late on school nights. You're still living under my roof."

"Fine," he said, walking away.

Later, as he came out of his room to go to the bathroom, he heard Motti in the kitchen. "He's a good kid. He's been through a lot this year. Frankly, I think he's allowed some concessions."

Yoni stayed in the hallway, motionless.

"I'm going to find him some help," his mom said.

"Ask Zohara," Motti said.

"I'll call Mika tomorrow. I have her number somewhere."

"Mami," Motti said. "You need to speak to Zohara."

"It's not like she's calling me either."

"You're the older sister. It's been weeks."

He heard her walking away, out the kitchen door. He slipped away back to his room.

WITH HIS MOM tightening up his curfew, he had to jump through hoops to get to the peace rally in Tel Aviv on Saturday night, a school night. He made up an elaborate story about a science presentation he and Shlomi had to prepare for the next day, told his mom he'd be sleeping over there; they had so much work and they started late. That way, he could sneak in at night and tell her the next morning he changed his mind, felt like sleeping at home after all.

He didn't like lying to her, but what other choice had she left him?

Baruch was pumped about the rally. They were going to be a minority this time, representing the opposition. That's why it was important to have a decent-sized group. Either way, Baruch said, it couldn't get as rowdy as it had in Zion Square. "They already think we are violent and hot-tempered." Secretly, Yoni wished for a little shoving and pushing, especially knowing Rabin and Peres would be there, on stage, in close proximity. Whenever he saw Rabin's smug face on the news or in the paper, he was filled with rage. How arrogant he was when he spoke about the protestors, calling them hooligans and "peace cowards"— what did that even mean?

The cafés on Ibn Gabirol Street were bustling with people who couldn't be bothered to take a stand, sipping espressos and beer and smoking cigarettes. Kings of Israel Square was packed, but the energy was different than other protests he had attended. People seemed happy, elated. There were a lot more women in the crowd, families too, children on their fathers' shoulders waving flags, boys and girls his age carrying signs—*Peace Now* and *Youth for Peace*—some even jumping into the city fountain as if this were a party. How naive they all appeared to him.

At the end, only six of them made it, Yoni, Baruch and four students he'd known from other protests. When they made their way through, people glared at them, policemen watched them closely, their kippahs attracting attention. Yoni nodded at the policemen hesitantly to defuse the tension. At some point, he saw cops pushing around a religious man. "What do you want from me?" he yelled. "This is a democracy." Two of the students removed their kippahs and stuffed them in the pockets of their jackets. He and Baruch exchanged looks. Wordlessly, they left theirs on.

They tried crying out slogans, but their voices were drowned out by the masses, so they just stood there with their signs held high over their heads: *This Is Not Peace* and *Only the People Will Decide*, which made one protestor chuckle in dismissal, pointing at the crowds surrounding them. "Looks like the people did." Baruch chain-smoked and muttered under his breath. "What kind of government puts up a demonstration against the people? And what's with all the singers? They need to draw people so badly, they made it into a music show. It's pathetic."

A group of Likud youth huddled across the street holding signs. "Should we be standing with them?" Yoni said.

Baruch shook his head, glancing at them with contempt. "That's the problem with the Likud, right there. They agree to be relegated to the fringes. They are going soft."

Still, two members of their group packed up their signs and walked over with an apologetic shrug.

The rally was moving at a leisurely pace: artists performed, politicians spoke and Yoni was growing bored. He knew it was going to be tamer than what he'd been used to, but he expected more passion. Why did they even bother coming? Even when Rabin gave a speech, thanking everyone for showing up, Yoni found himself tuning out. "I have always believed most people want peace, are willing to take a risk for peace," Rabin said in his monotone voice, and the crowd cheered, some chanting, "Rabin, King of Israel!" which made Baruch grunt. A long-haired blond singer Yoni vaguely recognized sang in a raspy voice about peace. The crowd sang along. Soon Rabin and Peres joined her, grossly out of tune.

When the song ended, the mayor was making closing remarks and people started leaving, including the remaining two students from their group. "Best to beat traffic," they said. Baruch raised his sign higher in some last, desperate attempt. Yoni did the same.

A burly guy with a ponytail and a tight T-shirt that read *Peace* walked by them a couple of times, then stood and read Yoni's sign demonstratively. "Why are you here?" he said. "To cause trouble?"

Yoni stared past him.

"You and your friend are not welcome here," the guy said.

"We have the right to be here like anyone else," Baruch said. A few people watched the interaction, but no one interfered.

"Take your stupid signs out of here." The guy lightly shoved the sign Baruch was holding. "Or I will make you."

Yoni sneered. Was this guy for real? Wasn't he aware of the irony? This was a rally against violence. The sneering caused the guy to refocus his attention on Yoni. "Did you hear what I said?" His face was so close, Yoni could smell his hot tobacco breath. Instead of backing off, Yoni took a small step forward, puffing his chest, even though the guy was much bigger, even though they were outnumbered.

"Yoni," Baruch said with a raise of his eyebrows.

The standoff lasted a few seconds. Yoni's heart raced. Finally, the guy dismissed him with a flick of his hand and walked away. Yoni was almost disappointed.

A festive song started blasting from the speakers. "Eretz Tropit Yafa." A Brazilian song that had been rewritten in Hebrew. *I have a beautiful tropical country.* People began dancing. Yoni felt enraged and reckless, annoyed at these people and their stupid songs. Under his feet, a discarded sign stamped with shoe prints read *Peace Now.* He picked it up and hollered to Baruch, "Matches!" and Baruch tossed him a pack. The fire caught quickly. Yoni threw the burning placard to the ground, satisfied by the warm glow, invigorated by the sight of the flames consuming the words. Baruch wrapped his arm on his shoulder, and he did the same, the two of them jumping and cheering as the sheet burned, screaming from the top of their lungs, "The people didn't sign!" Passersby looked at them with disdain.

A loud popping sound pierced the air, startling Yoni.

Once. Twice. Three times.

Yoni and Baruch exchanged quick looks.

The sound came from the direction of the stage. Louder than the murmur of the departing crowds, louder than the honking cars on Ibn Gabirol Street. Firecrackers? Gunshots? Could it be gunshots? Almost instantly, there was a shift in energy. The crowd scattered out, people ran, shoving him on their way out of the square. "What happened?" they yelled to one another. "Did you hear that?"

Men in dark suits rushed urgently to a spot by the stairs to city hall, falling to their knees, circling something on the ground. Someone. Yoni saw feet. He could swear he saw feet. An awful sinking feeling in his guts.

Someone was lying on the ground. Someone was shot.

Rabin?

Could it be?

Tata had been wearing her slippers when he found her, blue and furry, her feet splayed open.

The sounds of sirens moved closer, overlapping, their flickering lights reflected on the surrounding buildings, the entire square beating like a giant blue heart.

The big guy with the peace shirt was back, angrier now. "Look what you guys did!" he screamed in Yoni's face, spraying spit. His eyes were red and wet. Yoni shoved him lightly, just to get him off, and was baffled when the guy stumbled back. He sprung back up and shoved Yoni. Yoni lurched at him with renewed vigor. The guy threw a badly aimed punch, lost balance, and Yoni wrapped his arm around his neck. They stood entangled in a strange embrace. "You piece of shit," the guy muttered under strained breath. "You ruined this country. You ruined everything."

A strong hand pulled Yoni by his collar and dragged him out of the crowd, pushing him to the ground, hard, face down. "Let me go!" Yoni shouted. "Don't touch me!"

"Bastard," someone said, spitting on the sidewalk beside him. "Shame on you."

Cold metal fastened around his wrists. A bony knee pressed on his back. To his right, Baruch was being handcuffed, chin to the ground. A flurry of running feet. A twisted cigarette butt, a popsicle wrapper. The policeman muttered through clenched teeth, "Stop resisting. You're making it worse."

Yoni remembered the guidelines to protestors and told himself to let go, surrender onto the filthy ground. When the cop loosened his grip, Yoni looked up and saw a half-circle of faces watching him, terrified, tearful. He let his cheek drop back onto the dirty pavement and closed his eyes.

CHAPTER 29

ZOHARA

THE BEDOUIN BEACH camp in Sinai that Iggy and I used to go to remained the same, a large restaurant tent set by the water with sun-faded rugs, cushions and low tables, surrounded by a few straw thatch-roofed huts, and a building with common bathrooms and showers.

After we dropped our backpacks in the hut, we reclined on the cushions in the restaurant, smoking, sipping dark, sweet coffee and staring into the sea, its deep blue color richly saturated against the faded yellows and reds. It was perfectly, startlingly quiet, no traffic, no electronics, just the buzzing of flies and the murmur of conversation. The visibility was great. You could almost see people walking on the Saudi Arabian shore.

After lunch, when the sun blazed, we waded into the water—cold even in the sweltering heat of August and much colder now. We stood there a minute, ankle deep, watching colorful fish swirling around our feet. Back at the restaurant, we sank lower into the cushions as hours passed, the heaviness of the pot weighing on our eyelids. There was nothing to do in Sinai but this. We spent the afternoon playing backgammon and chatting with a couple of Brits on vacation. I browsed through a historical novel someone left behind. At some point, I lay down, resting my head on Iggy's thigh.

"It must be freezing in New York now," Iggy said.

I let myself imagine New York for a moment, me strutting on its sidewalks in my peacoat and boots, leaves crinkling under my feet. "I love fall in New York. It's my favorite season."

Iggy lit a smoke, nodded in a distanced way.

"This beats New York, though," I hastened to add. "Something about the desert; it instantly makes me feel calmer. And my curls look perfect here. Every day in the desert is a good hair day."

Iggy eyed my hair. "You're right. They do look perfect."

"See? I should move here."

He gave a short laugh. "And do what?"

"Write a book?"

"Your dissertation?"

One of the Brits from before jumped into the sea without hesitation and started swimming, splashing water. "Honestly, I'm not sure I'll ever finish that."

"Just like that?"

"No, not just like that," I said, slightly annoyed. "I've been agonizing about this for a long time." I pushed his shoulder slightly and he swayed dramatically. "Why don't you stay here with me? We can wait tables. Live a simple life."

His laugh was discordant. "Seriously though, are you thinking you might stay? In Israel, I mean?"

I gazed at the water. "I don't have a good reason to go back."

Iggy raised his chin and scratched his growing beard. His beard grew so fast. I used to love watching him shave, maybe because I'd never seen that at home. My dad had a thick white beard, stained turmeric from traces of Yemeni soup. I loved the way Iggy tilted his head to see his neck. It was a gesture that mirrored the appreciative way he looked at me when I got out of the shower wrapped in a towel or got dolled up to go out. I missed that look.

"Sometimes I wonder what would have happened if I'd never left," I said. I was talking about moving to New York, but also, I was talking about us.

Iggy gave me a doubtful look. "You were always going to leave."

"Maybe not."

"The first time I came to Sha'ariya, you had that poem by Dahlia Ravikovitch written in watercolor and taped to your wall." He closed his eyes in concentration. "'Don't leave traces . . .' Something something, 'I'm not staying anyway . . .'"

"'Do not leave traces,'" I recited. "'Do not scatter signs. I'm not staying in this place anyway. Do not write letters. Do not collect souvenirs—'" I stopped. "Are you sure it was this one?"

"I read it and thought, Shit, this girl is going to leave you and break your heart into tiny pieces. If anything, I might have slowed you down."

My heart ached hearing this. "Don't say that. You were perfect."

He smiled. "That's beside the point."

The pot knocked us out. We headed to the hut for a nap. When I woke up, it was dark out and my belly was rumbling. I touched Iggy's shoulder. "We should get up."

He leaned on his side to check his watch. "Shit, yeah. It's getting late." He sat up and started rolling a joint. I remained lying, staring at the straw roof.

Iggy glanced at me. "You okay?"

"Just thinking of what you said."

"What did I say?"

"About me leaving. I don't know. Maybe staying in Israel could be a good change. Break the pattern."

He chuckled.

"What?"

"Don't be mad."

"Why would I be mad?"

"It could also mean the opposite. Like, by staying here, you're leaving again. New York, school, Zack."

"It's different."

"How?"

I wrinkled my forehead, trying to articulate it. "Because it feels like a return to something that is more me. It's not driven by the same motive. If it makes sense."

"You're not running away this time is what you're saying."

"Exactly."

We smoked the joint lying down, fingers touching when we passed it. I could hear our inhales, the crackling sound of leaves burning, an occasional popping seed, the whooshing of waves. The evening deepened and now there was no light at all, only a thin belt of moonlight creeping over our bodies on the bed. Soon, the generator would start its loud humming.

Iggy glanced at me. "It's so good talking to you, Zorki. I've missed you."

"Really?"

"You sound surprised."

"I've hardly heard from you lately."

"Work's been crazy. But whenever I did call, I got the machine. I thought you needed space. That you wanted to be alone."

"God, no." I sucked on the end of the joint, feeling the sting of fire on my lips. "Grief is fucking lonely."

"What about Lizzie?"

"We're not speaking."

"What? Why?"

"A stupid fight. Doesn't matter. Besides, I had Lizzie and my mom when my dad died, and I still felt alone."

"Truth."

I stared at the wooden beam along the roof. "Everyone says time helps, but honestly, it's getting worse. I keep finding out how little I knew of my mom and it's killing me." I inhaled deeply. "Did you hear of that woman who died in the pigua in Jerusalem?"

Iggy shook his head no.

"For a few days after she died, her identity kept fluctuating. First, she was the terrorist, then, she was a German tourist."

"What? How?"

"They couldn't identify her because nobody, not her daughters, not her ex-husband, not her friends, thought she had a reason be on that bus at that time. For a whole week, no one even knew she had died."

"Sad."

"It made me think of my mom."

"Your mom saw Yoni and the girls every day."

"I know. But still, this woman died, and no one knew why she was on that bus or where she was going. Did she have a lover? A job? It feels like that with my mom. Like every day her story keeps shifting. And there's so much I don't know. Might never know." My voice quivered. "I'm just so mad at myself. Why didn't I ask? Why wasn't I here?" I broke down in tears.

Iggy pulled me toward him and hugged me hard, as though he was trying to squeeze the pain out. I buried my face in his chest, and when I raised my head, his sweater was completely soaked with my tears. "Shit," I said. We laughed.

I looked at Iggy, his beautiful, rugged face, and he held my gaze, no longer laughing. He closed his eyes, eyelids fluttering, as if he couldn't bear to look at me. My breathing shallowed and quickened. I leaned over his chest and kissed him. He opened his eyes. "Zorki, that's a bad idea. You're not okay."

"This is helping." I leaned to kiss him again, but Iggy moved his face away and then swung his legs down to the floor.

Oh, shit.

He got up, grabbed his smokes and lighter. "I'm going out."

What the fuck just happened?

I placed both palms over my head. Shit. Shit. Shit. This wasn't how it was supposed to go. When I recomposed, I stepped out. The night was quiet and chilly, the sky studded with a million stars. I clutched my sweater around me as I trudged toward the restaurant, found Iggy smoking on a hammock, facing the sea. "Um, it's super late. I'm going to order some dinner before they close the kitchen."

"I think we should head back." His voice was flat.

My heart sank. "Right now?"

"Yeah."

"Are you mad at me?"

He turned to look at me, forehead wrinkled. "Come on, Zorki. I'm with someone. You know that."

"Didn't stop us before."

"What are you talking about?"

"When I was visiting, remember? You knew I was seeing that guy in New York. And there was that other time when you were dating . . . what's her name? The actress? You practically jumped me then."

"This is different."

My chest caved. "It is?"

"Neither of us were serious back then," he said sharply.

"How was I supposed to know?"

"I told you I'm thinking of settling down."

"With *her*?"

"Why do you say it like that?"

I folded my arms over my chest. "I'm just surprised."

He sighed deeply. "God, Zorki. You can be so insensitive sometimes."

"So you *are* mad at me." Tears leapt into my eyes.

"No." He sat up on the hammock, slouched, legs on the ground. "I'm not trying to be a dick. I'm mostly mad at myself."

"You can go if you want. I'm staying."

"How will you get home?"

"I'll figure it out."

I wanted to say I wanted it to happen. That it meant something to me. But suddenly I wasn't sure. Was I confusing our friendship for something else? Seeking an easy fix to make my grief more bearable?

He got up. "I'm going for a walk."

I ordered dinner and sat down by the fire one of the waiters had started, fighting tears. Iggy was sitting on a rock by the water now, chain-smoking. I could barely eat, kept shooing emaciated cats from my left-over fish, then ordered coffee from the waiter.

The coffee was taking a while, even by Sinai standards. When I turned to look back, I noticed a commotion in the small, brightly lit kitchen. The workers had their ears to a transistor radio. The owner shushed the staff and glanced at me. Then they all looked at me.

He came out with my coffee. "Some bad news from your country," he said. "I'm sorry to say."

"What happened?"

"Someone shot your prime minister."

His words didn't arrange themselves into a coherent sentence. I wanted to believe he misunderstood, but I had this chilling knowledge in my guts that it was true. "Rabin? Who shot him? Is he okay?"

"I don't know. I'm sorry."

I walked toward Iggy in a daze.

. . .

ON THE DRIVE back we didn't speak. The road curved around bays and inlets, revealing glimpses of the sea, silver glimmers of the moon on its glassy surface. There was no life. The only light was the car's head-lights ahead. Above me, there were so many stars it was dizzying. I felt small and alone.

I tried finding a radio station, but it was all in Arabic. For the mil-lionth time in the past month, I wished I understood the language. At one point I managed to find a Jordanian station in English, but the re-ception was terrible. My arm got tired. I turned off the radio, opened the window, stuck my head out and screamed into the night.

Iggy gave me a startled look.

"Everything is so fucked." I leaned my head on the window ledge, tears streaming down. I was never good at praying but now I squeezed my eyes shut and prayed. Please, God. Or whatever. Please.

THE BORDER CROSSING glowed fluorescent in the dark. A clump of teary Israelis stood at the entrance. We walked toward them, steeling ourselves for the news. "Rabin is dead," a long-haired guy said to us, his body shaking with sobs. "They just announced."

I put my palm on my mouth. Iggy held me, both of us crying.

"This country is finished," someone said.

We wept and we hugged: a bunch of strangers at a fluorescent-lit border crossing in the desert in the dead of night. A crossing made pos-sible thanks to another peace process fifteen years ago. To our right, the waters of the Red Sea gently lapped the shores.

By the time we got into Eilat, we knew the murderer was a twenty-six-year-old from Herzliya, a law student, a religious guy. He shot Rabin three times at the end of the peace rally at Kings of Israel Square. The radio played some of Rabin's last words, "I was a military man for twenty-seven years. I fought for as long as there was no chance for peace. I believe there is a chance now, a great chance, and we must take advan-tage of it." I couldn't stop crying.

"I'm going to stay with Shuli tonight," I said. "I'll take the bus to Beer Sheva tomorrow to pick up my car."

Iggy looked at me tiredly. "Are you sure?"

"If you're okay to drive alone, that is."

"Sure."

"I mean, you're welcome to stay, too." God, the awkwardness.

"No, no. I need to go home."

He wanted to be with her.

Iggy pulled over by a pay phone and made a call. I waited in the car, looking the other way. When he finished, I dialed Shuli's number. "Zorki, hayati. Are you okay?"

"No. Are you?"

"Can you believe the murderer was Yemeni? Shame."

I said nothing.

"I can't believe it," she said. "How could he have been one of us? Yemenis aren't violent. We are known for being quiet, moderate. We don't make a fuss. Everyone always says that. That is why they took our children."

"It's just one person," I said. "One lunatic."

I thought of how my mother used to tell me every time a Yemeni Jew made the news—singers and actors, of course, but also a high-school student who won the International Bible Contest and a woman who died in a terrorist attack—with pride, with sorrow. As though all Yemenis were her long-lost siblings.

Shuli sighed heavily. "Nir called for you. Twice in the last hour. What a sweetheart. He said it was urgent. He left a message on your machine."

I called my mom's number to retrieve the message. "Zohara," his voice was colorless, grave. Still, I was so happy to hear it. "Yoni was arrested. I'm with him. He doesn't want to call your sister. I told them I'm his lawyer. Just get here as soon as you can. If you can."

"Change of plans," I said to Iggy when I got in the car. "I need to get to Tel Aviv ASAP."

CHAPTER 30

YONI

THEY WERE ESCORTED to the police car cuffed like criminals, Yoni staring down at the sidewalk, to avoid the glares. When they heard the confirmation on the police radio that Rabin had been shot, his stomach knotted.

"Don't say anything," Baruch mouthed to him.

What could he possibly say?

The officer shoved him roughly into the back seat and bent down to remove his cuffs. A cigarette dangled from his lips, acrid smoke blowing in Yoni's face. Yoni rubbed his sore wrists. His palms were scraped and bloody from the fall. When the cop came around to Baruch's side, Baruch said, "You know he's a minor, right?" The policeman gave Yoni a long look. "ID?" Yoni pulled it from his back pocket.

"Doesn't justify your behavior." The officer handed Yoni back his card. "You people think you own this country. You don't go to the army, but we have to fight for you and protect you."

You people? Did he mean religious?

As they drove through the jammed streets, accompanied by the whining of the sirens, Yoni looked at the bars separating him from the two policemen in the front, the large studded hamsa dangling from the front mirror. How did he get here? What was he doing inside a police car?

A wave of anger toward Tata washed over him. Maybe he wouldn't have ended up here if she hadn't died. If she hadn't left him all alone.

An official statement came on the radio, from Rabin's bureau chief outside Ichilov hospital. The driver turned up the volume and both cops leaned in. It felt like the entire country quieted down a notch in anticipation. "The government of Israel announces in dismay, great sadness and deep sorrow the death of Prime Minister and Minister of Defense Yitzhak Rabin, who was murdered by an assassin tonight in Tel Aviv." A deep collective wail from the surrounding crowd followed. *"Noooo!"*

"These fuckers." The driver slammed the dashboard with his fist. "May they go to a thousand hells."

Yoni felt the echo of that wail amplified in his own heart. A chill went through his body. Baruch turned to look at him, eyes widened in an exaggerated shock. Yoni didn't know how to read his expression. He looked away, blinking back tears.

The protests he'd been to these past few weeks all ran through his head, the gleeful chants, "Death to Rabin." The coffin carried by protestors, supposedly to symbolize the death of Zionism. The death curse Hodaya told him about.

How could he not have seen any of this coming? How did he get here?

Dear God. How did he get here?

"Did they say who did it?" The other cop asked. "Arab? Jew?"

The driver shot Yoni a disapproving look through the mirror. "I bet you a million bucks it was one of them."

AT THE STATION he was placed in a room on his own. "Don't worry. I'm going to call Nir," Baruch yelled as they pulled him away. "He's a lawyer."

The room was small and bare. A table and two chairs. It smelled strongly of antiseptics. He paced around the room, counting his steps. There were exactly thirty-two. He could feel the familiar scratch in his throat. When he tried making a sound, it came out raspy. He sat down, practiced breathing from his belly, eyes closed. Every few seconds he remembered: Rabin was assassinated. He had been arrested. This was a police station. Weariness overwhelmed him. He wished he were at home, in his bed.

He leaned his head on the table and cried.

HE WAS WOKEN up by the metallic echo of the door of being unlocked. A gruff old detective with a head of silver hair heaved himself opposite him.

"I'd like to see a lawyer," Yoni said immediately.

The detective narrowed his eyes. "Why, do you need one?"

Yoni hesitated for a moment, but then repeated, his voice breaking, "I want to see a lawyer. Also, I'm a minor."

The officer sighed. He got up, dragging the chair back loudly and muttering as he walked out.

When Nir walked in an hour later, Yoni almost fell into his arms with gratitude. "Don't worry," he said. "I'll get you out."

The clock at the station read 4:30 A.M. when they stepped out of the investigation room. Zohara sprang up from the row of plastic chairs and rushed to him, her face ashen, her eyes puffy. He was so much taller than her now, she had to pull him down to embrace him properly. "Are you okay?" she whispered, slapped a kiss on his cheek.

He teared up. "I didn't want this to happen."

"Of course you didn't."

"We were just protesting. I didn't think it would get to this."

Zohara grabbed his face with both her hands. "It's not your fault." She sent Baruch an icy glare over Yoni's shoulder.

"What are you looking at me for?" Baruch said. "It's not like I pulled the trigger."

"I wasn't talking to you." His aunt took a step toward Baruch, pointing a finger to his face. "And don't you ever, *ever*, come near my nephew again. Do you understand?"

Yoni gave her a look: surprise and appreciation. He'd never seen that side of her. Baruch raised both arms. "Whatever." He muttered, "Psycho," as if to himself.

"Hey." Nir's voice was very deep and loud. "Don't talk to her like that." He put his arm on Zohara's back, lightly turning her away from Baruch. "Come. I'll give you two a ride."

NIR DROPPED ZOHARA and Yoni off outside Yoni's house. The early morning air was cool, and sunrise tinted the sleepy street a soft pink. Birds started singing. Yoni looked up at the building and then down at the asphalt. "I can't go in," he whispered, his voice now almost gone. "She's gonna kill me."

"She might." Zohara gave him a half smile. "But you'll be okay."

He perched against the stone fence, arms folded on his chest. "I don't know." Everything he thought he knew these past few weeks had crumbled, like a carefully constructed tower of cards, built of his convictions, his unwavering truths. He was left standing in the wreckage, unable to make sense of it.

Zohara joined him by the fence. "I'll let you in on a little secret. Nobody knows anything. All the adults around you? We know nothing. And those who claim they do are full of shit."

He snickered.

"Personally, I think it's much more interesting that way." Yoni looked at her, hopeful. "If you already knew everything, what's the point of living? That's why I used to like academia. Before it sucked the life out of me, that is. It was a place to ask questions."

Yoni liked following guidelines. He liked that the map had been laid out for him. He needed things to be structured, planned, so he wouldn't get lost. He thought of the term *hozer betshuva,* used for those who became religious. He knew it literally meant returning to God, repenting; but *tshuva,* commonly, also meant an answer. It made sense to him. By becoming religious, one was offered answers. Now he understood, also, why those who abandoned religion, turned toward a secular life, were said to be "returning to question." He used to find it sad. Why would anyone want that? Choose that? But now he reconsidered. Maybe a life of questions was, at the very least, more realistic.

Zohara wrapped her arm around his shoulder. "Your mom loves you so much. Do you know how lucky you are? To have her as your mom?" She pulled him closer. "I know it's hard to believe but I remember being seventeen"—Zohara rolled her eyes dramatically—"and feeling misunderstood and alone. I mean, I *was* actually alone. You know I was sent away to a boarding school when I was fourteen, right?"

He eyed her. *Sent away* was never how he thought of it. The story he heard growing up was that his aunt—his privileged, distant, American aunt—attended this fancy school in Jerusalem.

"I guess what I'm trying to say is that I know what it's like to feel like an outsider in your own family."

Tears welled up in his eyes again. He looked away, tried to steady the quiver in his lips.

"You're not alone," Zohara said, softly.

CHAPTER 31

ZOHARA

LIZZIE WAS SCRUBBING the kitchen cupboards so hard, I was worried their color might come off. The smell of bleach was overwhelming. Just like my mother. Cleaning as a form of meditation. Cleaning as a way to gain control. Cleaning to calm the mind.

Just like me.

The radio was on, so she didn't hear us until we were standing at the door. She dropped the rag on the counter, grabbed Yoni, then pushed him away, looking him over as if to make sure he was in one piece. She smacked his arm with her open palm. "What were you thinking?"

"I'm sorry, Ima," he said, bursting into tears.

She clutched him again, this time not letting go.

Eventually, Yoni went to shower and sleep, and Lizzie turned to me. "Coffee?"

"Yes, please."

She turned on the kettle and grabbed two cups from the cupboard. "Thank you for bringing him home."

"Of course."

"What happened?"

"It got a little rowdy," I said. "You know how demonstrations can get."

She shook her head in disbelief. "It doesn't sound like Yoni." These were my exact thoughts when Nir had told me at the station. But how well did I know Yoni, really? I didn't know my mom. I barely knew my sister. I thought I knew Iggy.

I did not know my country anymore, either. Our prime minister was assassinated last night. This was the kind of thing that happened in other places. Unstable, fucked-up, faraway places.

The kettle boiled. Lizzie poured water and milk into two cups and heaved herself on a chair beside me. "You warned me about that Baruch guy. And I didn't listen."

"You've had a lot on your plate."

"I'll call Mika, ask her to recommend a therapist," she said, and pushed the sugar bowl toward me.

I sweetened my coffee and stirred. "I'm sorry I haven't been more helpful. I'm sorry I was self-centered."

She leaned over the corner of the table and squeezed my hand. "It's okay," she said. "Your mom just died."

I laughed and cried simultaneously.

THE NEXT DAY, Tali picked me up from the bus station in Beer Sheva. Her face was crestfallen. We didn't have to say anything. Everywhere I looked, I saw the same expression on people's faces: disbelief, sorrow, despair. We were all orphaned now. Not just me. She dropped me off at the garage and waved at Khaled.

I leaned toward her window. "Thank you for everything."

"You know, Nir called after you took off."

"Yeah, I saw him since."

"I told him you went to Eilat with some guy."

I chuckled, not understanding. "Some guy?"

"What was I supposed to say?"

"No, it's all good." What was she getting at? The exchange felt oddly hostile.

"Listen, Zohara. You seem like a nice person, so I'll be frank. I've known Nir for a long time. We're like family."

"Okay?"

She gave me a level look. "He likes you."

"We're just friends."

"He likes you," she repeated. "And he talks about you. He called to tell me you may be coming. Then he called to ask if you came. He was checking on you."

I said nothing.

"What I'm saying is if you're not into him, don't string him along, and . . . you know, don't be an asshole."

I twisted my face in part confusion, part offense. "You don't know me—"

"But I know *him*. He's the greatest guy I know. And I don't want to see him get hurt."

I resisted the eye roll. "Duly noted."

"Anyway, don't take it the wrong way. I'm just looking out for him."

"I get it." I didn't know what else to say.

ON THE DRIVE back, the radio was broadcasting Rabin's funeral from Jerusalem. The sky was yellow, fittingly grim. Clinton finished his speech with "Shalom, haver." *Goodbye, friend.* I inserted one of my mother's tapes into the player. Her mournful voice filled up the car, somehow comforting right now. I drove and wept.

When I got to Sha'ariya, I saw Nir carrying cases of produce into the store, his biceps bulging out from his sleeves. The sky clouded over in the west. He stopped to chat with Goreni, the box still in his arms, and burst into a generous laughter at something Goreni said. My heart quickened. Could Tali be right? As I was about to turn into my mom's street, he saw me and waved.

I rolled down my window, turned the music down.

He leaned over to look at me through the window. "How's it going? How's Yoni?"

"Okay. You?"

"You know. Everything is terrible. Smoke?"

"Um . . ." I looked at the rearview mirror but there were no cars behind.

He followed my gaze. "Or not. You sure you're okay?"

"Yeah. It's just, like you said, everything."

A car sped down the street behind me.

"Go," he said, tapping the top of the car.

I turned the music back up. The car crunched gravel as I inched down our street. As I parked by the gate, I could see Nir behind me, grabbing more cases. I realized that during the past few weeks, the one thing I could count on to be easy and effortless and reliable and, yes, delightful, was my relationship with Nir.

My mom stopped singing abruptly as I was about to turn off the engine. I heard her breathing, the familiar sound of our house door opening. I tensed. This was the first time I'd heard anything on the tapes other than her singing and the occasional creaking of her chair. My heart clenched at the sounds of her alive. I heard the tapping of foot-steps, a man's voice humming. Who? Then my mom called, "Yaqub? Is that you?"

What?

My skin broke into chills. I turned up the volume to maximum and stared at the tape in anticipation, afraid to move, to disturb the moment. There was shuffling, a chair being pushed back. *Please don't stop. Please don't stop.* And then, the quiet tap of my mom's finger pressing the stop button as she rises to embrace her returning lover.

No, no, no. I rewound, listened more carefully in case I missed something. I picked up the tape cover with trembling fingers, but it was unmarked. It looked newish. I rewound again, to the beginning of the session. There was nothing else.

I hurried inside the house, rummaged for no good reason at the pile of envelopes in the basket by the door; nothing but bills and junk. I paced in her room, opened her bedside drawer and searched through it again. I couldn't call Iggy. Shuli already told me everything she knew. Bruria was the only one who could help me.

What I really wanted, I realized with startling clarity, was to go back to the grocery store and have that smoke with Nir, tell him everything.

Then I remembered something I'd just seen. I went back to the bas-ket and grabbed the stack of mail, flicked through it until I found the envelope, and held it up.

It was a bill from Beit Ora, addressed to Mr. Yaakov Hason.

CHAPTER 32

ZOHARA

"ZOHARA, COME IN," Mr. Hason said, as if he was expecting me. I had knocked on his door so lightly, thinking he must not be home. I hadn't seen him at all these past few weeks.

The room was tidy and sparsely decorated: a bookshelf neatly arranged with books, a single bed with a checkered blanket. One window, facing the same guava tree, provided diffused daylight. A stainless steel Turkish-style coffee pot glinted on the stove, smelling like fresh coffee. He gestured at it. "Coffee?" I nodded.

He stirred a spoonful of sugar into the pot and let it boil again.

"You're a writer," I said, as if this was what mattered.

He chuckled. "I don't know about that."

"The stuff you have at my mom's . . . it's really good."

He turned, spoon in midair, eyes rounded. "You read it?"

"Twice."

"Well, that's embarrassing." He took off his wool flat cap and scratched his head. It was full of white hair, not a bald spot in sight. I could see him adding up everything, understanding.

"I hope you don't mind. I didn't know it was yours when I found it."

"I never share my work with anyone. I mean, except for your mom."

His face crumpled; loss written all over it.

He poured coffee into two small glass cups. "Hawaij?" He held open the jar. I nodded, though I never took it. He mixed some of the fragrant Yemeni spice mix into our cups and gestured toward the two chairs that constituted his living room. I sat upright, hands on knees.

Everything I wanted to ask him was jumbled in my head. Every now and then, I had to reimpose his body, his face, on the stories I read, the things I imagined, the poems she wrote. It was him, all along. Mr. Hason. This small, elegant man who lived in our shed for the past couple of years.

"Have you written anything else?"

He motioned at the wooden desk in the corner. A towering pile of papers was stacked against the wall.

"What do you write about?"

"Yemen, the camp, my childhood." The Hebrew in his mouth was richly accented.

"A book."

He squirmed in his seat. "I'm not sure what it is."

"And these stories you gave my mom? Were they a part of the book?"

"Maybe." He looked at his cup. "Your mother loved when I read to her. She loved hearing it over and over again. Sometimes we read other things, too, poetry, novels."

"Really? I had no idea my mom read."

"She taught herself the alphabet too, eventually, but it was too hard for her beyond a newspaper headline. She preferred when I read to her. We watched a lot of movies together, too. It was something we shared, that love of stories, the curiosity about the world."

I scoffed a little. "Are you sure we're talking about my mom?"

He looked at me with surprise. "Absolutely."

I sipped from my coffee. It was both sweet and spicy. "I just never saw that side of her. I mean, you moved around, you studied . . . She stayed with him all those years. Why didn't she leave?"

Mr. Hason's face hardened. "You cannot compare. I'm a man. She was a married woman. A mother in a very traditional society. And divorce wasn't common or acceptable back then. It was different times. A different culture."

"Of course." I was filled with shame. "You're right."

"She traveled," he said. "She sang. She wrote. She took some liberties in her songs. She was being rebellious within the confines of what she was allowed."

"Rebellious? How?"

"Just voicing a woman's pain in a culture that silenced their voices was subversive. That alone was a form of protest."

I thought of the lines Nir found explicit. Of the way Shuli described my mother as a girl. I reexamined my memories of her from the last few years, how happy she was when I saw her in New York, her wide smile in the photos I found from Rome, her new love of gardening. Rain started tapping on the roof, hesitantly at first, then harder.

Mr. Hason looked at me and his eyes reddened. "I'm sorry," he said, looking away. "You just . . . you look so much like her."

"I know," I said. We sat in silence for a minute. I glanced at him again and back at my cup. "How could you stay in love with someone after all this time?" I blurted.

Mr. Hason laughed, a big, kind-hearted laugh. "Don't be mistaken, I lived my life. Saida kept popping into my head every now and then. Sometimes these were the times I wrote. Other times, I'd push the thought away and go on with my life. I loved my wife. And I believed I was over Saida. But when I saw her . . ."

"Where was it?"

"In Beit Ora." He closed his eyes and inhaled as if still unbelieving. "She was standing at the counter like a regular person, not a figment of my imagination. It was a miracle. Truly." He stared out the window as if reliving it. "I wrote about it recently."

"Can I read it?" I said, leaning forward in my seat. "Please?"

YAQUB

Petah Tikva, 1993

HE HAD KNOWN for some time he needed to put Ruth into a home. Weeks. Maybe months. Every time, he delayed it. Just a bit longer. It was his job to take care of his wife, after all.

He had already been grieving her by the time the stroke happened. The early onset Alzheimer's had stolen her from him piece by piece. But there were days, moments, when she was back, where he saw glimpses of her spirit, of her character, of the girl she'd once been.

Now, she needed twenty-four-hour care. The woman with whom he'd shared thirty-five years of his life. The mother of his children. Strong, dedicated, hard-working, loving Ruth. Gone.

Beit Ora had an excellent reputation. Eventually, he'd rent a cheaper place nearby so he could walk to visit her daily, sell their four-room apartment in Ramat Gan to help pay for the care facility. It was too big now anyway, too lonely. And he liked the idea of living in a Yemeni neighborhood again, craved the companionship, the community, after years of living in Ramat Gan, where everyone around them was Iraqi. When he first walked the streets of Sha'ariya, the sounds of prayer from the synagogue were comforting in their familiarity, and on Friday evening, Shabbat songs emanated from the houses, along with the aroma of Yemeni soup. Everything about this place already felt like home.

For the first month, he went straight to Ruth's room on the third floor, took the stairs to keep himself active. They watched TV together, him holding her hand, commenting on things on the screen as if they were at home and she could respond. Some days his sons would join him, and they'd chat over her limp body.

That day, he came earlier than usual. He had taken the morning off to go to the passport office. His sons were taking him for a weekend in Paris for his birthday. He and Ruth had dreamt of going together. When he arrived, Ruth was having lunch in the dining hall with her nurse.

"Go eat," the nurse urged him. The food wasn't appealing, but he got up anyway, just to move around, rather than watch his wife being spoon-fed by a nurse the way she used to feed his sons. He idled by the display as if considering the flat pale schnitzels, the bean stew, the yellow lentil soup, the mashed potatoes, and then he raised his eyes, and she was there.

Saida.

Time didn't stop. The enormity of that moment, a once-in-a-lifetime kind of moment, got crushed by the mundanity of life, the humility of the setting, the murmur of people, the dull clanking of plastic plates piling in the dish pit. Numbness took him over. He didn't fall to his knees. He didn't drop his plate (was he even carrying a plate?). He stood there thunderstruck, frozen, and then she saw him too. She gasped and placed a hand on her heart, and he said, too quietly, like an exhale, "Saida," shaking his head in disbelief, and then he placed his palm over his eyes, pressing onto his eyelids, thumb on one eye and middle finger on the other, as if to restart his vision, but when he removed them a second later, she was still there.

All these years he thought he'd seen her in crowds, on buses, in the market. He never imagined a care facility, a counter with sad-looking food between them, the fluorescent light in the corner flickering erratically. Saida smoothed down her apron, tucked a stray curl from underneath her hairnet, and he knew she did it for him. It filled him with satisfaction, that she cared, that she wanted to look beautiful. And she was. My God. Even with the hairnet, the stained apron, the wrinkles fanning from the corners of her eyes, the cheeks that had drooped, her forehead glistening with sweat. She was still so, so beautiful.

"Yaqub?" she said, her eyes moist.

He laughed and nodded, tears leaping into his eyes too.

Still the counter between them, the hum of appliances and the flickering fluorescent. A woman in scrubs walked by with a tray and asked, "Are you waiting?"

"No," he said, waving her ahead of him, and in his mind, he was thinking, I *have* been waiting. For over forty years. How is it possible so much time has passed? And Saida awoke from her frozen stance and wiped her face, now thoroughly wet with tears, and somehow managed to fill the woman's plate. More people lined up, pointing at the display, and Saida sent him an apologetic look, and he walked away and sat at Ruth's table and watched Saida's every move, and when the nurse spoke to him, he didn't answer because his heart wouldn't stop beating like a million clocks ticking *now, now, now, now.*

Eventually, he fled outside. He couldn't sit on that plastic chair next to his demented and infantilized wife and watch Saida who was still strong, still beautiful, and for whom he still had feelings, deeply buried, persistent and unspoken. That desire, that ache, that unfulfilled love—reignited.

How unbelievably stupid.

Sitting on the concrete bench in the courtyard, he could see her eyes searching for him while dishing out mashed potatoes and beans on people's plates. He was pleased. Let her be tortured for a moment.

He looked at his wife. Her glassy eyes were looking straight ahead, as if seeing him, accusing him, and he was washed with guilt. His wife, whom he loved, who was beautiful once, too, in her own way. Not like Saida, but who was? Saida's beauty was the kind that turned heads, that took men's breath away. But then again, her own husband preferred his first wife.

And it dawned on him.

Her husband.

She was married. They were both married.

He stood up abruptly, but instead of walking back in, he rounded the building and skipped over the bushes, scraping himself on a spiky shrub. He drove in a daze. At home, he found his calf was bleeding. He had left a trail of blood in the car, in the stairway, like a wounded animal on the run.

The next day, he drove all the way from work on his lunch break, but Saida wasn't there. "Works Sunday to Wednesday," said a heavyset woman with a thick Russian accent. Which meant he had to wait an entire weekend before seeing her again.

THE FOLLOWING WEEK, he came back. He took special care with his appearance. Pressed pants, a sweater vest that was tight on his belly. His tweed wool hat. He made himself see Ruth first, sat by her bed feeling guilty for his impatience, raised her hand—smelling different, of hospital soap and detergent—to his lips. He whispered he loved her.

When it was close to lunchtime, he walked downstairs, heart racing, entered the dining room and spotted Saida from afar, stirring a large pot by the stove. Graceful, slender. His heart thumped so fast he was worried; he wasn't a young man. He pressed his palm against it, imploring it to slow down. As if she could feel his eyes on her, she looked up and beamed. He walked toward her, feeling shy, awkward. "Yaqub," she said. "Why did you leave? I went looking for you!" And it took him a second to understand she meant last week, not forty years ago. Before he had a chance to reply, she wiped her hands on her apron and rounded the counter. They faced each other for a moment. Then she opened her arms with a question in her eyes and they hugged. Her small figure in his arms. Even after all these years, her smell was familiar, intoxicating.

"What are you doing here?" she said.

"My wife." He pointed at the ceiling. "Third floor."

"I'm so sorry. You know, my husband, he passed away many years ago."

"Sorry to hear that." Should he be feeling such glee at her loss? He forced down that feeling.

They stared at each other. Her wrinkles complemented her. So did her silver curls, which poked from underneath her net. He shook his head. "This is unreal."

Her eyes shone. "Wait." She went back, returning with her purse, dug out her wallet and pulled out the photo he had tucked in Rafael's crib all these years ago.

"You found it!" he exclaimed. "And the note?"

"It's at home. I think I started learning the alphabet just so I could read it."

"I wasn't sure. I worried the nurses might have found it before you did."

"You know, Rafael . . ." Her lips quivered and her eyes welled up.

"I heard." He was tearing up, too. "A few years ago, I saw Daud Sanani on the bus in Tel Aviv, and he told me. I am so sorry, Saida."

They embraced again, both crying.

"Can you take a break?" he asked her.

"I can't." She glanced at the clock. "But I'm finished in three hours. There's a nice café on the corner . . . if it's okay with you, I mean." Her face flushed. He made her blush.

"It's a date," he said, casually, as if it was all an ordinary exchange. "I will see you there."

CHAPTER 33

ZOHARA

BY THE TIME I got to Bruria's street, it was pouring. I ran until I stepped onto her front porch, catching my breath. Her hanging flowerpots swung wildly in the wind. She must have heard me because she opened the door before I knocked and looked me up and down.

"I'm wet," I said.

"That's okay," she said, pulling me into her arms.

We sat facing each other on her sofa, which was draped in a red embroidered spread, two cups of fragrant mint tea and a plate of ka'adid cookies on the coffee table in front of us. Bruria had given me wool socks to replace mine. A tuxedo cat napped next to an electric heater on the carpet.

I didn't waste time. "Why didn't you tell me about Mr. Hason?"

She bowed her head slightly. "It wasn't my story to tell."

"So my mother had an affair. My father had an affair," I said. "No wonder I can't hold a relationship."

Bruria shifted in her seat. "Your father didn't have an affair. I was his wife. Did you know my mother was the one who found your mother? Who introduced her to your father as a potential second wife?"

"Seriously?"

"Yeah, once it became clear I couldn't have children. And God knows, we tried and tried. I kept miscarrying, until even that stopped."

"Oh, Bruria. I'm sorry."

"At first Hassan said that if God wanted us to have children, he would have given them to us. He didn't want to take another wife. But his mother insisted. Your grandmother, may her memory be a blessing, was a force of nature." She smiled faintly. "She wasn't always easy on me, but it could have been worse."

"What do you mean?"

"Some women had awful mothers-in-law, who beat them—"

"Beat them?"

"Sure. On one hand, women were so oppressed in Yemen, and in that sense, our lives became better here. But on the other hand, in Yemen, as women grew older, they were the queens of the house! When we got married, we moved to our husband's family's home and were subjected to the reign of our mother-in-law. They had a lot of sway. At least, in their domain. And yes, some mothers-in-law abused that power."

"I had no idea."

"My mother met Saida at the well a few times, heard her singing, saw how good she was with her younger sister. She took a liking to her. She inquired and found out she was an orphan, and she thought, why not? This would save your mother, help your father and me. It was a perfect solution."

Against my better judgment, I blurted, "That's messed up."

Bruria exhaled loudly. "Zohara, try to be more open-minded."

I recoiled. Was she really asking *me* to be open-minded?

"Yes. I said open-minded. You're looking at this through the lens of today. Let it go. You're not a child anymore. Your father and I loved each other. It was so unfair we couldn't conceive, so painful. And to have to share him with your mother, and watch her give him a boy, see how joyous he was and know I couldn't give him that. And after all this, we came to Israel and realized our way of life was unacceptable here. That was such a shock." She stopped and looked away, out the darkened window. "And then we lost Rafael."

We. I had never thought of it as her loss, too. "Your parents grieved very differently. It just got them further apart. Your father was a shell of a man after that loss. He never got over it." Her bottom lip quivered.

"When you and Lizzie grew older, your parents worried about how you two might take our . . . arrangement, how it could affect you socially. I had to move out. I understood the reasoning, but it still hurt."

It seemed like she had been aching to tell me all of this for a long time. I never thought of her side of things.

"We were lucky, your mother and I. We loved each other. Other women weren't so lucky. Your mother was like a sister to me."

I swallowed tears. "I always thought of you as an aunt."

The cat climbed the sofa and settled in my lap. I laughed, surprised. "Do you mind?" Bruria said.

"Not at all." I patted him and he started purring instantly. "I'm sorry, Bruria," I said. What I really wanted to say was "I miss you."

"It's okay, binti," she said. "It's okay."

LIZZIE OPENED THE door and took one look at me, my wet clothes, my frizzy hair, my puffy, red face. "Oh my God, now what?"

She grabbed an old bottle of white wine from the fridge and poured it into two glasses. We sat on her balcony, wrapped in blankets. Lizzie chain-smoked, listened without interrupting me, shaking her head in disbelief.

"You really didn't know any of this?"

"No," she said and immediately reconsidered. "Well, maybe. I may have had a hunch about Mr. Hason. I saw them in the yard once. It was dark, so they didn't see me. Something about the way they were laughing and . . . I don't know, there was an intimacy there. And I'd seen her with other tenants she'd been friendly with. Men too. This was different. But I wouldn't admit it even to myself. Because it didn't make sense. That's not who my mother was. I saw what I saw, and I dismissed it as impossible, know what I mean?"

"I know exactly what you mean." From an apartment nearby, I heard Peres's booming voice, a replay from Rabin's funeral earlier that day. "It makes me sad. That we didn't know her. Or that *I* didn't know her."

"How many of us really know our parents? Especially old Yemeni parents. Especially women. They didn't want to be known. They were taught to be quiet, to take no space. They believed their stories had no value. I used to ask Ima about her life, and she kept saying, 'There's nothing to tell.'"

"I remember when I first realized it didn't have to be like that." I fiddled with the fringes of the blanket. "That some people actually talk with their mothers. Like, Mika and her mom. Or Shuli and her boys. I never thought to consult with Ima on anything, you know?"

Lizzie blew out smoke. "When I was talking to Yoni earlier, I realized I was in danger of mimicking that kind of relationship with him. It's not what I want for my children."

"I always assumed you and Ima were closer."

"Only in the last few years, but even then, never like a friend. Like, I would never confide in her if I had issues with Motti. And she never shared anything intimate. The only thing I'd consult her on, really, was the kids." She squished her cigarette in the ashtray. "I can't believe she's gone," she said quietly.

I drank my wine, staring at the flickering blue of TV screens lighting up apartment windows. "The other day I was sitting at the beach with the staff and somehow we got into a conversation about first words. Someone's niece just said her first word, and people started saying, oh, my first word was this. My first word was that. Aba. Etz. Mayim. And I realized I had no idea what mine was, and even if Ima were alive, she probably wouldn't have remembered. She wasn't that kind of mom. Maybe it's both cultural and generational. Like, our parents never played with us on the carpet. We walked ourselves to school. We read ourselves bedtime stories. We were running around outside playing ball and dag maluach all day."

Lizzie chuckled. "I loved that game."

"And I got so sad," I said, unable to stop the tears from flooding my eyes. When she first died, I felt like I wasn't crying enough. Now all I did was cry. "That I don't know what my first word was, and now I'll never know."

"Your first word?" Lizzie frowned. "I can tell you that."

I sat up in my seat. "You can?"

"It's nothing exciting."

"Tell me!"

"It was otsa."

I stared at her. "That's not even a word!"

She laughed. "It was short for lo rotsa. I don't want. And you said it with one shoulder raised, pouty lips. Otsa. Otsa."

"So how did I get from that to being so obedient?"

"You?" She puffed air from her lips. "You were never obedient."

"Maybe not compared to you! But I went to the school she sent me to, and I was a good student. I did everything right."

"That school was a good choice for you," Lizzie said.

I made a face.

"You still don't think so? Even now, with the perspective of time?"

"Actually, I see more clearly the damage it has done. It distanced me from my background. It made me feel ashamed of my parents, of being Yemeni. I know it gave me better education, but honestly, I think the best thing for me would have been to stay home with my mother. I was a child. Can you imagine sending Lilach or Ortal away? And she did that after she'd lost a child! I can't wrap my head around that. Aba would have never let her send me."

"What are you talking about?" Lizzie gaped at me incredulously. "She did it for him!"

I twisted my face. "What?"

"He always spoke about how smart you were, how far you could go if only given the chance. Not me, of course, with my mediocre intelligence." She rolled her eyes. "But she truly thought that's what Aba would have wanted. In her mind, she was fulfilling his dying wishes."

I stared at her. "I never thought of that."

"For someone so smart, you can be such an idiot sometimes." She smacked the side of my head.

"Ouch." I laughed, rubbing the spot.

Lizzie downed her wine and eyed me. "Yaffa mentioned you and Nir have been hanging out."

"Yeah, a little."

"Interesting." She smiled in a meaningful way. "You know, I went to thank him for being with Yoni all night. He did it for you, didn't he?"

"Oh, I don't know. He's just a good guy." I didn't make eye contact. My cheeks tingled.

Lizzie gave me a narrow look. "Why are you being so weird?"

"I'm not," I said, a little too passionately.

"That's a strong reaction."

I squirmed. "I don't know. He's not like the guys I usually go for."

"You mean, Yemeni? From the neighborhood?"

"That's not what I meant," I said quickly. "Though he is *really* Yemeni. He even speaks in *het* and *ayin* sometimes, like, it slips into his speech. It's adorable."

Lizzie grinned, enjoying this a bit too much. "You like him!"

I pulled the blanket up to cover my face. "I guess I'm a little surprised by that myself."

We went back inside. I stood at the kitchen door so I could watch the TV in the living room, which kept playing clips from Rabin's funeral. Every time, a jolt of shock.

"I still can't believe it," Lizzie said, piling dishes into the dishwasher. I wasn't sure what she was referring to.

The camera panned over the grim faces of world leaders who flew in for the funeral. "Honestly, I feel like anything could happen now, and I won't be surprised anymore."

"Yeah," Lizzie said. "I keep thinking of Ima and Mr. Hason. Like, seriously, how could none of us have known?"

Yoni sat up from the living room sofa. He had been lying there the whole time, watching TV in the dark, and we hadn't noticed him.

"I knew," he said.

CHAPTER 34

YONI

HE WAS GROUNDED, his mom said. For life. But she didn't seem angry with him. It's not like he wanted to go anywhere or see anyone. He didn't even feel like going to synagogue anymore. The day he came back from the police station, he unceremoniously folded the kippah and hadn't put it back on since. Whatever resolve and certainty he had felt in the past few weeks had melted away. Strangely, there was some lightness in the unknowing, like a clenched fist had been unfurled.

At school, he sat alone at the far end of the bleachers eating his lunch and reading a book he had taken from the school's library. Despite his anger at Tsafrira's comments, her advice to read more books stayed with him. The librarian was eager to offer some of her favorites. *Scapegoat* by Eli Amir, *The Book of Intimate Grammar* by David Grossman, *The Kites* by Romain Gary.

The rest of the time he was plunked in front of the screen, watching the news. Maybe by watching closely, he could understand how he got there. How *they* got there. Pinpoint the moment everything changed. The world. His life. As if he could have done something to change the outcome, reverse history. As if he singlehandedly could have saved Rabin.

The same futile way he wished he could have saved Tata.

He watched boys and girls his age sitting on the ground at the square, the scene of the murder, where Yoni had been just a couple of days ago, feeling so righteous then, so sure of his way. The youth lit candles and sang. Many cried. Candles fringed the fountain and illuminated the stairs leading to city hall. Yoni wondered if joining them could have given him closure, but then he remembered the man in the shirt that read *Peace*. He was afraid of more glares. Especially looking the way he did. Even without the kippah, Yoni could see that the murderer looked a little bit like him. Yemeni. Dark, slim and tall. He could have been in any of the demonstrations Yoni attended. Any of the meetings. Yoni couldn't help feeling ashamed. Guilty by association.

The camera panned over the notes left by children and visitors. One note caught his eyes: *Father Yitzhak,* it said in childish handwriting. *We love you and miss you.*

Father?

"What will we do now?" one teenage girl sobbed, a little too fervently, he thought. "Who will guide us?" A psychologist on the news called it a collective orphanhood, which Yoni found odd. Rabin didn't strike him like a fatherly figure. Was everyone yearning for a father figure? Feeling deprived as he was? Was that a national sentiment? Feeling forsaken? Left behind?

It was then, lying in front of the screen in the dark living room, that he overheard his mother and aunt talking about Tata and Mr. Hason.

TATA DIDN'T TELL him everything. He was, after all, a child, and her grandson. She rarely spoke about Rafael, his uncle, but some days he found her sitting by the window, staring blankly at nothing, the house darkened. "Tata? Can I read the paper for you?" he'd try. "We can play cards, or shesh-besh."

"Not today, hayati," she'd say, her voice tired and hollow.

Other days she'd be angry, snappy. She'd walk around the house performing tasks with a permanent scowl grooved in the middle of her forehead. "It's this stupid bill," she'd say. "I don't understand this charge." Or, "I called the bank, and they dismissed me. They hear my accent and think I'm stupid."

When he was thirteen, he fell in love with Yaara, a serious, freckled girl he met at the conservatory, back when he was learning to play the flute. The day he confided in Tata, she told him about Yaqub, the boy she loved when she was young, who wrote beautifully and dressed well. "He was smart and curious," she said. "He wasn't like the other Yemeni boys." Tata sighed. "It was the best time of my life." She did not burden the story with the fact of her marriage, didn't mention the timing of it. He figured it out later, on his own.

"Why did you break up?" he asked.

She opened her eyes, busied herself with the laundry she was folding. "Sometimes even love can't prevail," she said, finally.

Some things he discovered by himself. Mr. Hason, for example. Being quiet, he had learned, gained you access to a world of secrets. He understood why Tata felt the need to hide it from him, from the world. People judged. Some things are better kept for yourself, she had said before. The whole world doesn't need to know your business.

One day, he came over and saw them sitting in the yard, drinking tea. "This is Mr. Hason," she said, her face open, beaming. "He's renting the back shed."

Mr. Hason shook his hand enthusiastically. The two of them buzzed with an inexplicable delight.

Later, he heard his mom talking to Motti about it. "It's good she has companionship. It's a good arrangement for her."

"Do you think there's more going on?" Motti asked.

"Don't be ridiculous," his mom said.

Yoni was in love with Sivan Damari then. Her hair smelled of green Hawaii shampoo, her curls burst out of her high ponytail like a fountain. After she moved away to Ra'anana, he walked around downcast and glum.

"If it's meant to be," Tata said, "you will find a way back to one another." It was a different outlook on love than what she had previously professed. And Tata herself was different. In a better mood, less angry, prone to bouts of laughter. Some evenings they'd watch sitcoms together and she laughed and laughed, tears running down her face.

Then, one afternoon, as he was making himself a cup of tea in her kitchen, he heard her calling, "Yaqub?"

Astounded, Yoni looked through the window at the yard, where his grandmother was crouched by the flower plants, wiping her forehead with the back of her hand, leaving a streak of earth. She looked up at someone. "Can you please get me some cold water, galbi?"

Yoni easily added up the facts. He filled a glass of water from the jug in the fridge and walked out, running into Mr. Hason in the hallway. "I got this."

When he handed Tata the water, she eyed him with surprise, and then slight alarm as she recognized her slip. "I forgot you were here, hayati," she said. A short, uneasy laughter. "You've been so quiet."

"Just doing my homework," he said.

She drained the glass and handed it back to him.

"Yaqub?" he asked quietly. She looked at him, her hand shielding her eyes from the sun, and there was a flash of confirmation in her eyes. She raised a finger to her lips. *Shhhh.*

He never asked more. He told no one. He added that story to the arsenal of stories he kept for her. He liked keeping her secrets; it made him feel special. Around Yoni, Tata and Yaqub were a little freer. They sat in the dining room together, watching TV side by side, an air of relaxed domesticity about them. He walked in on him reading to her. He saw Tata rubbing Yaqub's back in the kitchen, as he was making tea. Saw the way she looked at him, the love in her eyes, the glow on her face.

Yoni liked that he was able to bestow this upon her: this act of witnessing, this safety and ease, a space in which to love freely, with no judgment. In return, their story made him hopeful, believe love was possible.

THE PSYCHOLOGIST HAD AGREED TO SQUEEZE HIM IN ON short notice thanks to Mika. Her name was Miri. She was older than his mom, her silver hair wavy and down to her shoulders. Yoni thought they would talk about Tata, about his arrest, but she wanted to start in the beginning. She wanted to talk about his dad.

"I don't really know him," Yoni said. "He left before I was born."

"Do you wish you knew more?"

He picked at the upholstery with his nails. "I don't care."

"If he were here right now, what would you say to him?"

What would he say to him if he could? Was that why he lost his voice as a kid? Because of all the things he couldn't say to the man who wasn't there to listen? Who couldn't be bothered? Who never, not once, sent a birthday card? Seriously. A fucking birthday card. He felt the familiar tingling of heat spreading through his body, his jaw locking, his teeth clamping.

"Think about it," she said. "You can write it down if you like. Your mother tells me you're an excellent writer."

He looked up. She did?

ON THE DRIVE back, he peeked at his mom. She glanced back. "What's on your mind, hayim sheli?"

The traffic slowed down, the brake lights turning red one after the other. "Did my father hurt you?"

His mom turned her head sharply and looked at him, wounded.

"I'm not a kid anymore," he said. "You don't need to protect me."

She was quiet for a while, the muscle in her cheek taut. "He was always a bit possessive, but I thought it was romantic," she said finally. "What did I know? I was so young. But it got worse. I know it may be hard to understand how I let it get to this—"

"Not at all," he said. He knew what it felt like to have your life spin out of control, to look back and wonder, How did I get here?

"I didn't want to tell Tata. I didn't want anyone to know." She took a deep breath. "One day it got so bad the neighbors called the police. There was a policewoman there. She took me aside and told me to go to a shelter. While they took him to the station, I packed my stuff and went back to Tata."

"And he never came back for you?"

"He tried. Eventually I got a restraining order. I still worried. I hardly left the house during the last few weeks of my pregnancy. Then, one day, poof—" She blew air out. "He disappeared."

"Where is he now?"

"Last I heard he was living in Florida. But honestly, I didn't look.

Didn't want to know." She eyed him carefully. "But I can look into it. Help you find him if that's what you want."

He watched the reflection of the traffic lights on the wet pavement. "No," he said.

His mother seemed relieved.

"Do you ever look at me and see him?" His voice cracked.

"God, no." She grabbed his left hand, squeezing it. "You are *good*. You could never be like him, you hear me? You are kind and gentle and sweet."

His throat tightened. "I get angry sometimes."

"You're growing. And you've been through a lot. It's normal. You're such a good kid." This time, he liked her calling him that. "Sometimes I forget to worry about you because you're such a good kid. I'm sorry. I'll do better."

At the stoplight, she grabbed him by the shoulder and drew him closer to her, and for a moment he leaned sideways, over the gear stick, breathing in her familiar smell: baking and schnitzel and oranges.

"Listen," she said. "I hope you don't mind, but I read your essay."

"You went through my things?"

"Your teacher gave me a copy."

"And?"

"I loved it," she said. She turned the signal on to turn into Sha'ariya. "You know how I said your teacher's opinion is what counts? I was wrong. I bet Tata would have loved that you told her story so beautifully. That's what counts."

He nodded gratefully. "I think so too."

YAQUB

Petah Tikva, 1993

FOR A LONG time, all they did was talk, catching up on a lifetime of stories. They sat at the little café outside Beit Ora, more of a kiosk really, after her shifts. She drank tea stuffed with mint leaves and he drank black coffee spiced with hawaij. Saida pulled a small Tupperware from her purse with ka'adid cookies to dip. Sometimes their fingers touched as he grabbed a cookie or passed her the sugar bowl.

She told him about her daughters, her grandchildren. Zohara was doing a doctorate in New York, she said, beaming with pride. "Smart," he said. "Like her mom." And she laughed, bashful.

He told her about his three boys; the youngest, Shai, was studying to be a journalist. "He got the writing bug from you!" Saida said.

He told her, choked, about his cousin Saleh, who died in the Yom Kippur war, a war from which Yaqub had been spared when he broke his leg that same morning, test riding his bike with his sons in preparation for the holiday. He recounted his years of teaching in the desert, their move to Ramat Gan.

"And your writing?" she asked. "What ever happened with that?"

"Life happened," he said. "And you? Do you still write songs?"

"Sometimes." She blushed. "Just for myself."

The first time he grabbed her hand over the table, she drew it back and looked around nervously. He stared at his cup, cheeks burning. She removed imaginary lint from her dress.

"Would you walk with me?" he said one day when their cups were emptied, and he didn't want to say goodbye yet. It was a balmy winter day after a series of dreary ones, and the afternoon light was soft. Soon, they were walking together almost every day, through the fields that bordered the neighborhood, in the paths between the crops of corn and strawberries. They were alone, like they had been on the riverbank. And one day after many walks, as they strolled along, he took her hand and she let him. Their hands grew moist. She pulled it away eventually, wiped her palm on her skirt.

"Your wife," she said.

"Ruth was a wonderful wife. But she's been gone from me for years."

They stopped by the chipped wooden fence at the end of the fields. From there, they could see the highway, the cars zooming toward the airport, the curved hills of Rosh HaAyin, big-bellied clouds in the east. She drew circles on the ground with her foot like she used to do by the river. "I need time."

"I understand," he said.

What was time for him, anyway?

SEASONS CHANGED, SPRING arrived, the strawberries had all been harvested. Soon, summer would descend like a bully, making it too hot to walk outside.

"I've been writing again," he said to her.

"What about?"

For the first time, he told her he'd written their love story. "I dug it out and I've been revising it."

She stopped walking, eyes wide. "You must read it to me!"

On that riverbank a million years ago, she had said to him, "You are a writer. You should write a book." Many times in his life he had lamented the curse of his sharp memory, envied Ruth for her forgetfulness. But what if there was a reason for this affliction? What if he were meant to remember through writing the way the women remembered through song?

He started bringing his pages, reading out loud as they ambled along. When he read her of their first kiss, his voice quivered. He looked up and saw she was crying.

"Should I stop?"

She shook her head.

He wiped her tears with his finger. She didn't look away, didn't move. So he leaned over and kissed her wet cheek, then the other, tasting salt. When she didn't pull away, he kissed her forehead, then her eyes, then, finally her lips. Softly, again and again and again. And she kissed him back.

She kissed him back.

BY FALL, HE found a buyer for his apartment in Ramat Gan and Saida was helping him look for a place in Sha'ariya. "His wife is at Beit Ora," she explained to people, some who knew her. And they all nodded empathetically and congratulated Saida for her good deed. Yaqub felt fleetingly guilty.

One evening, after they saw a few apartments, they sat in his parked car outside her house, reluctant to part, and she said, "I've been actually thinking—I'm not sure whether it's appropriate to suggest."

He looked at her expectantly.

"You know the rental unit I have in the back? It's small and not fancy. And it's probably a crazy idea, but my tenant is leaving at the end of the month, and people are used to me having tenants, so maybe it won't look too suspicious . . ." She spoke fast, nervously.

"Yes," he said.

"Are you sure?"

He had never been more sure of anything in his life.

CHAPTER 35

ZOHARA

MIKA GAVE BIRTH to a baby girl on Shabbat morning. A swift birth, Avner had said on the phone, sounding deliriously happy. "You should have seen her, Zohara," he said. "She was amazing."

I got in the car and drove to Hasharon hospital. Mika was calm, beautiful, motherly, a new smile I had never seen before drawn on her lips. The baby, still unnamed, had a shrunken face that resembled no one but other babies. I watched in awe as Mika breastfed her, resenting the tug in my own nipples, and later, the strange vacancy I felt when I went to the bathroom and found a red stain in my underwear.

It wasn't the time or place to tell her everything that had happened these last few days, but I told her I found Yaqub. That couldn't wait. "Mr. Hason!" She gasped. "Oh my God. I spoke to him at the shiva. Lovely man."

"I barely remember him there."

"Imagine meeting the one person you know you're meant to be with," she said, wistfully, "and not being able to be with them for over forty years."

"Imagine thinking you know the person you're meant to be with," I said. "And then realizing you're an idiot."

Comprehension washed over her face. "Iggy?"

I told her what happened. "I feel so stupid. I can't believe I've risked our friendship."

She stretched out her free arm so I could hold her hand. "Maybe you needed to do that to really know."

ON THE WAY back, I drove by Nir's store, but he wasn't there. The academic year had started, as it does in Israel, after the High Holidays, so he must have been back at school. His mom caught my searching look and waved. I waved back. A car came from the other direction, and I swerved to avoid it.

At home, my mother's answering machine was blinking. I pressed the button, anxious. I had left Iggy a jumbled, apologetic message a couple of days ago, and he had yet to respond. When I heard his voice now, I sank onto the armchair, steeling myself. *Hey Zorki. What's up?* He sounded normal, good old Iggy. *Michal and I are heading to London for a few days tomorrow so let's talk when I get back, okay?* He paused for a moment. *Everything is fine. We're fine. Don't worry, okay? Love you, dumbass.*

I exhaled, my chest dropping with relief.

Another message. My subletter in New York offered condolences for Rabin. "I can't imagine what you're going through over there." She and her sister were interested in staying on, "if that's at all an option for you," she chirped in American, so out of place in my mom's living room in Sha'ariya. Their sublet was ending in January. Originally, I had planned to be back by then.

But I didn't want to go back. Despite everything, I wanted to stay.

THE WOMEN WELCOMED me with joyous cries. "Zohara! Our young blood!" There was Bruria, and Yaffa and her sister, Malka. We sang some songs I knew, and I was pleased to discover I remembered the melody and even some of the lyrics. Then, Yael taught us a new song, a henna song specific to a southern region, and I wasn't the only one who had to learn it.

Earlier that day, I had gone to Tel Aviv University to send my advisor and the department head in NYU an email. Since talking to Shoshi, I couldn't stop thinking of renegotiating the subject of my dissertation. I wrote and rewrote the email, described my feelings toward my topic, explaining my passion for it had died out, that I wished to examine it from a different angle. I wrote about my discovery of the women's songs and how I saw it fitting within my exploration of feminist voices in Israeli poetry. I said I had already been writing about it, which I had. My journal was filled with thoughts, observations, questions, quotes from songs. Turned out, writing was not torture when I was invested in the topic. It was even enjoyable.

It was late to change course, and it was a stretch, but I had to try.

While there, I looked at some research about oral literary traditions. Singing together, I read, released positive neurochemicals in our brain, improved immune response, lowered stress. Cheaper than therapy, healthier than drugs and alcohol.

I thought of that while I was singing with the women. When I sang, I forgot. And that forgetting manifested in my body too. It was a feeling I remembered from when I used to sing with Mika, how, for a moment, the awkwardness of my teenage body with its long, skinny limbs had disappeared, and I was just voice.

When I sang with the women, I felt lighter, carried away with the sounds my vocal box produced even though I didn't know the meaning of the words. It was as if my body knew the songs, as if they'd been folded in there, imprinted, as if the other voices, my ancestors' voices, became my own. I opened my mouth, and they flowed through me.

Some days, singing was the only thing I could do when grief knocked me out. Not a metaphor, but an actual, physical pain in my body, a heavy lead blanket over my chest. Grief didn't care that I'd experienced loss before; it resisted linearity; it laughed at the face of any supposed stages.

Is that how my mother felt when she sang? As though the burden she was carrying was lifted for the time being? Singing made me feel closer to her, understand something about her, a woman I rarely understood when she was alive. A woman, I realized, who was much more complicated than I had given her credit for, filled with contradictions. A woman who was content with her role as a second wife, but also committed the worst crime a woman of her generation and culture could have committed: falling in love, having an affair, wanting, desiring, dreaming. A woman who wrote and recorded her own songs but never wished to perform. Who wore the headscarf, kept the Shabbat, believed in God, but was living in sin.

I sang in her kitchen, as I washed the dishes. I sang along with the radio. When I drove. When I cleaned. One day at the beach, I swam to the rocks, climbed on top, sat facing the sunset and sang my heart out. I could almost hear my mother's voice accompanying me, harmonizing.

When the meeting finished, I hovered close to Yael as she packed up. She looked up at me in question.

"I was wondering," I said quickly, before I could regret it. "If you might be willing to teach me privately. About the songs. The history. The pronunciation."

She put a hand on my shoulder. "Of course, Zohara. You know, I was thinking about you last week. I was going to ask if you wanted to join some of us to sing at a henna in the neighborhood, but I remembered you're in your year of mourning."

"Me?" My face stretched in astonishment.

"Why are you so surprised?"

"I didn't think I was ready."

"Well, next year you'll be ready for sure! You have a beautiful voice, and it would be good to have a younger woman join the singing. It's fun, and it's a mitzvah to make a bride happy. A privilege." She packed up her papers. "And call me about lessons. I'd love to help."

WHEN I CAME out of the building it was dark and cool out. A silhouette was leaning against the fence. When he saw me, he stood up and stepped into the orange ring that poured from the streetlamp, his face revealed. Nir. In a pair of worn blue jeans and a gray V-neck sweater. My heart leapt at the sight of him. Behind us, the women lingered, chatting loudly. One asked about the song we just learned. "Is it like this?" She sang the line with its last note rising up. "Or like that?" Her voice went down. A chorus of women demonstrated the line, their voices overlapping.

I sauntered toward him, stuffed my hands inside the pockets of my gray wool New York peacoat. "Waiting for your mom?"

He grinned in a way that showed the dimple in his right cheek. "Waiting for you."

"Oh?" I tilted my head, looking at him sideways. "Are you going to walk me home?"

"If you let me."

Yaffa glanced at us with a smile as we left. We walked slowly, as though wishing not to arrive. The neighborhood was alive with the sounds of evening, dinners being prepared, dishes clanking, baths being filled. The air smelled fresh, crisp, and the asphalt glittered orange under our feet. I stole a look at Nir. He looked back at me. Again, that flip in my stomach. We both looked down.

"How's school?" I said, at the same time that he said, "So how have you been?" We laughed.

I hooked my arm through his, moving closer until I could lean into him. "I have so much to tell you."

"I can't wait," he said.

Behind us, the women started singing, their voices carried along by the cool evening breeze, accompanying us as we walked.

Acknowledgments

FIRST AND FOREMOST, I'd like to extend my profound gratitude and appreciation to my Yemeni Jewish community, a main source of inspiration in my work. This book would not have been possible without the dozens of Yemeni women (and some men too) who invited me into their homes, spoke candidly with me about their lives in Yemen and Israel, and shared their food, recipes and songs with me. Every woman I met also willingly sang to me from the repertoire of women's songs, some accompanying themselves with tin drums or a simple cooking pot.

Immense gratitude to my editors, Jennifer Lambert from HarperCollins Canada, and Noa Shapiro and Andrea Walker from Penguin Random House US, for their respective keen eyes and insights, and for championing this book through its long journey. To my agents, David Forrer and Kim Witherspoon of InkWell Management, for their guidance and faith in me. I feel very fortunate to have this dream team behind me. Thanks to the production crew at HarperCollins Canada: Angela Hill for overseeing the production stage and Catherine Dorton for her meticulous copyedit. And thanks to the publicity team at Random House, led by Windy Dorresteyn.

A Chalmers Arts Fellowship (administered by the Ontario Arts Council) allowed me to spend several weeks during two research trips in 2015 and 2016 studying the oral traditions and rituals of Jewish Yemeni women.

It was during these trips that I interviewed many of the women I mentioned. In addition to conducting individual interviews, I met women in community centers and senior day care centers around Israel. The group settings helped re-create the environment that had inspired the women's songs, as the rituals of storytelling and singing were how women in Yemen came together to express their joys and sorrows. It shaped a safer environment for them to share their stories with me and grant me entry to a sisterhood. So many of the accounts in this book, as well as the description of Zohara's conversation with Saida's singing group, are based on these gatherings. While I cannot name all the women for reasons of privacy, I would like to acknowledge and honor their generous, indispensable contributions to this book.

The following people helped me get access to interview subjects: Shoshana Yael Yigal, Yael Tzadok, Zehava Jovani, Ohaliav Naaman and, chiefly, Tuvia Sulami, a dear friend of my father's and a fine poet in his own right, who has assisted me generously throughout the years with all my research needs, and whose essay about the subversive nature of the women's songs gave me a new perspective on the practice. Tuvia, whose sister had gone missing in 1945, also encouraged me to write about the Yemenite, Mizrahi and Balkan Children Affair—as he phrased it, sharing stories about it is "a calling." Thank you, also, to Sarah David, Rachel Zehavi, Saida Kubani and her mom, Kadia Z"L, and to the women of the Midrakh Oz and Gilor day care center in Megiddo.

A subsequent Chalmers Professional Development grant awarded me the enormous privilege to take singing lessons from the unparalleled Gila Beshari, a professional Yemeni singer who's been trained in both women's and men's traditional songs. (Stop everything and go find her on YouTube.) Gila provided me with Yemeni lyrics written phonetically in Hebrew, the proper pronunciation of the Judeo-Arabic dialect, and the translation and context for each song. Her expertise in the field of Yemeni music and poetry and her willingness to pass on her knowledge are extraordinary. Thanks to Gila, I was able to join the women I met while they sang, and they reacted with joy and surprise. These two grants were instrumental to the development of this novel, and I'm deeply grateful to the Chalmers Family Fund for its generous support.

An Access Copyright Foundation research grant afforded me the opportunity to delve further into the tradition of the women's songs and to study their literary characteristics and the context in which they were written, so that I could create original poems in Saida's voice. As a nod to the spirit of the tradition, the poems that appear in this book, attributed to Saida or to an unknown Yemeni poetess, are rooted in and based on existing women's songs. To create these poems, I studied the songs my teacher Gila Beshari had taught me and consulted Nissim Binyamin Gamlieli's comprehensive book, *Arabic Poetry and Songs of the Yemenite Jewish Women,* originally published by Afikim in 1974 (the same book Yael gives Zohara on page 161). Although I have been studying Arabic (and share Zohara's frustration at not speaking it fluently) and could understand some of the lyrics, the easiest way for me to approach this task was by first translating the songs from the Hebrew translation into English, and then reconstructing them by keeping some original lines, borrowing lines from other poems and composing a few lines of my own. This process was a way for my own writing to become an extension of the tradition, and for me to become part of the collective voice of Yemeni Jewish women who remember through storytelling.

A subsequent book written by Nissim Binyamin Gamlieli's son, Dr. Benny Gamlieli—*Wake Up, Utter a Song: Perception of Jewish and Muslim Women via Their Oral Poetry and Songs* (Association for Society and Culture, Documentation and Research, 2021)—further deepened my understanding of the tradition. I also consulted folklore scholar Dr. Vered Madar's fascinating and important doctorate work, "Yemeni Women's Songs for Childbirth and Their Laments for the Dead: Text, Body and Voice" (2011). Some of the anecdotes relayed by women in Madar's work found their way into the novel. Dr. Tova Gamliel's essays about the Yemeni wailing culture also helped me understand this element of the women's songs. Gamliel's book *Aesthetics of Sorrow: The Wailing Culture of Yemenite Jewish Women* was published in English in 2014 by Wayne State University Press.

The Canada Council for the Arts and the Ontario Arts Council granted me the rare gift of uninterrupted writing time. For these generous grants and their continuous support of my writing, I am grateful. Thank you, as always, to the Sami Rohr family and foundation—the Sami Rohr Prize for Jewish Literature launched my career and changed my life—and to Carolyn Hessel for her support.

Two films by Israela Shaer-Meoded were instrumental to my research. *Queen Khantarisha* (2009) features Naomi Amrani, an elderly Yemeni poetess who continued to write songs in the women's songs tradition, and poet Bracha Serri. (The quote by Bracha Serri on page 137 about how there was no greater insult for a Yemeni woman than to be considered unquiet is taken from this movie). *Mori: Shabazi's Riddle* (2018) is an attempt to shed light on the seventeenth-century enigmatic Jewish Yemeni poet Shalom Shabazi.

Ofra Haza was one of the first Yemeni Israeli singers to bring Yemeni Jewish music to the forefront with her album *Yemenite Songs* (1984). Haza's groundbreaking work made a huge impact on me as a child and continues to do so to this day. I'd like to honor her memory and thank her family, especially her sister, the charming and adored Shuli Haza. In recent years, there has been a renewed interest by Yemeni women and men of my generation in the women's song tradition. A-WA (a band of three sisters, Tair, Liron and Tagel Haim) remixed songs from the tradition to international acclaim and wrote original songs in the spirit of the tradition. Shiran Karni (whom I was fortunate enough to study with) also performs renditions of the women's songs with her funk band, Bint El Funk. I'd like to thank Shiran for her expert voice lessons and insightful conversations on voice and identity. I'd also like to honor my cousin once removed, Miriam Naaman. Although I met her only once at her apartment in Eilat, stories of her music career and her beautiful singing voice inspired me when I imagined the character of Shuli.

Thank you to the archivists, librarians and scholars at the Ben-Zvi Institute in Jerusalem, Beit Ariela's newspaper archives in Tel Aviv, the Zionist Archives in Jerusalem, the Museum of the Jewish People in Tel Aviv, and the city archives in Rehovot and Petah Tikva for their dedicated assistance.

In my research into the Yemenite, Mizrahi and Balkan Children Affair, supported by an Access Copyright research grant, I was assisted and inspired by activists Shlomi Hatuka, Naama Katiee, Maayan Mahari and Tom Mehager. The Amram Association, founded in 2013, has been collecting survivors' testimonies and has information in English on their website. You can find and support them online. I'm also grateful to filmmakers Eyal Balachsan (*Meshulam,* 2015, with Noam Sheizaf) and Reut Klein (*Severed Ties,* 2011). I interviewed several people who lost children and family members, and some of their stories are embedded in this book (like in Zohara's conversation with her classmates on pages 63–64). I am indebted to them for sharing their painful stories.

The only book written in English about the Yemenite, Mizrahi and Balkan Children Affair is *Israeli Media and the Framing of Internal Conflict: The Yemenite Babies Affair* by Shoshana Madmoni-Gerber (Palgrave Macmillan, 2009). The disturbing statements made by head nurses on page 42 are real quotes from real head nurses, taken from interviews done by Madmoni-Gerber in 1995. You can read about this in her article, "The Yemenite Babies Affair: What If This Was Your Child?" published July 11, 2013, in *Haokets* and translated into English on *+972 Magazine,* available online. In Hebrew you may read Shoshi Zayed's *The Child Is Gone: The Yemenite Children Affair* (Gefen, 2001), and *Children of the Heart: New Aspects of Research on the Yemenite Children Affair,* edited by Dr. Tova Gamliel and Dr. Nathan Shifris (Resling and the Association for Society and Culture, Documentation and Research, 2019).

Dr. Bat-Zion Eraqi Klorman read segments of this novel that had to do with Yemeni history, culture and traditions, offered generous advice and corrections, and answered my many questions patiently. You can find several of her illuminating essays on Yemeni Jewry in English online. Other researchers, scholars and authors who've helped me in my research are Dr. Menashe Anzi, Dr. Carmela Avdar, Dr. Amnon Ma'abi, Dr. Tom Fogel, Dr. Sigal Nagar-Ron, Dr. Pnina Motzafi-Haller, Yaakov Gluska, Rabbi Mordechai Yitzhari and Ora Yitzhari Z"L. Additional resources I consulted in my research into Yemeni immigration and the ma'abarot were the books *The "Magic Carpet" Exodus of Yemenite Jewry: An Israeli Formative Myth* by Esther Meir-Glitzenstein (Liverpool University Press, 2014), *1949: The First Israelis* by Tom Segev (Owl Books by Henry Holt and Company, 1998) and the docuseries *Ma'abarot* (2019), directed by Dina Zvi Riklis and produced by Arik Bernstein.

I have attended a few Judeo-Yemeni language lessons on Zoom with Dr. Uri Melamed, run by Lashon Habayit (Mother Tongue Project), as well as an informative introductory course to Yemeni Jewish culture offered by the Association for Society and Culture, Documentation and Research.

To accurately describe life in academia, I interviewed PhD students, academics and university professors, amongst them Danielle Drori, Zohar Elmakias, Maayan Eitan, Dana Llyod (who also shared insights on voice and absent fathers), Roni Mazal, and Yonit Naaman. I'm grateful to them for sharing their experiences. Thanks to those who kindly read segments about Zohara's academic life and provided feedback: Hamutal Tsamir, Mimi Haskin, Leonarda Carranza, Angy Cohen and Sharon Shahaf.

Shoshana Madmoni Gerber was so helpful and inspiring to me in writing this novel that I named a character after her. In our many conversations in Boston and Tel Aviv, she shared reflections on Yemeni identity, her boarding school experience, her work as a journalist and her research into the missing children affair, which was spurred by a personal family loss. Her sister, Galit Madmoni Landau, also spoke with me about attending a boarding school. Their stories (along with others that I found online) formed the foundation for Zohara's high school experience.

Profound thanks to Adamit Pereh for carefully reading the entire manuscript and providing invaluable notes and insights. Thanks also to Khulud Khamis, Tom Mehager, Na'ama Klorman-Eraqi and Matti Friedman, for reading segments of the novel and providing feedback.

The following people have either advised me on topics relevant to their fields of expertise, referred me to helpful materials or shared their stories, experiences and art in ways that were significant to me in the writing of this book: Erez Naaman, Efrat Cohen-Noyman, Naama Perel-Tzadok, Chana Kronfeld, Gili Meisler, Zion Ozeri, Avishag Ben Shalom, Tair Haim, Gali Agnon, Mirit Barashi, Yigal Nizri, Aya Elia, Dana Rosenfeld and Miri Shacham. Thank you to Leah Hadad for the apt painted bird metaphor.

I'd like to thank Amichai Serri-Menkes and Niki Serri, Bracha Serri's children, for their support, and to Amichai for his generous permission to translate and use an excerpt of his mother's poem as an epigraph; Ido Kalir, Dahlia Ravikovitch's son, for permitting me to use and translate lines from his mother's poetry; Joshua Sobol for his permission to translate a quote from his legendary play, *The Night of the Twentieth;* and Benny Szames-Levy of Kneller Artists Agency, who represents Nathan Alterman's estate, for permission to translate and use Alterman's words.

The following people kindly hosted me for mini-retreats in their homes or spaces. Thank you to Noa Raveh, Noa Harari Stoler, Noa Aaronsohn Ambar, Hadassa Tron, Elian Lazovsky, Paddy Laidley, Dafi Grossman, Inbal Achiron, Hagar Levi, Evan Fallenberg and Arabesque.

Deep gratitude to my beloved neighborhood singing group, the Eliyahu Sisters, and to our fearless leader, Udi Raz, for the weekly dose of endorphins and the joy of sisterhood and song.

To my friends around the world: you know who you are. Thank you for your friendship. I love you. Special thanks to my heart sisters who've been listening to me talk about this book for years: Aya Ortal, Yonit Naaman, Nadia Hedar, Elsin Davidi, Tal Savoray, Eufemia Fantetti, Yifat Jovani, Sacha Levin and Carlin Sandor. And to Yossi Zabari, who joined me on several research trips and shares a curiosity about our heritage and a love for language and singing. Gratitude also to Maya Tevet Dayan, Mira Sucharov, Minelle Mathani, Gurjinder Basran, Sarah Hedar, Kelly Thompson,

Rachel Rose, Betsy Warland, Lishai Peel and Kamal al-Solaylee for their artistic friendship, moral support and encouragement in writing complex stories in difficult times.

Over the years, I interviewed and recorded the stories of my dear aunts and uncles, Mazal Cohen, Sarit Damari and Aharon Levi; my uncle Shmuel Sabari, who, like me, is the keeper of stories in his family and a lover of Yemeni music and singing; and my uncle Dr. Avi Levi, who was our local synagogue's cantor and its unofficial leader for many years, and who shared his knowledge about the Yemeni synagogue experience. I am grateful to them for their vivid memories and their love. I'm grateful to my beloved grandmother and mighty matriarch Salha Mahdun (Esther Levi) Z"L for telling me about her experiences as a second wife and for showing me what feminism could look like in a traditional, patriarchal society. I miss you.

My two eldest aunts who were born in Yemen both passed away this year. My father's sister Bracha Tanami Z"L told me stories about my paternal family and read her own poetry to me. My maternal aunt Rivka Levi Z"L spent numerous hours answering questions for me and telling me remarkable stories, and was a pillar of our family after my grandmother passed away. Some elements of Shuli's character (mostly how cool she was) and of Saida's character (like her love of travel) are inspired by her. May their memory be a blessing.

I'm grateful beyond words to my family: my partner, Sean, my first reader (who's unimpressed by the fact that this book isn't dedicated to him) for his love, strength, humor and undying support. My brilliant daughter, for putting up with her writing mother and for making everything in my life a million times better. Thank you both for allowing me to take many weekends away to get this book done. To my mother and my awesome siblings—my four brothers and my sister—for their endless, unwavering support of me. (It should be noted that it was a WhatsApp poll in our family group chat, along with thoughtful reasonings from my siblings, that determined the title of this book.) My wise, beautiful mother told me about growing up in Sha'ariya in the fifties, and when I agonized over how hard it was to write a love story that took place in a conservative society, said, "These things happened, even if nobody talked about it. People are people." These words helped me more than she'll ever know.

This book, like everything I write, is in memory and honor of my father, Haim Sabari, a poet, lawyer and community activist and advocate, whose love of words, kindness and generosity are the legacy I carry with me forever.

ABOUT THE AUTHOR

Ayelet Tsabari was born in Israel to a large family of Yemeni descent. She is the author of the memoir *The Art of Leaving*, winner of the Canadian Jewish Literary Award for memoir. Her first book, *The Best Place on Earth*, won the Sami Rohr Prize for Jewish Literature and the Edward Lewis Wallant Award, and was longlisted for the Frank O'Connor International Short Story Award. Her work has appeared in *The New York Times*, *The Globe and Mail*, *Foreign Policy*, and elsewhere, and has won a National Magazine Award. She's the co-editor of the anthology *Tongues: On Longing and Belonging Through Language* and has taught creative writing at Guelph MFA in Creative Writing, The University of King's College MFA, Tel Aviv University, and Bar Ilan University.

ayelettsabari.com